Always,
JESS

ALWAYS, JESS

MISSISSIPPI QUEEN TRILOGY

TRACY BROEMMER

Always, Jess

Mississippi Queen Trilogy, Book 3

by

Tracy Broemmer

Contemporary Romance

Published by Tracy Broemmer

Edited by Lexie Broemmer

Cover by Vanilla Lily Designs

CHAPTER 1

He cut his hair.

Margo lowered her gaze to the pint glass in her hand and watched the amber liquid fill it, careful to limit the foam at the top. She hadn't given anyone good head in a damned long time, but a Mississippi Queen customer wasn't a good place to get back in the game. She snorted and rolled her eyes and then realized Jess Covey had just walked into the bar.

Hadn't he? God, was she hallucinating now?

Scared to look up—what if she was imagining things? Was she so desperate for Jess to come back that she was dreaming him up and seeing his face on every guy in the bar now?—she pushed the tap back and set the pint glass on the bar to nudge it toward Leah's friend, Dante.

"Thanks." Dante's voice drifted to her over the bar. Rather than look around, rather than scope out the guy who had walked in wearing the black leather jacket and Jess' face,

Margo offered Dante a smile. Glass at his lips, Dante's brown eyes warmed, and he arched his eyebrows in response. His olive-colored skin was smooth, and his thick dark hair was slicked back neatly. He wore a beige dress shirt, open at the collar, with a brown sport coat over it.

She wondered if Leah had ever slept with him.

Probably not. Dante had asked Leah out not long before their friend Kenzi had a stroke. Leah happened to be with her and her husband, Joe, at the time, and the experience had been traumatic for her. Maybe she had been attracted to Dante, but the timing hadn't worked out, and then along came Nashville—

Margo realized she was still staring at Dante. Afraid that she might have given him the wrong impression—he was much too pretty for her taste—she blinked and laughed and prayed that he didn't notice the heat rush her face. She wasn't interested in sleeping with him, but he was easy on the eyes—

Suddenly aware of someone standing a few feet down the bar, she stepped back and looked away from Dante.

When Jess left last year, he'd worn his black hair long. When he made love to her, it would fall around her face, like a curtain affording them privacy. She wondered now if he had left it loose with the other women. How many of them had run their fingers through the long, dark silk while he pumped his hips over theirs?

He wore it short now, cut in a quiff style. Margo might have decided again that she was projecting, thinking too much about Jess and seeing him in men she thought attractive, but Jess turned then to look at her. His golden-brown eyes flipped a switch inside her, and suddenly, her belly and her lungs and her heart seized and flared with electricity.

"Hey."

The irony of standing behind a fully stocked bar where she could have any drink at her fingertips while her mouth was suddenly dry wasn't lost on her. She tried to swallow and worked to calm her racing heart, to breathe around the clenched fist that held her stomach in a tight grip. A shock of thick black hair fell over his forehead and dipped over his left eyebrow, almost giving him the same rakish appeal the longer hair had.

Back when they were lovers.

She wasn't ready for this.

He had been gone for over a year, and though they spoke on the phone sometimes, she wasn't prepared for *this*. He wasn't supposed to just show up like this and catch her off-guard. She might have spent the last year lying to herself that she was over him, immune to his charm, but still, a head's up would have been nice.

"What're you doing here?"

She wanted to sound tough, at least, if not mean. Unfortunately, the words came out on a rugged, breathless whisper. Margo was glad for the ornate wooden bar she stood behind, because it hid her legs, which trembled a bit now under his stare.

"Hey."

Trace Dixon—her cousin Leah's unofficial fiancé—appeared at the end of the bar. God, where was her army? Where were Leah and Stevi? She needed them now; just their silent support would go a long way toward getting her through the next few minutes.

Jess narrowed his eyes as Trace sidled up next to her and dropped his arm around her shoulders. Margo leaned into him and snuck a deep breath, comforted by his familiar scent.

"You okay?" Trace tightened his fingers around her upper arm in a gentle squeeze.

"Mmm."

"Duncan and Stevi are digging out Halloween decorations," he told her. Jess was still watching them, his eyebrows slanted in a harsh frown. Stomach still churning under that intense stare, Margo had to snort at Trace's words. Duncan hated the Halloween tree. Stevi loved it. They had been bickering about it for over a week now. Apparently, Stevi had won the battle. Margo wondered what she had surrendered to get her way.

Not wanting to go too far down that rabbit hole, she straightened and patted Trace's chest. Jess wasn't going to go away, no matter how badly she wished he would. She wanted him to leave, right? Didn't that uneasy feeling in the pit of her stomach mean she wanted him to leave? Or did she want him to stay? To talk to her?

The phone calls had been about Berkley, mostly. Jess called now and then to update her on his sobriety. To promise her he had a steady job. To ask her about their daughter.

But maybe showing up here unannounced was something else. Was he jealous? Of Trace? Could the scowl on his face be anything other than jealousy?

"Trace." She cleared her throat and lifted her hand to tuck her hair behind her ear. In case either of them was looking closely, Margo tucked that same hand into her hip pocket so they wouldn't notice the slight tremble. "This is Jess Covey."

It hurt to say his name, to toss it out there casually in an introduction. Because she had to add those other things. Other words. My *ex. Berkley's father*. She didn't have to say them for Trace's benefit. But maybe for Jess. Maybe for herself. Maybe she needed to be reminded of the way Jess had hurt her. "Jess is Berkley's father," she mumbled, and Trace moved again to offer support. His hand stroked her back, much the same as Leah's would if she were standing here right now.

"Jess." Trace was contained, his face impassive.

Not Duncan. If Duncan were standing here right now his hand might be fisted and swinging for Jess' face.

"Good to meet you." Trace offered his hand to Jess now, and Margo noticed that he said *good* to meet you and not *nice* to meet you. Because maybe it was good that he now knew what face to protect Margo from.

"And you are?" Jess tipped his head a bit, the dark look softened just a bit by the hint of a smile.

"Trace Dixon."

Margo knew Jess wouldn't recognize Trace's name. He wouldn't know Tanner Dixon, either—Trace's younger, country-music-star brother. Jess' musical taste leaned toward classic rock with a bit of metal. He wouldn't know country from polka.

"We agreed that it would be weekly."

Duncan's voice carried from the back of the bar and wound through Margo's shoulders and neck. She loved her stepbrother to the moon and back, and she loved his protective side, but the last damned thing they needed was a brawl here in their bar. It was early yet, but Dante wasn't the only patron here, and a standoff between Jess and Duncan would be enthralling entertainment.

"You have five freebies," Stevi reminded him. "I don't care how or when you use them. But the number doesn't change."

Margo pressed her lips together as she considered what sort of freebies they were talking about. Also something that didn't need to be done in front of their patrons, a conversation about sexual favors in any form.

"You'll have to handcuff me, Stevi," Duncan told her. Margo glanced at Trace, amused by the smirk on his face, and then looked past him toward the back of the bar. Duncan led with his back; he and Stevi carried the boxed

Halloween tree between them. "I can't keep my hands off you."

"Duncan and Stevi?" Jess' eyes popped open and made Margo think of a cartoon character. She trilled an honest laugh and then covered her mouth with her hand when Duncan shot her a look over his shoulder. She breathed easier when he looked back at Stevi, not noticing or not recognizing Jess at first. Jess glanced at her and arched his eyebrows in question. She gave him a quick nod and a shrug and realized there was someone standing by him. The woman stood to his right, her head bent over a smart phone.

Without bothering to explain to Jess who Trace Dixon was, Margo slipped in front of him and braced her hands on the bar.

"Can I get you something?"

A cute ponytail flipped as the woman lifted her head to look at Margo. Big green eyes, thick long lashes, and creamy skin dotted with a smattering of freckles, the girl —not a woman; she looked younger than Stevi—tipped her lips up in a sweet smile.

"Oh. Can I—"

"She's with me," Jess said distractedly. He glanced at the girl with a warm smile and then looked back at Margo. "Since when?"

Margo felt a wave of nausea sweep her from her head to the soles of her black boots. This kid was with Jess? She was cute; not a lick of makeup on, but Margo thought she was adorable. Glowing with natural beauty or health. Or sexual satisfaction. Margo knew Jess Covey knew how to please a woman. She supposed he had the same finesse for girls.

She felt a stab of guilt for the rush of hate she felt for the girl on the opposite side of the bar. She didn't hate easily, but she had found that where Jess was concerned, it had become doable.

Jess moved his mouth again, but Margo didn't hear him. She wasn't listening. How could she listen? Two minutes ago, she had considered the possibility that Jess had gambled and shown up here to sweep her off her feet. That maybe he hadn't been calling just about Berkley but that he had wanted to be part of her life again.

The joke was clearly on her. Jess didn't need her if he had that sweet little body warming his bed now.

"What're you doing here?"

Margo processed the words. Duncan's voice. The sound of the box hitting the floor as if it was dropped from knee-high.

A hand smoothed over her back, but this time, that same hand curled possessively around the curve of her waist. She smelled Stevi's perfume as her cousin pressed into her side.

"Hey." Stevi squeezed her waist. "You okay?"

"Yeah." Margo stirred. "Yeah. I'm fine." She wasn't fine, but she sure as hell wouldn't let on to Jess that something was wrong. That once again, he'd yanked her heart out. After all, this one was on her. He had no idea she had this ridiculous fantasy that he would come back for both her and Berkley.

She turned to look at Stevi, careful not to meet her eyes, and let her gaze skate over to Trace.

"You and Duncan?" Jess asked with a laugh.

"Yep," Stevi answered without hesitation. "This guy is the love of my life."

Margo hoped her words were enough to calm the angry beast. As tempting as it was to sic her stepbrother on Jess, it really wasn't the time or place.

Or Jess' fault.

"How are you, Stevi?" Jess' voice dropped to that low, sexy tone that used to drive Margo crazy in bed.

"She's good." Duncan suddenly appeared at Margo's other shoulder. "Why are you here?"

"Duncan," Stevi chided him softly. "Maybe he's here to see Berkley."

"She's not here," Margo mumbled. She brought Berkley to the Queen with her now and then before their business hours, but most of the time, her mom watched her.

Margo appreciated the show of support—the very same one she had wished for a few minutes ago—but now, she felt smothered. She stepped away from Stevi and cut a glance at Duncan. He stood like a brick wall, legs spread wide and his hands braced on the bar now. Hulking and aggressive, like he was considering climbing over the bar and knocking Jess' face in.

She wanted to tell him to stand down, but then again, that would only draw attention to her and Jess and what was already a tense, awkward situation. Instead, she looked back at Jess, surprised to find him ignoring Duncan, eyes on her.

"Do you want something? Water? Soda?"

Was he still sober? Should she offer him a beer? Would she give him one if he asked for it?

"I'm fine." Jess shook his head slightly, but he glanced at the girl at his side and arched his eyebrows in askance. Margo couldn't hide the surprise when the girl asked for a beer. Seemed kind of rude if she was sleeping with Jess to order alcohol when he was a recovering alcoholic.

Rather than comment, Margo simply nodded and leaned into the cooler to grab a longneck for her.

Jess started to speak, but Margo held her hand up to stop him.

"Excuse me? For a second?"

He nodded. She stared at him a moment longer. Catalogued his intense golden eyes. The thick, dark eyebrows she used to brush her lips over. The dark stubble on his cheeks and his chin. His soft, generous lips that used to glide over her skin.

She turned and slipped away in one move, aware as she hurried on impossibly steady legs to the ladies' room that she was leaving Jess to Duncan and his anger. She knew from the click of the heels behind her that Stevi was following her. Needing to be alone, she pushed the door open and let it close. But Stevi caught it and stepped into the room behind her.

Margo stood with her back to her, but she heard the door click closed. Heard Stevi flip the lock.

"I'm…" Margo stopped talking and tried to draw a deep breath and push the emotion back down her throat. "I'm so stupid."

"Margs."

"So fucking stupid, Stevi," she whispered.

"Margo, no." Stevi's fingers gripped her arm just above the elbow and turned her around. Margo ducked her head, embarrassed by the tears that welled in her eyes. "No, you aren't."

Stevi still held her elbow. She reached with her other hand to tip Margo's chin up, but Margo tossed her head the other way to escape her. There was a harsh knock on the door, quickly followed by Leah's voice.

"Let me in, guys."

Margo didn't want an audience. She didn't want to cry in front of Stevi or Leah. She didn't want to talk about how naïve she was. She couldn't admit that she had secretly hoped that Jess would eventually come back for her.

But she didn't want to be alone, either.

Stevi loosened her hold on her—wasn't like Margo could escape—and reached back to unlock the door. Margo watched the gold doorknob turn, and then the door cracked open, and Leah slipped inside. She pushed the door closed and leaned back on it, reaching back to twist the lock.

If either of them was going to lecture her about wasting time and letting an ass like Jess hurt her—again—it would be Leah. Margo drew herself up to full height and drew in a deep breath, ready for Leah to rip into her. And let it roll off her shoulders. Because she couldn't help the way she felt about him, could she? God, she'd kicked him out over a year ago, and her heart was still in love with him.

"You okay?" Leah asked softly.

Her kindness was Margo's undoing. She covered her face with her hands and sobbed quietly.

"Hey. Hey." Stevi moved in close again. "Not here. Don't do this here."

"I can't help it." Margo sniffled and dabbed at her eyes. "Who the hell is she? She looks like she's fifteen."

"Sweetie, you have to go back out there." Stevi's voice was gentle but firm. "You have to go back out there and face him."

"Give her a minute, Stevi." Leah pushed off the door and reached out to touch Margo's arm.

"I thought…"

"I know." Leah nodded. Margo swiped at her nose and swallowed hard.

"I can't believe he brought her here."

"You need to get back out there with Duncan." Leah cut her eyes to Stevi. "He looked ready to whale on Jess."

"Trace is out there." Stevi shook her head.

"Trace is tending bar, because Duncan is standing there staring Jess down like a junkyard dog."

Margo groaned out loud and wished she were at home. It was early, and even if her cousins suggested she go on home, she wouldn't. No way in hell would she let Jess or his new woman think they had run her out of her own territory. She blew her nose on a paper towel and then checked her eyes in the mirror over the sink.

"I look like shit," she decided. "But then, whatever I was before wasn't enough—"

"Stop it!" Stevi grabbed her by the wrist this time and swung her around to face them again. "This is on Jess."

"Nope." Margo shook her head. "Not this time. That other stuff was on Jess. This is me." She swallowed hard and shrugged. "I never could learn a lesson."

CHAPTER 2

WHEN JULIE CARMICHAEL HAD INVITED HERSELF ALONG ON his drive to Adam's Bay, Jess Covey wasn't sure it was a good idea. Now, standing opposite Duncan Marks and this other guy—who the hell was Trace Dixon?—Jess was kind of glad he had agreed to it. Jess was a big boy, and being the drinker he used to be, he had handled himself in his fair share of bar fights. But Duncan Marks was the total package in a protective brother way: brooding, mean, and angry, and even when Jess and Margo had been happy, Jess had never been too sure of what Duncan thought of him.

He leaned on the bar now, itching for a beer. He hadn't touched alcohol—hadn't had a drop—in ten months. When Margo booted him out after Berkley was born, with the condition of him cleaning up his act and quitting drinking before he could be part of his daughter's life, Jess had slinked away with no hope. His alcoholism had no basis in family, either genes or experience. His parents were social drinkers; his sisters liked to party, but neither of them needed alcohol to have fun. The family was close, and if there were deep, dark reasons for Jess getting hooked on first beer and then hard liquor, those reasons were still too deep to find.

Still. When he left Adam's Bay, he assumed he might never see Berkley. He hadn't thought it possible to quit drinking, mainly because he didn't believe he had a problem. He hadn't *wanted* to quit; he wanted to fight Margo, argue that he didn't have a problem, and that he had the right to see Berkley no matter who or what he was.

And then he'd met Julie, and for whatever reason, he had stopped thinking so much about the injustice. He'd stopped thinking so much about Margo, about assigning blame, and about where his next drink would come from.

Julie had scooted back to sit on a barstool, but Jess still stood. His feet didn't hurt; his legs weren't tired. He could stand forever if needed. But the scowl on Duncan's face had his shoulders hitched up in knots, and the damned leather jacket was hot, and there was sweat on the back of his neck. Where the hell had Margo gone, and why had Stevi followed her? Where was Leah?

"I don't know you." Jess turned his head toward the other guy behind the bar, but he still felt Duncan's scowl.

"Moved here from Nashville," the guy told him. As if that explained anything. Had they hired a musician from Nashville to try and pull in more business? Or was the guy a cook? A bartender?

Or was he seeing Margo? The Nashville guy had been the first one to approach the bar earlier when he and Julie walked in. He had been the one to slide his arm her and draw her in, as if to shield her from Jess.

Jess narrowed his eyes at the guy. Margo had curled into him easily, comfortably. But, then again, the two of them hadn't whispered anything to each other, and the guy hadn't kissed her or followed her from behind the bar, either, to make sure she was okay.

"Hey." Stevi's voice, thank Christ, floated across the open room. Still stunned by this development, Jess watched Duncan's rage melt into something like appreciation as he turned to watch Stevi approach. Margo's cousin still favored the spiky heels, and with each step, the click of those heels was like a hammer whaling on Jess' head. He flexed his fingers and counted to five.

At his side, Julie tilted her bottle up and drank from it. She reached her free hand over to him and closed her fingers around his. Jess glanced at her; when their eyes met, she tipped her head just slightly and reminded Jess to breathe.

Grateful for her support, he drew in a full, deep breath before looking back at the crew. At the end of the bar, Stevi stood motionless, eyes on Julie's hand around his. Jess felt another flash of panic when she lifted her gaze to look him in the eye. Margo and Leah strolled up behind Stevi, Leah speaking quietly to Margo and Margo laughing softly.

Jess studied them, the Mississippi Queen crew. He had loved Margo. And he'd liked her cousins, wanted to be part of their group. Leah had never really warmed to him, but he and Stevi had hit it off okay most of the time. But he and Duncan had never been friends. Jess missed the place, the atmosphere. Not the liquor, though God knows, today was proving to be his toughest challenge since the last swallow of whisky not quite a year ago.

He missed the bar; the girls ran an awesome business. For the short time he was part of it, Jess had become friends with some of the regulars. He missed Stevi and Leah, and hell yes, he missed Margo. He missed every damned thing there was to miss about a woman when it came to Margo Nevin.

But at the moment, with all of the accusing eyes pointed his way, he was ready to slink right back out the door and walk away. Maybe they were right. Maybe he wasn't good enough to be a father. Maybe Berkley Nevin was better off never knowing who he was.

"Hey, Jess." Leah trailed her hand over Stevi's and Duncan's backs as she moved to claim a spot behind the bar. "How ya doing?"

"Leah." Jess nodded and offered her a tight smile. Now they were all lined up behind the bar. Five against one. Julie moved then to pull her hand from his, but she smoothed her fingertips over the back of his hand as she did so, in a subtle reminder that she was here with him. She was on his side. Five against two, he corrected himself. Still not the best odds.

"You met Trace?" She stepped closer and pressed herself against the new guy's side. Jess fought the automatic response—the way he almost sagged his shoulders in relief—when Trace dropped his arm around her and turned his face toward her to kiss her hair. If that guy was his competition for Margo, he was fucked. The guy had movie star good looks, and it was obvious he was an accepted member of the Mississippi Queen crew. Jess was thrilled to realize the new guy was Leah's boyfriend.

"I did."

"Hey, I'm Stevi."

Jess turned as Stevi reached over the bar to shake Julie's hand. Another bit of weight off his shoulders. Julie didn't deserve any of the hatred or rage directed at his side of the bar. He was relieved that someone had acknowledged her.

Well. Margo had earlier, hadn't she?

"Julie."

"It's nice to meet you." Stevi flashed a big smile. "That's my sister, Leah. Her fiancé Trace."

"Fiancé?" Jess looked back at Leah, gaze automatically going to her ring finger. She wore a ring, though without Stevi's announcement, Jess wouldn't have assumed it was an engagement ring.

"It's not official yet," Leah said with a soft smile.

"Better start making it official soon," Duncan muttered.

"If I'm gonna be that kid's godfather, I might insist his parents are married when he's born."

"What're you gonna do when she's a girl?" Leah leaned around Trace to see Duncan, face painted with amusement.

"You're pregnant." Jess frowned.

"We are." Trace nodded.

"Congratulations."

Jess was thrilled for them. He really was. So why did he feel like Stevi had just gutted him with a machete? Like she'd hooked him and then given one big yank and left him hollow?

"And our cousin, Margo," Stevi continued with the introductions. "And my…" Stevi slipped her arm around Duncan's back and turned to press a kiss to his upper arm. She grinned and laughed when Duncan narrowed his eyes impatiently waiting for her description of him. "Boyfriend, Duncan."

"That sounds so high school." Duncan winced and shook his head.

"So buy her a ring," Trace suggested.

"Too soon!" Stevi laughed. Duncan turned sideways at the bar and tipped his head at Stevi.

"Too soon? I've been in love with you forever. Hell of a lot longer than Trace and Leah."

Jess watched the exchange behind the bar curiously. Hard to decide if he was happy for Stevi, because mostly, Duncan Marks was an asshole, and Stevi could do better. Not to mention, walking into the Queen today felt like boarding the Love Boat. Jess sure as hell hadn't been prepared for this. Maybe it was something in the water.

"Jess."

Her thick, buttery voice drew his attention immediately. Brought to mind all sorts of memories of the two of them together. The way she said his name in her sleep sometimes. The way she said his name when he kissed her. When she wanted his touch. Jess straightened at the bar as his eyes met Margo's, relieved that he was hidden at the bar and no one could see his dick waking up to Margo's presence.

"Can we talk?"

He hadn't expected that.

He nodded before she changed her mind. Jess had expected that he would have to be the one to ask for her time. He assumed he would have to do some damned fancy talking just to get her to listen, and he figured once he said what he wanted to say, she would ask him to leave.

"Is it cold outside?" she asked quietly. The antics were still playing out behind the bar with Stevi and Duncan being cute and lovey-dovey. Jess was almost fascinated enough to stick around and watch Duncan make an ass of himself. Leah and Trace had their heads together, but their conversation seemed a bit more serious.

"Chilly, but not too bad," Jess answered. She nodded and wended her way back through her family and around the end of the bar. Jess glanced at Julie, who still sat at the bar, one hand wrapped around the beer, and the other propping her chin up.

"Go." She nodded. He brushed his fingers over her back as he slipped by her to follow Margo to the back door.

There had been two tables occupied inside and a guy at the bar, but the patio was empty at this hour. Jess noticed a couple of heaters spaced among the tables, but obviously none was in use now. Rather than sit, Margo led him to the rail around the patio. Greedy for the sight of her, Jess took the opportunity to look at her. She wore dark wash skinny jeans and boots with heels that were less deadly than Stevi's, but still sexy. Then again, Jess had seen her in those boots, and probably those jeans—down around her knees as he knelt before her—and a look of ecstasy on her face.

He'd never seen that look on Stevi's or Leah's faces, and though Margo had once thrown that at him—phrased as a question, but Jess wasn't dumb—he never wanted to see that look, to watch Stevi or Leah in such an intimate moment.

He had cheated. Biggest mistake he had ever made. But he had never been attracted to or flirted with Margo's cousins.

Maybe that didn't mean a flying fuck to Margo, but Jess thought that it would have been a special sort of asshole move if he had ever come onto someone close to her.

"Why are you here?"

She didn't even bother to look at him when she spoke. Jess stood at the rail at her side, closer to her than he had been in a year. But the two feet that separated them now might as well have been an ocean between them.

"Margo."

Arms folded over her chest, she turned to face him.

"Why? Why are you here?"

His mouth was suddenly bone dry, and not from arousal. He had cleaned up his act, as per Margo's ultimatum. He quit drinking. He had a steady job; Margo didn't need to know he was considering giving his notice, that he'd already talked to Derrick Carmichael about leaving. *That* was a different story. Jess needed to pace himself. Start with this, with his desire to see Berkley, and move up from there.

Margo had been so strong when she'd asked him to leave. For fuck's sake, Jess had never been convinced she needed him around. Not even in the beginning. She was independent to a fault, and she had made it clear there was absolutely nothing she couldn't or wouldn't do for herself—even sex. She had a well-used and well-loved vibrator, and there had been rare occasions when Jess couldn't satisfy her, so she took care of things herself. At first, her strength, her power had turned him on. Until one day, it didn't. She didn't love him; they'd been intimately involved and created a baby together, but they'd never said that stuff to each other. But when Jess had realized she didn't even *need* him, he had made the mistake of looking for someone who did.

"I want to see my daughter."

Margo's eyes flashed with emotion at his words. Was she angry? He wasn't sure. Rather than hold his gaze, she ducked her head.

"You were gonna call first," she reminded him.

"You would have said no."

"I wouldn't have said no," she argued. "We've talked about this. This is why you quit…drinking. Right?"

The tip of a knife grazed him when she angled her head to look at him.

"Right. Yeah." He nodded. He had changed his lifestyle for his daughter, yes. But he wanted more. Again, different story. One he wasn't ready to get into.

"I just…" She drew in a quick, short breath and shook her head. "I'm not ready for this."

"You're not ready for me to see Berkley?" He felt a sharp pain in his chest and stepped back from her, as if distance from Margo would make it ease.

She closed her eyes and shook her head, but she didn't speak. Jess waited for her to rail at him, to tell him to get the hell out of the Queen and leave her alone.

"Are you sober?"

"Ten months, three days."

She nodded, eyes open now and scanning the parking lot behind the building.

"She's at my mom's, Jess."

He had assumed Berkley wouldn't be here. Margo had told him over the phone that she brought her to work with her sometimes, but not during the bar's open hours. He didn't particularly relish the idea of tangoing with Margo's mother to see her.

"Please let me see her."

He stepped closer to her when he realized she was shivering.

"And then what?" she whispered.

"What does that mean?" He shrugged out of his jacket and laid it over her shoulders.

"Don't." Margo shook her head. "I don't need—"

"You never did," he said quietly. But he rested his hands on her shoulders, and Margo tugged the front of the jacket closed over her middle.

"I will never give her to you." Her whispered words hung between a threat and a promise. "Do you know that?"

Jess stepped back as Margo whirled around to look at him. Her eyes were bright with angry tears.

"It doesn't matter to me that you quit drinking or if you have a great house with a swing set and a sweet, little fuckable wife, Jess Covey. You will never get custody of my daughter."

"Margo, I don't—no, it's not like—"

She shrugged her shoulders as she shoved by him. Jess caught his jacket before it fell to the ground, eyes on Margo's retreating back, sputtering to argue with her.

This was more like what he had anticipated when he had climbed into his truck earlier. An angry Margo warning him that even if he saw Berkley, he would never really be part of her life. What he wasn't prepared for, though, was the rush of indignant rage that ripped up through him, tagging his gut and his heart and his lungs.

"I just wanna know my daughter!" he called after her.

He headed back over the patio, his booted feet punishing the ground with every step. He and Margo had rarely fought when they lived together. Because he had always given in. He had known he would never be right, and he'd walked away to let her simmer. Tired of being the pussy that let her run the show, Jess was ready to dig his boots in and fight.

"I don't wanna take her. I didn't come down here to grab her and throw her in the truck and run. I just want to see her. I've done what you asked me to do, Margo—"

She held her hand up and pressed her lips together.

"I'll call Mom. She'll bring her down." She nodded. "But, Jess?"

All the anger crashed at his feet as Margo swiped at her eyes.

"Don't do this again, okay?"

"Do what, Margo? Drive down to see my daughter?"

"Stop it." She shook her head. "Stop saying that. Okay? Just stop."

"Berkley is my daughter," he reminded her.

"Don't bring your women here. Okay? I don't know if this is gonna work. But—"

"What?" He stepped closer to her, that rage creeping up his throat again. "If what's gonna work? Are you suggesting that this is it? You won't let me see her again?"

Margo dropped her gaze to his fingertip on her chest. When had he done that? Backed her up against the door and pinned her there with his finger? He wouldn't hurt her. He had never raised a hand to a woman in his life. He wouldn't start now. But dammit, if she didn't make him lose his shit. He was tired of Margo Nevin running the show.

"I don't know if you're gonna like this. Or if you'll get tired of playing daddy. If you plan to keep visiting her. But if you do, don't bring the girls, okay? Don't do that to Berkley."

"What?"

"Because she'll love them. All of them." Margo shrugged. "And if you're just fucking around with them, you're gonna hurt her."

Jess rocked back on his heels. "You sure you're still talking about Berkley?"

"Fuck you, Jess." Her words quivered, and if he knew Margo, she hated that she had let him see any weakness.

"Do you wanna do that, Margo?" He moved his hand, turned it to cup her chin and hold her still. "Do you still wanna fuck me?" He leaned in close enough to feel her breath on his lips.

"If I wanted to fuck you, I'd tell you to go back home without seeing your baby girl."

Jess stroked his thumb over her lip and pressed it gently to her teeth.

"Your eyes get really big and round when you're aroused."

She closed her eyes, but her rapid, choppy breathing didn't change.

"Does she know?" She blinked. Spoke softly. "That sweet little thing in there? Does she know who you are? What you do to women?"

"Just you and me here, Margo." His voice was gruff. "Not woman enough to deal with that? You keep throwing—"

To his surprise, she straightened from the door and leaned into him. He slid his fingers from her chin to the back of her neck. The warm, soft skin there brought to mind thoughts of her smooth, silky thighs under his fingers and his mouth.

Her lips were warm and firm on his. He closed his eyes, moved to touch her with his other hand. To grip her hip.

"Jesus, Margo." He groaned when she opened her mouth over his.

"You haven't changed a bit." Her voice was thick and sultry, but Jess felt his dick stand down when he realized what she'd said. Instead of sliding her tongue over his lips and into his mouth, she sunk her teeth into his lower lip and bit him hard enough to make him yelp.

"What the fuck—"

"I'll call Mom." She laid her hand on his chest and shoved him backwards. "But don't do it this way again."

CHAPTER 3

MMARGO'S HEART RACED LIKE AN OVERWORKED ENGINE AT the Indy 500. The hell of it was, she wasn't sure why. Anger? Oh hell yes, she was pissed at Jess. What the hell right did he have to just show up this way, without talking to Margo first, without establishing some kind of rules about when and where he could visit Berkley? And what the hell was he thinking waltzing into the Queen parading that fresh, dewy-faced girl in front of Margo and her family?

She was so angry with Jess at the moment that she kind of wanted to climb his damned body like a fucking tree and slap that damned smug look off his face. Trouble with that was, she'd already gotten too close to him, and *she'd been the one* to put that damned smug look on his face in the first place. First by letting him believe she was jealous of his little friend and second by kissing him.

Granted, she hadn't kissed him because she wanted to.

Well. Not really.

She'd leaned into him with thoughts of inflicting pain. Since a much-deserved knee in the balls would have drawn too much attention—what would the gang think when they, well, she walked back inside and Jess hobbled back inside with his face blue and his hands wrapped protectively around his balls?—she had bit him instead.

Unfortunately, she'd tasted him first. What had made her think she needed to lick him before sinking her teeth into his lip? Because now, Jess was at a tall table with his girlfriend, all smiles and laughter as they waited for Margo's mom to deliver Berkley so they could meet her, and Margo was tied up in knots—revved up to go a round or two with Jess. She just wasn't sure if she wanted to hit him or—

Fuck him.

He'd called it.

Hell yes, she still wanted him. She'd never stopped *wanting* him. But that didn't mean she wanted him *here*. Hanging out in her bar.

"Do you think they're dating?" Leah asked quietly. Margo drummed her fingers on the back of her phone laying face down on the bar. She let her eyes roam over the large open space in the bar, but she refused to give in and look at Jess. Because each time she did give in and look, his smile—the flash of his straight, white teeth and the warmth in his eyes—was like a dagger in her heart.

She looked back at Leah and shrugged.

"I mean, she looks like she just got out of high school," Leah continued. "She looks too smart to get involved with someone like that."

"Ouch." Margo flinched. "Thanks, Leah."

"That's not what I meant." Leah shook her head. "You know that's not what I meant. She just looks so young."

"Can we stop watching them? Please?" Margo cleared her throat. "I'm gonna go check on Tony. Make sure dinner prep's a go. We have two reservations for six."

"Sure." Leah nodded. "I'm gonna help Stevi with the Halloween tree."

Margo couldn't help the snort that escaped her lips as Leah turned to study Stevi at the front window. She squatted by the big box she and Duncan had carried upstairs, hands pulling artificial limbs with black needles from the box.

"She had to give him five freebies for that."

"Yeah, but if the sex is good, it's not like she can lose." Leah glanced at Margo over her shoulder. "Right? I'd rather give Trace five freebies than five nights of not doing the dishes."

Five nights of feeding a baby. Bathing a baby. Five nights of getting up in the night with a crying baby. Five nights of lying awake and alone in her bed. Missing Jess. Reminding herself why she missed Jess and that she was better off without him.

"Yeah, you're right," Margo mumbled. She turned and headed to the opposite end of the bar before Leah could say more. It wouldn't take her mom long to get here. Might take her a while to get Berkley's stuff together and to buckle her in her car seat. Just because her mom was torn on the subject. Of course, Margo's parents wanted Berkley to have both parents involved in her life. But neither of them was ready to forgive and forget the things Jess had done.

Margo peeked into the kitchen, though she didn't really need to. It was a rare occasion when things didn't run smoothly there. Things had gone a bit off the rails last week when Tony had gone home sick, but their second in command had stepped up and handled things after a shaky hour or two.

She slipped out the back door, thankful to see the patio was still quiet. There was just no way she could be inside right now. The Queen was a big bar, but apparently not big enough for her and Jess and another woman. No matter that there were three stories in the building and two sides to the bottom floor—and Margo pretty much ran the restaurant side, where Jess definitely was not sitting—she couldn't stand inside the building with him and not get all itchy and bothered and feel that need to look at him.

Them.

The girl.

She did look young. Leah's words had stung a bit, but Margo knew she hadn't meant them as they sounded.

Either the kid had just gotten out of school or she had a damned good skin care routine. No, Leah's words stung because Margo knew she had never been terribly crazy about Jess, and apparently, even though Leah was now over the moon for her own guy and her own happy ending, she was still going to be hard on Margo and her decidedly unhappy ending.

Well. Margo had a beautiful, healthy baby girl, so she couldn't say she had an unhappy ending. But, still. As happy as she was for Leah and Trace and for Stevi and Duncan, she would love to find that kind of love for herself. Unfortunately, her brain and her heart hadn't learned as far as Jess was concerned.

Were they dating? Margo doubted it. Because Jess didn't really date. He flirted. He found his way into a woman's pants. And he moved on. Except with her. She'd been stupid enough to have him move in with her, even when they'd never said the big L word and even though she knew what he was doing with the other women. He'd had it made when he lived with her.

Were they sleeping together, though? Really? But would Jess bring a woman here with him, to meet Berkley, if they weren't...something? Had he finally fallen in love with someone? The thought wedged sideways in her throat, and she had to fight to swallow, to breathe.

Why had she believed that when Jess figured his life out, that when he came back for Berkley, that he would be coming back for her, too?

"Margo."

She took a deep breath when she heard Duncan's voice behind her. Hunched her shoulders and tipped her head up to the evening sky. She loved this time of year. There was something so refreshing about autumn. The chill in the air and the changing leaves made Margo feel alive. She couldn't wait to take Berkley trick-or-treating; she was going to be adorable in her puppy costume.

"Hmm." She leaned into Duncan when he stepped up beside her. He put his arm around her and rested his chin on top of her head.

"You okay?"

"Yep."

"Want me to break his knee caps?"

She laughed softly and patted her hand on Duncan's chest.

"No."

"You really okay with him and Berkley?"

At a loss as to how to answer him, Margo sucked in a deep breath. She considered her words. Duncan was a hothead, especially when it came to protecting her and her cousins. She didn't want to say something that would send him back inside to kick Jess's ass and send him home. On the other hand, Stevi had softened Duncan a bit, and for just a second, Margo was tempted to tell Duncan exactly what she was thinking.

Right here, right now, she wasn't okay with Jess and Berkley. She was still reeling from Jess's sudden appearance, and the girl with him had knocked the wind out of her, like Jess had sucker punched her in the belly. Because she had assumed Jess would come back for her and Berkley together, and that the three of them would heal and be a family.

Admitting that even to herself made her feel stupid. There was no way she would say it to Duncan. Or Jess.

Instead, head still resting on Duncan's chest, she nodded.

"Yeah. Berk needs her daddy."

"Berk's got two uncles who would do anything in the world for her."

"I know that." She nodded again. "I do, Duncan. But she needs her daddy. And he…" She straightened and shrugged. Afraid of Duncan's reaction to what she would say next, she dipped her head to avoid his eyes. "As angry as I am with…as bad as it was, if Jess quit drinking, then he deserves time to be with her. To build a relationship with his daughter."

Duncan bit off a slew of curse words, but he didn't turn around and march inside to take Jess' head off. Instead, he leaned forward and rested his elbows on the rail around the patio. Margo stared at his back, at the muscles bunched beneath his shirt.

"Stevi told me a while ago that you're in love with him."

A little bit surprised to think about Stevi and Duncan taking time to discuss her pathetic life, Margo could only stare at him, mouth gaping open, when he glanced back at her. She waited for a tirade, at the very least an admonition for being stupid, surprised again when Duncan looked back at the parking lot without a word.

"Your mom's here." He spoke so softly, Margo barely heard him. She winced at the thought of her mom inside with Berkley, even though Stevi and Leah were in there to run interference.

"Who's got the bar?" She took a step backward.

"Trace."

She nodded, even though Duncan wasn't looking at her. Backed away slowly, curious about what Duncan was thinking and afraid to go back inside. Where Jess and his girlfriend—Julie—waited. Where, once again, her life was about to change. There would be no going back from here. Jess—good or bad—was truly about to become Berkley's father. Time would tell if he proved to be a good daddy.

Margo stood for a second at the back door to summon the courage, the strength to see the scene through. No matter how today played out, Margo would take the lead. No way she would give up control of her life or her little girl's life to anyone, much less Jess Covey.

Her mom was at the bar with Leah and Stevi, Berkley in her arms. Margo felt a jolt of love zap through her body. Berkley, thumb in her mouth, stared at Stevi, mesmerized by her teasing. Margo's mom was talking to Leah, but she was tugging absently at the zipper on Berkley's windbreaker. Berkley jerked in her arms and turned her head as Margo approached them. A gummy grin broke over Berkley's face, around her thumb, the pink hood of her windbreaker poked up over her head.

"Mamama." Berkley flopped forward in Margo's mom's arms and reached for Margo.

"Hi, baby girl." Margo took her daughter as her mom handed her over. She propped her on her hip and leaned close to kiss her forehead.

"Say *Mommy, take my hood off. I look like a conehead.*" Stevi stepped closer and tugged at the tip of the hood.

"Cutest conehead ever," Margo said with a laugh. She turned purposefully to give Jess her back and pulled Berkley in against her. She snuggled her tight enough that Berkley squirmed and squealed.

"Hey." Stevi touched Margo's hand as Leah finished the task of pulling Berkley's jacket off.

"I'm fine." Margo nodded. She wasn't fine, but she couldn't let on to her mom and her cousins that she was anything but fine. And she sure as hell wasn't going to let Jess see how badly he had rattled her.

"You sure you're ready for this?" Her mom wedged herself in close enough that her thigh bumped Margo's. She smoothed her hand over Margo's back.

"It's been a year." Maybe if she kept repeating this, she would start to believe it herself. "It's time. If Jess is… sober…this is only fair."

"Don't let him hurt my baby girl." Her mom cocked her head and arched an eyebrow.

"Nobody's gonna hurt Berkley, Mom," Margo promised her.

"Call me later." Her mom patted her back as she stepped away from her and snatched her purse off the end barstool. Margo nodded and watched her go, her heart racing again and stealing her breath away.

"Why don't you go upstairs?" Leah suggested. Margo dragged her eyes from her mom's receding figure as she neared the front door. She glanced at Leah and then looked around the bar. Still not packed, but a few people had come in while she had been outside a few moments ago. She hated the idea of being alone with Jess up in the office. They'd made out up there once or twice, back before they broke up, and the last thing she needed right now was to be reminded of the heat the two of them could generate. Then again, she hated the thought of introducing Jess to their daughter down here in front of their patrons, too.

"Yeah," she finally agreed. "Good idea."

"What about—?" Leah cleared her throat. "Her? Do you want me and Stevi to…"

Good question. Margo had no idea what she wanted in regards to the girl with Jess. Short of packing her ass back out the door and down the road, Margo had no idea what to think of her or what to do with her.

Or what Jess wanted.

She answered Leah with a dramatic shrug. "I dunno."

Leah nodded. "Okay. If she stays down here…Stevi and I will…"

Margo tipped her head and waited curiously to see how Leah planned to finish her sentence. Leah only grinned.

"Well?" Margo bounced Berkley on her hip when she started babbling. "You'll what? Tar and feather her? Ply her with alcohol? Make her scrub the floor?"

"Well, I was going to say…talk to her."

"Yeah, no. He's doing her. I don't need my two favorite people in the world getting cozy with her."

"Never happen." Leah's whisper was gruff. "You know that."

Margo did. If they were in junior high, Leah and Stevi would be steadfast Team Margo. But they weren't in junior high anymore, and Margo's cousins were too nice to be rude to anyone, and besides all of that, they were business owners. None of them would treat Jess's girlfriend as anything other than a customer.

She nodded and turned away from Leah. No more hedging. Time to get this over with. Margo cringed at the thought. Not a good way to start this…relationship. Even if she and Jess were never getting back together—and they weren't, not now—they were Berkley's parents. She wanted this to work for Berkley's sake, so she had to be mature about this and she had to start now.

Stevi nodded at her as she turned her back to the bar and took a step toward Jess and Julie. They weren't touching;

they sat on opposite sides of a tall table. Julie lounged back in her chair, her face guileless and sweet as she listened to something Jess was saying. Margo hesitated, unwilling to interrupt them. Didn't seem like Jess could hurt her any more than he already had today, but if she overheard him saying something sexy or sweet to this girl, it would kill her.

She already felt ancient and irrelevant in comparison.

Admittedly, they didn't look...cozy. Or sexy. Margo watched Jess's face as he spoke. He looked amused, and Julie was laughing, but it didn't look like an intimate moment.

Not that that meant anything.

"Oh my gosh."

Margo swallowed hard as a wave of heat touched her cheeks. Julie had noticed her standing near the table, and she was making eyes at Berkley now. Jess turned and scooted his chair back at the same time. The smile on his face dimmed a bit and then froze. He climbed to his feet and stared at Margo with wide eyes.

The proverbial deer in the headlights.

Margo cleared her throat and patted her hand gently at Berkley's diaper-clad butt.

"Um."

The smug look was gone now, but Margo wasn't sure this was any better. She hadn't often seen a lot of emotion paint Jess's face when they were together. Happy. Laid back. Indifferent. They'd laughed together, a lot, and obviously, they hadn't always worked. In the end, nothing about them worked. But he'd never seemed invested enough in her, in their relationship, to get worked up or angry about anything.

Jess stood there now—a couple feet away from her—in his black boots and his leather jacket, his face pale and stricken.

Margo didn't know what to do with a vulnerable Jess Covey.

"She's beautiful."

The words gushed out of his mouth in wonder. Margo prepared to step back, away from him, but Jess only tucked his hands in his jacket pockets. Instead, she took a deep breath and made herself step forward.

Berkley lost interest in the top button of Margo's blouse. Now she turned her attention to Jess and stared at him with the big blue eyes that melted Margo's heart a gazillion times a day.

"This is Berkley." Margo's words were nothing more than a thick whisper.

Berkley cut loose with a squeal and then beamed at her father, as if waiting for his praise. Margo felt prying eyes on her, and it wasn't just Julie watching, either.

Jess fumbled trying to get his hand out of his pocket. Margo stepped back, heart in her throat. She couldn't just hand Berkley over. Not here. Not with so many people watching them. She needed another minute. Jess looked at her sharply, his eyes suspiciously glassy.

"Margo." Brows drawn down in a severe frown, he held his hand out, palm up. Was he reaching to take Berkley or to take Margo's hand?

"Let's go upstairs," she suggested. When he looked at Julie over his shoulder, Margo held her breath. Even if he was sleeping with her, even if he was in love with her, Margo thought she and Berkley deserved a few private moments with him. She didn't want his new girlfriend's eyes on her hands as she passed her baby to his waiting arms. She didn't want the girl to notice that she was shaking, that her eyes burned with tears.

She didn't want Julie to think about her hands on Jess' body. Not because she cared about Julie's feelings, because right at the moment, she didn't give a flying fuck about the other girl. But because she'd loved this man once, and she didn't want the love they had made or the product of that love to be an object of curiosity.

"I'll be fine," Julie promised him.

Margo watched with interest as Jess dug his keys from his pocket and tossed them to Julie.

"Take a spin, if you want."

Julie nodded. She turned her bright eyes to Margo and offered her a small, but friendly smile.

"I'll be fine. Take your time."

CHAPTER 4

JESS TOLD HIMSELF HE WASN'T GOING TO WALK INTO THE
office upstairs with Margo and remember the things they
had done together there before she kicked him out. He
was here to see Berkley; he was finally going to hold his
baby girl in his arms. Today wasn't about the memories he
and Margo had made. They weren't kids; they had never
been kids together, and Jess realized now that was part of
what had been wrong between them. Margo had wanted
an adult relationship, and Jess had been reckless and
immature from the beginning. He'd forced her to be
independent, because he hadn't been reliable. And then
when she handled things on her own—whether it be
cleaning out the gutter or delivering their baby—he had
reacted badly and blamed her.

But when Margo led him into the office, he couldn't help
but look at the big leather couch where they had snuggled
and kissed late into the evening on more than one
occasion. And it wasn't about getting naked and getting

lucky. He and Margo had been in love without knowing it, without sharing it. They had created a life together, and now Jess wanted more than visitation rights to the baby they created together. He wanted that life back; he wanted to be in that love relationship.

Margo cleared her throat, reminding him to move. He stepped aside as she curled her fingers around the door and swung it closed. Jess was glad for Berkley's little singsong voice babbling away. His baby's presence cut the tension in the room, at least a little bit, though Jess jumped and groaned out loud when Margo gave him a gentle nudge further into the room.

"Do you wanna hold her?" Margo asked as she held Berkley toward him. Not ready for it, not ready to take his baby's weight in his arms and make her real—instead of the fantasy he'd carried in his head for a year now—he hesitated. He half expected Berkley to twist away and bury her face in Margo's neck, to hide from him. But she didn't. He stared silently at the pudgy baby hands that reached for him. His throat tight with emotion, he lifted his hands to take her. Margo looked away as Berkley threw herself at him. His hands propped under her arms, she lifted her head and blasted him with a sweet baby grin, complete with the nubs of a few baby teeth and a whole lot of drool.

Margo cleared her throat again as Jess pulled Berkley in closer and settled her against his chest. She was warm, her skin baby soft; and Jess pressed his lips and his nose to her fine, black curls to breathe in the scent of baby shampoo. He couldn't speak. His lungs ached with pent up emotion, and his throat was tight. He squeezed his eyes closed.

Berkley was rattling again, this time in a low monotone. Jess didn't look for meaning; he simply held his daughter close and tried to breathe in the days he had lost with her before he had come back.

Julie had asked if she could ride along. Moral support for him. Genuine curiosity about Margo. A love of babies and the desire to see Berkley. Jess had waffled on bringing her with him, right up until the moment they climbed into his truck for the hour and a half drive. They were friends, and yes, he needed the moral support, because an outraged Margo was terrifying. Not to mention Duncan, Stevi, and Leah. But he hadn't wanted her here, either, because who needed an audience when he was confronting a former lover and meeting his daughter for the first time?

He had felt a stab of guilt downstairs, when he and Margo had closed ranks to come up here and left Julie there at the table. Julie didn't need a babysitter; she had either won the whole bar over down there, or she'd taken his keys and his truck and gone for a spin. Either way, when the two of them left the Queen later, she would have her own observations, her own stories to share, and she wouldn't begrudge him a second he spent with Margo or Berkley.

He was glad for that now. Glad that she had stayed downstairs, because no matter that Margo wasn't looking to reconcile, no matter that there was nothing intimate between them up here, everything about this moment was intensely personal and private and intimate in a way someone who hasn't created a life together wouldn't understand. He and Margo and Berkley, they were a unit. They were a family, albeit a broken family, and Jess was grateful for the moment alone with his ex-girlfriend and his daughter.

Margo moved somewhere behind him. Jess stood with his forehead pressed to the top of Berkley's head, not willing to rush this moment. Berkley might not remember it, but he would never forget it.

"What do you wanna know?" Her voice was a bit gruff. Jess heard her clear her throat, and then he heard the squeal of the chair as she sat down. She had chosen to sit behind the desk. For a second, Jess let himself believe that it was because she wanted the protection, the distance from him. That maybe she was afraid she would get too close to him if she didn't have a big slab of wood and metal between them.

He didn't answer her. He didn't dwell in his delusions, either, because Margo would control herself, even if she had any thoughts of moving closer to him, of touching him. And he knew better than that, too.

"She was…"

Margo's hesitation, the way she caught her breath before she continued was a knife in Jess' chest. His heart.

"Born in August."

Berkley was still singing softly, and now she was batting his face with her little hands.

"Seven six," Margo continued. "She was born August fourteenth—"

"I know that." Jess spoke so softly, he doubted Margo heard him.

"She weighed seven pounds and six ounces. She was seventeen inches long." Margo's voice dropped to a whisper as she shared the clinical details of Berkley's birth.

"Margo."

"And, um." She coughed. "She—"

"Stop."

"She was a little bit—"

"Stop," Jess repeated, louder this time. When Margo didn't try to speak again, he turned to look at her. Elbows propped on the desktop, her hands plastered over her mouth, her big eyes brimmed with tears.

"I figured you would want to know—"

Jess lifted his head from Berkley to give Margo a stern look when she started talking again.

"Not like this." He shook his head.

"What?"

"I don't wanna know like this," he said again.

"What does that mean, Jess?" Still hunched over the desk, she shrugged. "What does that mean? Do you want me to be excited? To be happy to have to share this stuff with you like this? Because you weren't there?"

"Margo." He dropped his head back and squeezed his eyes closed. Berkley patted her hands on his exposed neck, drawing laughter from both him and Margo.

"She likes that."

"What?"

"The scruff on your face," Margo mumbled. Jess covered Berkley's hand with his own and then looked at Margo. Seemed to him that she had liked the scruff on his face and his neck, too. Margo used to smooth her fingers over his face and his lips, and she liked the feel of it against her skin when he kissed her.

She looked away first, turned toward the window.

"She's fascinated with Duncan and Trace."

He watched her struggle not to look at him. She rolled her lips inward, and he wondered if she wanted to say more. Jess wanted to ask about Duncan and Stevi. And Leah's new guy. But it wasn't the time. Sadly, he wasn't sure it ever would be the right time for small talk, to catch up on what had been happening at the Queen.

"How long were you in labor?" he asked.

"You really wanna ask me that?" She turned cool eyes on him, the tears gone now.

He shrugged. Turned to move back to the sofa and lowered himself slowly to sit. Berkley beamed at him and stuck her fingers in her mouth.

"I wanna know." He nodded. Well aware that it was a dangerous question, and that Margo was sure to take some skin in exchange for her answer, he still wanted to know.

"Longer than it took you to fuck whoever you were with that night."

He opened his mouth to argue, but when their eyes met, he simply closed it again. He hadn't been with a woman when Berkley was born, not like that. But he had cheated, and guilty was guilty.

"Seven hours." She flopped back in the chair and stared at the ceiling. "My water broke after about five hours. Spent nearly an hour with my feet in stirrups."

She was trying to bait him, but he didn't react. He had never witnessed a live birth, but he had overheard horror stories, turned incredible birth stories. For whatever reason, women seemed to like talking about birthing rooms and stuff that had always sounded gory to him. Now, though, he wanted to know. Every last detail. He wished he could flip a switch and go back in time to that day, so he could be with Margo while she delivered their daughter.

Except, if he did flip a switch and go back in time, he would still be drinking.

He had come a hell of a long way from that guy, and as badly as he wished he had seen his daughter's birth, he didn't want to be that guy again.

"What?" Margo pressed.

Jess shook his head.

"Tell me," she demanded. "What are you thinking?"

"I was just wishing I could go back and be with you for that." He shrugged his right shoulder, kept his eyes on Berkley. "But that I wouldn't trade the world for my sobriety."

When she didn't answer, he took a chance and lifted his gaze to look at her. Head turned toward the window again, Jess studied her face in profile. In the year that he'd been gone, she'd lost the baby weight and then some. Her cheeks were lean, as was the rest of her long, slender body. She looked down now, and her long, thick lashes swept her cheek. Jess felt that same knife in his heart when she reached to dab at her eyes with her fingertips.

"I'm glad you're sober, Jess," she whispered. "But I'm not sure I can ever forgive you for not being there when she was born."

Her words twisted that knife in his heart. Never mind that she hadn't given him the chance to be there when Berkley was born.

"I had Leah and Stevi." She sniffled and swallowed hard. "Berkley does, too. But every baby girl needs her daddy."

"I'm here now, Margo," he reminded her.

Her nod was slow in coming. She stared out the window for long, quiet moments, and finally, in slow motion, she swung her face back around to look at him.

"What do you want with her?"

"What?"

"I'm not gonna let you take her."

"I don't wanna take her from you." He shook his head. "I just want to be involved."

"Involved like you might drive down with your girlfriend once a month and cluck her chin and parade her around because she's the best thing you've ever done? Or involved like choosing her preschool and watching her tiny tot soccer games and tucking her in at night?"

"She's not my girlfriend," he said quietly, "and Berkley isn't the best thing I've ever done. You are. What you and I had together created this baby—"

"Save it, Jess. What we had was sex." Margo stood up. "And it wasn't even good enough to keep you faithful."

He sucked in a deep breath and turned his attention back to Berkley, who was bouncing on his lap now.

"Your mom's seen her," Margo told him. She paced to the window and stood with her back to him. He'd known that; his mom had called him the night she'd bumped into Margo at the grocery store. Margo had been cordial with her, but she hadn't been friendly, and she hadn't offered for his mom to hold Berkley, and his mom had been a wreck that night.

"I know."

"Kinda messy dealing with your family," she announced. "None of them wanted to believe you cheated. They all wanted to excuse your drinking. Of course I'm the bitch keeping you from your daughter."

"I told them the truth. I told them how it was."

Margo's shoulder jerked. "Moms don't want to believe bad things about their babies, Jess."

"You still haven't said what you want with her," she reminded him after a few seconds of quiet. "Involved. Involved, how, Jess? You live an hour and a half away. I won't entertain you when you visit her on a whim, and you will take her from Adam's Bay over my dead body."

"Why don't you just cut my dick off, Margo?" He climbed to his feet. Berkley seemed to sense the anger brewing in him. Her lower lip quivered, and she strained to see Margo. "I wouldn't ask you to let me take her to my apartment. I'm not asking you to drop everything and entertain me. Just let me be around? Let me spend time with her?"

Margo perched on the edge of the desk. "You gonna hang around the Queen?"

"If that's what it takes."

"Won't it bother you? Being around the booze?"

"No."

She stared at him for a long time and finally, she stood, and gave him a nod.

"Suit yourself."

CHAPTER 5

"Hey." Margo stood at the end of the bar and watched Stevi adjust a strand of purple garland on the Halloween tree.

"Hey." Stevi flashed a big grin her way and then took a few steps back from the tree to appraise it. The same as she'd done every day since she and Duncan had put the tree up. "What do you think? Is the witch crooked?"

Margo chuckled as she stepped up beside her cousin to eyeball the crazy-looking witch at the top of the tree.

"I think it's great," she decided.

"You know what Duncan told me last night?" Stevi asked as they moseyed back over to the bar.

"Where is Duncan, anyway?"

"He and Trace went to the farmers' market," Stevi waved her hands impatiently. "He said he thinks the tree looks great."

Margo grinned, but she couldn't help the eye roll.

"Mm-hmm. And what were you doing when he said this?"

"Giving him—"

"Nope." Margo shook her head. "Stop. Don't want to know."

"A massage," Stevi yelped and laughed. "I was giving him a massage."

"Right."

"That ended up—"

"Can I ask a favor?"

"Please don't ask me to never share sex stories just because he's your stepbrother. There are times he blows my mind—"

"And I'm sure you blow him," Margo winked at her. Stevi snorted. "But that's not what I was going to ask."

"No? What's up?" Stevi scooted onto the end barstool and tipped her head at Margo.

"Um." Margo fiddled with a pint glass. She flicked her eyes up over Stevi and around the empty room. Leah was upstairs in the office, working on an order. Tania was on the schedule, but she and the other two waitresses scheduled weren't due to come in for hours.

"Margo?" Stevi coaxed her.

"I…"

"You..." Stevi arched her eyebrows. "Are scaring me. What? Just ask."

"Set me up? Find me a date?"

Stevi stared at her thoughtfully for a moment. Margo prepared herself for whatever Stevi might say; true, Leah was generally the one with opinions about Jess, but Stevi observed the same things Leah did, and surely, she had an opinion, too.

"Okay." She nodded. Margo watched her work her lower lip with her teeth.

"It's just that you know a lot of guys," Margo said quietly, "and I know they have to be good guys, because you wouldn't hang out with jerks."

Stevi chuckled. "Oh, there's one in every bag, believe me."

"Not someone you slept with."

"No kidding," Stevi mumbled.

"Which is unfortunate, because Grant is pretty hot."

"Oh, he is," Stevi agreed. "Good guy. But yeah, totally sailed that ship many times, Margo. Not to mention, Duncan kinda has it in for him."

"Anyone?"

"Yeah." Stevi tossed her hands up quickly as if to settle Margo. "I can get you a date in a heartbeat, Margo. You can get a date in a heartbeat. Just start looking around the bar any given night."

From the corner of her eye, Margo saw Leah coming down the sweeping staircase on the northern wall of the building.

"I don't wanna go out with a barfly."

Stevi grinned. "Bar hawk?"

"What's a bar hawk?" Leah asked as she sidled up to the bar.

"You know what I mean," Margo told Stevi.

"I do." Stevi nodded. "Okay."

"What's going on?" Leah leaned into the bar, folded her arms over the edge.

"Tired?" Stevi smoothed her hand over Leah's back.

"No. I'm hungry."

"Whatcha want?" Margo asked. "I'll go see what we have."

"Hot fudge."

"A sundae?" Margo tipped her head.

"No. Just a big bowl of hot fudge. And some potato chips."

Margo cut her eyes to Stevi's and saw that Stevi was trying not to laugh.

"It's not funny," Leah groaned. "I'm gonna weigh four hundred pounds by the time I have this baby."

"And then when you're running your butt off, chasing said baby around, you'll lose it all and be skinny and sexy again."

"I feel like I'll never be sexy again," Leah mumbled. "Do you have stretch marks?"

"Yep." Margo shrugged. "I also have a little doll baby girl."

Leah nodded. "What's a bar hawk?"

"Margo wants me to set her up on a date."

"Too bad you and Grant have done the deed." She glanced at Stevi. "He's pretty hot."

Stevi laughed softly.

"Does he have the v?"

"What?" Stevi yelped.

"You know…the way a guy's abs are so cut and the v…" Leah raised her eyebrows. "At his waist. Leading to the package?"

Stevi opened her mouth to answer Leah, but she could only groan out loud.

"Does Duncan?" Margo surprised herself by asking. She wanted to know, but she also didn't particularly want to picture Duncan naked.

"Mmm." Stevi cleared her throat.

"Better than Grant?" Leah nudged her with her elbow.

"Yes. He also knows…"

"Okay." Margo knocked her fist on the bar and stepped back. "I'm—"

"Why would you ask?" Stevi glanced at Leah. "I used to hear you praising every deity I've ever heard of when I lived with you and Trace."

"I dunno." Leah shrugged. "Maybe because I haven't... heard or seen that with you guys. I hope it's half as good for you—"

"Stop." Stevi shook her head. "Stop. I told you I could live happily with him if he only kissed me the rest of our lives."

"If you guys need me, I'll be in the bathroom," Margo told them. "Barfing my lunch."

"Margo." The tone of Stevi's voice stopped her in her tracks halfway down the bar.

"Hmm?"

"Just...um..."

Margo glanced at Stevi over her shoulder, but she drew up short when she saw the uncertainty on her cousin's face. They were done teasing, done talking about sex.

"Nothing left?" Stevi asked quietly.

Margo wanted to snap an answer back at Stevi to convey both irritation and nonchalance, but she also knew she couldn't feel both things at the same time, and they would call her on it. She stared at Stevi for a second, glanced at Leah, and pressed her lips together. She shook her head and lowered her gaze to the floor.

She hadn't talked to either of them the day Jess had been here. She and Jess had had the showdown in the office—

the memory left Margo cold, because there had been so much left unsaid and now they had moved into the next phase of their lives, parenting but not together—and then she'd suggested Jess bring Berkley downstairs so he wasn't completely abandoning Julie. She had heard him claim Julie wasn't his girlfriend, but if she believed it, it was only because Jess didn't really do girlfriends. He did girls. Women. Margo had been an exception, maybe, for a while, but she hadn't been anything special in the end, and he had moved on while he still lived in her house.

"What did he say? What happened?" Leah finally slid onto the barstool to her right. Margo thought she looked tired. Because it was easier to worry over her cousins, easier to care for them than herself, she fetched a glass of cold water and put it in front of Leah.

"Do you want me to fix you something to eat?"

"Not unless you can warm me up some hot fudge and find a bag of potato chips."

"Really bad craving, huh?"

Leah shrugged helplessly.

"Does Trace indulge you?"

Stevi snickered beside Leah.

"With the cravings?" Margo rolled her eyes.

"Yeah."

"So if you called him now and asked for hot fudge and chips, he would deliver?"

"Already called him."

"Wow." Margo nodded. "You know what? That's really..."

"Crazy?" Stevi suggested.

"No. I was gonna say romantic." Margo propped her hands on the bar behind her and leaned against it. "He loves you so much."

"Either that or he gets tired of me whining."

"Imagine that," Stevi mumbled.

"Is he coming back?" Leah sipped her water.

"To see Berkley."

"Bringing his girlfriend?"

"I didn't ask."

"Did he apologize? Did he say *anything*?"

"What would he say?" Margo straightened. "He's moved on. He wants to be involved with Berkley. So." She drew in a deep breath and tossed her hands up helplessly. "After wasting another year on him, thinking he would come back for me, I'm ready to move on, too."

"Did you tell him that?"

"You're kidding, right?" Margo narrowed her eyes at Stevi. "*Hey, Jess, I know you've got a cute girl up there who's probably sweet and tight and hot, but what if we tried this again? Why* would I put myself through that?"

"Yeah." Leah nodded. "Why would she? Stevi." Leah was

staring at the Halloween tree now. "Your witch is crooked."

CHAPTER 6

Sunlight lit the farmhouse, bounced off the white siding, making Jess' head feel like it might split in two. He pulled his insulated hooded jacket on and tugged the zipper up and then took a look around at the trucks parked in the gravel drive. Only three, so far. He leaned back into his truck and grabbed his phone from the console. Not quite seven. Good. He had a few minutes. Derrick Carmichael's truck was the first one in the drive; Jess straightened, shoved the phone down in the pocket of his work pants and zipped it closed. The phone had taken a beating, but not for lack of trying to keep it safe.

A cold gust of wind whipped around the corner of the house. Jess squinted up at the sun and cupped his hands around his mouth to blow on them. They were dry, chapped already, and it was just October. Margo liked his rough hands, the way they felt on her skin. She used to, anyway. Not enough to give him total control, but she'd told him more than once that she liked his callouses.

Derrick stood in the backyard, head tilted back and eyes on the gutter of the two-story house. Josiah Wies stood with him, but Jess headed toward them. He'd hoped the sun would bring some heat today and warm things up a bit. October had been decidedly cold, and being on a rooftop during daylight hours didn't help. Judging from the bite in the wind and the forecasted high of 41, Jess decided the sun was just a cruel tease again today.

"Jess." Derrick turned as he approached.

"Looks like another day of freezing our balls off." Jess glanced accusingly at the sun and then turned his head to survey the gutter above them. A tree had come down in the last big thunderstorm earlier this month and bounced off the roof before hitting the ground. The gutter and roof had suffered minimal damage due to the tree being young and spindly, rather than ancient and thick and strong.

"Coffee in my truck," Derrick told him. He nodded appreciatively. Coffee did sound good, but more than that, he needed to talk to his boss. Just to touch base.

"I'm gonna go get some," Josiah decided. He turned and yanked an orange stocking cap down over his ears. "Jess?"

"Thanks." Jess shook his head. "I'll get it."

Josiah wandered away, leaving Jess alone with Derrick. Derrick wasn't really old enough to be his father, and Jess wasn't looking for a father figure. He had a perfectly good dad back home in Adam's Bay. But he'd learned early on—from Julie—that Derrick was wise beyond his years. A recovering alcoholic, Derrick had made every mistake Jess had and then some. Thankfully, Ginger—his wife of thirty years—had been patient and forgiving, and Julie—his daughter and Jess' current closest friend other than Derrick—had rebounded and learned a variety of life's lessons from her dad's drunken escapades and her parents' tumultuous marriage.

"You got somethin' on your mind, son." Derrick didn't look at him, but Jess knew he listened. If any of his crew needed anything, they knew they could count on Derrick. "Spit it out."

"I went to Adam's Bay the other night." Maybe it was the way the words just gushed out of him in a heap, like he'd been holding them in forever, that made Derrick turn toward him. Jess had done the drive often—just over an hour, it wasn't bad—to see his parents and his sisters, though he had finally admitted to Derrick that those trips were sometimes harder than staying away. His family didn't judge him, but they sure as fuck didn't get him, either. His mom was a worrier, always hovering, and that made him want to drink. One sister was so busy being superwoman that she breezed in and out of their parents' house and rarely had time to exchange two words with him. Jess was proud of her nonprofit work at the community center, but now and then he felt like Lori thought he was beneath her. Not just because Margo had kicked him out and issued the ultimatum, but because he hadn't used his degree for a real job. Lori thought she was *making a difference*, and she obviously thought Jess was just getting by. Melissa never belittled him, but Melissa ran her mouth with mean things about Margo often enough that the air around her blistered his skin.

"Did you see Margo?" Derrick asked him.

The wind kicked up again. Jess wished now that he would have grabbed some coffee, although there was little satisfaction in standing outside with a tiny Styrofoam cup of coffee that cooled off in the time it took to lift it to his lips.

"Yeah. I did." He balled his hands into fists and shoved them in his pockets.

Derrick's grin was immediate and sincere, and Jess felt something inside warm a bit. This is why he talked to Derrick about this stuff rather than his parents. Julie had told him stories about Derrick and Ginger, but Jess would never have admitted that to Derrick. But eventually, last year, once Jess had alluded to his ex and his little girl a time or two, Derrick had warmed to him, and the whole sordid truth had come out. Not the tiny details that Julie sometimes shared. Derrick didn't tell Jess about a neighbor woman giving him a ride home form the corner bar and blowing him on the front porch, while Ginger stood inside waiting for it to be over with.

But Julie had.

Derrick's truth—his ugly version and Julie's grittier version told through a child's eyes—had given Jess hope. If Ginger could love Derrick through that mess, maybe Jess had a chance at getting Margo back.

"You look like a new man." Derrick studied him closely and let out a whistle. "How's the baby?"

The words hit Jess like an arrow in the heart. God, how he'd wanted the opportunity to field a question like that. He'd fucked things up with Margo, and then when she threw him out, he'd blamed Margo, and it had taken a kid like Julie to make him see sense. But he wasn't a bad guy. He wasn't the dick Margo's clan had made him out to be. Strip off the leather jacket and the heavy black boots, and he was just a guy who made immature choices and hurt the wrong woman.

"She's beautiful." He surrendered to the grin and shrugged helplessly. "Black hair. Big blue eyes. I think she liked me."

"You hold her?"

Jess had confessed to Derrick one night last fall when they were first getting to know each other that he'd cried like a baby the night Berkley was born. When Stevi called him *after* Margo delivered her. After he'd taken that long-legged brunette out to the alley behind Grisham's, a grungy bar a few blocks south of the Queen. He'd skipped the foreplay and flipped the girl's skirt up—silently thanked the stars she wasn't wearing underwear—and shoved his pants down enough to roll a condom on and fuck her.

Somehow Margo had found out about that and used it as ammunition against him. Twisted things around to make it sound like he'd been fucking someone else while she delivered, when he would have hauled ass to Adam's Bay Mercy to be with her if he had known it was time.

Overcome with emotion—again—he swallowed hard and gave Derrick a stoic nod.

"I will give that little girl my heart if she ever needs it." His voice was pinched, his words quiet.

"No better feelin' in the world than the way you love your own child," Derrick agreed. "Except when you know they love you that same damned way."

Jess nodded.

"Only thing that comes close is when your baby's mama loves you, too."

"Mm." Jess arched his eyebrows and shrugged. Of course, he'd told Derrick he wished he could go back in time and undo the mistakes he'd made. That he wished he could earn Margo's forgiveness. That had sparked countless conversations conducted in early hours like today or sometimes in the afternoon, when the whole crew climbed down from the roof and headed to their trucks and went home.

"Did she know you were coming?"

They'd talked about that, too. Was it best to make solid plans with her? Work around her schedule? Tiptoe around her so as not to piss her off? Or sweep in and catch her off-guard?

"No."

Derrick wagged his eyebrows and cut loose with his hearty laugh.

"She happy to see you?"

"No." Jess shook his head. "I don't think so. I mean...the..."

Derrick meandered back across the yard. Jess heard more engines and truck doors out front. It was time to get to work. He jogged a few steps to catch up with him, saw that Derrick was waiting expectantly for him to continue.

"The tension's still there."

"The sexual tension," Derrick clarified.

"Yeah. She kind of launched herself at me and bit me." He laughed now, though that nip had both surprised and hurt him. "She's still the same bossy, pushy Margo."

"You still attracted to her?"

"Absolutely."

"But she's not…"

"I don't know. She's still so angry."

"If she's still angry, you still have a shot, Jess." Derrick shrugged. "Is she gonna letcha see your Berkley?"

Jess sighed as they rounded the house. The whole crew was assembled now, all of them in various stages of dressing for the weather. He was ready to work, ready to get through today and the next and the next. Until he could get his ass back to Adam's Bay to see his girls.

The thought of Margo bristling at those words made his heart beat a little quicker. He turned to Derrick with a big grin.

"She said if I'm sober, she won't keep her from me."

"Congratulations, Jess." Derrick offered his hand. Jess shook it, well aware several of the other guys—even Tito from Rabe Gutters was here—were watching the interaction curiously. "You're a father."

"Thank you, Derrick." He nodded.

"You say the word." Derrick squeezed his hand before letting it go. "Whenever you need to."

Jess answered with another quick nod and then he sauntered back to his truck. He opened the driver's door and leaned over the seat for a moment, as if searching for something. In reality, he simply needed a moment to himself.

Technically, he had been a father for over a year now. But hearing Derrick say it had puffed him up big and proud, and afraid he would get emotional—most of these guys were single, no kids and maybe wouldn't get it—he lingered at his truck for a few moments.

He would start with being a father, but Jess couldn't wait for the day his sweet baby girl called him Daddy.

CHAPTER 7

Jess sipped his black coffee as he steered his old Chevy truck down the familiar streets. When he had lived here with Margo, he hadn't known a lot of their neighbors. He hadn't really bothered to look around much past the bottle and the women. Not that he'd slept with all of them. In fact, that had only happened twice. Still, he had hurt Margo, and it had taken a long time for him to really understand that. To understand that choosing to sit in a bar with this woman or that had hurt the woman he had committed himself to. Choosing to laugh and talk and yes, flirt, with other women had hurt her. Spending his time with all those bottles and the women—it didn't matter if he was in bed with them or not. He had made the choice over and over again to spend his time away from Margo, and though he'd never once felt anything other than friendship and simple physical attraction for them, he had committed emotional infidelity.

He had packed his bags without argument and hit the road when Berkley was born. Margo didn't know it, but he'd gone to the hospital to see her. Berkley, not Margo. He figured by that time, Duncan Marks would have called the cops on him and had him escorted out of the building if he tried to get near Margo. He had loved Margo too much to stick around and make her miserable. But he wanted to see Berkley. Just once. He wanted to know if his daughter was born with dark hair. If she had blue eyes. If she looked like him or Margo. He had wanted to count her baby toes and stroke his finger over her hand and cradle her against him just once. He had promised himself he would walk away from both of his girls—for their own good—if he could just press his baby girl to his chest and his heart just one time.

He hadn't made it into the nursery area. The fancy security system on the labor and delivery floor required passcodes to get in. And even if he had been able to slide in on some other daddy's shadow once a passcode was put in, he noticed through the small, rectangular windows in the doors that the new dads had hospital bracelets on just like the moms and the babies, and the nurse scanned those bracelets each time a dad approached the nursery window.

Already wrecked because Margo had given him his walking papers, by phone, no less—at that time, he still blamed her for being judgmental and unforgiving—he had jammed his hands in his pockets and stalked back to the elevator.

Remembering the way he'd jabbed the button for the first floor, Jess tightened his left hand on the steering wheel as he slowed at a four way stop up the block from Brassfield Elementary. He had gone to school there when he was a kid. It also happened to be two blocks up from Margo's house.

That day at the hospital, he had slipped out of the elevator as two old women got in. Knowing he looked like hell—hung over and desperate for a drink—he had rushed by the women and headed out of the elevator bay. For some reason, he had lifted his chin just in time to see the large collage photo frame on the wall. Stickers of the words *New Beginnings* were plastered to the wall over the frame; Margo had some of those fancy script stickers on the walls at the house.

The collage frame was filled with photos of the babies born in the hospital. Berkley's picture was already there. Jess didn't know how long he stood gazing at that small photo of his baby girl, but probably long enough to make people suspicious of him.

He had considered taking a picture of the frame with his phone. Thank God, he had come to his senses before trying that, or someone else would have called security and had him hauled away. Instead, he had looked his fill at Berkley's fiery red cheeks and the perfect little O of her lips. She had a mohawk of black hair; her tiny fists were smooshed up by her face. She appeared to be dressed in pink, and she was bundled up in a white blanket with pink and yellow hearts on it.

Moved to tears—which had blown his mind, because Margo had asked him to get out, and so he was pissed not hurt, and ready to watch her flail at motherhood—he had decided to buy her flowers. Berkley, not Margo.

Jess groaned out loud now at the memory. He eased the truck to the curb at the end of the block. He couldn't sit here now. School was in session, and though he had worked hard and changed all the stuff he had grown to hate about himself, it still wouldn't fly to linger outside an elementary school.

He took a healthy drink of the coffee this time and let the hot liquid warm him. Even with the sun out, it was another chilly morning. Jess watched the wind lift a pile of leaves and scatter them a few inches down the sidewalk.

Frustrated with himself now, Jess tucked his chin to his chest and pinched the bridge of his nose. God, he had been such a dick. The hell of it was, he hadn't been brought up that way. His parents were social drinkers, so he had no idea where he had learned to overdo it. No idea when he had started using alcohol as a crutch. When he had started blaming everyone else—especially the people he loved, including his parents and Margo—for his failures.

That day at the hospital, he had hurried down the corridor by the emergency entrance. He remembered smiling at people as he passed them on the way to the gift shop. He'd been ridiculously happy and naïve once he had decided to send his baby girl a gift. No, he couldn't walk it up to her, like he wanted to. But he would send a little pink rose to her via the hospital volunteers.

Shame and indignation making his gut twist now, Jess swallowed more coffee, dropped the truck in drive again, and eased away from the curb. He drove cautiously in the school zone; though it was after nine, so there were no kids out on the sidewalks or playgrounds now, anyway. It was one thing for Margo to kick him out when Berkley was born. But he was still a little angry over the way she had reacted last week when he had gone to the Queen to see her.

He had found a little pink teddy bear in the gift shop, and imagining that one day, Berkley would hug that teddy bear when she slept, he had grabbed it from the shelf and carried it to the register. Asked for a pink rose and that teddy bear to be delivered to Margo Nevin's room for the baby, all the while thinking of the big *fuck you* he was sending to Margo with the gift for their baby.

I care enough to say goodbye to her, but fuck you, Margo, for making me leave.

All the houses on Margo's street were decked out for Halloween. Jess drove slowly, one arm slung over the wheel and the other hand resting in his lap, fingers wrapped around the paper coffee cup. He eyed the porches decorated with hay bales and pumpkins, the mailboxes and light posts done up with cornstalks and orange ribbons. He even noticed a scarecrow on one porch swing. The doors were all closed to keep out the chill, he supposed. Or maybe to keep unwanted visitors away.

He hadn't sent the rose or the teddy bear. The memory made his cheeks burn with shame. He'd been all chatty, talking to the grandmotherly woman at the register, bragging about his new baby as if he had the right to do so. The woman had been so happy for him, asking for details about the birth. How much did she weigh? How long was she? What was her name?

Jess couldn't answer the questions. Because he didn't know. And he couldn't pay for the teddy bear and the flower, because he'd spent his last ten on a twelve-pack the night before. The single in his wallet wouldn't even buy his baby a candy bar if she were old enough to eat it.

Margo's house looked the same, but different. Jess braked and turned his indicator on. Though Margo lived in the city limits of Adam's Bay, she didn't live in the heart of town. There hadn't been a single damned car on this road until now, when Jess was stopped in front of her house. He imagined her watching him out the window and running through the house, pulling the curtains and locking the doors.

When he killed the truck engine, the morning quiet roared around him. Living here—he had thought it was the middle of nowhere back then—had been hell. He had been the guy who needed noise and lights and cars and music. He had needed stimulation, and he had been restless, and that was maybe a symptom of his alcoholism and a cause for his break up with Margo.

Head turned deliberately away from the house—he didn't want to see Margo watching him through the windows— he opened his mouth and tried for a deep breath. Sucked in a huge breath and let it fill his lungs before letting it out slowly and evenly.

The day after Berkley was born, he had ducked his head and slinked out of the hospital gift shop. Embarrassed and ashamed, he'd hightailed it out of the hospital, afraid the woman behind the counter would expose him for the fraud he was. He had climbed into his truck and floored the gas, daring every fucking cop in Adam's Bay to pull him over.

None had. Apparently no one wanted him around here.

With one last sigh, Jess climbed down out of the truck and then swung the door closed, flinching at the noise. Who would have thought this drive would be so hard? He had survived that initial encounter with Margo last week. He had even landed a hit or two of his own. He'd worked hard to change who he was, or maybe he had just remembered who he was deep inside and found that guy again. Margo didn't know he had hoped to come back to Adam's Bay and claim her as well as Berkley; she would never have to know. But there was no reason for him to slink around now, uneasy about dealing with his ex.

Julie would tell him to grow a pair and deal with it. There had been a time when she would have been sympathetic to how he felt, but she wouldn't let him wallow in the memories. Not the way he had on the drive down this morning. Those memories had been drowning him back when they met, and Julie had spoon fed him encouragement and friendship and dignity, and when he'd finally emerged from the deep end, their friendship had evolved into a two-way street. She expected the truth from him at all times—even if it meant him telling her the dress she was wearing made her look fourteen or that she looked like she was trying too hard if she was wearing lipstick.

And Jess expected, needed the same from her. For instance, right about now, he could do with a little kick in the ass. He chuckled, considered texting her now to tell her that. But she would be at work, and he still had the paper cup in one hand, and by now, Margo had to know he was in the driveway.

What was left of the coffee in his cup had gone cold, but he still carried it to the back door with him. He rapped his knuckles on the glass pane in the door and then jammed his hand in his hip pocket to wait. There was no sound coming from inside, but he would bet she was home. No doubt, she would be getting ready to head out soon for the Queen, but he would bet she was home at the moment. The Margo he knew was not an early riser. She could do it; she hated to be rushed or worse, to run late. But she also loved lounging in bed in the mornings, especially on mornings like this.

She would have the window open. He could imagine her propped up in bed, her pillows stacked against the headboard, and a book in her hands. She loved mysteries and thrillers, the darker, the better. Her hair would be messy, but sexy, and he could just see the strap of her tank —the light blue one, maybe—sliding off her shoulder. The swell of her breast peeking over the edge of the material.

The door swung open cutting his memory-fueled fantasy off. Too bad his dick was still in dreamland, thick and hard for the woman staring at him now with about the same level of enthusiasm she had shown him last week at the Queen.

"What?"

He feasted on the sight of her. Maybe he had been dead wrong about the sexy, tousled hair and the tank with the strap slipping down her toned upper arm. But his dick still liked what he was looking at. Skinny jeans—to his knowledge, Margo didn't own a dress, but damn, her ass did wonders for denim—and a crème-colored blouse, open low enough that he saw a brown tank and even shiny brown lace under that. Her dark hair spilled in luscious curls over her shoulders, and her eyes stared at him blankly, as if he was a stray dog on the stoop.

"Can I come in?"

He expected her to argue, so when she stepped back without a word in response and held the door open for him, he was surprised. He heard music as she leaned around him to close the door, but it wasn't familiar to him. Though it was just past nine in the morning and full daylight outside, the overhead light was on. Jess smelled coffee and toast.

"Did we plan this one?" She slipped by him and went to the sink, where the faucet was running. He watched her tap it off and then dip her hand into the soapy water in search of the dish sponge. The sarcastic edge in her voice almost amused him.

"I have the day off."

"What kind of work do you do that you can just take a day off?"

"I didn't just take a day off," he told her. "And you know I'm working with a roofing crew. It's storming at home."

A loud squeal and a crash came from the living room. Jess felt a wave of warmth bowl him over. Margo groaned and dipped her chin to her chest.

"Is she okay?"

"Yep." She withdrew her hand from the water, squeezed the sponge, and set it on the back of the sink. Jess took a few steps toward her as she dried her hands on a towel and then tossed it aside, too. Margo glanced at him over her shoulder as she went to the living room. He didn't know if it was an invitation to follow her, but he chose to read it as such and stepped into the living room behind her.

Berkley stood in a playpen, hollering what had to be four-letter words in baby speak. A stuffed koala bear was on the floor a few feet away.

"You are not funny," Margo told her, but even as she spoke, Berkley stopped the noise and beamed up at her mommy. Jess thought she looked angelic in her purple shirt and little denim pants. Instead of picking Berkley up, Margo moved to grab the bear and dropped it back in the playpen. "Play with Dunny."

Dunny? Jess arched his eyebrows and watched Margo go back to the kitchen sink. Berkley didn't pay any attention to him. She simply took a shaky step to her left—her fat little fingers white-knuckling the side of the playpen—and picked the bear up. Jess snorted when she launched it again and followed that up with an angry bellow.

"Mommy will be there in a minute," Margo called.

Berkley shrieked, her cheeks flushing pink with anger. Jess loved the little flare of temper, but he knew Margo wouldn't think it was funny or cute. Without considering what Margo would say, he shrugged his jacket off and tossed it on the arm of the wooden rocker in the corner of the room. The movement or the slap of the leather on the wood drew Berkley's attention.

Her lip quivered, but her bellows quieted to soft sobs. She watched him curiously for a moment, her big blue eyes glassy with tears.

"Hey." He squatted down to put himself at her level and studied her the same way she studied him. The fingers of her right hand were still curled around a fist of the playpen netting. Her cheeks were fiery red, and her wet lashes were spiked with tears. "What's the matter?"

She worked her mouth like she was talking, but she didn't make a sound. Instead, she reached her other hand over the top of the playpen. Jess eased to his knees and let her press her fingers to his face.

"Mum!" Her shrill voice still sounded angry, but her eyes were wide now with wonder. Jess smiled and covered her hand on his face with his own.

"Mommy's busy," he told her. "She'll be in when she's done."

Berkley rattled off something that sounded serious, her little fingers inching over his face as she talked. Jess let her explore. The music he had heard earlier was kids' stuff, he realized now. Margo had some kind of little kid stuff playing in here with Berkley; he heard the words to "This Old Man."

He wanted to pick her up, but he hesitated. Margo might have a routine established, and if he picked Berkley up now without her permission and threw a wrench into that routine, it would piss her off. Berkley looked over his shoulder and then put her eyes back on him.

"Mum," she said softly.

Jess rested his chin on the playpen and breathed deeply. She smelled like baby shampoo and fruit. Now she gripped his face with both hands. Before he knew what he was doing, he reached over the side of the playpen and slipped his hands under his arms. He hefted her easily and climbed to his feet, but he stopped when he turned and saw Margo, propped in the doorway, watching him with a guarded expression.

He hated to ask permission, because he refused to be a pussy who took orders and cowered in the corner when a woman wasn't happy with him. But he didn't want to be an asshole, either, and carelessly blow up Margo's organized life.

"This okay?" His voice was a little gruff. Hell if he would admit it, but he was afraid she would tell him no.

She nodded and rolled her lips inward.

"Yeah. It's fine."

CHAPTER 8

FOR ALL THE SQUEALING AND TANTRUM THROWING OF JUST seconds ago, Berkley rested her head on Jess's shoulder now, her thumb in her mouth and her big eyes glued to Margo. Beast to angel, as usual, but it usually took Margo longer to calm her down. Because it took her longer to get to her in the morning routine, and often by the time she did, Berkley was in full-blown meltdown.

Margo let her eyes wander over Jess's shoulders and arms —he'd taken his jacket off, treating her to a peek at his hard, muscular biceps and strong, sinewy forearms—and watched him pat her baby girl's back. The same way she always did.

When she lifted her gaze, she found him watching her. His eyes were warm, and a faint smile touched his lips. Behind him, the room looked the same—playpen, toys, and flat screen TV on the wall—but it was different now, too, because he was back. He had once fit inside this house and inside her heart, but he'd been gone for a long time, and Margo hadn't had time to slow down. She'd missed him. Hell yes, she had missed Jess, but she was a single mom and a businesswoman, and broken hearts and lessons learned or not, as the case may be, were time consuming. She didn't have time to stew over the hurt; she had moved on. Alone with Berkley.

Lessons learned, she reminded herself, as she cleared her throat and stepped back into the kitchen. She surveyed the table and the counters, disappointed to realize she was finished cleaning up their breakfast mess. Nothing left out here to keep her away from him.

The music segued from "This Old Man" to "London Bridge." It felt ridiculous to stand here with her little girl and the man who had helped her make that little girl and listen to someone belting out little kid songs. She had wanted so much more with Jess, and she had loved him, and she'd been so hurt that he had never loved her back. In hindsight, what they had was dark and maybe even tawdry, and conversations between them should be conducted in dark, seedy bars over hard liquor. Not a living room with a playpen and board books and "London Bridge."

"Are you alone?"

She hated herself the second the words came out of her mouth. The last damned thing she felt was anything at all to do with Jess's girlfriend: worry over her being out in his truck alone or jealousy that she existed. And the last damned thing she wanted was for Jess to think it mattered to her one way or another.

"Yeah."

She glanced at him over her shoulder and saw him nod. Before she could say something mean—crossed her mind to ask if Julie was in school today—she bit her lip and ducked her head. She raised both hands to her neck and rubbed viciously at the tension, but it did no good.

"Do you need to go to the Queen?" he asked her.

"Not for a while."

"Would you rather I just drove down on the weekends?"

She started to say yes, but she caught herself. What difference did it make? She worked a full schedule. The Queen was closed on Sundays, so they were all off on Sundays. But other times, she and the crew took whatever personal time was needed.

Besides. When she'd told Jess he could come back if he quit drinking, she had envisioned a little something more than a weekend only daddy. Then again, she'd envisioned something more than Jess being Berkley's daddy, and that hadn't played out well.

"No." She stepped into the living room with him and slipped her hands in her hip pockets. "Whatever. It's not like you're interrupting her school routine."

"What can I do?" he asked after a few moments of quiet. Berkley lifted her head to look at him and then stroked her fingers over the scruff on his chin. Margo laughed softly.

"What do you mean? What can you do about what?"

"To prove to you that I have good intentions?"

Margo frowned and shook her head. "I guess it's just gonna take time, Jess. You have to show me you can do this. That you're in it for the long haul."

"Does she do this every morning?"

"You mean throwing stuff? Pouting for attention?"

He grinned without answering her.

"Not every morning. She's a little grouchy. She might be teething."

"Are you grouchy?" Jess looked at Berkley, who gazed at him with adoration and a brilliant smile.

"Good grief, Berk, Mommy's gotta teach you to play hard to get."

"You are the best at that damned game," Jess mumbled.

"I'm sorry?" Margo tipped her head.

Jess dropped a kiss to the top of Berkley's head and avoided Margo's eyes.

"So." She took a deep breath. "Do you get a lot of days off?"

"No. Forty hour week," he answered absently. "I told you it's storming. Pretty nasty. And it's cold. Little bit dangerous to be up on a roof when it's that bad."

"How'd you end up in roofing?"

Jess had been in construction when he had lived in Adam's Bay. He had a business degree, but he had never seemed too interested in using it. Not that he wasn't a hard worker; Margo couldn't fault him his work ethic. He had showed up every day at work and put in a hard eight, sometimes ten hours. The problem was after work when he decided he would stop for one beer. Because one beer was too many and any more was never enough.

A good-looking guy like Jess with a quick smile and sexy eyes got friendlier and friendlier with every beer he swallowed.

"I needed a job," he answered. "I took the first offer I got."

She felt a sharp pang, sort of like an arrow just nicked her heart. What had it been like for Jess to pack his bags and not just move out of her house, but move out of town and start over? What had he been doing for the past year? Besides roofing and not drinking?

"Do you…" She nibbled on her lip. This was necessary. Talking. They absolutely had to talk to each other and get to know each other again if they were going to parent Berkley together. Even if Jess was just Berkley's father and not her daddy, they needed to get to know each other again.

But damned if she could do it here. The room felt too small and quiet, "London Bridge" be damned. She needed some space, and she needed Jess out of the house, because even though he was holding her baby, she wanted to touch him. She wanted to run her fingers over the scruff on his chin the way Berkley had just done.

"Do you wanna take her for a walk? She loves stroller rides."

"Um." He shrugged and nodded.

"Are you in a hurry? To leave?"

"No. Of course not."

Margo felt a wave of heat engulf her when he swept his eyes over her from head to toe.

"Are you coming?" He arched his eyebrows. Margo's mouth went dry at his words. Because he hadn't meant anything dirty by what he'd said, she ducked her head and hurried by him.

"Let me get my shoes."

Once in her bedroom, Margo took a minute to breathe. She stood just inside the closet; one hand gripped the doorframe, and the other she pressed to her stomach. The shiver that Jess's innocent question had chased through her lingered in the backs of her knees and low in her belly. Lower, still, in parts where Margo hadn't felt much at all lately.

She refused to even glance at the bed where she and Jess had slept together. Nope. Thinking about the good times with Jess wasn't going to get her anywhere, except maybe heartbroken again.

Besides, Stevi was going to set her up with someone. Any night now, she could have a date. And that date might lead to another.

It had seemed like a good idea when she mentioned it to Stevi. Not so much now. Not just because of Jess being here, because he'd just unintentionally melted her panties with that look. But because she was a mom, and she didn't want to be the mom who dragged boyfriends—flings or serious—in and out of her daughter's life. Berkley deserved better than that.

She should wait. Once Berkley was older, she would have time for dating and fun.

"Margo?"

She jumped when she heard Jess's voice behind her. Turning her head slightly, she stayed where she was—the chest of drawers between them—and eyed him warily. Berkley, the little traitor, still looked content and angelic with her thumb in her mouth and her cheek pressed to Jess's shoulder.

"You okay?"

The look they shared was unbearably intimate, but Jess's eyes were bold and hypnotic. She couldn't look away. Couldn't breathe either, with him in the room with her. The room where they had slept together, made love.

She simply nodded and tore her eyes away. Her heart thundered in her chest and her fingers as she reached for the long, well-worn brown leather boots she had planned to wear to the Queen. Low-heeled, they would be comfortable for a short walk. She couldn't be bothered to think past the act of perching on the edge of the bed and sliding her feet inside the boots. Pulling the zippers up. Her hands still shook, and once she was ready, she smoothed them over her thighs and rested them on her knees and opened her mouth to draw in a long, deep breath.

Afraid, suddenly, that Jess might still be standing there, that he might be watching her struggling to gain her composure, she looked up at the doorway. Relieved to see he'd gone back to the living room, she squeezed her eyes closed, counted to three, and then climbed to her feet. This is what you wanted, she told herself. Deal with it.

Well, it wasn't what she had wanted. But maybe it was better this way for all of them.

And besides, she was tired of living with the anger and the humiliation Jess had caused her. She would never find her own way, her own happiness if she didn't figure out how to let the bad stuff go. Her belly flip-flopped with nerves at the thought. Who would Stevi set her up with? She loved Grant Deavers, the guy was nice and so easy on the eyes. But she would never look at him and not think of him with Stevi. As much as she liked the guy, she couldn't go out with someone Stevi had slept with.

Not to mention, Duncan might kill him.

Duncan might kill Jess, too, she reminded herself.

She found him in the living room. He sat on the couch now, Berkley in his lap. Jess read to her quietly, an open board book in his hands. Berkley's little butt was perched in the crook of his right elbow, so she had her back to Margo. But she seemed content. Margo watched for a moment as Jess's smooth, gentle voice rose and fell with the words, and Berkley looked from the book to Jess's face.

Margo startled when Berkley stirred and patted his cheek. She wasn't sure how long she'd been standing there, listening to Jess's voice, but she sort of thought she could do it a lot longer. The grin on Jess's face lit her up inside, so familiar to her. He was happy. Cuddled up there on the couch with Berkley, Jess Covey seemed content.

She must have made a noise to clue him in—she had probably laughed, because it tickled her how much Berkley liked the scruffy whiskers on his face—because he turned his head, and those golden-brown eyes zeroed in on her.

"She likes books."

"She loves to be read to," Margo answered with a nod.

"She'll probably be reading those thrillers you always read by the time she's ten."

"Yeah, not so much." Margo watched him set the book aside and stand again. Berkley pitched a fit and flopped sideways to grab the book. Jess shifted her in his arms, grabbed the book for her, and handed it to her. "Let me get her jacket."

"It's chilly," he agreed.

Margo moved down the hall to Berkley's room, sensing when he followed her. Rather than stand there and face him—Berkley's room was small, and she didn't relish the idea of being that close to Jess—she rummaged through the closet quickly for the windbreaker.

"Is this heavy enough?" She turned, holding the windbreaker up for him to see. Jess stood in front of Berkley's chest of drawers, hungry eyes greedy for the framed pictures there. He glanced at her, and rather than blow her off with a quick yes, he pursed his lips in thought. "Maybe with a blanket?"

"Yeah. That should work."

She approached them cautiously, as if Jess might turn and grab her. Or maybe as if she might lose her head and get too close to him. Her fingers ached to touch him. To feel the heat in his skin. The slide of muscle under his shirt.

"C'mere, Berk."

Careful not to do that, not to even accidentally bump him—she was still hung up on the taste of his lip the other day when she bit him—she reached for Berkley and tried to wrestle her away. Berkley squealed in protest and clutched a tiny fistful of Jess's t-shirt. He let out a small yelp when she apparently got some skin under the shirt. Margo snorted and arched her eyebrows when he glanced at her.

"Let Mommy put your jacket on you." Margo felt the smirk lingering on her face when she looked back at Berkley. "We'll go outside for a while."

Berkley turned her big eyes to Jess.

"Jess can go, too."

His name felt awkward in her mouth, but she couldn't call him daddy. Not yet. Because they were still way too early in this game, and there was no guarantee that Jess would stick around and not hurt Berkley.

"You gotta put your jacket on." Jess stroked his fingers over Berkley's hand. Margo wanted to roll her eyes when

Berkley let go of his shirt and held her arms up for Margo to take her. Berkley was no more immune to his charm than any other female of the species. All the more reason Margo needed to protect her.

Jess passed her over easily, as if the two of them had been doing this from the beginning. Margo thrilled at the feel of Berkley's weight in her arms. She dropped a noisy smooch on Berkley's curls and then stood her in her crib.

"I bet you need a diaper change, don't you?"

Berkley shrieked and rewarded Margo with a big grin.

"When was she baptized?" Jess still stood at the chest, his eyes still memorizing details of the pictures there. Margo felt another pang of guilt.

"She was six weeks old," she answered. She moved closer to him again, but she was still careful not to touch him. Berkley, holding on to the crib, wobbled her way to the end and hollered at them.

"Kenzi and Joe are her godparents?"

"Yeah."

This time, the pang Margo felt had nothing to do with guilt. But it was sharp, and it took her breath away. She bit her lip. She and Kenzi had gone to school together, and they had been friends for years. Leah, Stevi, and Duncan had loved Kenzi and Joe, too. And now their friends lived on the East Coast, Joe with their three kids and Kenzi in a nursing home, after a debilitating stroke.

"This was her first Halloween." Her words came out in a choked whisper, because she was still thinking about Kenzi. No desire to talk about that, to share that story with Jess, she pressed on. "And, of course, her newborn picture."

He nodded absently and pressed a fingertip to the glass.

"I've seen that one," he mumbled.

Margo stepped back in shock. Berkley rattled off a litany of what sounded like curse words, so she scooped her up and then laid her down to change her diaper.

"You've seen that one? When?"

It was easier to not look at him as she waited for him to tell her how the hell he had seen Berkley's newborn picture when she sure as hell had never shared it with him. Berkley had calmed her voice to a sweet little singsong, and she twisted on her side to snatch a stuffed bunny from the corner of the bed to play with.

"I..."

When he hesitated, Margo shot him a quick look. He tore his eyes away from the pictures, jammed his hands in his pockets, and hunched his shoulders. She hated that look, the real, raw pain in his eyes and the slight downturn of his lips. But she couldn't look away, either. Her fingers deftly worked Berkley's pants down and unsnapped her shirt, but she stared at Jess expectantly.

"I was at the hospital the day after she was born."

CHAPTER 9

HE LET MARGO PUSH BERKLEY'S STROLLER, WHICH MEANT he was the one to go after Berkley's stuffed bear whenever she decided to toss it. Funny, if asked, he would have said he was in pretty good shape, but after a few minutes of walking and bending over and squatting, he was already feeling the burn in his legs and his stomach. He didn't mind, though. In fact, he loved it. He loved that Berkley had warmed to him as she had, and not because it obviously annoyed Margo.

That first day, when he and Julie had driven to Adam's Bay, he had worried that Berkley wouldn't like him. Not that she would seriously dislike him, because she was just a baby. But he had worried that she would cling to Margo. At the moment, after snuggling Berkley at the house, he felt bulletproof. Margo had noticed the ridiculous grin on his face, because he had seen her roll her eyes at least seven times in the past twenty minutes. But he refused to apologize for being happy to be with his daughter.

"Why were you at the hospital the day after she was born?" Margo asked now.

Jess eyed her silently and then raised his eyebrows when she didn't say more.

"I came to see Berkley," he finally told her. "Why else would I be there?"

"You saw her?"

"No. I didn't. The labor and delivery floor has a high-tech security system. I didn't have a hospital ID—" He stopped talking when she nodded and looked away.

"I'm sorry," she mumbled. "Maybe that was a mistake, Jess."

Maybe.

She wasn't looking, but he shrugged anyway. Maybe just to remind himself that he hadn't been ready to be a father when his daughter was born, and most likely, if he had been involved in any way, things would have gone south really fast.

"I was just so damned angry with you," she continued, still avoiding his eyes. "So hurt."

Those last whispered words hit him with the force of a baseball bat in the gut. He flinched and then looked away when she finally turned her head to look at him.

"Are you still?" His question shocked him, because he hadn't realized he had the balls to be so bold so quickly. But he had to know where he stood with her. If for no other reason, he would like to be friends. Seemed like it would be better for Berkley if the two of them could at least be friends.

She was slow to answer. Jess counted seven jack-o-lanterns on porches and three ghosts hanging from trees and finally dragged his eyes back to her. He watched her fingers tighten around the stroller handles and caught her nod from the corner of his eye.

"Yeah. I guess I am," she admitted. Her voice was gruff, so she cleared her throat. "I'm sorry that you missed so much, but everything you missed hurt me, too."

"I know."

They walked without conversation for a while. Berkley had mysteriously stopped throwing the bear, so Jess peeked around the canopy of the stroller. Tucked up under a mint green blanket, windbreaker hood a stiff point over her head, she was sound asleep. So overcome with emotion, Jess held his breath and looked away again, unwilling to let Margo see how the morning had affected him so far.

"She always goes to sleep on stroller rides," Margo said quietly. "Unless the neighbor's dog is outside. Then she spends half her time yelling at the dog. And half trying to climb out of the stroller to pet him."

Jess chuckled, but again, Margo's words hit him hard and took his breath away. He had been so desperate to know the big things about his daughter—the details of her birth, the struggles Margo might have gone through during delivery, the challenges she faced now as a single mother, and how they had celebrated her first birthday—that he hadn't stopped to wonder about the every day little things he was missing. Like seeing her entranced while someone —most likely Margo—read to her. Or watching her try to climb out of her stroller to pet the neighbor's dog.

Suddenly, all those moments that Jess had missed that first year of Berkley's life were heavy around his shoulders and his neck. He ducked his chin to his chest and breathed deeply, in and out and in and out again. Even if he and Margo were to be friends, even if he did become part of Berkley's life now, he had lost so much that he could never get back.

There was a time when he would have blamed Margo for that. And a time when he would have carried all of the blame himself. Now he wondered if they weren't both at fault.

"How's Kenzi doing?" he asked after a while.

Margo whipped her head around, apparently startled by the question.

"Kenz had—"

"I know." He nodded.

Margo tipped her head and narrowed her eyes at him.

"How do you know?"

"I do have family here, Margo," he reminded her. "My life started here just like yours."

She looked chagrined, which made him feel better and then guilty. He didn't want to hurt her. But he wanted her to know that he regretted the way things had worked out, too.

"Who told you?"

"Mom."

His mother had told him Margo's friend had suffered a stroke, and that her husband had packed her and the kids up and moved them all to the East Coast. But he and his mom and sisters had all talked about it. Jess had considered stopping in from time to time to check on Margo, because he knew how close she and Kenzi were. But his mom and sisters always stopped him. Mom and Lori reminded him that Margo had asked him to leave until he was sure he could be responsible enough to stop drinking and start being a father. Melissa had argued that Margo wasn't worth his worry after the way she had treated him.

"She's made some progress," Margo spoke so quietly, Jess had to strain to hear her. "But, I'm not sure she'll ever make a full recovery."

"Joe?"

Jess had liked them both. At one time, he had been a trusted friend of their family; he'd taken the kids bowling and skating, and he'd been invited to all the birthday parties. He wasn't sure what Joe or Kenzi either one thought of him now, if at all with their world imploding as it had, but he still thought about them often.

Margo sniffled and shrugged her left shoulder.

"He's been amazing." Her words were small in the big outdoors, but they smacked him between the eyes this time, as if reminding him that he hadn't been man enough to be present at his child's birth, let alone to adjust to a new life with a disabled partner and three kids to care for.

"I can't imagine."

Jess shot a glance back over his shoulder. They were a block away from the house, from his truck. He felt bad about bringing Joe and Kenzi up now, and he had the fleeting thought that he could rush back, climb into his truck, and get out. Maybe Margo was talking to him, but that didn't mean she wanted to.

Then again, running away now would only be proving that he didn't have the balls to deal with messy life and emotions. He could ask about Joe and Kenzi's kids, but maybe poking around there wasn't a good idea. Maybe she would share more when she was ready, and then again, maybe Margo didn't know much more than he did. Even if she talked to Joe often, Jess doubted the guy would complain much about anything.

"Do you come back a lot?" she asked as they slowed at the four way stop. Up ahead at Brassfield, a bunch of kids were running and playing on the playground. Jess assumed it was a morning recess. He had played hard back in his school days, always up for an adventure. He jammed his hands in his pockets and wondered if he wished he could go back. Didn't think so. He'd had fun, sure, but what mattered to him most right now was the present. And the future, currently conked out in the stroller.

"Here?"

She nodded. "To see your family?"

She hadn't moved, though there was no traffic. Jess wondered if she wanted to turn around and go back to the house.

"Not a lot," he answered honestly. "I was here for the holidays. It was kind of hard."

"How so?"

"Everybody needs a drink over the holidays." He peeked under the stroller canopy again, but Berkley hadn't moved. "I partied for Halloween. And then remembered I was supposed to be getting my shit together. So I tried to clean it up for Thanksgiving."

"And did you?"

"No." He sighed. "I didn't. I was home for the weekend, and I was drunk every night I was here."

"And then?"

Julie had come to see him when he'd gone back. And the look of disappointment on her face had been the wake-up call he needed. How did he tell Margo that? When her love, when the birth of their child and her ultimatum hadn't phased him, how did he tell her that crushing some kid's faith in him had been what made him grow the fuck up?

"I quit."

"Just like that."

He shrugged the corner of his lips and tipped his head. Why were they standing outside on a street corner a block from Margo's house discussing his sobriety? He looked around, uncomfortable, even though they were absolutely alone on the sidewalk.

"No." He met her eyes. "Not just like that. It took me a bit, Margo, and there are still days when I don't get it."

"What do you mean?"

"Do you wanna keep going? Or head back?"

She whooshed out a deep breath and held his gaze. "Honestly, I don't want you in my house, Jess—"

"Gonna be pretty hard to move forward like that—"

She cut him off with a quick shake of her head. "I didn't mean…I just…the house is so small and we were so…big. And talking about this stuff with you there makes me feel like I'm suffocating."

He stared at her silently. Temper flared through his gut and his blood, but he gritted his teeth until it passed. Sort of.

"So you wanna keep going?"

She shook her head. "No. I need to get moving. I need to get to the Queen."

He waited while she turned the stroller around.

"So. What did you mean? That you don't get it?"

He groaned softly, knowing they were venturing into

dangerous territory. He figured it wouldn't matter what he said, he was going to piss her off.

"I didn't drink to forget things. I didn't drink because I hate my life. I didn't drink because I was bitter and angry."

She nodded when he shot her a quick glance.

"I drank because I liked a cold beer. Because I liked talking to the people at the bar."

"Yeah. We know that."

"And there were times when I wanted a drink. And since I wasn't drinking to forget a life I hated, I didn't get what was wrong with me having that drink. It pissed me off that I had to quit."

"Do you still get pissed off?"

He considered his answer before opening his mouth. "I don't get pissed off. I guess mostly it makes me angry that you called the shots."

"I didn't, though," she corrected him. "I *asked* you to stop, Jess."

"You gave me an ultimatum."

"I asked you to choose me," she whispered. "And a hundred times or more, you chose a bottle. You chose the next bottle. It was your choice to be drunk half the time we lived together."

"Margo—"

"I watched you once." She glanced at him. Jess felt his heart pitch so hard in his chest, he actually pulled his hand from his pocket to rub his knuckles over the tight spot.

"Watched me what?"

"Drinking," she answered. "Talking. You were the life of every party when you were drunk, and you thrived on that. Every guy in the room wanted to talk to Jess Covey, and every woman in the room wanted to fuck Jess Covey, and you ate it up."

He wanted to argue. He wanted to tell her she was wrong.

She wasn't.

"You chose that adoration. You chose a bar full of strangers over me every damned night you left me alone, Jess."

He had. But how did he tell her he knew that? That he had finally worked through his anger, his petulant anger over being kicked out, and he finally understood that even before he'd climbed in bed with another woman, he'd been unfaithful to Margo.

"There's no way I will let you do that to your daughter. Ever."

"Margo."

"Because no woman should be rejected that way, and no little girl should ever, ever feel like her daddy loves a crowd more than he loves her."

They walked for a few moments in silence. Margo sniffled once or twice, but her eyes were dry. Her face was a hard mask of anger, and though he desperately wanted to say something, anything to fix all the broken things between them, he kept his mouth shut.

When they reached the house, he expected her to tell him goodbye and take Berkley inside to get her packed up to go to her mom's house. He hated the thought of an hour visit and the drive back home with nothing solved and so little time spent with Berkley. But he made up his mind he wouldn't argue. There would come a time when he would stand up for himself and push back, but it wasn't the right time yet.

Margo was still the boss, and as much as it irked him, he wasn't about to lose the opportunity to spend more time with Berkley.

"Do you…" She slowed as she passed his truck, and Jess felt that ball of anger expand in his stomach again. He had every right to be here.

Unless.

Had she put his name on Berkley's birth certificate? Melissa had questioned him before, but he had insisted Margo wouldn't fuck him over that way.

"I know you and Duncan don't hit it off," she tried again. "But. I'll take Berk with me to the Queen for a while. If you want…if you wanna hang out down there."

He couldn't help the grin that tugged at his lips.

"Margo, I'm a hell of a lot more afraid of you than I am Duncan Marks."

"Duncan's a bartender, Jess. He's had his share of bar fights."

"So have I." He shrugged. "I'm not afraid of his fists."

"But you're afraid of me." She arched her eyebrows.

"You can take her away from me."

Margo winced and looked away. "I won't do that. I told you to come back to her when you quit drinking."

CHAPTER 10

"So, you're just gonna let him hang out here all day?" Duncan eyed Jess over Margo's shoulder as he walked out from behind the bar and headed back to the steps. Margo followed him as far as the door to the cellar, but there she stopped. She told herself it was because she didn't particularly want to go down and hash this out with Duncan while he did whatever he thought needed doing in the wine cellar. Had nothing to do with the fact that she didn't trust Jess up here in the bar with Berkley.

She sensed that they'd left a lot unsaid this morning, but then, she had no intention of speaking her mind. It was one thing to let him know that he'd made her angry, that he hurt her a hundred times over when they were together. Maybe another to let him know that she was angry now that she had to feel guilty for depriving him of the first year of Berkley's life, when she'd done it to save Berkley the same hurt she'd suffered at his hands. But it was something completely different for her to spill her guts to him about how she'd been stupid and naïve enough to envision Jess working away and getting clean so that he could come back and be the missing piece of the puzzle for her and Berkley.

"What else am I gonna do, Duncan?"

"Send his ass home, Margo."

"He's her father. He deserves the chance to get to know her. She needs to know him."

Duncan turned his back to her and rolled his shoulders.

"Whatever. I'll be down here for a while."

She heard him grumble something else as he disappeared down the stairs. Margo stood for a moment, torn with the need to soothe her stepbrother's ruffled feathers and the need to keep an eye on her ex with her daughter. She laughed at herself, because what the hell did she think Jess was going to do if she wasn't watching him like a hawk? He wasn't going to walk out of the bar with Berkley in tow and leave. She knew without a doubt he would never do that. He wouldn't hurt Berkley. So what did that leave? Love her? Read another book to her? Tickle her tummy? Find the ticklish spots just above her chubby little knees that made her cut loose with that beautiful, healthy laugh that warmed Margo's heart?

Still.

She didn't want to argue with Duncan. She didn't want to go down to the cellar and defend her decision to let Jess spend time with Berkley. She didn't want to have to defend Jess, and she sure as hell didn't want to try and hide her feelings from Jess or defend any feelings that Duncan might read on her face, because she didn't *know* *what* she felt. And the tumult that his return had caused had left her feeling vulnerable and inside out, and that just pissed her off.

Knowing Duncan expected her to follow him and hoping like hell Stevi could talk him out of his cranky mood, Margo retraced her steps to the bar. The Halloween tree caught her eye as she reached for her iPad. Jess had told her he'd been drunk last year on Halloween. She wondered what his plans were this year. If he would want to see Berkley in her puppy costume.

Jess had Berkley plopped in the middle of a table surrounded by toys. Margo watched for a few seconds as she picked them up one by one and handed them to him, as if she wanted to share. Jess seemed to be completely unaware that she was watching him, totally entranced by the big blue eyes that already worshipped him.

"Hate to break it to you, Mama, but baby girl's in love."

Margo glanced at Leah as she joined her at the bar.

"I know."

"Are you okay with that?"

"Don't I have to be?" Margo's throat closed on her words, because she wanted to be okay with it. Even though it scared the hell out of her.

"Do you?" Leah leaned into her and rested her head on her shoulder.

"Don't I owe him a chance to do the right thing?"

Margo felt Leah's head move on her shoulder, so she assumed it was a nod.

"Did you ask him about his friend? Julie?"

"No."

"Why not?" Leah straightened and eyed her carefully.

"First of all, why would I? And second, I don't…I don't wanna know. That's his business."

"Okay." Leah nodded. "Fair enough. Are we solid on the Halloween party?"

"Um." Margo blinked and tried to switch gears from personal to business mode. She tapped her iPad and brought up her memo app. "I think so." Finger hovering over her list of things to do for the party, she read each item carefully. "We've got entertainment."

"Boy, do we," Leah agreed.

Margo lifted only her eyes to look at Leah. "Do you have to brag?"

"Imagine it, Margo. Those hands. Those fingers on his guitar—"

Margo snorted and rolled her eyes. "Stop it!"

"Stevi found you a guy," Leah announced. "Did she tell you?"

"No." Margo felt a stab of nerves and regret. Yes, she wanted a life. A normal life that included entertainment and good hands and love and laughter. But suddenly, weekends with Berkley and kiddie TV and movies and stroller rides were terribly appealing.

"You'll like him."

"Who is it?" Margo asked her.

Leah shook her head. "I'm not telling. She'd kill me. She'll kill me anyway. I thought you already knew."

"I haven't seen Stevi today."

"She had an appointment this morning."

"Mmm." Margo nodded. "Ob-gyn, right?"

"Yeah."

"Is she pregnant?"

"Annual." Leah shook her head in response. "She'd kill you if she heard you say that."

Margo laughed softly. "Maybe a kid would soften Duncan Marks up a bit."

"You kidding me? The guy is putty in her hands." Leah pulled Margo's iPad from her hands and started typing something to add to the bottom of the list. "It's kind of gross, really."

"I find it fascinating," Margo admitted. "I never in a million years thought Duncan Marks could fall in love like that."

"Sheila at the bakery called," Leah told her as she passed the iPad back to her. "They had a glitch, but I guess everything's okay now. Should have the cupcakes delivered that afternoon."

"They should? On Halloween? That's cutting it kind of close." Margo repeated.

"Why didn't we just do them here? Tony can bake."

"You've never had Cake's pumpkin and cream cheese cupcakes, have you?" Margo eyed Leah sharply. "They're incredible. I mean, food orgasm."

"Okay, but Tony can bake, too."

"Food orgasms are all I've got right now, Leah. Let me live a little."

"Not true. You have a vibrator."

"Maybe I like a little action up here, too." Margo puckered her lips and winked at Leah.

"Margs, live a little." Leah tapped the iPad screen as she turned to walk away. Margo turned her attention to the screen to see what Leah had added to the list.

He looks pretty hot with that haircut.

Margo blinked. Cheeks burning as if Jess might be watching her or as if he could somehow read over her shoulder, she looked up at Leah in time to see her look back at her over her shoulder. She wasn't sure it was possible, but when Leah arched her eyebrows suggestively, the heat in her face turned up a hundred degrees.

Leah didn't even like Jess. Margo wasn't sure how to take what she had said. Sure, the haircut was hot. Jess was movie star good-looking; no one had disputed that fact. With the dark hair—long or short didn't matter, apparently—and the thick, dark eyebrows, and golden-brown eyes, he had a pretty face that had charmed her into his bed in a matter of days that first time.

When she glanced at him now, he was laughing, talking gibberish to Berkley. But as if he could feel the weight of her stare, he looked at Margo over the top of their daughter's head and offered her a small, sheepish grin. That grin could charm her right back into his bed if she wasn't careful. Complicating things like that was the last damned thing she needed.

But his eyes. Women always swooned over baby blues, but Margo loved Jess's warm, cognac gaze. A look from those eyes was more dizzying than a hit from any bottle behind the bar.

He stayed out of their way. Entertained Berkley for hours. Gladly put her bib on her, held her on his lap, and fed her lunch. Margo tried to concentrate on the job, mostly because she didn't want to hear it from Duncan about how distracting it was to have Jess around. Stevi sat with him for fifteen or twenty minutes when she first came in. Margo wasn't exactly jealous of that, but it kind of sucked that her cousin could sit and have what sounded like a fun conversation with her ex, when she was bound and determined not to have any kind of fun with him.

She also found him talking to Trace later in the afternoon, just before they opened. She wondered exactly how that conversation was going, but she refused to join them to find out. It was one thing for Jess to hang around now to spend time with Berkley; no way was she going to let him think she wasn't busy and that she had nothing better to do than entertain him.

Not to mention, the last thing she needed was to get attached to him again and watch him live a life completely separate from her again. Still, she had to get Berkley over to her mom's house, so as soon as Trace walked away and headed to the bar, Margo meandered over to the table and perched on the edge of a chair.

Jess had carried Berkley around for a while, looking at things. He had pointed things out to Berkley—she'd watched him for a minute—like the paintings on the walls and the ghosts on the Halloween tree. With her permission, he'd strapped Berkley in her stroller to take her outside and across the street for a ride through the park. Duncan had eyeballed her with obvious irritation, while Leah had propped herself in the front window to watch Jess.

Margo wondered what Leah was thinking, but she hadn't asked. Talking about Jess in front of Duncan was never going to be easy, so she would rather just avoid it when possible.

"I need to take her to Mom's." Margo heard the apology in her voice and chastised herself for it. She was Berkley's mother; she had a job to do, and she needed to get her daughter out of the bar.

"Okay." Jess nodded. Berkley was snuggled up against him again, her back to his chest, a lift the flap and see book open, upside down in her hands. "I'll get out of your way."

"Do you..." Margo rolled her lips inward, surprised at what she was about to say. But the words tumbled out in a rush. "Wanna ride with me?"

She wished she could take them back, because of course Jess had better things to do than ride along with her to her mom's house. It sure wasn't like they were going to welcome him with open arms. From all of her observations, he had enjoyed the day with Berkley. That didn't mean he wanted anything to do with her.

"Really?" His eyes—the ones that could turn her on with one look—lit up now with childlike excitement. "You wouldn't mind?"

Margo swallowed hard and offered him a tiny smile.

"No. I don't mind."

"Okay."

Jess passed Berkley to Margo as she stood. Berkley fussed and dropped the book, but she latched onto a fist full of Margo's hair and rested her head on her shoulder. Margo stood for a moment and watched Jess pack up Berkley's toys and load them in her diaper bag.

"Hey!" Leah hollered from above them. "Where're you going with my favorite baby?"

"You can't say that much longer, ya know," Margo answered. She watched Leah move carefully down the staircase to join them at the table. Jess handed Margo Berkley's windbreaker.

"She can be my first favorite baby," Leah said with a grin. "Isn't that right, Berk? I love you."

Margo got a whiff of Leah's orange scented body lotion when she leaned over to kiss Berkley's cheek. She breathed deeply, needing something familiar to calm her nerves. Once she dropped Berkley off at her mom's, she and Jess would be alone in her car. What the hell had she been thinking?

"Will you do me a favor?" Leah laughed as Berkley lunged for her. She took Berkley smoothly into her arms and settled her on her hip. Margo watched with concern; Leah had had complications early in her pregnancy, and they all tended to baby her now. Which only pissed her off. "What? I'm not gonna ask you to hunt down chai tea or something crazy."

Margo snorted and lifted her eyes to meet Leah's gaze.

"Let me take her."

"Margo—"

"Then sit down."

"For God's sake, I'm pregnant, not old and frail."

"Leah."

"Will you get me some ice cream?" Leah grinned.

"So today you want ice cream? Not just the fudge?"

Leah tossed her back and laughed out loud. Margo and Jess shared a laugh when Berkley, adoring eyes on Leah, mimicked the move.

"Yes."

"Okay." Margo nodded. More time in the car with Jess, which she would thank Leah for later. Or maybe she'd exact a favor in return or some sort of revenge.

"You're my favorite cousin." Leah beamed.

"I'm telling Duncan." Margo took Berkley back as Leah shifted her toward her.

"Oh, God, no. Don't." Leah rolled her eyes. "That guy's had a burr up his ass all day."

Jess cleared his throat. Margo glanced at him in time to catch the smirk on his face.

"Yeah, well, you know it," Leah mumbled with a look in Jess' direction. "You mess this up, he might kill you this time."

"Noted." Jess flashed Leah an easy-going grin.

Leah sighed and groaned out loud. "Okay, dammit." She waved her hand in front of her eyes and looked at Margo from the corner of her eye. "These damned pregnancy hormones."

"You're feeling sad about Duncan killing Jess?" Margo tipped her head to stare at Leah.

"I'm glad you're back, Jess," Leah said quietly. "Berkley should know you."

Jess, clearly touched by Leah's words, blinked in surprise. He nodded his thanks and hugged Leah back when she slipped her arms around him.

"Okay, enough of that, or Duncan might kill me, too." She dabbed at her eyes. "Don't screw this up. Please."

"I'm not gonna hurt Berkley." His voice was quiet, but firm. Margo drew in a deep breath and turned her attention to Berkley and the windbreaker.

"What kind of ice cream?" she asked Leah.

"Surprise me."

"Yep, and when I come in with chocolate, you'll say you wanted vanilla."

"Am I that bitchy?"

"No, but I was pregnant once, too, and I know how it is. What do you want?"

"A scoop of cotton candy in a sugar cone," Leah answered deadpan.

Margo stared at her blankly for a moment, and then she snorted and laughed and nodded.

"Are you kidding me? Cotton candy?"

"Don't judge." Leah took her hand and rested it over her belly.

"Can't even tell she's pregnant, can you?" Margo rolled her eyes at Jess. "I felt like I was showing at six weeks and huge at twelve."

"The baby wants cotton candy." Leah giggled.

"Does Trace fall for that?"

"Heck, no." Leah rolled her eyes. "I don't have to say a word about the baby. Trace does it for me."

CHAPTER 11

J ESS FELT LIKE A JUNIOR HIGH KID—A LITTLE BIT IN LOVE and a little bit in lust—as he watched Margo drive. Funny that denim loved her ass and that when she leaned just so he could see the lace of her bra under her tank, and she smelled like cocoa beans, and her throaty laugh stroked his dick like a hooker's hands. Because all he could think about now was her hands.

She drove with one hand on the wheel, her elegant fingers wrapped casually around the bottom. Before she dropped Berkley off at her mom's, she had glanced in the rearview at every stoplight to look at her. She'd made sweet faces at her and talked to her—both in that sweet baby talk and in a regular voice—and she'd laughed softly when Berkley rattled in answer to her. Now, she paid attention to the music playing, and she kept her eyes on the road, and all Jess could think about was the way it felt when she used to put her hands on him.

"So." He cleared his throat, suddenly a little uptight being alone with her. He had no idea what he was about to say, but he hoped to God he didn't rattle off some asinine thing about parking by the river to make out. God knows, he'd love to get Margo into the backseat of the car and get his hands in her jeans, but if he suggested it, she might throw him out of the car and run over him. "Stevi and Duncan."

Well, okay, that wasn't so bad. He probably shouldn't bring up Duncan, but the idea of Stevi and Duncan sleeping together blew his mind. Margo's soft laughter took the edge off the tension in the car that had exploded in Berkley's absence. By unspoken agreement, he had waited in the car while Margo carried their daughter inside, but Jess had been touched when Berkley shrieked with rage when Margo took her from the car seat. She had been mollified when Margo moved to stand at Jess' window and leaned in so Berkley could touch his face again. The feel of her soft, warm hand on the scruff on his face had almost been enough that he hadn't noticed the up-close peek at Margo's lacy bra and the smooth skin under the lace.

"How?" he asked now, braver after her laughter.

"Oh, man." She turned the music down and then rested her hand on her leg. Jess eyed her fingers, curled into a fist, and then her lean thigh in the denim. He commanded his own hands to stay right where they were, because damned if he didn't want to reach over and touch her. "I don't even know, Jess. They just…they started flirting. I mean, they were flirting a little bit right after you left."

He bit his tongue before he could correct her. He hadn't *left*. He hadn't packed his bags and left Margo and his child; she had kicked him out. Maybe—okay, yes—she had been right in doing so, but it was important to him that there was a difference.

"They fought it, I think," she continued, unaware of the mental battle playing out in his head. "They were…afraid of what might happen. You know. If things didn't work out."

"I don't get it," he mumbled. "She's adorable. And he's—"

Margo held her hand up to stop him. "Don't tell me you think my cousin is adorable, Jess Covey, because I know you have wandering eyes, and I don't need to know you have a thing—"

"I like Stevi, Margo," he interrupted her. "That doesn't mean I've ever wanted to screw around with her."

"They work," she said quietly after a few seconds of silence. "They had a hell of a blow up a couple of weeks ago, and then they figured things out. And now." She shrugged.

"Maybe she'll soften him up."

"Duncan's a good guy, Jess." Margo glanced at him. "Just because he doesn't like you doesn't make him an asshole."

"He was always like a guard dog with you."

"He was there when you weren't." She shrugged.

"When you had Berkley?"

"No. Leah and Stevi were with me." She sniffled, but she kept her eyes on the road this time. "But he was there after. Everyone was crazy for Berkley, and I get it. Of course everyone's going to love a baby. But Duncan was there for me."

Jess grinded his teeth together to keep from saying something to piss her off. He drew in a long, deep breath through his nose and reminded himself that she was right. She had the right to be angry with him for missing all of those moments. She had kicked him out, but he had driven her to it.

She stopped at the Creamery and climbed out of the car in a hurry. Jess followed her but at a slower pace. He told himself he just wanted to watch the sway of her ass as she hurried inside, but as much as he liked the sway of her ass, he was slower to move because he needed time to think. To process what she had said.

Duncan Marks would never forgive him for the way things had played out between him and Margo. If he ever won Margo back, Duncan would always be a sticking point between them.

She looked at him over her shoulder, hand propping the door open, waiting for him. Her cheekbones were sharp, and her eyes were cool, and he remembered that she would never forgive him and take him back, so nothing about Duncan mattered anyway.

"You gettin' any?" he asked as they stood side by side at the counter. When she didn't answer, he glanced at her to find her staring at him with wide eyes. "Ice cream? Are you ordering anything?"

She laughed softly, and before she looked away, he noticed the slight tinge of color in her cheeks. The show of emotion pinged him right in the heart, but it also reminded him that Margo was a beautiful, vibrant woman, and just because he had been working his ass off to come back for her, it didn't mean she had been waiting for him. She could be involved with someone right now, for all he knew.

"No." She shook her head.

He watched her as she stepped forward to order for Leah, his hungry eyes roving over her backside when she wasn't paying attention. Had she been with other guys while he was gone? The thought of another man's hands on her smooth, pale skin and another man driving into her slick heat made his head pound.

"You want anything?" She turned to him and met his gaze. Jess curled his hands into fists—his body still vibrating with jealous anger at the idea of Margo moving on—and stepped up to the counter beside her.

He didn't want anything, but if he ordered, he could share it with her. His dick twitched at the mental image of Margo's talented tongue sliding over a scoop of ice cream. He felt Margo's eyes on him as he studied the tubs of flavors in the freezer. The girl behind the counter offered him a big smile when he lifted his eyes to hers.

"Can I get a scoop of the vanilla caramel swirl?"

"You bet." The blonde moved efficiently to fill their order. Jess felt Margo still watching him, but she was quick to look away when he turned to her.

"You can't help it, can you?" She spoke so softly, he could barely hear her.

"Help what?"

"The charm. The flirting." She folded her arms over her chest and narrowed her eyes at him. She didn't look angry, though; in fact, she almost looked a little flirty herself.

"I'm not flirting." He shrugged, careful to keep his voice low, too.

"She's pretty cute," she argued. Jess didn't have to look back at the girl to agree. She was cute. But she looked like jailbait. Not to mention, she wasn't Margo.

"Men still flirt with you at the bar?" He cocked his head and watched her expectantly. But she only rolled her eyes.

"No one flirts with me, Jess." She stepped up to the counter again to pay for the ice cream. Took the cone and asked for a small cup, too. "I'm a single mom."

Sexy single mom, he thought. One he'd like to fuck. In the backseat of her car. Against the wall. On the bar.

"What're you doing?" he asked as she dumped Leah's cone into the cup the girl handed her.

"Right?" The girl giggled and shrugged as she gave Jess his order, but he didn't make eye contact with her. He didn't need to be accused of flirting. Getting Margo's attention, winning her back would be hard enough without her thinking he wanted to put his hands on every other woman he laid eyes on.

"Trust me." Margo flashed them both a cool smile and led Jess back out to the car. She looked at him over her shoulder, her gaze catching on the ice cream cone at his mouth. He caught the look on her face—longing? desire, maybe—though she tried to hide it from him. "Leah will take it and crush the cone on top of the ice cream and eat it like that."

"But not with pickles?"

"I've never known a pregnant woman who actually craved pickles and ice cream."

"How about Cool Ranch Doritos and chocolate milkshakes?"

She hesitated at the car. Jess waited for her to look at him. He needed her to look at him and acknowledge the memories. He'd missed Berkley's birth, but he had been there through Margo's pregnancy. Things hadn't always been perfect, but they'd had good times, too.

She didn't look. Jess's heart dropped a bit when she pulled her car door open and climbed in without so much as a glance in his direction. The ride back to the Queen was quiet. Margo was either miffed at him for the way the girl at the ice cream shop had looked at him or else his gamble on mentioning her craving when she was pregnant with Berkley had been a bad idea.

Hell if he knew. Maybe it was both.

When her phone buzzed and danced around in the console between the seats, he eyed it curiously. Wondered if it was Leah or Stevi. Or if she had guys who called her. Even if she didn't date, he knew Margo had a lot of friends. She'd had guy friends call her now and then and flirt with her at the bar back when they were living together. Now she was single, angry, and still so fucking beautiful it took his breath away. Of course, there were guys who wanted to ask her out. Get in her pants.

She hadn't flinched when her phone buzzed, but when Jess did—uncomfortable with the thought of her with someone else—she shot him a quick glance. Their eyes met, but neither of them said anything. She let the phone call go, which only made Jess more curious about who it might be.

Just as Margo had said she would, Leah hugged her, kissed her cheek in thanks, and then crushed the sugar cone over the cup of ice cream and dug in. Margo greeted a few guys at the bar, back to Jess, completely oblivious to the way all three of them watched her every move.

"I'll walk you out," she told him. Still eating the cone, he nodded. He didn't want to leave, but he had no excuse to be here now. He said goodbye to Leah and followed Margo to the back door.

"You don't have to walk me out, Margo."

"We should talk about Berkley," she mumbled as she stepped out to the patio. Jess followed her.

"Okay."

She led him out to the parking lot, though there was no one on the patio at the moment. At his truck, she stopped and turned to him.

"I'm sorry," he said quietly.

Her smile was sad. "For what, Jess?"

"Not calling this morning."

"Why didn't you?"

"I guess I was afraid you would tell me not to come."

He watched her swallow and then tip her chin to her chest.

"I'm not gonna keep you from seeing her," she whispered. "Unless—"

"I'm not gonna fuck it up and drink now."

She nodded and lifted her eyes to his again.

"Do you…do you know when you'll come back?"

"Can I come this weekend?"

"I'll be here Saturday," she reminded him. "Home on Sunday."

"And do you want me to call first?"

She shrugged. Jess's mouth gaped open when she swiped the last bite of his cone and popped it in her mouth. His dick grew hard and thick when she crunched it down and then licked her lips.

"You totally flirted with her."

"Why would I flirt with her when I was standing right by you?"

"You always did," she reminded him.

Frustrated, because he wasn't suggesting he wouldn't flirt in front of her, he shook his head and let out a long, low growl.

"Margo, you are a fucking wet dream in those jeans." His voice was gruff with need. "I don't need to look at anyone else. Never have."

Her eyes went big and round at his words. Jess stepped closer to her, so close he could feel the brush of her thighs against his. Margo stared at him uncertainly as he lifted his hands to cup her face.

"Jess." She shook her head, but he leaned in and rubbed his lips gently over hers.

"Thank you." He cleared his throat. Stepped back and lowered his hands to his sides.

"For what?"

For the day with Berkley. For carrying Berkley. For giving birth to his child, even though he hadn't been responsible enough to be there for her. For the kiss.

He wouldn't say any of the above. He couldn't.

Instead, he huffed out a quick breath and raised his eyebrows.

"For the ice cream," he said quietly.

CHAPTER 12

"So?" Margo sat back in the chair and lifted her feet to rest on the desk. "Who is it?"

Perched on the arm of the sofa across the room, Stevi waggled her eyebrows. "You sure you're ready for this?"

"Well, I don't know, because now you're making me nervous."

"Wait." Leah tossed her hands up as if to stop both of them. She shook her head, stared at Stevi long enough for Margo to sense unspoken communication between them, and then turned to Margo.

"You know who it is." Margo cocked her head. "Don't you? You know who she wants to set me up with?"

"I told you the other day I did." Leah shrugged and waved Margo's question away. "But you're really gonna do this? Go out with someone else?"

Margo stared at Leah silently for a moment. Long enough that Stevi slipped off the couch and paced across the room to the desk. Margo watched, strangely comforted, as Stevi leaned on the front of it, her hands propped on the desk at her sides.

"I thought you wanted me to start going out." Margo frowned. "You don't? I'm supposed to just wait? For how long? Until Berk's twelve? Sixteen?"

"What about Jess?"

Stunned that Leah was playing the Jess card, especially when there shouldn't even be a Jess card, Margo slowly lowered her feet to the floor and rolled the chair in under the desk so she could lean forward and really look at her cousin. Stevi scooched a bit and turned sideways on the desk so she could see Leah and Margo both.

"What about Jess?" Margo shook her head slightly.

"Well, I mean…" Leah shrugged dramatically.

"Leah, he brought a girl here with him the first time he came back to see his daughter. Seriously? Why are we talking about this?" Margo rubbed her fingertips over her forehead. "I thought you hated him."

"I don't know what I think, Margs," Leah admitted. "He's Berkley's father."

"Yeah. He is!" Margo snapped as she shoved the chair back again and climbed to her feet. "And he's moved on. Why can't I?" She paced around the front of the desk and propped her hands on her hips. "What does me wanting to go out with someone and do something fun have to do with Jess being Berkley's father?"

"He's changed, Margo," Leah argued quietly.

Margo narrowed her eyes at Leah and shook her head slowly. With a glance at Stevi—who didn't look as confused as she should have—Margo sighed and tossed her hands up in defeat.

"Who are you, and what have you done with Leah Hague?" She took a step toward Leah but hesitated there. "It's too soon to know if anything's changed."

"He kissed you."

Leah's soft words were met with total silence. Margo wanted to argue, to throw the words back at Leah. She wanted to deny it, and when she couldn't—Jess had kissed her the other day, hadn't he?—she had to squeeze her eyes closed and hold herself completely still for a moment, in case she broke apart.

"What?" Finally able to speak around the knife in her throat, Margo tipped her head and waited for Leah to go on.

"I saw him. The other day when he was here with Berkley. He couldn't keep his eyes off you. And then you guys were gone for a while, and then—"

"Gone for a while?" Margo's voice was sharp and loud. "Gone for a while? When I took Berk to Mom's? And got you ice cream?"

Leah ducked her head sheepishly and shrugged.

"What do you think happened? Do you think we parked by the river and made out in the backseat of my car?"

"Stevi?"

Margo jumped when she heard Duncan's voice behind them. She looked over her shoulder to find Duncan, hands braced on the doorframe, leaning in—eyes on Stevi. He flicked his eyes to her, but embarrassed by what he might have overheard or what he might just be assuming, since Leah and Stevi had apparently made the same assumption—she looked away.

"What's up?" Stevi asked softly, but she made no move to join him at the door.

"You have a call."

Margo listened hard for an edge, for anger in his voice, but she didn't hear any.

"A lady wanting to talk to you about having an anniversary dinner."

"So, wouldn't she want to talk to me?" Margo cleared her throat.

"Stevi usually does the initial planning, Margs." His calm made her feel worse.

"Can you get her number, Duncan?" Stevi asked quietly. "We're kind of in the middle of something here."

"You bet."

"Margo—" Leah started the second Duncan's footsteps faded away from the door.

"Here's what happened when we were gone for a while. I drove Berkley to my mom's house. I carried her in, after she had a fit and had to tell Jess goodbye. Jess asked me about Stevi and Duncan, because he can't wrap his head around that. I got you ice cream, and Jess flirted with the kid serving. And then we came back here."

"She's not a kid," Stevi corrected her. "You just wanna make it sound worse than it was."

Margo rolled her eyes. "How do you know? And what difference does it make? He can't help the flirting with women. He can't keep his dick in his pants. Why are you doing this to me?"

"First of all." Leah unfolded herself and stood from the window seat Stevi usually chose. Margo found it interesting that Leah had sat there, as it made her sick with nerves when Stevi did. "I didn't say anything happened when you guys were gone. I didn't suggest that you two might have gone somewhere to make out. But you were alone. Without us around. Without Berkley." Leah shrugged. "Sometimes, when people have a shared past together, they talk when they're alone. And second, I doubt he was flirting with the ice cream girl—"

"A few weeks ago, you hated him."

"Yeah, so, I'm pregnant and hormonal and emotional. Humor me."

"Nothing happened!"

"But when you walked him out of the Queen, he kissed you goodbye."

"What?"

"Before Nashville and I slept together…before there was anything between us, he kissed my forehead. We had talked, and he leaned in and kissed my forehead, and Margs, it was…the most tender thing anyone has ever done, and I don't know. Maybe I fell in love with him then."

"We can't all have that tender perfection you do, Leah," Margo said quietly. She looked at Stevi. "And we can't have that utter devotion you do. Some of us get guys who cheat. Who forget that they have a baby coming. Who would rather hang out at a bar all night and get drunk and play to a crowd than go home to their girlfriends."

"I saw him kiss you, Margo," Leah said stubbornly. "That wasn't about sex. He's in love with you."

Margo's stomach felt funny, a little like butterflies before a ball game and a little like she might be sick. Irritated with both of her cousins, she was tempted to stomp her feet and rush out of the office. But she couldn't just walk away and ignore them; they owned a business together, and they had to communicate to run the bar.

Besides, if she stomped out of here now, they would only assume they were right.

The hell of it was, it was entirely possible that they were. Right. Not about Jess. Not about him being in love with her. But maybe Margo was rushing head first into the dating thing because he had come back, and something about his presence threatened her.

She wasn't rushing, though, was she? She had waited over a year for him to come back, and now that she had seen him again—well, after seeing him with Julie—she was ready to move on.

"He's not in love with me."

"How do you know?"

"How do you know that he is?" Margo looked at Leah and tossed her hands up helplessly. "You've seen him twice. Does that ring on your finger make you wise? Do you think now that you know something I don't?"

She felt a pang of regret the second the words left her mouth. Leah flinched and folded her arms over her chest.

"We had a baby together," Margo continued. "No, actually, we didn't. I had his baby. End of story. We never had what you and Trace have. Never, Leah. It was never like that with us, and you know it."

Leah stared at her silently and finally gave in with a small nod.

"Okay." She shrugged and sniffled. "Then by all means, go out and have some fun. You deserve it."

Margo stood, shoulders tense, as Leah slipped around her and left the office. She waited for Stevi to move, to follow her but when seconds passed and Stevi was still perched on the desk, she finally glanced at her.

"Kind of harsh." Stevi was hoarse.

"I get that you guys see rainbows and hearts everywhere right now, but—"

Stevi cut her off with a quick nod. "Still. You didn't have to go for her throat."

Margo dropped her head back and cut loose a long, tired sigh.

"I agree with Leah," Stevi mumbled. "He seems different. But I know he hurt—"

"He didn't hurt me," Margo argued lifelessly.

"He did hurt you, Margs." Stevi straightened and teetered on her heels for a second. "He did hurt you. And I know how hard it is to get past that kind of hurt."

Margo bit her lip to remind herself to keep her mouth closed. Duncan and Stevi were committed to each other, but it hadn't been that long ago that Duncan had ripped a hole in Stevi's heart. Revenge. Over a misunderstanding.

She and Jess didn't even have that much together to cause that sort of pain.

Margo had lost out to brown bottles, loud music, and big crowds. The women were extra. Jess had never been in love with her, and though there was a tiny bit of her that wanted to believe it, he wasn't in love with her now. He did seem different, although, they were just beginning this new phase and who knew what would happen next. But different didn't mean a damned thing to her anyway. Jess only mattered to her in regard to Berkley.

"So, I haven't talked to him yet, but what about Shawn Perry?"

Margo crossed her arms over her chest and turned away from Stevi. She moseyed to the window where Leah had been sitting and propped her shoulder on the wall. The overcast day matched her mood; she shivered in her navy sweater and wished she could go home and start the day over.

Head and heart—though she wouldn't discuss that—still reeling over the talk of Jess and that kiss, she couldn't begin to think about someone else. Not right now. A month ago, even just a week ago, the idea of that new attraction and the fun dates and the buzz of a new crush had sounded exciting. Now she craved the familiar touch of the man she'd lived with, the man who had never loved her more than anything.

Jess had kissed her, and it had been the perfect way to say goodbye to her the other day. He had shaken her up and left her wishing he would stay. To be with her. They could have sat on the patio for a while. Or they could have walked down to the riverfront and snuggled up together for warmth. His lips had been surprisingly warm after eating the ice cream. Soft and firm and gone before Margo could process that he had kissed her.

She had been outraged at first that he'd done it, and then when he climbed into his truck and drove away, she had been outraged that he had kissed her so softly and walked away, and she wanted more. She had wanted his hands on her back and his arms around her and the warmth of his body pressed up to hers.

That night, she dreamt of that moment, of the kiss. And she'd kissed him back, and even now, she could taste the ice cream on his tongue and feel the heat of his face pressed close to hers. She had managed to shove the kiss —the real one and the dream one—down inside and forget about it, sort of, until Leah brought it up again.

What if he had kissed her and gone home to Julie? What if Margo hadn't been enough to hold his interest and make him happy at home, but Julie was?

"He's a loan officer at—"

"I know who he is." Margo nodded. She knew Shawn Perry; she'd met him and talked to him on several occasions. Nice guy. Dress shirt and tie kind of guy. Probably had manicures and probably didn't know the working end of a hammer and probably preferred the missionary position in bed.

All things that were okay, maybe.

But they weren't Jess Covey.

"He looks like Hugh Grant," Stevi reminded her. "He's kind of sexy."

"Maybe." Margo laughed. "If you like the Hugh Grant type."

Stevi moved up behind her and rested her hands on Margo's shoulders.

"You prefer the bad boy type."

"I like the rough edges," Margo admitted, "but they're bound to scrape you up and make you bleed, right?"

"I don't know." Stevi gave her a gentle squeeze and dropped her hands. "If you love them enough, you can round those hard edges out a bit and still have just enough left to love."

"Are you comparing Jess to Duncan?" Margo asked in disbelief. She spun around to look at Stevi.

"Maybe."

Margo felt her phone buzz in her pocket. Joe had called the other day when she and Jess were driving back to the Queen. She hadn't answered it, because she didn't want to have any phone conversation on Bluetooth with Jess in her car. And she hadn't even looked at her phone, because she didn't want Jess to ask who it was. She watched Stevi slip out of the office and then slipped around the desk to sit down again.

Maybe she *had* hoped Jess would wonder who it was. Maybe a tiny part of her had hoped he would at least consider that it might be a guy calling her and feel that deep green jealousy she'd felt the day he'd waltzed into the bar with Julie at his side.

She lifted her butt from the chair and pulled her phone from her pocket. The text was from Joe—*...telephone silence...pretty sure I still have service...*

Feeling a little raw after the exchange with Leah, she opted to text him rather than call.

Sorry, Joe. Jess is back.

I know.

How—? Leah?

Jess.

"What?" Surprised by the last text, her phone slipped from her fingers. "Jess?"

She glanced at the office door and picked up the phone to tap his name.

"Hey. God, Margo, I thought maybe you were dead."

She hung her head and held her breath. Kenzi had been her best friend—she'd loved her the same as she loved Leah and Stevi, still did—but that sharp ache of loss had dulled a bit over time. Not to mention all that had happened here in the past year, sometimes there was so much going on, Margo couldn't think past the moment. She couldn't call and talk to Kenzi now anyway, not even if she made time. Kenzi was physically disabled after suffering a stroke during the delivery of a surprise baby. She suffered from aphasia, so while Joe put them on speaker phone now and then to say hi to her—she'd shocked them all recently with a few words—she couldn't call her bestie and cry to her about the situation with Jess. Or ask Kenzi how she was doing, because while Kenzi would hear her perfectly well, she might never again be able to put words together to share her thoughts.

Still, she was close to Joe, too, and her stomach plunged now with guilt for not checking in with him.

"I'm sorry," she whispered. "I'm sorry, Joe. I suck. There's so much happening, and now Jess is back."

"I know." He sounded calm, unflappable as always. "I get it. I just miss you."

"How're the kids?"

"Always on the gro. Liam is costing me several thousand dollars a month on groceries."

Margo laughed out loud and flopped back in the chair. "He is not."

"Okay, maybe not, but that kid eats everything that's not nailed down. The other day I considered nailing down my kitchen chairs. I need them."

Margo snorted.

"You okay?"

"Um." She squeezed her eyes closed for a moment and swallowed the words she wanted to say. No need to dump everything on Joe; his plate was full already. "Yeah."

"Kenz sends her love."

"Oh, Joe," she sobbed. "I miss her so much. I miss all of you guys."

"The kids and I might…visit over the holidays."

She caught her breath and clamped her hand over her mouth. Joe's family lived in Adam's Bay, so it made sense that they would come back for a visit. And Kenzi's family had moved east several years ago, so Kenzi had someone there to keep her company if and when Joe was gone for a few days. The thought still broke her heart.

"Okay," she finally whispered. She dabbed at her eyes. "I wanna see you if you do."

"Of course," he agreed. "I need to meet Leah's guy. Get a look at her pregnant—"

"She's so cute, Joe," Margo chuckled.

"And I damn sure need to see Duncan and Stevi. I gotta see a kiss or something to believe it."

"You don't wanna do that," she warned him. "They can't stop. Once they get started, they're—"

"Jess texted me. The day he drove down to see you and Berkley."

Margo had no idea what to say to that, but Joe seemed to be waiting for her to say *something*.

"Are you guys in touch? Does he text often?"

Was she hurt? Jealous?

"Not that often, but he's kept in touch. He sends notes to tell Kenzi hi."

Margo nibbled on her lip, a little bit touched that Jess had kept up that contact, that he apparently truly cared for Kenzi and Joe.

"I didn't know that." She huffed out a sigh and swallowed another mouthful of guilt. Jess had been in contact with Kenzi and Joe, and she had been too busy to slow down and check in with them lately.

"I just wanted to tell you I think you're doing the right thing."

"What?"

"With Jess. Letting him be part of Berkley's life. He's earned that, Margo. I know the rest of the crew might argue, but Jess loves her. He'll do right by her."

Margo cleared her throat, still unable to process the thought that Jess—lying, drinking, cheating Jess—texted to check in with Kenzi and Joe.

"I gotta go. Don't be a stranger."

What would Duncan say, what would any of them say if they knew this about Jess? Did it mean he was capable of love and commitment or was this just another example of fun-loving, friendly Jess needing all eyes on him?

CHAPTER 13

Jess glanced at Julie, but her eyes were glued to the phone in her hand. He looked back at the road and then flicked a quick glance at the clock on the dashboard.

"What's wrong?" he finally asked her.

"Nothing." She looked up quickly and shook her head. "Why?"

"You had this weird look on your face," he said with a shrug. "Like you were reading an article on Facebook that was telling you which planet your descendants would live on."

Julie's light laughter filled the cab of his truck, but she rolled her eyes.

"Neptune." She shrugged. "That's easy."

"What's so important on your phone? You've hardly talked to me tonight."

In the interest of not wrapping his truck around a tree, he kept his eyes on the road. Still, he chanced frequent glances at her as he waited for her to answer.

"I shouldn't have come," she finally announced. He waited for her to explain, but she simply turned her head to stare out the passenger window.

"You wanted to come with me."

"Yeah, I know, but I shouldn't have."

He had decided that rather than wait for Sunday, rather than wait for Saturday even, he would drive to Adam's Bay Friday night. Even if he didn't see Margo or Berkley, he could hang out at his parents' house and catch up with *someone*. They had a basement bedroom open that he had planned to use, but when Julie had dropped by his place Thursday night to find him packing and asked if she could come along, he figured she could have the bedroom and he would sleep on the couch.

"Is he texting you?"

"What?" Julie whipped her head around so fast, Jess worried she would get whiplash.

"Is Brent texting you?"

"No."

From the corner of his eye, Jess saw the sign for his exit, though he didn't need it. Adam's Bay had been his home for thirty-two years; he could find it with his eyes closed. He also noticed the frown on Julie's face. That one was a bit harder to navigate. He was learning to understand women—sort of—and he was learning to read Julie, but she was aware of it, so she fought harder to keep her secrets.

"Jules."

"He did this afternoon," she answered. "He's going to a music festival tonight. Up around Chicago."

"He didn't invite you?"

"No offense, Jess, but would I be here with you if Brent invited me anywhere?"

Jess chuckled.

"You need to tell him how you feel about him." He had told her so at least seven times this past week. Now, as she had every other time he had said so, Julie simply rolled her eyes.

"Margo isn't going to be happy to see me."

"What?"

"She didn't like me."

"Everyone likes you, Julie."

"Well, apparently not Brent or Margo," she mumbled. "She was ready to serve me poison at the Queen the first night you were there."

"What?" Jess shook his head. "Margo's not like that."

"Jess?" Julie turned sideways in her seat and tipped her

head to study him. "Are you really that dense? She thought we were together."

"You and me? Together?"

"I know," Julie said with a snort. "Blows the mind, doesn't it? Seriously, she thought we were together. How did you not see that?"

"But you're so much younger than me."

Julie shrugged. "Yeah, I'm not your type, either, but ask her."

It felt like the truck was creeping now that they were in the outskirts of the city. That and the fact that Julie was watching him now and she'd thrown down some personal stuff to ride in the truck with them.

She wasn't his type, but then Jess didn't know that he *had* a type. There were women. And there was Margo. He liked women. Christ, what man didn't like women? Their eyes and their curves and their inner thighs pressed around his waist? Blondes, brunettes, short, tall.

But Margo was different.

He didn't want just any woman. He didn't want a bunch of women. He didn't want Julie. Not as more than a friend.

He wanted Margo back.

And she *had* referred to Julie as his girlfriend, hadn't she?

The thought made him squirm now.

"I kissed her."

"What?" Julie drew back as if he had slapped her. Why had he opened his mouth? And why now? Trapped in the cab of the truck? Pulling up to a stop sign? He and Julie had talked candidly about a lot of things, he and Margo being front and center. He admitted to Julie that he had cheated on Margo, and he had even admitted that half the reason he had done it was because Margo refused to need him for anything. Desperate for a drink that night, he had sat on the hood of Julie's car and confessed to the fact that Margo's independence made him feel useless. He had confessed to the three shots of tequila he had done before he did the blonde in the alley behind the bar the night Berkley was born, too. *After*. After Stevi had called him, *after* Margo had delivered her.

Julie hadn't cut him any slack; she had gone inside her apartment and come back with a cold can of generic Doctor Pepper and told him he was a jerk for being unfaithful to his girlfriend. And an even bigger jerk for blaming her for it. When he'd heatedly asked what the hell he should have done differently, she got in his face and suggested that he could have talked to her.

"You're too skinny for me," he told her.

"I'm not Margo," she reminded him. "And let's not go there."

"Good idea." He nodded. The light changed to green so he eased his foot off the brake and tapped the gas. "You hungry?"

"Yep."

"Let's go to the Queen."

"Great. I can get a burger and a shank."

Jess laughed softly.

"It's not funny!" Julie leaned toward him and punched his arm. "When did you kiss her?"

"Why do we need to talk about it?"

"Hello? I'm your trainer, remember? When?"

Jess gritted his teeth and hissed with frustration. So, it was still a little uncomfortable talking about personal stuff, especially with someone like Julie. Then again, she had given him a lot of insight into Margo, into himself, and their relationship.

"The last day I was here."

"And?"

He groaned and shrugged. "I didn't call her. I came down the day we had all that rain at home."

"I know. Fast forward to the good part."

"There's no good part."

"You kissed her?"

Jess glanced at her with a nod.

"There's a good part. Proceed."

"Like, you think kissing me would be good?"

"God, no." She rolled her eyes. "I think kissing you would be like smooching my brother if I had one. And don't do that. You're deflecting, and you're flirting, and that would piss Margo off."

"I'm not flirting."

"In what world does a man say something like that and it's not considered flirting?"

"I'm just having fun. Not trying to get anywhere."

"Well, thank you for that." She laughed. He caught her eye roll again. "But it's still flirting."

"She was pissed at me. For flirting with the girl at the ice cream place."

"Wait." Julie held up her hand to stop him. "You guys got ice cream together?"

"Why? Is that better than kissing her?"

"Ice cream dates are romantic."

Jess narrowed his eyes and sighed. "I thought dinner and drinks were romantic."

"Eh." She shook her head.

"Is the Queen okay? They have good food."

"It's fine. So was there an ice cream date or not?"

"No. We stopped to get something for Leah after we took Berkley to Margo's mom's house. And then when we got back to the Queen, she walked me out to the truck—"

"She did?"

"Just to talk about Berkley."

"Still."

"I kissed her."

"What kind of kiss?"

"No." Jess shook his head. "Nope. Not doing this."

"Oh, come on. I'm not asking if you got to second base, Jess."

"It was a kiss. Just a kiss."

"Did she kiss you back?"

"No. But I didn't really give her the chance."

"Oh. So, like a drive-by kiss."

Jess turned in to the parking lot behind the Queen and crept through the packed lot until he found an open spot at the far end.

"It was just a kiss," he argued.

He climbed out of the truck and waited while Julie did the same on the passenger side. As she rounded the bed to join him, he beeped the locks and they headed together to the back door of the bar. Three patio tables were occupied, all of them pulled relatively close to the space heater, though far enough apart that there appeared to be three different conversations going on.

"That's the best kind," Julie told him as he pulled the door open and waited for her to go inside.

"What? What does that mean?" He followed her, but his voice was drowned out by the music and the din of the crowded bar. His eyes moved quickly over the crowd around the bar and stopped when he found Margo.

Dressed in painted-on-denim, as always, and a red blouse, she stood at the end of the bar. Right foot crossed over her left, she rested her hand on the forearm of the guy next to her, eyes intense as she listened to something he was saying.

Jess felt a sharp stab of jealousy again. He had heard Stevi and Margo talking the other day about Stevi finding Margo a date, and he'd wrestled with that thought every night since then. Had she been involved with anyone seriously since he had been gone? Had she gone through another breakup? Was she playing the field? Was she inviting her dates into her house? When Berkley was home?

She shifted on her feet as he and Julie approached the bar. Lifted her face toward Leah's boyfriend at the register when he hollered at her. Jess didn't hear her laughter, but he knew when she tilted her head and grinned, that she was laughing at whatever Trace had said. Her face was bright and happy; she had no idea how beautiful she was.

He was an idiot. He'd had her all to himself and rather than love her, he'd let her go.

She turned her head slightly. Jess knew the moment she noticed him, because her whole body tensed up and the easy smile on her face disappeared. She didn't even try to pull it back; she simply met his eyes and watched him approach.

Damn Julie for making him think about that kiss just before walking in here. She'd probably done it on purpose. For a moment, he smelled Margo's perfume—the spicy, rich scent of cocoa beans—and he felt the press of his lips over hers. His dick throbbed at the memory of that kiss and a hundred others.

Julie had said *just kisses* were the best kind, but he doubted Margo would appreciate it much if he swaggered up to her right now and kissed her. As much as he liked the idea —wrapping his arms around her and sliding his tongue inside her mouth—he figured that was a sure way to piss her off. Maybe not so much that she would deny him the right to see Berkley, but he had more at stake here than Berkley.

"What're you doing here?" She turned all the way to face him as he stopped at the bar. She had drawn her hand away from the guy next to her. Crossed Jess's mind to get a good look at him, but now that he was this close to Margo, he didn't want to look away. Dark liner and thick, heavy mascara made her eyes pop, and it crossed his mind again that Stevi had said something about setting her up with someone.

Had he interrupted a date? But she was working. Right?

"Thought I'd spend the weekend in Adam's Bay."

"Don't you work Saturdays?"

He did, yes, but not every Saturday. Besides, the crew was currently caught up and would start a new project on Monday, weather permitting.

"Can I get a beer?"

Margo stared at him silently, eyes wide with surprise.

"Not for me. For Jules."

"Jules," Margo repeated and lifted her gaze to look over his shoulder. "Julie. Hi."

She hadn't been particularly warm with him, but now that Julie had mentioned that Margo hadn't liked her, he noticed the cool, professional tone.

"Hey, Margo." Julie ducked her head around his arm to see Margo. "How are you?"

"Great, Julie," Margo said quietly. "I'm doing great."

Jess watched her slip away and grab a longneck from the cooler for Julie. She twisted the top off and handed it to her with that same, robotic smile.

"Do you want anything?"

"Water."

"Hey. I'm gonna go grab that table." Julie touched his arm and nodded to a two-top table across from the bar. There were dirty glasses there, but they appeared to have been abandoned. Jess nodded and looked back at Margo. He watched her move down the bar, stretch to her tiptoes to say something to Trace, and then lean over the bar for an exchange with two girls there.

"Do you wanna start a tab?" she asked him when she moved back to stand beside him.

"Sure." He pulled his wallet from his pocket to give her his credit card, but she shrugged him off.

"Just close out with Stevi when you leave," she told him as she squeezed between him and two more patrons who were now crowded up behind them. Jess turned to watch her when she moved through the crowd of people and saw that she had ducked into the kitchen.

"Hey." Leah appeared out of nowhere. "You here alone?"

"No." He returned her smile. "Julie's with me. Can we get menus? You guys still serving?"

"You bet. Go sit. I'll bring them to you."

He stood a moment longer, but when it became obvious she wasn't going to engage in small talk, he wound his way through the crowd to sit.

"You know any hot single guys here?" Julie asked, bottle at her lips.

"Um." He frowned. "I've never been one to check out those possibilities. And the only single guy I knew around here was Duncan. You don't want Duncan."

"Well, no, he's not single, anymore, is he?" She rolled her eyes. "He is hot, though."

"Duncan?" He was glad he hadn't taken a drink, because he would have sprayed it all over the table when he snorted and coughed.

"Mmm. Yes."

"That's your type?"

"Well, no, but he's hot."

"He's a tool. Total dick with women, but holier than thou about Margo."

"And yet, he and Stevi are a thing."

"Well. We'll see how that ends up."

Julie nodded her head toward the bar. Jess peeked over to find Duncan watching Stevi; he looked completely pussy-whipped. If he were a cartoon character, his eyes would be the shape of hearts.

"I'm gambling on true love," Julie decided.

"Well, it would be hard not to love Stevi Hague, but I still can't see Duncan treating her right."

"Jess."

Head still turned to see the action at the bar, he dragged his eyes away and looked back at Julie when he felt her fingers on the back of his hand.

"If you really want a relationship with Margo, you have to figure out how to deal with him."

"He's a prick."

"He's her brother, and he's trying to protect her."

"Stepbrother," he corrected her, though it made no difference if Duncan was Margo's brother or stepbrother, and they both knew it.

"What if it were me?"

"What?"

"If Brent and I were living together, and you knew he was out running around on me?"

Jess drew in a deep breath to launch his defense again, but when Julie shook her head, he closed his mouth without a word.

"Reasons don't matter. If I were at home and he was out with other friends and girlfriends all the time, what would you do?"

"I'd be pissed, Julie. I'd probably tell him about it, too."

Julie shrugged and nodded. "And you're not even my stepbrother. You're just my friend."

"Hey guys!" Stevi chirped. "Leah said you were here. The Mississippi Burger is on special…" Jess looked at her as her voice faded away. Followed her gaze to Julie's fingers still resting on the back of his hand. "It's…um….really good."

Julie drew her hand away and took the menu Stevi held in offering over the table. Panic surged through him and left a trail of dread. If Julie was right—if Margo thought he and Julie were together—Stevi seeing that innocent touch was bad. Trying to explain himself out of it would only make the situation worse, so he simply took the menu Stevi handed him and watched her walk away.

"You should go talk to her."

He glanced over the menu and finally looked at Julie.

"Stevi?"

Julie rolled her eyes. "Jess, you're not stupid."

"You think she told Margo she saw that?"

"I know she did." Julie nodded. "Fix it. Or I'm going home."

"How are you going home? We're in my truck."

"I'll steal it. You can find a way to get your ass home."

CHAPTER 14

"So, don't look now." Stevi stepped in front of Margo, but Margo automatically strained to see around her. "I said don't look now!"

"Really?" Margo shook her head and rolled her eyes. "Does that ever work?"

"Well." Stevi shrugged.

"So? What? Is he here?"

"What?" Stevi blinked and looked down the bar. "Is who here?"

"Shawn Perry."

"Wha—no? I thought you weren't interested."

"Maybe I am." Margo twisted around to pick up her pint glass from the back bar. She raised it to her lips. "Yeah. Maybe I am interested."

"Maybe you're not really, but he showed up with Julie again," Stevi whispered.

"Dammit, Stevi."

Of course, her cousin was right. She wasn't sure she wanted to date someone now. Not since Jess had shown up with that slick new haircut and those compelling eyes and that smile. But maybe she did, because he'd shown up with that cute brunette twice now, and that was a definite turn off.

"Margs, don't do this." Stevi bit her lip. "I get it. But you're gonna get hurt. No matter what you do, you're gonna get hurt. And Shawn's a good guy. I don't wanna watch you two play for a bit and then see you walk away from him—"

"Really? You're worried about him?'

"Look. You gotta figure this out."

"There's nothing to figure out." Margo heard the flippant tone of her voice. She took a healthy swallow of her IPA and shrugged. "Shawn's a nice guy. But. You know me. I don't like 'em pretty."

"Boy, I do," Duncan announced as he cut between them. He leaned over to drop a kiss on Stevi's cheek and kept moving to the other end of the bar.

"That's gross, by the way," Margo told Stevi.

"That he kisses me here?"

"No. That he's so frigging sappy over you."

Stevi snorted. Both of them watched Duncan for a second as he pulled a draft beer and handed it over the bar to a big guy in a Bills baseball hat.

"He lost his man card." Margo tipped her head. "You know that, right?"

"Margo, he doesn't need a man card." Stevi winked. "You know what I mean?"

Margo grinned. "I'm just giving you shit. But on the other hand, it really is weird to see him so in love."

"But not with me."

Margo looked at Stevi in time to see her bite her lip.

"Right? You don't have a problem with me and Duncan together?"

"Nope."

"Margs, I have to tell you something."

"Okay, sticking to bottled drinks." Margo put her glass down again and cocked her head at Stevi. "Are you? Pregnant?"

"What?" Stevi drew her eyebrows down in a deep frown. "No. God, no. That might make Duncan run."

"Maybe." Margo pursed her lips. "Maybe not. He'd be a good daddy."

Stevi blinked and rubbed her eyes, careful not to mess up her makeup.

"I'm not ready for that, either."

Margo didn't point out that she hadn't been ready for Berkley. Instead, she swept her gaze around the bar, lingered on Jess and Julie for a second, and then looked back at Stevi.

"They were holding hands."

"What?"

"When I took their menus to the table…" Stevi gulped a deep breath. Obviously miserable to have to tell Margo the news, she met her gaze and waited for Margo to say something. Except Margo couldn't. The hole inside her had grown so big, it sucked her lungs and her voice down inside it and rendered her mute.

Stevi's misery only made her feel worse. Anything she said at the moment would break her. Margo, eyes burning, simply nodded and turned to walk away. The music played on behind her, something folksy and easy to listen to, except right now the particular riff the guy kept hitting made a spot between her eyes throb painfully. Her legs felt limp, and she worried that they would give before she could slip away from the crowd. But they carried her to the cellar door, and she moved steadily down the wooden stairs, careful not to think.

Her brain turned on when her foot hit the last step, though. She wondered where they were going to sleep. He planned to spend the weekend here, so Julie would be here all weekend, too. Were they staying at his parents' house? Would they sleep together there? She and Jess had never stayed a night at his parents' house, but they'd had sex in the basement bedroom a few times.

Her stomach dropped at the thought. Jess and Julie tangled together in the sheets. Julie, lithe and sexy, riding him, her head thrown back and her perfect breasts on display for his eyes and roaming hands.

She covered her face with her hands and gasped for a long, deep breath. As much as she wanted to break, to rage and cry and throw things, she couldn't do it here. This was her place of business, and the bar was crowded, and she couldn't shatter their inventory and hide out down here for the rest of the night, tear-stained and heartbroken.

When she heard footsteps on the stairs behind her, she sighed and pressed her fingertips gingerly to her closed eyes. Figuring it was Duncan, she hustled across the uneven stone floor to the other side of the cellar and looked around, desperate to find something to make her look busy.

"Hey."' Jess's voice chased shivers up her spine. Standing at a closed metal cabinet, fingers wrapped around the handles, Margo couldn't hide her surprise when she looked at him.

"What're you doing down here?" The words tumbled out before she was ready to speak, and her voice was thick with the emotion she wanted to hide.

"Looking for you."

"Jess, I—" She shook her head. "I'm working. Whatever it is can wait."

"It really can't," he argued.

"I'll be back up in a few minutes."

He didn't turn around, though. Didn't appear ready to leave her alone. Instead, he stepped closer to her and watched her with an intensity that burned deep into her bones.

"I don't know what game you're playing, Jess," she whispered, "but I can't. I can't do this—"

"No game." He shook his head and took a final step to stand toe to toe with her. She averted her eyes when he reached to stroke her face with his fingers.

"Julie—"

"Is fine upstairs," he interrupted her.

"But—"

"It's not like that, Margo."

With finesse that she had nearly forgotten, he swept his fingers from her cheek down under her chin and turned her face back toward him. His golden-brown eyes were warm and tender. Margo sobbed softly at the press of his warm skin when he rubbed his thumb over her lower lip.

"Don't." She tried to shake her head, but he held her still. She let her eyes close as he leaned in and kissed her. His warm lips brushed hers, the spot where he'd pressed his thumb still throbbing.

"There's so much left unfinished, Margo."

"No, there's not." When she lifted her hands, she meant to set them on his chest and push him away. Instead, she sought out the soft leather jacket and curled her fingers around his arms. He played there at her lips, making several soft, sweet passes over hers. The scruff that had fascinated their daughter just the other day felt good against Margo's face.

"We need to talk."

"There's nothing to talk about, Jess," she whispered. "Just Berkley. She's all that's left between us."

"You don't believe that, or you wouldn't have come down here the second Stevi told you what she saw."

"I came down to get something for the bar."

He drew back just enough to look her in the eyes. Knees weak with longing, Margo fought to keep the desire from her face.

"Do you want to kiss me as badly as I want to kiss you right now?"

She found her voice immediately. "No." But the word was barely a whisper, and her hands moved without her approval. Now they were on his chest, but rather than push him away, her fingers curled around his shirt and dug into his skin.

"Liar."

"Jess—"

She moaned softly when he cut her off. His lips covered hers again, but this time, he opened his mouth, and Margo felt his warm breath on her face. Need stirred inside her, pounded in her chest, and her heartbeat throbbed in her fingertips. His fingers trailed like feathers over her neck and inside her blouse. Margo closed her eyes and reveled in the feel of his fingertips at the hollow of her throat and over her collarbone.

The stroke of his tongue at the center of her upper lip made her gasp out loud. She smoothed her hands over his shoulders and held on as she kissed him back. Hungry for his touch, she pressed into him, but Jess kept his hands in place—one at the open collar of her blouse and the other, tangled in her hair at the back of her head.

He kissed her slow and sweet and deep. Every sweep of his tongue over hers nudged her closer to the edge, closer to him, and she cried out in protest when he broke the kiss and leaned back to look at her.

"I thought you didn't want to kiss me."

"I don't want to want you," she corrected him. The kiss, the intimacy made her desperate for honesty, but she regretted her own the second she spoke.

"Margo?"

She jumped when Stevi hollered down the stairs.

"Yeah?" She stepped away from Jess, saddened by the space, by the loss of his body heat and his touch. The loss of this moment, because she couldn't think when he was that close to her, and now there was distance between them and she could think, so she had to say no.

"Not coming down." Stevi's words were punctuated by the sound of her heels hitting the first step hard. Margo rolled her eyes, but she stood with her back to Jess, now, so the gesture and the attitude went unnoticed. "Just wanted to tell you Leah and Trace are heading home."

"Is she okay?" Margo made her way back to the stairs and looked up at Stevi.

"Yeah. She's just tired."

"I'll be up in a second."

"No rush." Stevi shook her head slightly. "We're okay up here. Just wanted to tell you that."

Margo nodded. Stevi widened her eyes and nodded her head toward the other side of the cellar.

"You okay?" She spoke so quietly, Margo barely heard her.

"Yeah."

Stevi studied her for a moment and finally, with a nod, she turned and disappeared up into the bar.

"When can we talk?" Jess slipped up behind her. Margo held her breath when he slid his hands over her hips and pulled her back against his body. She bit her lip when she felt his erection against her backside.

"There's nothing to say as long as you keep bringing another woman with you when you come here." Her voice shook with pent-up emotion, but her legs were steady as she climbed the steps to get away from him.

CHAPTER 15

Margo didn't bat an eye when she opened the front door to him Saturday morning. She didn't flinch when she realized Julie was with him. He would have felt better about the night before, about the kiss they had shared in the wine cellar, if she had reacted in some way to his *other woman* on her porch.

Instead, she led them both inside and offered them both coffee and then went back to her daily business. Jess and Julie entertained Berkley in the living room—maybe it was more accurate to say Berkley entertained them— while Margo cleaned her house and did laundry. She kept up a pretty steady conversation with them, with Julie, mostly, and the fact that she sounded happy made him wonder if he'd actually dreamt the kiss last night.

He hadn't told Julie. She'd insisted he find Margo and talk to her, that he promise her that they weren't an item, but what she didn't get was that Jess's promises meant nothing to Margo. They hadn't for a long time. Words thrown about carelessly tend to lose their meaning, and he'd thrown a lot of words at Margo when they were together.

Margo asked Julie about school and what she did now, and Julie made Margo laugh at her stories about working in a health club and the crazy lengths some people went to for a fast fix. The conversation was natural and fun, and Jess found himself feeling like a third wheel. He listened to every word Margo said and paid attention to the tone of voice she used, and he jarred his teeth together to keep his mouth shut when she spoke about some of the guys who nosed around her down at the Queen. She referenced a date with one of them, and she and Julie shared an inside laugh about needing a safe word and having a friend on standby in case rescue was necessary. But Jess was hung up on the guys nosing around her at the bar and the date, and he was desperate to know who it was and if she had slept with him.

When Margo packed Berkley up and left for the Queen later in the afternoon, she and Julie seemed to be in good spirits. They parted with a friendly goodbye and see you later, and Jess was surly and irritated when he drove back to his parents' house. They spent the evening with his family, which was alternately fun and miserable because he could see each of them—his parents and both of his sisters—trying to work out if he and Julie were a couple or simply friends.

They hung out there for dinner, because Jess didn't have the heart to drag Julie back to the Queen for a second night in a row. Twice, he had seen her deeply involved in something on her phone, and he wondered if Brent Willer would ever see how perfect Julie was and ask her out. His parents had fixed dinner, so Julie insisted on helping with clean up. Rather than subject her to alone time with his sisters and subject himself to his parents' sly glances, he jumped in and helped dry dishes and put them away.

"So, what're you going to do?" Julie asked him later. His sister Lori had gone home to her family, and Melissa had gone to meet friends. He didn't know where, but he did know they wouldn't be at the Queen. Melissa had no more love for Margo than Duncan did for him.

"About what?" He aimed the remote at the TV and flew through seven channels before Julie could speak again.

"Do you learn that skill in school? Or is it just something men are born with?"

"What skill?"

"Channel surfing." She stretched out on the couch and watched him, clearly amused.

"Born with it," he mumbled with a shrug. Propped on the end of the couch as she was, her hair falling forward over her face, Jess decided Julie was pretty. Always before, she was cute, but something had changed. Maybe it was seeing her interact with Margo. Knowing there were things Julie kept from him, even when he had assumed they had become close friends and shared everything, made him as curious about her as he was Margo. He also wondered how the hell Margo had flipped the switch to defrost and been friendly to Julie today after her ultimatum last night.

Had it been an ultimatum? Had she hinted that if he stopped bringing Julie around, she would give him the time of day? Or was she simply reminding him—again—that she would never trust him around other women?

"He's an idiot," he told her now.

"What?" Julie snapped her head around to look at the TV. "That dude?"

"Brent."

"Mmm." She slumped her head back on the sofa and shrugged her lips. "Maybe I'm the idiot, Jess. He's out of my league. I've always known that."

"Why? Why is he out of your league?"

"He's gorgeous. Remember that?" She tipped her head at him, but Jess only shrugged and rolled his eyes. "And he's got money. Last weekend? He and like two hundred of his closest friends partied on a yacht in the—"

"He doesn't deserve you."

Julie sucked in a quick breath and then let it out slowly. "Thank you. But please tell me you're not sitting there thinking about hitting on me, Jess. Because I don't wanna do that. I like you too much as a friend."

"Nope." He shrugged. "I'm sitting here thinking about Margo and how do I get her back, and I'm thinking it's pretty shitty of me to bring you here and spend all of my time thinking about her."

"It's why you're here," she reminded him.

"She's not gonna forgive me. She's—"

"She's letting you spend time with Berkley."

"That's different. She's willing to let me be Berkley's father. But she's not gonna let me back in."

"Then you keep knocking," Julie said simply. "Keep trying."

"If you were Margo, would you ever forgive me? Would you take me back?"

"Depends on how good you are in bed."

Jess dropped his head back to the cushion back of the recliner and laughed softly.

"Pretty sure that's not the problem."

"You hurt her, Jess. You have to be sorry for that."

"I regret what I did, but it didn't hurt her. Margo is tough as nails—"

Julie, shaking her head enthusiastically, struggled to sit up. "No. It doesn't matter if she's immortal, Jess. You were in a committed relationship with her. Regardless of what you two did or didn't say, you were living together. Sharing a bed. And you cheated on her twice. That hurts. Hell yes that hurts."

"Happen to you?" His voice was gruff.

"No." She frowned and rolled her lips inward. "Not really. There've been breakups, and there's been…someone else, but not exactly the same."

"But."

"Jess." Julie tossed her hands up. "Turn it around. You're living with her. You sleep with her every night. You hold her. You're skin to skin, even when you aren't making love. That involves deep, heavy trust. You wake up with her. You share a bathroom. You don't have to be head over heels in love, but you share all of these intimate moments every day. Wouldn't it hurt you if you found out she'd been with someone else and kept it from you?"

Jess came off the chair and paced the small living area in the basement.

"I think I'd want to kill any man who touched her."

"Then how can you shrug off what happened and tell me it didn't hurt her? Just because you guys never said I love you?"

"She's just so damned stubborn. So independent."

"My dad." Julie rubbed her face and then dragged her fingers through her hair. Jess stood still to listen. Julie's dad was Jess' boss, and he knew him well. Jess looked up to the guy. Apparently, though Jess still doubted it now and then, they were cut from the same cloth. "He would get so fucking drunk that he didn't know his own name. And Mom would go get him from the bar. Other times, he'd drink enough to be the fun guy. And he wouldn't come home at night."

Jess held his breath as Julie struggled to continue. He'd heard the stories before, but it wasn't often that Julie dug so deep into her own experience to soothe him or coax him back to Margo.

"They fought all the time. She would rant at him for coming home so drunk. For going home with other women, when he couldn't…" She shrugged and shook her head. "When he was with her."

Jess felt a stab of guilt. No one wanted to think about their parents this way, and no one sure the hell ever wanted to talk about it. To share that humiliation.

"Okay." He nodded.

"Okay, what?" She looked up at him, her eyes glassy with tears.

"I know I hurt her. Intellectually, I know it was wrong. I just…I needed to see that, Julie. I needed to see that she could cry. That it mattered."

Julie climbed to her feet and dabbed at her eyes.

"That's not what I meant." He groaned and ducked his head. "I didn't do it just to see if she reacted. I just needed—"

Julie dropped her hands and shook her head.

"You need to tell Margo. Not me."

"I can't."

"Why not?"

"Because she's at the Queen. Because you're here. Because it's not something I can just say and walk away from. I need time—"

Julie nodded. "I'm fine here. I have a couch. A pillow and your blanket. The TV."

"She's at—"

"So go to the Queen."

CHAPTER 16

Margo shouldn't feel guilty for coming home from the Queen early; she'd skipped out early a few nights a week since she had Berkley. No one minded, and she more than made up for the time missed in the evenings when she worked earlier morning and afternoon hours. But she did feel bad, because Leah was tired, and Margo knew that sort of tired all too well. Add in the worry over the complications early in Leah's pregnancy, and she had almost turned around and driven back to the Queen to insist Leah go home instead.

Guilty or not, she loved the evenings she spent with Berkley. She had picked her up from her parents' house around nine. Sometimes, her mom left the bathing and the jammies to Margo, sometimes she had everything taken care of when Margo picked her up. Margo loved it either way. Tonight, she had picked up a sticky, messy baby girl who had apparently helped her grandma frost a cake. Margo had narrowed her eyes at her mother and asked her if she was nuts, letting Berkley have frosting. She was too tired to deal with a toddler's sugar rush at nine in the evening.

Her mom had promised her it had been just a taste that Berkley had managed to smear all over her face and her hands. And her hair, Margo had realized, once she got Berkley home and into the bathtub. Berkley had played in the tub as usual, and Margo stayed there on her knees at the side of the tub until the water was almost cold and Berkley was yawning and rubbing her eyes.

An hour later, Berkley in clean, soft jammies, fast asleep in her arms after a bottle and two story books, Margo crept into her bedroom to put her down for the night. Berkley rolled to her side immediately, and Margo pulled her mint green blanket over her and watched her sleep for a few moments.

It was the same blanket she had put over Berkley in the stroller the day Jess had come over and they had walked outside. Sad now, and a little bit lonely, Margo stroked her fingertips over the blanket, but she drew back quickly when Berkley wiggled and sighed in her sleep.

She tiptoed out of the bedroom and collapsed back on the couch.

She hadn't slept last night. Instead, she had tossed and turned and remembered the way Jess had kissed her and the feel of his hard body pressed against hers. When thinking about the kiss left her hot and bothered, she squeezed her eyes closed and remembered other times. The night they had played a Batman video game until they'd fallen asleep together on the couch. A rainy weekend when they binge-watched James Bond movies and fed each other grapes and popcorn and cookies.

The first time he had made love to her, when she thought she had felt his heart beating against her chest. In the end, she decided she had imagined it, because she wasn't sure Jess had a heart. Hadn't taken long for her to decide she didn't want him pressed to her heart when they had sex, and she'd demanded any position that kept things just a little bit impersonal.

Margo turned the lamp off now, but she didn't go to bed. No point in it, because she knew it would be a repeat of last night. She curled up in the corner of the sofa and picked up her phone. But she didn't look at it, choosing instead to turn the TV on and find some silly sitcom rerun to occupy her brain until she could at least get a catnap on the couch.

When her phone buzzed in her hand, she assumed it was Leah or Stevi, texting to check on her. On the TV screen, there was a black and white show with canned laughter, and even though she didn't readily recognize the actors, she welcomed the feeling of contentment and familiarity the show gave her.

Are you at the Queen?

Jess. It was dangerous to answer him right now, but she knew she would. She could set her phone down and walk away—better yet, she could put her phone in the freezer, but she would be back in the kitchen in five minutes or less to get it—or just answer it and get it over with. Something had to give.

And once it did, once she and Jess said everything they'd left unsaid, there would be no chance they would be friends, even. But at least Berkley would have her father in her life.

At home.

She waited for a response, and when none came, the feeling of dread grew bigger inside her. Nerves and anxiety drove her to her feet, and she paced the front room until she saw his headlights when he turned into the driveway.

For a moment, while she watched from the front door as he climbed from the truck, she was reminded of the nights when they lived together, and he would come home after drinking too much. Either he was all hands or he walked by her without a glance; she never knew which Jess to expect, and she never reacted the way she wanted to. If he was all hands, she gave him what he wanted, though she was dead inside. If he ignored her, she was a tangled mess of need and anger.

He looked up as his foot hit the first step on the porch. Propped in the doorway, she watched through the screen door as he lifted his other foot and hesitantly put it down on the next step, until finally he was just on the other side of the door.

"Everything okay?" he asked by way of greeting.

"Yeah."

In her tank top and loose pajama pants—feet bare—the night air outside the door was cold. Margo shivered and rubbed her hands up and down her arms. Jess's eyes roamed over her in the flickering lights of the TV; her nipples hard and tight now from his gaze and not the cool air.

"Can I come in?"

She thought about saying no. Sending him back home. But two things kept her from doing it. First of all, sending him away now would be pushing him into Julie's arms. Even if Jess had been sleeping with the girl since the day he moved out last year, she hated the thought of him leaving her like this and going home to someone else's arms. Besides, they needed to clear the air and move on.

With a sad sigh, she tapped the handle on the door and pushed it slightly outward. When Jess pulled it open, she stepped away and turned her back to him.

"Is Berkley here?"

"She's sleeping." She looked at him over her shoulder. "Is that why you're here? To see Berkley?"

Jess's stare left no room for her to think he was there for any reason but to see her.

"Do you wanna see her? Just peek at her?"

"I would love that," he admitted.

"Please don't wake her." She nodded as she led him back through the short hallway to Berkley's room. She stood back as Jess tiptoed up to the side of the crib. Rather than touch her or even place his hands on the rail of the crib, he simply tucked his hands in his coat pockets and tipped his head to watch her sleep.

Overcome with guilt for the days and nights she had deprived him of, Margo slipped out of the room and tiptoed back down the hall. She wandered through the living room but ended up in the kitchen. Yes, they'd had some intimate moments here, too, but at the moment, it felt like the safest room in the house with the cold, hard countertops and the stiff, uncomfortable chairs. A glass of wine sounded good, but the last thing she wanted to do was rub it in Jess's face that she could have a drink or tempt him, so she simply sat down at the table and waited. Moments passed before his gruff voice jolted her out of her thoughts. Sad thoughts about all of Berkley's firsts that he had missed.

"Are you seeing someone?"

"What?" She blinked and looked at him across the room.

He shrugged, but he stayed where he was, as if waiting for her to invite him to join her.

"No."

"But you have dated since we broke up."

She had an issue with the words broke up, because they sounded so high school. And what they'd done and what she'd done later—making a baby and then having that baby and raising her herself—wasn't high school, but so much more complicated.

But she only shrugged. "I don't know that I'd call it dating."

"You slept with someone."

She watched him curl his fingers into fists.

"Yeah." She nodded. "I did."

"How many?"

"Why?" She refused to answer.

"Just curious."

"I don't think I want to talk about it, Jess."

"Were you in love?"

"What?"

"Before me." Jess stepped into the room finally, but he hesitated before joining her at the table. "Were you ever in love?"

Margo propped her elbow on the table and rested her chin in her hand.

"Why do you wanna know?"

"I just do. I wanna know."

She sighed and raised her eyebrows. "I dunno. I was involved with a guy when I was fresh out of high school. Thought it was love. Figured we would get married."

"What happened?"

"I don't know. We just kind of…fizzled out. Nobody's fault."

She looked up at him silently when he stood before her and reached for her hand.

"What?" She shook her head, reminding herself there was a reason she'd chosen the kitchen.

"I know what you're doing. Can we please sit in the other room? It's hard to relax in these chairs."

"I think they're fine."

"And what if I remind you of the night we went three rounds on that very chair you're sitting on?"

Margo closed her eyes when her face flooded with heat.

"Margo, we've made love in every room in this house. You can't hide from the memories if that's what you're trying to do."

She swallowed hard.

"And if you're worried something's gonna happen, I promise it won't."

Eyes still closed, she laughed sadly. "I stopped believing in your promises a long time ago."

"I was six the first time I fell in love," he announced. "She was my kindergarten teacher. God, she was so pretty, I asked her to marry me once."

"How'd that go?"

"She laughed at me. Tousled my hair and introduced me to her boyfriend."

"Ouch."

"Please?" He held his hand out to her again. She stood, but she avoided his hand. Led him back to the living room where she burrowed back into the corner of the couch.

"I had a similar crush on a teacher when I was thirteen."

"Did you ask her to marry you?"

"No." He grinned as he shrugged out of his jacket and tossed it down on the middle of the couch. Margo watched him sit at the opposite end. Found herself wishing he would move closer.

"I had a burning, insane crush on a guy when I was sixteen. He was a senior. He didn't know I existed. I thought I was alive to satisfy his every need. To have his babies."

"His loss."

"Right." She nodded and tucked her hair behind her ear. "Look. I don't know what we're doing. I don't know what you're doing. These are things we should have talked about a long time ago. It's too late, Jess. We'll never be more than stories in each other's pasts. Now you can tell your next girlfriend….you can tell Julie that you had a crazy year when you lived with a girl who had a bar and free booze and was occasionally good in bed. And I can tell whoever I choose to see that I lived with a guy who gave me a baby."

"Is that all I was to you?"

Margo's eyes filled, but she looked away and breathed deeply.

"And you think that? You think you were free booze and a mediocre fuck?"

Though he was rephrasing what she had said, his choice of words tore through her like a freight train.

"Wow." She sniffled and looked back at him. "Thanks, Jess. Obviously, I wasn't good enough to hold you here, but that's pretty harsh."

"You never cried."

Margo arched her eyebrows and dabbed at her eyes.

"You never looked hard enough to notice."

"I miss you."

"Funny." She nodded and wiped at her eyes. Her throat ached with the tears she desperately wished she wouldn't cry. "Funny thing to say now."

"I loved making love with you. You were bold and adventurous, and you were hungry. You wanted me just the same way I wanted you."

"Then why did you just call me a mediocre fuck?"

"You said it."

"I'm not gonna keep her from you." Margo swallowed hard, but the knot of emotion stayed in her throat. "I'm sorry that you missed so much, Jess. But I don't want to do this. We don't need to rehash—"

He moved with the stealth of a predator. Speechless, Margo watched Jess reach for his jacket and toss it aside. He moved down the couch so fast, his hands were on her before she could protest. His fingers were gentle on the back of her neck, and his right hand was at her hip and his fingers eased under the snug-fitting tank top to smooth over her bare skin.

"I miss you," he said again, and Margo wanted to answer him. But she didn't know if she wanted to argue or suggest that perhaps he missed her because she was willing to open her legs to him or even maybe he missed her because she wasn't mediocre in bed, but because they had been so fucking hot, they'd burned each other to the core.

When she did part her lips to speak, only his name slipped out on a desperate sigh. His hands still tending to the skin of her neck and her flat belly, he ducked his head and fastened his lips on her jaw. His erection pressed painfully hard against her thigh. Margo cupped him through his jeans, stunned not by her boldness but by how badly she wanted him.

He moaned her name with pleasure and pressed deeper into her hand.

"Jess." She wound the fingers of her other hand through the longer hair on top of his head and tugged roughly to bring his mouth to hers. His tongue was hot and daring, but she took each thrust eagerly, curling her own tongue around his when he moved to break the kiss.

So lost in the wet, velvet kisses, she was surprised to feel the cool air over her stomach and her breast as he pushed her top up.

"Hurry." She panted as she backed away. Jess moved his hand from her neck and grabbed the tail of the tank. Impatient for his touch, for his mouth on her, Margo took the shirt in her hands and whipped it off. She cried out with pleasure when he lifted her to his lap and her bare breasts brushed his soft, worn t-shirt.

The moves—their moves—came back to her, and she pressed her knees to the couch and rose up to offer her breasts to him.

"You taste so fucking good." He scraped his teeth over her sensitive skin and then sucked hard on her nipple. Margo whimpered and reached to push her pajama pants down.

"Margo."

"What?"

"Let me."

She blinked when she heard the command in his voice.

"I need to come, Jess. It's been so damned long—"

"Let me do it," he said again.

She nodded, hands at her waist, her fingers curled around the elastic in her pants. Jess had magic hands. He knew where to touch her. He knew the right amount of pressure. He knew when to stroke and when to curl his fingers inside her when they were lying together in bed. But when they were messing around like this, she'd always done it. Jess had played with her breasts, while she'd touched herself. Quick and easy for her, and she'd assumed he liked watching her.

"Okay," she whispered and nodded. "But I need it now. Please. I need—"

"I know." He leaned forward and licked a trail from her collarbone to her ear. "Trust me, Margo. I know how to love you."

Eyes locked with his, she nodded again. Her hands shook as she moved them to his shoulders, and the ache between her legs was enough to drive her closer to him.

"Let me," he said again when she grinded against him.

"Please," she whispered. She kissed him when he grazed her lips with his, but she tipped her head to watch when he traced his fingertips down over her belly. Something about watching his hand slide beneath the elastic of her pajamas, the black panties she wore was almost enough to make her come.

"You're dripping wet." His voice was low and sexy, and Margo felt it chase shivers over her bare shoulders and arms.

"I know."

"So hot." He whispered the words as he pressed his fingers over her center and slid them inside her.

"Jess."

"I know, sweetheart," he reminded her. "Let me make you feel good. Let me make you come."

"I need—"

"This?"

Fingers scissoring inside her, he pressed his thumb over her clit and rubbed a soft circle there.

"Yes."

"Margo?"

"Mmm?" She moved with him, arching into him as he withdrew his fingers and thrust them inside her again.

"I'm only gonna let you come if you we do this again. In bed."

"Yes. Please." She nodded.

"Tonight."

"Jesus, Jess, please. Yes. Yes. Make me come. Take me to bed."

He moved his fingers faster, but he kept the pressure on her clit steady, the movement slow and lazy.

"I think about this every night I close my eyes, Margo."

She lifted her head to meet his eyes again.

"I think about being balls deep inside you, your pussy tight and hot on my dick. I miss kissing you whenever, wherever I want."

A wave of pleasure climbed over her slowly, warmth spreading from her thighs to her toes. She moaned softly and arched her eyebrows.

"I trusted you," she whimpered as she slipped her hand inside her pajama pants. She covered his hand with hers, just as Jess increased the pressure between her legs and leaned over to press his open mouth to her nipple again.

Margo gasped his name, mindful of their little girl asleep in her room, as she shattered on her knees, straddling his lap.

"I've got you." Jess kissed his way from her breast to her neck until finally he nipped at her bottom lip. "Have I ever told you how good it feels when you come on my hand like that? I can feel you tightening around my fingers. I feel your heartbeat when I put my mouth on you here."

Margo wrapped her left arm around his head when he lowered his head to her breast again.

"Have I ever told you I love the way you fill me when you're inside me?" She pressed her lips to his hair, still breathing hard, her body still quaking with pleasure. "I want you inside me, Jess. Please. Balls deep." She smoothed his hair back and kissed his forehead.

Still holding onto him, she moved her other hand from his and worked the button of his jeans. Jess moved as fast as a snake, coiled his fingers around her wrist, and held her still.

"Not here."

"Right here." She nodded.

"The bedroom."

"Jess." She tried to shake his hand off her arm, but he held on tightly.

"In your bed."

Maybe it was because he said *your* bed and not *our* bed, and maybe it was because she was desperate and he refused to move, to let go of her hand, but she gave in and nodded and eased backwards over his lap. Jess wiggled his fingers one last time as he drew his hand away from her, and then rather than let her stand, he climbed to his feet with her in his arms and carried her to her bedroom.

CHAPTER 17

Jᴇss ʟᴀɪᴅ ʜᴇʀ ᴅᴏᴡɴ ᴏɴ ᴛʜᴇ ʙᴇᴅ ᴀɴᴅ ʀᴇᴀᴄʜᴇᴅ immediately to tug her pajama pants and panties down over her hips. Still struggling to breathe, Margo propped herself on her elbows to watch him strip out of his clothes. T-shirt first; he grabbed the collar and pulled it over his head. Tossed it to the floor. Unsnapped his jeans, but he hesitated when he noticed Margo's eyes go big and wide with expectation. She lifted her leg and touched the back of his hand with her toe.

"Hurry."

He hadn't come over here to fuck her. Not like this, anyway. He had envisioned a long heart-to-heart talk and then a night of slow, tender lovemaking. He had forgotten Margo favored rough and tumble, fast and furious, and her tears earlier had broken him down and then lit him on fire.

Fuck yes, he was gonna hurry. He shoved his jeans down and kicked out of them. Pulled his wallet from his pocket to retrieve a condom, suspecting that come morning she would comment on the fact that he had one ready. She watched, her breasts proud and bigger than he remembered—probably from carrying Berkley—as he ripped the condom open with his teeth.

"I wanna see you."

"No lights," she argued.

Her skin was silver and shaded, and her nipples darker shadows. Her hair fell in luxurious curls over her shoulders. Jess backed away from her and turned on the lamp at the side of the bed.

"Please?" She shook her head and reached her hand out to grasp the comforter to cover herself.

"Margo."

"Please turn the light off," she insisted. Her voice was sharp with anger, so he simply turned back to the lamp and turned it off. Before he faced her again, he heard her move. Afraid she had changed her mind, he looked over his shoulder to see her scoot forward and reach for him.

"Holy fuck." He gritted his teeth as she reached around him to cup his straining erection in her hands. Together, they worked the elastic down over his hips, careful of his cock that she gripped immediately as he stepped out of the underwear. Margo circled her fingers around his shaft and smoothed his head with the pad of her thumb.

"Balls deep," she whispered. "Fill me, Jess. Get inside me."

He rolled the condom on and reached for her.

"How do you want it?"

"I want you," she answered.

Jess spun her around and eased her to all fours on the bed.

"I don't wanna hurt you."

"Have you ever hurt me?" she asked. "Like this?"

Her words nicked at him, but she looked over her shoulder and rational thought went out the window. Jess stepped closer to her, curled his hands around her hips, and drove into her hard and deep, in one long thrust. Margo gasped and then moaned with pleasure. He loved this position, because he could press deep inside her, but mostly he loved it because she did.

He waited a moment to gain control of his dick and his head. She was tight and slick and hot, and if he wasn't careful, he would lose it and blow in three strokes, and he wanted this to take all night. He wanted to make her come again, he wanted her sobbing his name over and over uncontrollably before he let himself go.

"Fuck me, Jess."

That was all it took for him to move. Long, slow strokes out and in. He watched the movement, the way she took him in, and listened to her throaty moans, but when his control slipped after only a few thrusts, he reached around her to touch her, his fingers hungry to feel her hot and wet again. He pinched her sensitive skin and sent her over the edge. Jess watched her gather the comforter in her hands and hang on desperately as he drew the orgasm out for her. She lowered her face to the bed, chanting his name between moans of pleasure.

Jess drove her harder and faster as his own release built in his back and his balls. His thighs burned, and his dick felt so damned good inside her, he could die happy right now. Feeling the orgasm coming, he grabbed her hips again and held her as he erupted inside her.

The only thing better than this was riding Margo bare back, and the one time they'd done that, they'd made that beautiful baby girl down the hall.

"Fuck." He shuddered with the powerful release and eased forward to rest his knees on the bed. Margo sank back against him, still draped over the bed in front of him.

"You walked away," she whispered.

"You told me to go."

"But you were sleeping with me in this bed, and you went looking for something better."

"There's nothing. Nothing in this world better than fucking you, Margo."

She reached back toward him and took his hand.

"But you had to look. That's what hurt, Jess." She scooted away from him and turned over to lie on her back. "When you love someone, you trust that there's nothing better out there. Ever."

Jess watched her in the shadowed room. Still on his knees

on the side of the bed, he ducked his head and sucked in a deep breath.

"Margo." He ran his hands over his bare legs and then reached for her. Hungry for every inch of bare skin before him, he trailed his fingertips up over her calf and her inner thigh.

"Where is she? Where is she right now?"

"What?"

"Your girlfriend? Where is she right now while you're here fucking me?"

"Julie's not my—"

"Dammit, Jess, don't. Don't do that!" She pushed herself up on her elbow and planted her other hand on his shoulder to shove him away. "Don't do that. I know you. I know who you are, and I know what you do, and now you've made me part of it."

Margo climbed off the bed and leaned over to snatch her pajama pants from the floor. Jess scrambled to get up and get his pants on when she left the room. He heard her in the living room, just a rustle of movement, but he knew she was pulling her tank top on, and she was about to shut down and kick him out again.

"You never listen."

He groaned and squeezed his eyes closed as he stepped around the corner into the living room just as Margo turned the lamp on. Dressed now, she crossed her arms over her chest and glared at him.

"And you lie," she reminded him. "Over and over, and somewhere along the way, Jess, I finally understood you are the lie. You're so beautiful to look at, but that's all there is. I don't know if you're empty inside, or if you're just so full of yourself that there's no room to love anyone else. I'm done. My mistake this time."

Jess blinked at her and then yanked his shirt over his head. Margo's gaze flickered down to watch the soft material fall over his bare chest and stomach.

"You." He pointed at her and stepped toward her. Snatched her wrist to tug her forward when he saw that she wanted to slip away from him. "Don't know how to be loved, Margo Nevin."

Her breath hitched, but she stared at him boldly. Too proud to let him win.

"I gave you everything I had." His voice was gruff and tight. "Everything. I thought it wasn't enough. Now I know."

"Know what?"

"Wasn't that I couldn't give you enough." He held on when she tried to pull her wrist from his grip. "It was always that you didn't know how to take from me."

She rolled her lips inward and tried to breathe, but her body trembled with emotion that she still fought to control.

"I've taken it any way you've given—"

"I'm not talking about sex, Margo." He shook his head. "I'm talking about everything else men and women do in a relationship. You don't know how to feel."

She flinched like he hit her. The flash of fear on her face made him let go of her and step back.

"So you leave your girlfriend home with your family, and you come here and you fuck me, and now you're going back to Julie…Leaving me here alone…and somehow everything that went wrong for us is still my fault?"

"I don't know how to make you hear me," he whispered. "I'm not gonna stand here and fight with you about this. I'm not gonna go round and round, and I'm not gonna wake Berkley up because I'm shouting because I'm so fucking angry with you. I'm not doing this now."

"Of course you're not." Margo tipped her head and nodded. She rubbed the bridge of her nose and closed her eyes. "Would you do me a favor? Just one?"

"I would do anything for you." He shrugged when she looked up at him. "All you've ever had to do is ask."

"Right." She nodded as she stepped away from him. Jess watched, fascinated, as she pushed her hair back and hooked it behind her ears. Her eyelashes were wet with tears. She stared at him for several moments before she spoke again. "When you get back to Julie. When you take your clothes off and climb in bed beside her—"

"Margo—"

She shook her head quickly and held her hand up to stop him.

"When you touch her. Just remember she's still perfect because she's young. I had your baby, Jess. You and your baby did a number on my body. Just remember it's not fair to compare us."

"Margo, I'm not—"

She folded her arms over her chest again and stared at him silently, as if she was waiting for him to finish. He couldn't. He wasn't sleeping with Julie; he had never slept with Julie. Never would. But denying it now was simply dragging out the same old argument. It wasn't the right time to dig in. Not with Berkley asleep down the hall and Julie hanging out at his parents' home.

Tears streaked her face as she waited for him to speak or move or do something.

"How about that?" She smiled sadly as she swiped at her eyes. "I do cry. I do cry, Jess Covey. I just know how to hide it."

CHAPTER 18

W HEN HE LEFT—HE HAD STOOD FOR A LONG TIME, LOOKING at her, getting off on her tears, maybe, before simply taking two steps toward the couch, swiping his leather coat from the floor, and walking out (no yelling, no stomping his feet, no temper)—she considered changing her sheets. Before, she would have done just that. She would have paced the house, every footstep hard and angry, while the sheets—the ones they'd had sex on— sloshed around in her washer and then tumbled in her dryer. She would have fought to forget the sex, the way he played her body like an instrument, and she would have fantasized ways to hurt him. Ways to exact revenge for the harsh words he threw her way when they fought. For the way he could slide his body in and out of hers and then tuck his dick back in his pants and walk out and look for someone else.

Tonight, she didn't. She didn't change the sheets. She didn't try to forget what they had done. Instead, she tiptoed to Berkley's room and lowered herself to sit in the hard, wooden rocking chair in the corner. She never used it; she chose the rocking recliner in the living room when she wanted to put Berkley down to sleep. But tonight, she sat in the corner of her daughter's room and watched Berkley sleep. Berkley's black curls were matted with sweat, and Margo was chilled to the bone, but she didn't move to grab a blanket.

She watched for signs that the baby was hers, for some likeness they shared. Imagined that she saw Jess in Berkley, in the way she slept with abandon. On her back, one arm slung up over her head. She thought of her sweet baby girl and the way she had thrown herself at Jess, the way she had loved his face and his voice. Thought of the way they had made her; of the rough sex she preferred and wondered how often she and Jess had truly made love.

It was easier when it was hard. Less intimate. Margo hated missionary position, because she hated being trapped under Jess, with his eyes on hers. Why was that? Because she didn't want to chance seeing boredom on his face as he moved inside her? Because she knew that he looked at other women the same way, even when he lived with her? Or was it that she was afraid of what he would see when he looked into her eyes?

Not boredom. Jess Covey had never bored her.

Fear. Desperation.

Love.

So cold she was shaking, she finally left Berkley's room and turned the lamp and the TV off and went to bed. She hugged her pillow tight and squeezed her eyes closed and remembered the way she and Jess had just touched. The things he had said to her. She loved when he talked dirty; his voice and his words left her wet and quaking for his touch. Once, a long time ago, he had tried to whisper sweet things to her. Lying between her thighs, buried inside her, he had slowed everything down so slow, she remembered feeling the warm, wet drag of his cock as he worked solely to pleasure her. He'd kissed her—long, slow, wet kisses, tongues sliding and dancing.

She'd balked at the emotion. The intimacy. Which was ridiculous, because they had been well acquainted with each other's bodies by that time.

Now she craved that sort of connection with him. Tonight had been perfect, as far as the sex went. Jess had done her that way on purpose, because she liked it that way, and he had known she would come fast and hard. But tonight had been completely wrong because he had left his girlfriend to come to her. He'd left that poor kid— what the hell was he thinking dating a girl so young—at his parents' house while he'd come to his ex for sex.

Margo wished he hadn't left. That she could press her naked body to his. That he was there to wake her in the night with his fingers, insistent and skilled, between her legs. That she could wake to him dragging his lips, his scruffy jaw over her naked shoulder. To a kiss and his offer to make her coffee.

But she wished he hadn't come at all. She almost wished that he hadn't come back for Berkley. Because he hadn't come back to love her, and now she was stuck between a man who loved to fuck her and her baby girl, who deserved to be with her daddy.

Ridiculous to feel that way. Ridiculous to try and lay claims on him, to be hurt that he'd done nothing out of character, and to wish that she could change him. She was a mom now; Berkley's happiness was her number one priority.

She'd fallen off her own sad little wagon. Tomorrow she'd climb back on, buckle her seatbelt, and hold on tight. No more screw ups allowed, because she had the potential to hurt a lot of people.

She would save Berkley and herself.

"So." Stevi cleared her throat and tapped her fingers on her coffee mug. Margo had downed two cups already, and Stevi had picked hers up once. She wasn't much of a coffee drinker; she was more into expensive sugary drinks available from a drive-thru window.

"I know." Margo rubbed her eyes and dragged her fingers down over her face.

"Hey, that reminds me!" Stevi pointed at her and laughed. "What are we doing for Halloween? It's next week."

"What do you mean what're we doing? Taking Berkley trick-or-treating."

"I know. You want me and Leah to go? Think Duncan and Tania can handle the Halloween party at the Queen?"

Margo opened her mouth to say yes, but she hesitated. "I don't know, Stevi. Jess…might want to go."

Stevi's eyebrows jumped in surprise, but she recovered quickly with a firm nod. "Of course he would."

"I don't know. I'll figure it out."

"Okay." Stevi fidgeted with her cup again.

"Are we set for next weekend at the Queen?"

"Yeah." Stevi grinned. "Halloween last year was great. I think costume contests really draw people in."

Margo frowned. "If you say so."

"We were swamped last year."

"I know."

"What's going on?" Stevi finally looked around the room and then settled her eyes on Berkley, chasing Cheerios around on her highchair tray. "Not that I don't love you, but why did you call me at nine on a Sunday morning and ask me to come over?"

"I need you to babysit."

"Of course," Stevi agreed. "No problem. Can I take her home? Duncan would love to see her."

"Not Berkley. Jess."

"What?" Stevi flopped backwards in the chair and tipped her head to study Margo.

Margo licked her lips—she did not want to tell this story —and looked at the clock on the microwave.

"Any minute now, Jess and Julie will knock on the door to hang out with Berk. I can't be here."

Stevi winced. "I hoped you guys had worked something out Friday night. When he followed you down to the cellar."

Margo held her breath.

"So, he's really with her? Is she even out of school?" Stevi twisted her cup in a circle on the table and finally picked it up and sipped.

"I slept with him."

"What?" Stevi choked on the coffee. She set the cup down with a bang; milk-colored liquid sloshed over the rim.

Margo swallowed hard and worked her mouth to speak. "He showed up here last night. After I left the Queen."

"Margo." Stevi gritted her teeth and squeezed her eyes closed. "Oh, hon, why did you do that to yourself?"

"To myself?" Margo's laugh was harsh and loud. "How about to Julie? He left that kid at his parents' house, and he came here, and we went at it just like we used to."

"She's just a kid—"

"It doesn't matter if she's eighteen or thirty-five. She's here with Jess, and I…had sex with him last night." Margo glanced at Berkley as she successfully picked up a Cheerio. She lifted her finger proudly to show Margo, a sweet smile on her face. "I'm the other woman, and I don't like it any more than being the stupid girlfriend waiting back home."

"You're not stupid."

"I am stupid. I knew what he was doing, and I let it happen. And now, knowing who and what he is, I still did what I did, and I'm now a cheater."

"Okay." Stevi held her hands up to stop Margo. She closed her eyes and shook her head slightly. "Did you guys talk? At all?"

"Um. I really don't think you want to know the things we said to each other."

"I didn't ask if you talked dirty."

Margo shrugged. "That's about the only way we talked."

"Did he spend the night?"

"No. We got in a fight. He walked out."

"He walked out?"

"Whatever, Stevi. It ended badly. As always. I can't be here when they come today."

"You can't just avoid him. He's Berkley's father."

"No, but I can't hang out with him and Julie all day again. I can't watch them play with Berk and wonder if he left me and went home to her and made…if they…" Margo shrugged. "Because I can't stand to think about him touching her that way." Her voice broke on the last word, and she had to swallow and breathe and look away from

Stevi's big, kind eyes. "And I can't look at her and wonder if she knows what I did."

"I don't get that vibe from them."

"You said they were holding hands."

"Okay, but you and I have held hands before. Doesn't mean we're doing it."

Margo rolled her eyes.

"Bad example, but you get what I'm saying."

"Will you stay here? I know it's a lot to ask, Stevi, but I can't. And I can't tell him that he can't see her."

"Of course I will, Margo." Stevi pursed her lips. "What're you gonna do?"

"I don't know. I think I'll to the Queen. Check inventory." She shrugged. "Clean something."

"You could go hang out with Duncan."

"Nope."

"Are you gonna talk to Jess? Figure this out?"

"What is there to figure out, Stevi?" Margo shook her head. "We're not good for each other. And if we're not good for each other, we're not good together for Berk."

Stevi drummed her fingers on the side of her cup. The look of hope on her face faded, and finally, she nodded, as if giving in to Margo, which only made Margo feel worse.

"Okay." Stevi smiled, but Margo saw her disappointment. "Go. I'll hang out here until…they leave."

"If he asks—"

"Really?" Stevi blinked at her as she stood. "You really think he would ask me why you aren't here?"

THERE WAS SOMETHING SOOTHING TO MARGO ABOUT BEING at the Queen. Even before, just after Berkley was born and Jess was gone, Margo had found comfort at the Queen. Sure, there was something to be said for throwing herself into hard work, but the dark, polished wood of the bar, the shiny mirror that ran the length of wall behind the bar—even the smell of the place, the lingering furniture polish and the spirits at the bar and the smell of the potpourri in the office—made Margo happy.

Didn't hurt that she and her cousins had put their trust money from their grandfather together to buy the building and refurbish it. Margo supposed maybe that was part of what comforted her about being here, that connection to her granddad.

She loved the Queen all lit up, with people crowding the tables and the bar, and Duncan and Stevi flirting as they served their patrons and Leah mooning over Trace when he sang—and Trace's deep, well-worn voice pounding out the country tunes. But she loved it all locked down and quiet, too. The rest of the gang didn't know it, but she'd come here through the night a time or two when things had been bad between her and Jess.

She had come here and sat curled up in the corner of the leather couch in the office one night before she was pregnant. She didn't know for sure that Jess was with anyone else that night; in fact, she would probably bet that he wasn't. Jess' infidelity was more about his affair with attention and himself and his need to be seen. He'd been with other women; she wasn't stupid enough to think otherwise. But she knew there were nights he wasn't with anyone, and he simply chose not to come home to her.

She had passed the night she found out she was pregnant here at the Queen. Alone. The cold remains of the dinner she'd cooked for Jess congealing in the pots on the stove, an empty pint glass on the table at his place. A baby rattle in the middle of the table. True, they'd never said the big L word, never made any sweeping promises to each other. But Margo had been naïve enough to think they would one day. She had been so excited about the baby. A little nervous, but excited, and she couldn't wait to share the news with Jess.

The dinner hour had come and gone with no Jess. By midnight, when he wasn't home, she had slipped out of the house with her car keys and driven the streets of Adam's Bay. Not to find him. But to lose herself. She hadn't told her cousins or Duncan why she had asked to be off that night; she'd wanted Jess to be the first to know. So when he didn't come home, she had driven around for over an hour—alone—and waited until the Queen was closed and even Duncan had gone home, and then she'd gone there. To be alone.

Margo stretched now. She'd been sitting at the bar for over an hour, pencil in hand and a notepad on the bar in front of her. She wanted to revamp the menu for November and December. Halloween was planned; it was time to think ahead and jazz things up for the holiday season. Adam's Bay was the type of place people visited for the holidays. Lots of people moved away, sure, but those same people always came back to see family, and that was an incredible business opportunity for people like herself and her cousins.

And Duncan.

They'd talked about Duncan buying into the bar. Margo wondered now why he hadn't in the first place. It wasn't like he didn't believe in them; he'd been all in from the word go. He didn't have the money gathering dust in a savings account that his grandpa started for him, but he wasn't destitute, either.

Still. Now that Stevi and Duncan were a thing, he was pretty much a partner now. Not legally, but if he and Stevi married—

Well, there would still be paperwork.

Would they?

Margo sat back for a moment and crossed her arms over her chest. She had never seen her stepbrother as relationship material. The idea of him being married was as foreign to her as the idea of her being the Queen of England. And yet, she could see it now. Maybe whatever started between Duncan and Stevi had just been for fun, a fling—though that mental image made Margo's shoulder blades itch—but the two of them were as lovey-dovey, honey-dripping sweet as Leah and Trace.

She was happy for them. One hundred and fifty percent happy for all of them. But she hated that she'd assumed she would beat them all to the altar. She hated that she'd had such an immature thought when she realized she was carrying Jess' baby. That she'd thought Berkley would be what made them say *I love you*. That they would raise her together and give her siblings.

Now she doubted she would ever have another child, which made her sad for Berkley. She'd had a good childhood, but she'd been thrilled to gain Duncan as a stepbrother when her mom and his dad got married. They weren't kids by that time—though today she felt ancient, and that memory of herself and Duncan certainly did paint them as young and innocent.

Before she could change her mind, she scooted her phone over the bar, closer to her and tapped Joe's name. Wondered what he did on Sunday evenings now. Probably some variation of her same bedtime routine for Berkley. Might be both harder and easier with two older kids in the house, in addition to baby Edison.

"What if I told you I watched some gory horror movie last night and had nightmares?" He skipped a regular greeting and dove right into crazy conversation.

The laugh and the warmth it brought rolled over her and loosened her shoulders.

"I'd probably say you're a wuss."

"I hate sleeping alone."

"Well, I get that. Kenzi could slay any monster's ass."

"Edison's teething," he announced.

"Oh. Ouch." Margo laughed knowingly. She rested her elbow on the bar and ran the fingers of her free hand through her hair. "First tooth?"

"No, but it kinda looks like two coming through."

"Poor baby."

"Poor baby?" Joe yelped. "How about poor Daddy?"

Thoughts of Jess and what he had missed out on with Berkley hit her in the heart. Margo winced and dropped her free hand to press to her chest. Wasn't her fault. Jess had made his choices.

"Did you put something on his gums?"

"Did the same stuff we used with the other two," he answered. "It's not working. I'm considering straight whiskey in his bottle."

Margo snorted. "Then you should talk to Duncan so you can make sure you introduce him to the good stuff early."

"Wow." His laugh was loud and boisterous. "Note to self. Don't let Margo Nevin babysit."

"One time when I babysat Addelyn and Liam, we built the coolest blanket fort. And we played in it forever. Like five games of checkers and some board games."

"I know. Addelyn still talks about that."

Margo felt her lips twitch in a smile, but her eyes filled.

"Have you talked to Jess?"

"No." Joe sounded serious now.

"Promise?"

"Margo, I didn't mean to give you the impression that we text all the time."

"I slept with him," she whispered.

"Oh. Damn. I wish you could talk to Kenz."

"I do, too, but you know she'd only ask if it was good."

"She would," he agreed. "But then she'd listen to what's on your mind."

"Okay, well, Joe, it was so good. We fit together like we were made for each other."

"But."

"But we're a disaster outside the bedroom."

"Where is he now?"

"At the house with Berkley. Stevi's there. I'm at the Queen. Everything's so damned complicated. I don't know what to do."

"It's not, though, Margo," Joe argued. "Life's hard, and it can be ugly and lonely. Why do you keep pushing away that one man who loves you so much?"

"He doesn't love me."

"The guy I know does."

"The guy you know had a permanent barstool at every tavern in town. Doesn't sound like love to me."

"Maybe he got tired of trying, Margo. I married a strong woman, too. Kenz wanted to argue with everything I did and said. She was her own person, just like you are. That's probably why you guys were tight She had to let me love her, Margo. She had to let me in."

Margo pressed her lips together, Jess' angry words from the night before ringing in her ears.

"Are you pissed?" Joe asked after a few moments of silence.

"No."

"Kenz would tell you the same damned thing. You guys made a baby together, Margo. Figure it out."

"I gotta go," she croaked out. She could argue with him. Easy for him to say any of this. As far as Margo knew, Joe had never cheated on Kenzi. Regardless of the intimate struggles they might have had in the beginning, he'd never cheated, and he hadn't left and come back to claim his child with his girlfriend at his side, either.

She didn't wait for him to answer. Instead, she ended the call and set her phone down. Rested her head on her arms folded over the bar and cried. She wondered what Jess would think of her tears; if they would be proof enough that she loved him and wanted him around?

CHAPTER 19

Jess' hands ached from the cold. They'd started the new project this morning, and Jess had been ready for the labor. Stripping the old shingles from the rambling, old house was hard work, and he needed the distraction from his thoughts about Margo. Since Saturday, when he'd fucked up his good intentions with the same hard, fast sex they always had—just the thought of being buried balls deep inside Margo made him hard and working on a steep-pitched roof in miserably cold temperatures was not a good place for those thoughts—he couldn't get her out of his mind. He'd wanted to talk to her. He had wanted to strip away the barriers and the walls she'd built around herself and sink into their relationship and how they could save it.

Instead, he'd been stupid and greedy, and the incredible sex had led to more harsh words between them, and once again, they were back at ground zero. He hadn't told Julie. When he returned to his parents' house after leaving

Margo, Julie was sound asleep on the couch, with the TV off. He had noticed her fingers curled around her phone, and he wondered if she had been texting with Brent. He didn't look, though, and he didn't ask last night when they were alone in his truck, heading back to Greenville, back to real life.

She poked the bear once, asked him about the night before, how it had gone. Not in the mood to discuss it, he'd only shrugged and shook his head to dismiss the topic. The past year away from Margo and Berkley had been at times hard and long and then somewhat happy and productive. But he'd spent his time hoping he was bettering himself so he could go back to Margo and offer her the real deal. Love. Marriage. Family.

The fact that maybe she was still in the same place—in her head, in her life—twisted him up inside and made him miserable. Maybe she didn't want the same things he did. Maybe he'd spent the past year training for an Olympic sort of event that just didn't even exist. The thought dug a hole right through his gut and made him feel empty. He would be Berkley's daddy, and yes, his heart nearly exploded in his chest when he thought of a future with his daughter in his life. But after the weekend with Margo— after she'd pulled that evade and hide maneuver yesterday —he couldn't shake off the grief, the feeling that he had lost her. This time, that feeling was even more profound than when she'd asked him to pack his bags and leave.

His phone vibrated against his leg as he walked down the gravel drive to his truck. The crew had stripped the roof of the old shingles today. Tomorrow they would put on the underlayment to start the new roofing process, weather permitting. The sun had teased them early in the day, but it had been long gone by noon. The wind picked up not long after that, and Jess was miserably cold now. His bones ached with the cold, but it wasn't the flu dragging him down. Just Margo. Himself.

Mistakes made and repeated.

He climbed into his truck, pulled the door closed, and started it before tugging off the hood of his Carhartt coat. He figured the text was from Julie, and while he had nothing against Julie, he wasn't in any hurry to look at his phone. He'd dropped her off at her place last night and offered to walk her in. He thought she looked preoccupied, and as her friend, he figured he should ask after her. He hadn't, though. Because checking on her emotional status would lead right to his baggage, and he just didn't feel like going there. So they'd said good night as she climbed down from the truck, and Jess had watched to make sure she got inside safely, and then he'd gone home alone to stew over his latest mistake.

Maybe Margo had kicked him out, but Julie and her friendship had been the driving force behind his sobriety. Being with Berkley had been his goal—Margo, too, but he had known that wouldn't come easily—but Julie's support had been instrumental in him getting where he was now.

Still didn't mean he wanted to sit across a table from her and spill his guts about fucking Margo in a five-minute rush to the finish line. Julie wouldn't flinch at his words, but she would be disappointed that he hadn't fought harder to get through to Margo, either before or after the sex. He hadn't done well with lectures when he was a smartass kid; years later, supposedly all grown up, he still didn't enjoy lectures, and he sometimes bristled at lectures given by someone who wasn't even a quarter of a century old yet.

With the truck running, it didn't take long for the cab to warm up. Jess flexed his fingers in front of the vents and rolled his eyes when his phone vibrated again.

"Hold your horses, Jules," he mumbled as he pulled up the flap of his cargo pants. He dug his phone out and looked at the screen, shocked to find two texts from Margo, not Julie.

Maybe they were about Berkley, but after what had happened between them Saturday night and then the way she'd dodged him all day Sunday and had Stevi at her house to hang out and watch him hang out with Berkley, he had figured it would be a while before he heard from her again.

The texts were about Halloween. Margo wanted to know if he wanted to come down and take Berkley trick-or-treating. He wondered if that meant drive her around to Margo's mom's house. Stevi and Leah's mom's house. What would she say if he asked if he could take her to his parents' house? To see his sisters?

Or was she planning on splitting the night into halves? She would take Berkley to see her family, and maybe, if he was lucky, she would let him take her to see his family?

He could have texted her back, but he didn't. Too much could be taken out of context in a text message. And besides, the ache inside—the one that Margo had left there Saturday night—just doubled in size after reading her texts. He wanted to hear her voice.

She answered almost immediately, which made him wonder if she was sitting on her phone. Was she waiting on him to answer her? Or was she waiting for another call? Had Stevi found her a date? What if…

What if Margo went out on a date with someone else on Halloween while he spent the evening with Berkley? That would be all wrong—

"Jess?" She sounded irritated, as if she had already said his name a time or two.

"Hey."

"You could have just texted me."

"I wanted to hear your voice."

"Don't." She sighed. "Look. I just…thought you might want to see her. In her costume. She's going to be a puppy."

"Of course I want to see her," he answered quickly. "Are we taking her trick-or-treating together? Or what?"

"I guess so." She spoke softly, as if she was surrendering, giving in to him when she didn't want him involved at all.

"Where will we take her?"

"I don't know." Now she sounded distracted. "My mom's house. I'll take her to my aunt's. A few other—"

"What about my mom's? Can we take her there?" Jess barged in on her answer, purposely cutting her off. He wanted to catch her off-guard.

"What? No." Margo cleared her throat.

"Why not?"

"Because…"

He let her hang, waiting to see how she would argue against his parents seeing Berkley. She didn't, though. In the background, he heard low music playing, and a distant buzz of conversation. Two male voices, one of them distinctly Duncan.

"Are you at the Queen?"

"Yep."

"Do you remember that night we danced on the bar? When everyone else—"

She laughed. His heart soared at the quick flash of honest laughter on the other end of the call.

"I bet not everyone dances to George Thorogood the way we did."

"That was a long time ago, Jess."

"I miss you."

"You were just here," she reminded him. "And things didn't go so well. Remember?"

"I wanted to talk to you Sunday."

"Yeah? What were you planning to do with Julie while we talked about how we fucked like old times? This isn't going to happen, Jess. I'm not going to be your other woman—"

His phone buzzed in his hand.

"What time do you want me there for Halloween?'

"Whenever."

"Nope. You give me at time. Otherwise, you'll start without me and then tell me it's my problem that I missed so much."

"Jess." She sounded hurt. He felt a nagging sensation in his gut, but really, he didn't care. She'd done a number on him, again, and he needed her to feel something, to be invested in this—whatever it was—if they were going to fix it.

"What time?"

"Five."

He flinched. He would have to take off work early. Then again, they would be off the roof before then, anyway. Darkness came earlier in the fall and winter hours; they didn't linger on rooftops with darkness falling.

"I'll be there."

The text that had dropped when he was talking to Margo was from Julie, asking if he wanted to meet for pizza. There was nothing fun, nothing off-the-wall or Julie-like in the text. Usually, she sent him a goofy bitmoji or maybe a Monday meme. He wondered again if she was okay.

Derrick hadn't let on today that anything was wrong. Then again, if Julie was having personal problems, her dad might be the last to know.

He texted her. Told her he'd meet her at the Pizza Pad in an hour. That would give him time to drive home, shower, and then head back out. Her response—a simple k—came while he drove.

His parents had been pretty patient about Margo and Berkley. When Margo was first pregnant and then as her pregnancy progressed, they had asked after her, how she was feeling. He and Margo had seldom spent time with his parents, but that was more his fault than hers. Either they were hanging out at the house—and they did do things other than the things that led to Berkley's conception—or at the Queen. After Berkley was born and Margo asked him to leave, Jess had been evasive with his family about what happened.

He had told them simply that he and Margo were no longer together. That Margo had asked him to stop drinking, and that Margo had told him she would allow him to see his daughter once he was sober. Maybe his dad had been disappointed. He'd simply given Jess a firm nod as if to ask him what he was waiting for—to get busy getting sober so he could claim his daughter. His sisters had blamed Margo, Melissa viciously so. But his mom had been hurt for him, sad that Margo had banished him.

Sunday evening, when he and Julie had left Margo's and gone back to the house to tell his parents goodbye, his dad had pulled him aside and walked him out to his truck to ask him if he was really Berkley's father. Jess had bristled at the question. He'd been unfaithful to Margo, but he assumed she had always been at home, waiting for him to come back. When he'd answered defensively—arguing for Margo's sake—his dad shook his head and rephrased the question. Had Margo put his name on Berkley's birth certificate?

His mom and Julie had come outside then, and Mom hugged him and patted his chest and said how she sure would like to see her granddaughter.

Damned if he wouldn't take Berkley there to trick or treat. It was past time for his parents to see her, to hold his baby. If Margo was serious about respecting his rights as Berkley's father, then he was going to start pushing to claim those rights.

Julie was at a two-top table in the back of the Pizza Pad when he walked in. Head ducked over her phone, she didn't notice Jess sizing up the situation as he approached her table. A glass of soda on the table—the straw poking out so far, it looked as if it would fall out—Julie's hair pulled back in a messy ponytail, and her index finger in her mouth as she chewed the nail down to nothing.

He was a recovering alcoholic. Julie tended to bite her nails when she was stressed.

"Hey." He slid into the booth across from her and waited for her to look up at him. She never wore much makeup— she didn't need it—but tonight, she looked especially pale.

The hollows around her eyes made her look gaunt and waiflike. "What's wrong?"

She sighed and dropped her hand to her lap, because she knew he would rag on her for chewing on her nails. Jess watched her throat work as she tried to answer him, waited patiently while she sipped her soda—Dr. Pepper—and then took her phone when she passed it over the table to him.

"What's—?" He stopped talking when he looked down at the screen to find a picture of Brent Willer with two blondes draped over him. Julie had said the music thing he'd gone to was in Chicago, and being that Adam's Bay and Greenville were also in Illinois, he had to assume it was cold in Chicago, too. But the blondes wore skimpy tank tops, the color of their tanned skin more prominent than the black and silver tanks.

"I guess that's why I didn't get invited to go," she mumbled.

"I'm sorry, Jules." He sighed. He was. It broke his heart that his friend was so over the moon for someone who was blind to everything she was.

She nodded and dabbed at her eyes before taking the phone back.

"I'm done." She shrugged.

Jess felt a stir of hope. As often as Brent had hurt her in the past several months, he hadn't heard her declare that she was over him. Maybe now she would move on and be happy, whether that meant with a new guy or just as Julie. Jess wanted to see her happy.

"With men?" he asked with a grin.

"Maybe." She almost smiled, but at the last minute, she pulled it back and stared at him silently.

"He's not worth your time, Julie." He considered touching her, reaching over the table to touch her hand. But after the way Stevi had seen Julie do the same to him, because Margo apparently believed they were seeing each other, he couldn't do it. Even if they were a hundred miles away in Greenville, he couldn't do it.

She nodded and sat up straight. Jess watched her pull in a deep breath and then blow it out slowly. Probably her mediation and Yoga background or something. Jess admired her the healthy habits for dealing with stress and defeat. He was learning; for a long time, that picture—the fights with Margo—had driven him to drink more, when nine times out of ten, his drinking was the root of the problem. Now he went to the gym. Pumped iron. Went for a run. Put some heavy-duty elbow grease into the day job. Anything but the bottle.

"Have you talked to Margo?" she asked after taking a sip of her soda. The way she could fold her own sadness up and tuck it away always amazed him. Tonight, even though he was amazed, he didn't particularly want to go down this road.

"About Halloween." He nodded.

"Yeah? Did she say why she ducked out on your visit yesterday?"

"I was in Adam's Bay to see Berkley, not Margo." He lifted his eyes to look around the restaurant. Nothing fancy, but probably the best pizza in town. They were always busy; the servers always looked harried and exhausted, but they always greeted everyone with a smile. Jess made eye contact with their waiter and asked for water. He glanced at Julie as the kid nodded and went to get it.

"I ordered," she said before he could ask.

He wondered if he argued to Margo that he and Julie were just friends, if he ever got her to believe that, would it be a strike against him that they came to this place often enough, that they could order for each other?

"So. You never told me."

"Told you what?" he asked. He examined his hands, smoothed his fingertips over a few cuts. The cold weather was hard on his skin. Not that he was a pansy-ass who couldn't handle it. And Margo always told him she liked his rough hands—the way they felt on her stomach, between her thighs. Still, he had a degree. Maybe he wouldn't be filthy rich if he was working as a contractor, but there were days when he wondered why he'd thrown it away to choose hard, physical labor.

He still hadn't told Margo what he'd done. They hadn't gotten that far yet.

"Saturday night." Julie's stare was so intense, it made Jess fidgety. He picked up his silverware, still bundled with the paper napkin, and twirled it in his fingers. "What happened?"

He could say nothing happened, but Julie knew him too well. Again he wondered if that would be a strike against him in Margo's book. If she ever took him back, would she tell him he couldn't have friends who were women? He wanted to believe he would walk the line for her, but it didn't seem like a real relationship—one built on love and respect—if either of them were going to place those sorts of demands on each other.

"Same thing that always happens," he finally mumbled. He tossed the silverware down on the table.

"You fought?"

"Worse."

"You had sex?"

Jess only stared at her, though he thought he should get adulting points for maintaining eye contact.

"And then we fought." He hung his head and dragged his fingers back through his hair. "The sex was…everything I love about her but didn't want. And the fight was pretty ugly."

"Why—? I don't get why you guys can't work it out."

"Well, for starters, she totally believes I left her and went back to Mom and Dad's to climb in bed with you."

CHAPTER 20

Propped in the doorway of the kitchen, Margo watched as Tony dropped a handful of chopped bell peppers and onions in a hot skillet. Her mouth watered at the sizzle of the vegetables hitting the olive oil. She'd skipped lunch because she'd been on the phone most of the afternoon: two calls were customers who wanted to discuss private dinner parties and one was a distributor trying to sell her on a new olive oil for cooking. In between the calls, she'd carted Berkley around for a while as she worked to refill condiment bottles in the kitchen, bundled clean tableware in black cloth napkins, and sampled a new IPA Duncan had been raving about for months.

Leah had come in late, practically floating on cloud nine. She and Trace had seen her ob-gyn and received a good checkup. Though still frustrated with Leah and Stevi for throwing Jess at her now as a reason not to date—which was dumb, because if Duncan happened to make any negative comments about Jess, she got defensive—Margo felt guilty for the harsh things she'd said to Leah the other day in the office. Thankfully, Leah seemed to have forgiven her, but it still bothered Margo. And the fact that it still bothered Margo probably meant something.

Like maybe Leah was right. Leah and Stevi both. Come to think of it, her mom had kind of seemed on board with them when she'd come to pick Berkley up for the night, hadn't she? She hadn't come right out? and said *don't start dating anyone since Jess has been around.* But she'd commented on how different Jess had been the time or two she'd seen him. As if seeing someone a time or two in passing was enough proof that big, life changes had been made.

Still.

Margo drew herself up straight and slipped back through the restaurant to the bar. The doors were still locked. No one was at the bar. Margo figured Duncan was down in the cellar getting what he might need to stock the bar. Tuesday nights usually allowed for a decent business, better than Monday, but certainly not Thursday. She eased onto the end barstool and sat for a few minutes in the quiet.

Rather than summon the memories of the past weekend, the way Jess had positioned her on her hands and knees on her bed and gripped her hips possessively as he drove into her, she closed her eyes, rested her forehead in her hand, and remembered the kiss. The soft, barely there kiss he'd put on her lips the day they had picked up ice cream for Leah.

She loved the sex. Margo Nevin had always enjoyed sex, and Jess had taken the enjoyment to a new level. But that kiss. That sweet, chaste kiss had rocked her, and dammit, of course Leah had to see it and mention it out loud.

Leah had to compare that kiss to the forehead kiss Nashville had given her. The day she might have fallen in love with Nashville. Nothing like assigning such huge meaning to a simple kiss.

What had it meant? To Jess? What had that kiss been about?

"Hey!"

Stevi's voice was a needle in the back of her neck. Margo tensed and squeezed her eyes a moment before dropping her hand and looking up to see her cousin moving across the bar from the staircase to sit by her.

"You okay?" Stevi sounded concerned now.

"Yeah." Margo nodded. "I'm okay."

"I'm so excited for Leah and Trace," Stevi gushed in a whisper. "I know it's too soon for me and Duncan to ever think about babies. But I'm so excited about their baby."

Margo felt a slow, tired smile pull at her lips.

"Me, too."

"Berkley said Steefi earlier," Stevi told her. Margo laughed softly. Stevi and Leah were always arguing over whose name Berkley would say first. Margo figured it would end up being Duncan or Nashville, but she didn't say so.

"Can I ask you something?" When her whisper came out sounding thick and gruff, Margo cleared her throat. Rather than look Stevi in the eyes, she stared at the smooth, rich wood of the bar. Duncan had poured his heart into making this bar for them; he'd done an incredible job. The long, wooden bar, always polished and inviting, was the heart and soul of the Queen.

She swallowed a pang of guilt and made herself look at Stevi. She'd shut Duncan out, because she knew he didn't approve of her feeling anything toward Jess Covey. That couldn't go on. Even if she somehow ended up with Jess back in her life, even if he simply remained Berkley's father and nothing more ever happened between them, Margo had to clear the air with Duncan. She loved her stepbrother too much to let Jess come between them.

But Jess had the right to be with his daughter, and she couldn't let Duncan get in the way of that relationship.

"What's up?" Stevi pressed her lips together and waited for Margo to continue.

"When you…were with Duncan…I mean. In the beginning…"

"Sweet Jesus, if you're gonna ask me for sex details, I can't do it, Margo." Stevi stared at her with wide eyes. "Not this time."

Margo shook her head, but she laughed softly.

"No."

"Then spit it out."

"Leah had the kiss. The forehead kiss."

"Ah." Stevi nodded. "When did I fall?"

Margo shrugged, but she gave Stevi an almost imperceptible nod.

"There was one night." Stevi took a deep breath. "We were here late. Flirting. Pushing it. And I thought he was going to kiss me."

"And?"

"He didn't," Stevi whispered. "But I wanted that kiss so badly, I was shaking when I left. I couldn't drive. I knew then I was in trouble."

"But when did you fall?"

"I don't know when. But I know when I realized I was gone. Duncan and I spent a lot of time here. After hours."

"So did Jess and I," Margo mumbled. "Let's not compare stories."

Stevi's brows shot up in surprise, but she choked her questions down and tried to continue.

"He kissed me the next night." She licked her lips. "Um. It was…maybe the most intimate kiss I've ever had. Because I knew him. I knew him so well. He didn't lay a hand on me, but he kissed me. I love the way he kisses me."

"Don't off-road." Margo shook her head. "Is that when you knew?"

"No. It was a few nights later. I had been out with Grant. Nothing happened. I came home early, because I was hung up on Duncan. The next night here, something was different. With us. It was just off. Like when you button a shirt wrong."

"That night you went out with Grant, I thought he was going to kick the cellar down," Margo mumbled. Another stab of guilt at the memory of how they'd talked that night, how she'd gone to him and he had basically told her to back off. He hadn't wanted to talk to her about Stevi. His brush off had hurt her. Now she was doing the same to him.

"He told me the next night that he wouldn't share," Stevi said softly. Margo watched her slip back in time, her mind clearly back to that night with Duncan. "He…yanked me over to sit in his lap and let me know exactly what he wanted." Stevi shifted her gaze to meet Margo's eyes. "And let me know we could have what we wanted and walk away friends when we decided we were done."

"Mmm." Margo winced. "Yeah. I remember that."

"It's not romantic, like Leah's kiss. But that's when I realized I was in love with him. Because if I wasn't, that wouldn't have hurt like it did."

Margo took a deep breath. "Have you talked to Shawn? Perry?"

"No." Stevi bit her lip. "Are you sure you want—"

"No. I don't." Margo shook her head. "I can't. I can't date someone else when Jess is the only one I think about."

"So you're going to tell him? How you feel?"

"No." Margo shook her head. "I can't. But I can't pretend like I don't feel anything for him. I don't wanna hurt anyone else, and I'm just not ready to try anything else."

Stevi held the eye contact a few moments longer before she nodded and stood. "Did you guys actually have sex here?"

Margo laughed, but tears streaked her face. She wiped them away as she shook her head.

"No. We danced on the bar, though."

"You what?"

"There were good things for us." Margo's throat ached with emotion. She took a deep breath. "It wasn't all bad."

"Of course it wasn't." Stevi touched her arm. "Look at Berkley."

Margo nodded as Stevi headed back across the room to the stairs. Someone approached the glass door and knocked.

"Margs, that's Julie," Stevi announced over her shoulder.

"We're not open yet," Margo mumbled.

"Jess is probably with her," Stevi reminded her. "We have to let her in."

Margo swiped at her eyes and swallowed hard. "Great."

"Go fix your face." Stevi nodded toward the bathroom. "I'll let them in."

Margo watched Stevi move closer to the door and motion to Julie to wait a minute, but she didn't stick around to watch her traipse back across the room to get Duncan's keys from the opposite end of the bar. Instead, she turned and headed to the bathroom.

Thankfully, her mascara hadn't smudged. She wasn't wearing eyeliner today; she generally saved the big makeup routine for the weekends. Her face felt stiff and her skin dry when she patted at the tears, but she didn't think it was obvious she'd been crying. But that didn't make her any more excited about going out to greet Julie and Jess.

What was he doing here tonight, anyway? He would be back tomorrow for Halloween. She understood that he wanted to see Berkley, but he was putting in a lot of miles and a lot of gas money driving back and forth. Unless he took tomorrow off. Which didn't seem like a responsible thing to do.

Whatever. Wasn't her place to worry about his job or his money situation. She'd go out and see what they wanted, remind them that Berkley was at her mom's, and send them on their way.

She wondered as she pulled the bathroom door open if he'd slept with her since the night they'd been together. If Julie gave him total control, or if she was as feisty in bed as Margo was. Would Jess like that better? If Margo had been more submissive, would Jess have looked for other women to satisfy him?

Julie and Stevi stood at the end of the bar when she returned. Margo looked around, wondering where Jess had gone. She felt a brief moment of panic when it occurred to her he might have gone down to the cellar to talk to Duncan, but Stevi caught her eye and shook her head.

"Hey." Julie turned at the silent communication between them. She flashed Margo a sweet smile.

"Hi." Margo raised her eyebrows in anticipation. "What's up? Where's Jess?" She looked up the stairs toward the mezzanine floor and further up to the office. She could see Trace on the third floor, standing just outside the office door, back to them. Talking to Leah, probably.

"Just me today," Julie said quietly. Her words filled Margo with dread. Either Jess had told her what happened, or she'd figured it out on her own. Reckoning day. And guilty as sin, Margo had no words to defend herself.

"Jess didn't come?"

She could have kicked herself for asking about Jess. She didn't want to sound needy or afraid, and she did, even to her own ears.

"Do you have a minute?"

Margo sighed. She glanced at Stevi, who was hovering, waiting to see if Margo needed her.

"Sure." She nodded.

"I'm gonna go help Duncan," Stevi told her. "With the bar prep. Holler if you need anything."

Margo nodded. She wouldn't holler. Julie wasn't going to climb over a table and scratch her face off, though admittedly, there had been times Margo wanted to do that to women who flirted with Jess. Women who made it clear they were willing and ready.

Julie.

Margo hated that this kid—how old could this girl even be—made her want to launch herself at her and pull her hair and rip her ridiculously cute Under Armor pullover and hurt her. Make her ugly.

Doesn't get much uglier than you right now, Margo.

She wasn't this person. Even when Jess lived with her. Even when he came home with teeth marks and hickeys on his abs and thighs, she'd had fleeting moments of jealousy. Of violent revenge. But Julie seemed like a nice kid. And it wasn't her fault she'd gotten tangled up with Jess. In the middle of something even Margo didn't understand.

"Want something to drink?" Margo asked as she stepped behind the bar. Jess wasn't here, and if this conversation was going to happen, she needed a drink. Maybe it wasn't quite four here; it was sure as hell five o'clock somewhere.

"Thank you." Julie nodded. Margo grabbed two longnecks. She eyed Julie silently as she twisted the tops off and handed her one. Her short stature added to her youthful appearance. That and her perfect skin. No blemishes marred her face. No dark circles under her eyes. No wrinkles around her mouth. She wore her hair in a high ponytail; black yoga pants with bright green down the sides outlined perfect legs.

She didn't look angry. Jealous.

Instead, she looked nervous. Anxious. Like she was scared of talking to Margo.

Since Leah and Trace were in the office, and it was possible Duncan would be back at the bar with provisions for the evening, Margo nodded for Julie to follow and led her over to the restaurant side of the Queen. Rather than choose a table, however, she pulled a stool out from the coffee bar and nodded for Julie do the same.

Currently, the restaurant was lit only by fading daylight at the plate glass windows up front. Mildly depressing, especially when the bar on the other side was so warm and inviting. But Margo wanted this conversation to be private, no matter what Julie had to say, and it was unlikely anyone would join them over here.

"What's going on?" Margo hated herself. She puffed up her chest with false bravado and looked Julie in the eye as if she hadn't been naked and begging Jess for more a few nights ago.

Julie took a deep breath and stared at Margo bravely.

"Goddammit, Jess," Margo muttered. "I hate this."

"Hate what?" Julie asked quickly. Margo held her breath when the girl reached out and skimmed her fingers over the back of Margo's hand.

"Putting me in this position. That I put myself in his position."

"Do you love him?" Julie sounded curious, seriously concerned—about Jess?—but not angry or jealous.

"I can't do this." Margo sighed. "I can't sit here and grovel about what I did last weekend to someone who should probably still be in class."

Julie groaned. She set her bottle down on the bar and aimed an angry stare at Margo.

"I'm not that young." She pinched the bridge of her nose and shook her head. "You all either act like you're old and wise like the gods or like I should be at home watching the Disney channel."

"That's what you're mad about?"

"I'm not mad." Julie shrugged.

"Did he tell you?" Margo whispered. Her face flooded with heat. Maybe it was a good thing Jess wasn't here, because she might hit him if he was.

"Tell me that you guys were together last weekend?"

Margo dropped her chin to her chest and tried to stifle a moan of misery. How had she done to this girl the same things Jess had done to her? When it had shattered her world? How could she do that to someone else?

"Julie, I'm sorry," she whispered. "It shouldn't have—"

"Margo." Julie reached out again, but this time she rested

her fingers on the back of Margo's hand. "Jess and I aren't together."

"What?"

"We're just friends." Julie dragged her eyes away from Margo's and stared at her beer for a second.

"Friends with benefits?"

"No," Julie answered with a frown. "No. There's never been anything like that between us."

Margo nodded and rolled her eyes. "You're kidding yourself if you think a guy like Jess isn't biding his time before he gets you in bed."

Julie actually shivered as if the thought made her uncomfortable.

"Jess works for my dad," Julie explained. "We just started hanging out. And talking. I swear to you that's it. I'm not interested in him. He's like a brother. He gives me shit. He gives me advice."

"Then why do you come down here with him? If you're not fucking him? Julie, you're adorable. And I know Jess. I know how he thinks."

"No, you don't," Julie whispered. "Because he's spent this whole past year working his way back to you."

"Berkley."

"You."

"Look. Jess and I might've lived together for a while, but we weren't...I don't know that either one of us ever thought about the future. It wasn't a forever thing. We both knew that. I appreciate that he's worked to get back here to be involved in Berkley's life. But there's nowhere for us to go. What happened last weekend was a mistake."

Julie's nostrils flared as she drew in a deep breath. "Look. He doesn't know I'm here. And if he did, he would be pissed. But Jess has talked to me a lot this past year. Margo, just listen to him. Please?"

"Jess made a lot of promises when we were together. He might have kept five of them." Margo licked her lips and then rolled them inward. "His promises mean nothing to me. And I don't want to hear his excuses any more than I want to hear the empty promises."

"Give him a chance, Margo. You might be surprised."

CHAPTER 21

THE IMMEDIATE RUSH OF ANGER HAD EASED, BUT HE WAS still pissed off at Julie. She meant well, but he was a grown man, and he didn't need anyone to plead his case for him. Margo probably thought he had put Julie up to driving down to see her and promise her they were just friends. In the year that he and Julie had grown so close, they'd had a few intense conversations—usually about him and Margo and his asinine behavior. But they'd never really been sideways, and it felt weird to be so pissed as he slowed his truck in front of Margo's house.

He had gone to the gym last night for a workout. Monday night had been more tossing and turning, with catnaps thrown in here and there. The catnaps had been torture, because he dreamt about Margo. In one dream, they had been dancing on the bar, only someone else—Jess hadn't recognized the guy—had cut in and taken her from him. In another, they were on the patio, and he kissed her and then instead of him climbing into his truck and driving away, Margo walked back into the Queen and left him standing there like nothing had happened.

And then there were the smokin' hot, x-rated dreams. The twisted sheets and the hot skin and the smell of sex in the air. Margo's eyes hot and hungry, her thighs wrapped around his waist. Her long, low moans of pleasure. Nothing like being so aroused by the memory of the other night that he went to bed and had dreams so hot that he woke up painfully aroused and nowhere to go with his need.

He'd called Julie from the gym to see if she wanted to hang out. She couldn't bench quite what he did, but they did their fair share of workouts together. She hadn't answered, though, and then when he'd called her later—after he was back at home and showered—she still hadn't answered, and he had paced the floor, a little bit worried about her.

He let it go for a while. Watched some mindless TV. Threw a chicken breast in the broiler and ate it while he watched mindless TV. And then he called her again. This time, when she didn't pick up, he left her a message. Asked her just to text and let him know she was okay.

Depression wasn't her thing, but he knew Brent had hurt her. And he knew it took a lot to hurt her, because she was tough after all of the drama with her parents when she was younger.

She'd called back within fifteen minutes. Apologized for missing his calls. He let it go, teased her and waved the apology away, but she hesitated when he asked where she was. And then she'd come clean, because she hated lying. Apparently, she was okay with sneaking around since she'd gone to talk to Margo without him. But he was supposed to forgive her because at least she was honest about it after the fact.

A group of preschool-aged kids climbed the steps of Margo's house as he got out of the truck. He offered a smile to the parents walking slightly behind them and then turned his gaze to the late afternoon skies as he opted for the back door and headed down her driveway. She would be handing out candy, so he let himself in the back door. Pushed it closed behind him.

Immediately, memories of the last night he was here bombarded him. The way Margo had straddled him on the couch and pushed her pajamas down so he could touch her. The way she'd nudged him with her foot to hurry him along. The orgasm that had left her boneless on the bed and the way she'd looked at him when she reminded him that he had left. He had looked for something better.

She was right. He had wanted more. Better.

But not from anyone else.

From her. From himself.

The thought of Julie coming here last night to argue his case still chafed, and the questions about Margo and what she'd done the past year and what she wanted in life made his head pound. He reminded himself he was here to see

Berkley and shoved it all down as he stepped into the living room. Margo was just pushing the door closed.

Berkley let out a squeal of delight when she saw him. On a folded blanket on the floor, she dropped her toy cell phone and flopped over on all fours. Despite the heartache, Jess grinned as she crawled toward him. His mouth dropped open when she reached her playpen and grabbed a handful to stand herself up.

"You're early," Margo said quietly.

He considered reminding her that he worried she would leave without him. Considered a few sarcastic responses. Chose to keep his mouth shut.

"We just had dinner," she continued. "Um." She glanced at a slim silver watch on her wrist as she squatted down and started packing toys and books into Berkley's diaper bag. "I guess we can go ahead and go over to Mom's."

A swell of anger rose inside him, but he breathed through it, proud of himself for staying calm. Eyes on Berkley, he felt Margo look at him. She waited there, squatting by the couch, as if she expected him to say something. When he didn't, she cleared her throat and stood.

"I'm going to change her diaper," she said quietly. Jess nodded and watched her pick his daughter up and whisk her down the hall. He wanted to be near Berkley, but he didn't want to be close to Margo, so he waited for them in the living room. Berkley, oblivious to the dumb mistakes her parents had made and continued to make, sang soft and sweet while Margo got her ready. Jess stood at the window and watched another group of kids approach.

He wasn't sure what Margo thought about him answering her door, but he wasn't a dick, and he liked kids. So when a ninja and a pumpkin rang the doorbell, he answered it. He leaned over a bit and talked to the kids—both little boys.

"I was a ninja once," he told the first kid as he dropped two small candy bars in his bag. "And pumpkins are the most traditional costume ever." A big smile lit up the second kid's face as Jess tossed his candy in his bag. "Happy Halloween, guys."

Margo was watching him when he closed the door.

"She was pretty."

"Who?" Jess shook his head, confused by her comment.

"The mom waiting for them on the steps."

Jess shrugged. "I didn't see her. You ready?"

"Yeah." She looked at Berkley, perched on her hip, brown puppy costume on.

"Where's Berkley?" he asked as he walked toward them. "And who is this cute little puppy?"

Berkley beamed up at him when he clucked her chin.

"Um." Margo cleared her throat. Jess picked up the diaper bag and followed Margo to the kitchen. "Do you…want me to drive? Or do you want to take separate cars?"

Jess stared at the back of her head and counted to ten. Five days ago, he'd had his cock as deep as he could get it inside her body, and now she wanted to know if they should take separate cars to take their little girl trick-or-treating?

"Jess?" She glanced at him over her shoulder.

"I'll drive, if you don't mind riding in my truck."

"Okay." She nodded after a slight hesitation. "I'll have to get her car seat."

"Give me your keys, and I'll get it."

Her purse was on the table; Jess watched her dig through it in search of her keys. She met his eyes as she handed them to him.

"Are you okay?" She studied his face closely, but she appeared as uncomfortable as he felt. He couldn't take his eyes from her teeth nibbling on her lip.

"Yep." He turned away from her and went outside to get the car seat switched to his truck. He unlocked her car and leaned in to unbuckle the seatbelt threaded through the car seat. What exactly had Julie said to her? Had she simply promised Margo they were just friends? She swore up and down that's all she said. But she was gone all night. Didn't take that long to say those few words. For that matter, she could have texted Margo or called her.

Margo was waiting by his truck when he swung her car door closed and locked it. Berkley babbled as he neared them and then pulled his truck door open. He was thankful he had an extended cab now, because he wanted to drive. He wanted to be in control tonight. Even if they went up in smoke again over where they took Berkley trick-or-treating, Jess wanted to be in control.

The drive across town was quiet, and the quiet was irritating, and Jess wanted to strangle Julie. He loved the kid, but the idea of her begging Margo to take him back made him so mad, he could chew a bucket of nails. The hell of it was, this should have been a fun night.

Seeing Margo's parents wasn't fun, but he would have been able to handle it, if it hadn't been for the explosive sex last weekend and Julie butting in last night. Margo was acting funny, too, and though her parents were pleasant—her mom even gave him a quick hug—he was disappointed. He had wanted so much more for them, for all three of them.

They went from Margo's parents' house to her aunt and uncle's house. He expected to be welcomed there; after all, if they were okay with Stevi sleeping with Duncan, he would have thought they would be okay with Margo hanging out with the devil. Not so much, though. Her aunt had been friendly; her uncle had mumbled some generic greeting and disappeared.

Two down, he told himself when they climbed back into the truck. He did as she asked and headed to the Queen so the gang would see Berkley as a puppy. He hung back near the end of the bar closest to the back door as Margo paraded around the place and showed off his daughter. Duncan, tending bar, shot him a look that might have scared lesser guys. Jess simply ignored him. Trace hollered a friendly greeting, and Leah and Stevi finally made their way over to him to say hello.

Jess accepted their hugs, though he was careful as hell to keep his hands on their backs. Not that it was difficult. He wasn't into either of them, and he didn't want trouble with Trace or Duncan. But mostly, he didn't want Margo to have any ammunition later if she decided to open fire on him.

"Be patient with her," Leah whispered in his ear. She gave him an extra squeeze and stepped back before he could ask what the heck that meant. He watched her walk away, only for Margo to catch him. She only arched her eyebrows. Berkley reached for him. He took her and followed Margo out the back door to his truck.

"Where to?" he asked once Margo had Berkley buckled in and she was back in the front seat with him.

"Can I ask you something?"

"And here it comes," he muttered, expecting her to comment on the way he'd watched Leah walk away from him. He'd been lost in thought, wondering what the hell she had meant with what she'd said, not watching her ass and thinking about getting his hands on her.

Margo turned sideways in the seat to look at him.

"Why are you here?"

"What?"

"Tonight. Why are you here?"

"To see Berkley."

"Coulda fooled me." She shrugged.

"What does that mean?"

"You act like you're doing me a favor, chauffeuring me and the kid around for the night. Not like a daddy who's taking his little girl trick-or-treating."

Jess huffed angrily and looked out the driver's window.

"Do you even want to be here, Jess? Or did I make you feel obligated?"

"I wanted to be here."

"Then what's wrong?"

"Nothing." He shook his head. "Nothing's wrong. And she's the cutest puppy I've seen." He looked at Berkley over his shoulder. She was slumped sideways in the seat, eyes heavy with sleep. "Sleepy puppy."

Margo twisted around to look and then looked back at him with a small smile.

"Look, if I ask you to come down here for something, and you have plans…or you can't make it…" She licked her lips. "I get it. I mean, it's not like I'm gonna be a bitch about it and assume you'll turn into one of those dads who never has time for his kid."

"Margo." He sighed and started the truck. "Can I ask you something?"

"What?"

"Is my name on her birth certificate?"

Margo stared at him blankly for a moment and finally tipped her head.

"What?"

"Is it?"

"I don't get what you're asking me." She frowned. "Are you suggesting she's not your daughter?"

"No." He smoothed his hands over his jaw and his lips and finally turned his head to look at her. "I'm just asking if you put me down on her birth certificate as her father or if you left that blank."

Margo swallowed hard. "Your name is on her birth certificate," she said quietly. "I'll show you. If you don't believe me."

He sat for a moment, his body almost quaking with relief. He hadn't really believed she would have left the father's name blank—just because his sister posed the question didn't make it valid, but since his dad had asked, it been nagging at him. She watched him as he dropped the truck in gear and slowly eased out of the parking lot.

"Where are you going?" she asked after a few moments.

"I guess taking you back home."

"Do you want to take her to your parents' house?"

Jess pursed his lips. He nodded, too overwhelmed with emotion to speak.

"Do you want me to go? Or would it be better if I wasn't with you?"

"You don't want to go?"

This time, Margo groaned with frustration. "I do, Jess. I want to go."

He nodded. Wished that she wanted to go because she wanted to be with him, and not because she didn't trust him with their daughter.

CHAPTER 22

CINDY COVEY'S TEARS OF SURPRISE AND JOY MADE MARGO nauseas. She'd always liked Jess' mom; they'd gotten along fine. But they'd never discussed the hard stuff. Margo never mentioned that Jess spent more time holding down barstools than he did at home. She never wondered out loud if Jess had a problem, if there was a reason he needed the love of a bar crowd over the comfort of home and hearth. Jess' other women had certainly never been a topic of discussion.

So, of course, she felt guilty when Cindy's voice shook when she asked if she could hold Berkley. Thankfully, Berkley was on and hammed it up for Cindy and Travis. She did such a great job of entertaining them that Margo didn't have to say much at all. She had accepted the offer of a drink, but she opted for a bottle of water over a beer. As she drank it, she wondered about her choice. Jess had asked for water, too, but why did it matter what she drank? She had no plans for her mouth to be anywhere near his tonight or ever again.

Jess texted both of his sisters, and both texted back with big apologies. Neither of them could get over to see Berkley, but both of them—even Melissa, and Margo knew she had no use for her—asked if Jess could please bring her back to the house very soon. Margo watched with glassy eyes as Jess took a picture of Berkley with his parents and texted it to his sisters.

Maybe it should have upset her that his sisters couldn't make time to come and meet their niece. But instead, Margo felt guilty for keeping Berkley from all of them during the year that Jess had been gone.

When they left—Jess carrying Berkley—Cindy gave Margo a tentative hug. Margo hugged her back, but she was afraid to hold on too tight. Cindy thanked her for the hundredth time for bringing Berkley over, and when Cindy asked her to please not be a stranger, Margo had only nodded and turned away. Tears streaked her face as she climbed into the truck. Jess buckled Berkley into her car seat. The drive back to her house was as quiet as the drive to her parents' house earlier. But the silence hurt. Margo sat with her shoulders hunched and her hands in her lap, trying to hold the tears in.

Jess had come down here tonight in a bad mood, and Margo could only guess that it had something to do with Julie. Maybe that Julie had told Margo they were just friends. Despite what Julie said, Margo didn't doubt that Jess had his eyes on the girl. Even if he didn't, she doubted he would fight it if Julie decided to try him on for size.

And that's what Julie didn't understand about him. Maybe she thought they were just friends. Jess didn't know the meaning of the words *just friends*.

At the house, Margo unbuckled Berkley and carried her inside. She was pliant in her sleep. Margo left the car seat for Jess to handle and took Berkley straight to her bedroom to change her diaper and put her in her footie jammies. Berkley chewed on her finger and then shifted to sucking her thumb as Margo finished up and Jess lingered in the doorway.

"Do you have to go?" she asked quietly as she hefted Berkley up to her shoulder.

"I should go soon," he mumbled.

She nodded. "Do you wanna give her a bottle?"

Jess straightened like a schoolmarm had threatened him. He nodded, but Margo noticed his Adam's apple bob as she passed Berkley to him. He followed her to the kitchen and watched her warm a bottle of milk.

"Did you—?"

Margo glanced at him when he suddenly stopped talking.

"What?"

"Probably shouldn't ask," he mumbled. Margo watched his hand smooth small, gentle circles over Berkley's back. The lamp light from the living room shined in her baby girl's eyes. She stepped forward and smoothed Berkley's dark curls away from her face. In the quiet between them, the microwave hummed.

"I nursed her," she said quietly. "For three months. I couldn't take it after that."

Jess nodded.

"Is that what you were going to ask me?" She met his eyes. Wondered if he was remembering the times when she was pregnant and they would lay side-by-side and Jess would touch her. Just gentle massages over her belly and her breasts. His fingers had felt so good on her skin, but she wondered now if seeing her, touching her distended belly and her grossly misshaped breasts had turned him off.

"I just." He hesitated. "I have a million questions. About her. About you. I think of them all the time. When I'm working. When I'm running." He shrugged. "I missed so much, and I know. My fault. But I wish I could make up for it. I wish I could learn everything about you. And her."

"You had a long time to learn everything about me, Jess." She pressed her lips together. "We wasted that time."

She noticed the shine in his eyes as the microwave beeped. Jess cleared his throat as she turned away and snagged the door to open it. She felt his eyes on her as she tipped the bottle over and let the milk drip on her inner wrist. He took it when she handed it to him, but he waited while she washed her hands. Margo laughed softly when Berkley reached for the bottle.

"Ask," she told him when they sat in the living room. Margo chose the couch, a good distance from him— although her body and her mind certainly remembered the activities they'd engaged in on the couch last weekend —and let him have the rocker recliner.

"Did you like knock-knock jokes when you were a kid?"

"No. Still don't."

A smile touched his lips, but he kept his head bent over Berkley as she sucked from her bottle.

"Are you uncomfortable?" she asked.

"What?"

"With your jacket on?"

"Mm." He looked at her and nodded. "Kind of."

Without hesitation, Margo climbed to her feet again and moved to stand by him and help him wiggle out of the leather coat and jostle Berkley as little as possible. She carried it with her back to the couch and prayed he wouldn't notice that she laid it close enough to touch when she sat down.

"Why were you angry when you got here tonight?"

She wondered if he would ignore her. But he lifted his head and looked right at her.

"I'm angry with Julie."

"Because she told me that you're just friends? Is there more? Or do you just want more from her?"

"Because she overstepped. What's between us is between us, Margo."

She shook her head. "There's nothing between us, but that baby girl, Jess."

When he didn't argue, when he didn't respond at all, Margo felt a swell of pressure in her chest. He ducked his head again to gaze at Berkley while she took the bottle. Before Margo could remind him to burp her, he slipped the bottle from her and then lifted her to rest on his shoulder. He looked up when Margo stood, but he still didn't say anything. She hated that she wanted him to. She wanted him to argue, because at least if they were arguing, she had his attention.

Was he holding their daughter and thinking about Julie?

"What?" he asked as she all but tiptoed toward him.

"I'm guessing she's asleep." She reached for the bottle, careful not to accidentally touch his fingers when he handed it to her. "She won't want anymore."

She kind of hated that, because once they put Berkley down, Jess would leave. As she'd just told him, there was nothing between them but their daughter.

Unless you counted the sex.

Right now, her body was counting the sex. Jess' subtle cologne teased her as she leaned around him to look at Berkley's face. Just as she'd thought, her eyes were closed, her long lashes resting on her cheeks.

Dammit. She didn't want to want Jess. Not now. Not after the way they'd blown up at each other over the weekend. After the sex. The rough, fast, sweaty sex. Her nipples tingled as she turned away from him to carry the bottle to the kitchen. If he stayed for any time at all once Berkley was down, she would want to do it again.

Even though her heart knew it was a bad idea.

The thought brought her to a stop in the kitchen. Her heart? Since when had she let her heart make any decisions where Jess was concerned? If she wanted to climb Jess like a jungle gym and play for a while, she would. Same as always.

But why had she been so miserable for the past five days? Well, technically, she'd been a lot of miserable and sad mixed with happy from day one with him.

She wondered how he felt. How he really felt about her. If he did feel anything at all for her. If he ever had.

She took a deep breath, set the bottle down, and then turned to face him. He climbed from the rocker, hand protectively over Berkley's back, and followed her to her room. Margo watched him as he leaned carefully over the crib and lowered Berkley slowly, so he wouldn't wake her. Berkley sighed in her sleep as if she noticed the absence of that warm, strong shoulder she had rested on.

Jess cut a quick look at Margo and arched his eyebrows. Margo felt heat rush her face; he was putting their little girl down for the night, and she was thinking about what would happen the second they walked out of her room. She realized he was holding the lightweight blanket that lay puddled on the bed, asking if he should cover Berkley with it.

She nodded. Her throat grew tight when he pulled the blanket gently over Berkley and then leaned over to look at her. Rather than kiss her, he stroked his fingers ever so lightly over her head and then slipped away without another look at Margo.

A little shaky after the display of emotion, Margo took a second with Berkley before she left her room. If Jess was here now, if he was truly Berkley's daddy, hopefully her baby wouldn't suffer any ill effects of not having him present the first year of her life. But Margo fought yet another rush of guilt for what she'd done to Jess by keeping him from her.

He was pulling his coat on when she went back to the living room. He turned and met her eyes, but he didn't say anything. The guilt surged into disappointment. It wasn't even late. Toddlers didn't do the full trick-or-treating show; if Jess left now, Margo would go out of her mind, alone, thinking about him.

"Do you have to go?" Her voice was thick with emotion, though she sounded a bit sultry. As if she wanted to seduce him. As much as she wanted…that…again, she just wanted Jess to stay for a while.

"I should," he mumbled. He shrugged his shoulders, settled the worn black leather on them, and rubbed the back of his neck. "I'll come back over the weekend. I'm not sure if it'll be Friday or Saturday."

She nodded, but she didn't dare try to speak.

"Probably Saturday morning," he decided. He took a deep breath and nodded his head toward the hall and the bedroom. "Thanks for asking me to come tonight."

Margo opened her mouth to argue, to ask him to stay, but he turned away and stuck his hand in his pocket to find his keys. She nibbled anxiously on her lip as she followed him to the door. Jess stepped out to the porch before he turned to her.

"Jess."

Her eyes burned, and even with the memory of last weekend, of Jess telling her she didn't know how to love, how to need, she didn't want to cry. She knew all there was to know about needing someone, but damned if she was going to give in and let him see that.

Rather than answer her, Jess simply stared at her, his expression unreadable.

"I don't want you to leave." She barely had enough courage to whisper the words. Jess stepped closer, close enough that she could feel the heat from his body. She studied his face, his eyes, searching for truth or love or something. His jaw was set in a firm line, and his brows were drawn enough to express that whatever he was thinking was intense.

She gasped in surprise when his fingertips touched her neck. Leaned in when he lowered his face to hers to kiss her. The kiss was barely there, the softest press of his lips to hers, and then suddenly he backed up a step and then another, and Margo was so overcome with emotion, with need, that she couldn't react.

"I don't wanna be your stud boy, Margo." His voice was gruff. He stuffed his hands in his pockets and shrugged helplessly. "I wanted more."

She sputtered, tried to say something, anything, to call him back as he turned and headed down the steps and around the porch to his truck. He didn't look back, not even when he was in his truck, backing out of the driveway.

Margo stared after him for several long, cold moments, wondering what the hell had just happened. She hadn't even asked him to fuck her. To touch her. She had simply told him she didn't want him to leave.

CHAPTER 23

Jess didn't regret his decision to leave the roofing job. He didn't regret his decision to return to Adam's Bay. But he felt like he had swallowed a box of rocks as he climbed around the Hodges roof they'd been working on all week. Not a particularly good feeling when he was two stories off the ground. But his anger with Julie and his disappointment with how things had happened with Margo—again—made him feel off-balance.

Neither Julie nor Margo knew he'd given Derrick his notice. He and Julie had talked about it on occasion, but he had talked to his boss about a month ago. Told him he was thinking about taking that leap. Derrick had been supportive, and he had told him to keep coming to work until he jumped.

He was ready to move back home. Ready to be closer to his parents, to his sisters, and especially, closer to Berkley. Jess wanted everything Margo would give him with Berkley. The Halloweens and the Christmases and every other holiday and every other day she would allow him to be with her. He wanted to see her bang her hands on her highchair tray, demanding a bite of spaghetti or cake. He wanted to see her face the first time she tasted a lemon. He wanted to hear her sweet little voice say everything, including daddy. He wanted to watch her learn to walk and run and ride a bike.

He would never regret his decision to come back.

He just wished he felt better about where he stood with Margo. The more he thought about last weekend, the more it nagged at him. Margo always did have a healthy appetite for sex; she rarely said no when they were living together. So, maybe that hadn't changed. But he had, and he couldn't go back to that kind of relationship with her. He loved her too damned much to settle for something physical.

There were other women. And maybe someday, he would consider dating. Looking for love somewhere else. But it seemed like such a waste. Starting over with someone else, when he'd spent a couple years of his life in love with a woman, and a year realizing he was in love with that woman. It hadn't occurred to him—the whole time he'd been winning on the sobriety issue—it never occurred to him that Margo wouldn't want to be a family.

By the time Friday rolled around, he was exhausted from the hours spent at work. His back and his arms ached from lugging shingles up a ladder and then moving slowly and carefully over the roof, using the bulky nail gun to attach them to the felt they'd wrestled into place Tuesday. His legs were tired from bracing himself for balance, and mostly, his head hurt from chasing all these damned thoughts he'd been having since he had driven to Adam's Bay a few weeks ago to see Berkley.

The crew was off the roof by three, and he was home and showered by four. Plenty of time to head to Adam's Bay, but he wasn't sure he wanted to. Margo was likely at the Queen, so Berkley would be with Margo's mom. He could go now and hang out with his parents, but that made him feel like a pussy. Especially when he knew the whole time he was visiting with his parents, he would be hung up on thoughts of Margo.

Julie called him on his drive home from work, but he didn't pick up. He hadn't talked to her since she had confessed to him that she had gone to talk to Margo. Between being pissed off and driving down to see Berkley for Halloween and being tired last night after work, he hadn't had time to worry about it.

Now he felt bad for blowing her off. And truth be told, he could use an ear. But the idea of Julie feeding Margo his secrets made him second guess that idea. Then again, Julie might want to hang out because the whole thing with Brent had gone off the rails. Before he could make up his mind on whether to call her or not, his doorbell rang. Jess didn't move from his spot on the sofa—an extra his parents had loaned him when he had left town so hastily—because the door was unlocked and he knew Julie would let herself in.

Instead, he aimed the remote and his gaze at the TV and turned it on. He zipped through four channels before she opened the door. Glanced at her as she stepped inside and leaned on the door to close it. Dressed in loose-fitting sweats and a t-shirt, she looked frazzled enough to make him feel guilty. She tossed her keys and her phone on the end table—also on loan from his parents—and perched on the opposite arm of the couch.

"Are you planning to speak to me again?"

"Haven't decided yet."

She rolled her eyes. "Do you know when you might?" She shrugged and lifted her hands to her face. Jess watched her rub her eyes and then drag her fingers back through her hair. "I need to talk to you."

"What's up?" he asked quietly. He wasn't ready to forgive her, but he recognized that something was wrong. Anytime Julie needed him, his first thought was her dad and his drinking. Sobering thought, really. Was that how Margo felt the entire time they had been together? On edge, always waiting to exhale, to make sure the phone call or the knock on the door wasn't someone telling her Jess had wrapped his car around a tree or hit someone head on?

"I slept with him." Julie buried her face in her hands.

"What?" Jess tossed the remote to the floor and sat up straight. He could shove his anger with her down and deal with it later. "You slept with—? How did you sleep with him? You were ready—"

He stopped talking when she lifted her head at the same time she pulled her fingers down over her face, stretching her skin into a gross mask. She huffed out a sigh and dropped her hands to her lap.

"He was in the area, and he stopped by—"

"Jules. He wanted sex."

"I know."

"And you just—? You just gave it up to him? Just like that?"

"A little understanding would be nice before you lecture me."

"I *don't* understand it."

"Really? *Mr. Margo and I were together last weekend?*"

"That's different."

"How is it different? You want sex, and that's okay? If women do, it makes them bad?"

"No." Jess gave himself a mental shake. He wasn't comfortable with the idea of Julie wanting sex. Especially not from Brent.

"Look." She dragged in a deep, long breath to steady herself and wiped at her eyes. "I know what it was. I walked into it, eyes wide open. I just...I don't get why I'm good enough when he's horny. And not—"

"Don't use that word."

"Horny?"

He nodded, but he avoided her eyes. "Have you done this before?"

"Had sex?" she squeaked quickly.

Jess snorted and rolled his eyes. "With him."

"Mm." She climbed off the couch and wandered a path around the couch. "Once. Maybe right before we met."

"Before…we? Met?"

She nodded, her back to him. Jess watched her as she propped herself next to the window by the door.

"Is he worth it?"

Before she could answer, he scrambled off the couch. "Never mind. Don't answer that. I don't wanna hear about any incredible orgasms or the size of his dick. Save that for your girlfriends."

"I don't have any friends I'm close enough to say that to." She glanced at him over her shoulder and shrugged her eyebrows. "Except you."

"Damn." He groaned out load. "Okay. Say it. Get it all out now, because this is weird."

"He's good in bed," she said simply. "We have fun. I mean, it's not like…a…business thing. We're friends. We talk. We laugh. And…we're good together. But not good enough, I guess."

"Julie, maybe he just doesn't want to settle down."

"I know." She rolled her eyes. "Believe me, I know."

"I just don't get why you don't move on. You deserve so much better."

"People might have said the same to Margo," she reminded him.

Behind the kitchen counter now, Jess froze at the refrigerator. He stood for a moment, anger seething in his gut.

"Yeah. They did. Leah, Stevi, and Duncan all did." He sounded deceptively calm. "We're not talking about Margo anymore."

"Because you're not comfortable talking about sex and body parts with me?" Julie folded her arms over her chest. "I've been doing this for seven years, Jess. I'm not innocent."

"No, Julie." He dropped his hands to his sides and turned to face her. "Because I don't trust you anymore."

She flinched and turned away as if he'd hit her.

"Just because I wanted to make sure she understood there's nothing between us?"

"God only knows what she thinks now. Probably, she thinks I'm pissed because I was hoping to get my hands on you, and you messed it up. The thing is, it's my business. Not yours."

"It is my business, Jess." Julie stepped away from the door and marched toward him. "I like her. I like her family. I care about you. And I don't want her to believe that you and I are sleeping together. For you and for me."

Jess took her words like a blow to the gut. He bent slightly and rested his hands on the counter.

"Yeah? Sleeping with me would be that bad?"

"Don't you dare do this. Don't turn this into a dare. I love you. I like her. I'm not gonna fuck you just because you're pissed off and feeling reckless."

"I don't need you to fight my battles, okay? It's bad enough that I've emptied my guts to you on more than one occasion. It's bad enough that I've fucking cried to you about my kid. Margo. I don't need you to go marching into battle in my name."

Julie stared at him with wide eyes.

"Why is that bad enough?" she whispered.

"Julie." He shook his head.

"Why, Jess? Because I'm a girl?" She tipped her head and studied him with an intensity that made him uncomfortable. "Or because I'm eight years younger than you?"

"You overstepped—"

"Fuck you. I didn't tell Margo your secrets. I just wanted her to stop feeling guilty. You let her think that she was the other woman—"

"I didn't let her think anything!" Jess roared. "I told her you and I aren't seeing each other. I told her you aren't my girlfriend. She doesn't believe anything I say now, and there's nothing you can do fix that!"

The room was silent around them after Jess' outburst. Julie stared at him silently for a moment longer and then she ducked her head and nodded.

"Okay."

Jess watched her slip back around the couch.

"Okay what?"

"I'm sorry." She shook her head and picked up her keys and phone. "It was important to me that she know you and I aren't sleeping together. Good luck, Jess."

"Jules," he called as she opened the door and slipped out without another word. "Dammit."

He huffed with anger. Considered going after her but decided against it. He was upset with her, but maybe he was angrier with himself than anyone else. And if that was the case, it might be best to steer clear of company so he didn't say something he would regret.

A cold beer sounded good, but he didn't have any. He wouldn't do it anyway, but he couldn't deny that he wanted one. Instead, he trekked back to the sofa and dropped in a heap. Picked up the remote and flipped through the channels so quickly, he had no idea what was on.

His phone buzzed after he settled on a movie channel. Something with a lot of skin and a love scene that physically hurt to watch. He wanted Margo back, and he wasn't sure how to make his brain, his heart understand that it wasn't going to happen.

He stretched toward the end table where Julie had put her stuff. Snagged his own phone and drew it toward him. He figured it was Julie. Hoped it was anyway. He hated being at odds like this. Yes, he was pissed, but he cared about her. And if push came to shove, he would admit he knew she did what she did because she cared about him.

Are you in Adam's Bay?

He stared at the text from Margo for a long time. Wished he was there. Decided he was glad he wasn't. Pictured her behind the bar in painted on jeans and long boots, her hair falling in curls over her shoulders.

Pictured her in nothing on the bed they had shared, waiting for him to take her.

No.

CHAPTER 24

Margo hissed with anger. Loathing. All aimed at herself. She reached back to shove her phone in her pocket with enough force that she was surprised the denim didn't rip.

"Hey." Duncan set his hands on her shoulders and leaned in as he moved to step around behind her. "Careful where you're swinging those hands."

She looked at him over her shoulder and offered him a small smile when she saw the hint of one on his face.

"Sorry."

"Are you ever gonna talk to me?"

"I talk to you every day," she mumbled. She patted his hand on her shoulder and stepped away from him. The music playing was decidedly not country, and that was okay with her. Her soul felt a little darker than classic rock, but she would take what she could get. Leah and

Trace had already gone home for the night, so the rest of them were on their toes with the crowd. Margo would deny it if she was asked, but she'd been searching the bar consistently for signs of Jess and Julie.

She shouldn't have texted him. At least then each time she looked up and around, the wings of hope would flutter low in her belly. Now that she knew he wasn't even in Adam's Bay and she wouldn't see him until tomorrow, her heart felt heavy inside, and she was exhausted.

"About Jess." Duncan spoke to her out of the side of his mouth as he flashed a welcoming smile at the guy across the bar. The guy pushed two wine glasses at him and asked for another round. Margo marveled at the fact that Duncan had used Jess' name, except that her heart had sort of jolted at the sound of it. If that didn't make her pathetic, she didn't know what did.

"What is there to say?"

"You're in love with him." He said it softly, and there was music playing and a crowd congregated in the bar, but Margo still swept her gaze around the room. What did it matter if anyone heard him? Except that it wasn't true.

She didn't answer him, but as he poured the Dykstra cab, he studied her with a side eye. Margo felt her eyes tear up, so she looked away.

"I'm not," she whispered.

"The only way to get through it is to admit it."

She wasn't sure if she wanted to get through it. She wanted Jess, dammit. Jess, here. With her. Not the girl who had driven here alone to promise her they weren't a couple. She wanted Jess here to sit with her and tell her that himself. She wanted Jess to explain to her how he had ended up in a friendship with a girl so much younger than him.

She wouldn't say all of that to Duncan, though.

Never.

She couldn't bear the thought of him attacking Jess. Attacking her because she had some sort of feelings for Jess.

"Margo."

She blinked and realized that he had served the round to the man at the bar and now he was staring at her.

"The…I'm going to…" She shook her head and stepped around him, praying he would let her go. As much as she was hurting inside, she didn't want to put on a show for anyone.

She and Stevi stayed busy with the tables. Duncan stayed busy with the bar. Twice, Margo's phone buzzed and twice, she'd yanked and fumbled it out of her pocket with shaky hands, praying that it was Jess. Even if he wasn't here, they could text. Leah and Nashville used to text all the time before he moved up here to be with her. Maybe Margo would never rate that sort of devotion, but she and Jess had left too much unsaid. His parting shot the other night had left her seething with rage.

And his absence since then had cooled the rage enough that she missed him.

One text was from Leah, reminding her that they had a morning book club coffee meeting there tomorrow. As if Margo could forget it. She would be the one up and in here brewing the coffee first thing. And the other was from her mother. She sent a picture of Berkley with Margo's dad.

When closing time rolled around, Margo stifled a yawn and watched Duncan lock the doors. Stevi laughed at her as she stacked glasses to carry them back to the kitchen.

"Not used to these late hours," she said around a grin.

"I'm glad you're here," Duncan announced as he moved back to the bar. He tossed the keys down and pinned her with his steady gaze. "What do you want?"

"Good sex followed by six hours of uninterrupted sleep to start with."

Duncan twisted the top off a longneck and handed it to her.

"Cold beer. There ya go."

She rolled her eyes and took a long drink.

"Stevi and I have this closing routine down." He propped his butt on the bar at his back and crossed his feet. "But you can sit there and talk while I pick up glasses."

"If I'm here, I'm gonna work." She shook her head.

Duncan picked up his glass tumbler and eyed the bourbon bottle.

"Stevi? Want anything?" he asked when she appeared through the door again.

"Sex with Duncan?"

Margo groaned and leaned over to rest her head on the bar.

"It's a drink," Duncan said with a chuckle.

"I don't wanna know."

"Why are you avoiding me? Is it always gonna be this way now?"

"I'm not avoiding you, Duncan. We're together every day."

"Stop playing games." He shook his head. "I'm talking about Jess. You're sharing things with Leah and Stevi, but you're tiptoeing around me and keeping secrets."

"I'm not keeping secrets. I just have nothing to say."

Even with her eyes on the bottle, she noticed the way his eyebrows shot up in disbelief.

"You slept with him."

Margo covered her eyes with her hand and sighed.

"Thanks, Stevi."

"Oh, come on!" Duncan snapped. "So, she told me. We're all adults here."

"I'm really not up for a lecture." With another long sigh, she slipped off the barstool and picked up her beer.

"Margo—"

"Or your list of reasons why he's not good for me." She shook her head as she walked away. "Or…anything. Really."

"What about that girl? The one who was here the other day. That comes here with Jess."

Margo shook her head again. "They're friends."

"And you believe that?" Duncan called as she crossed into the restaurant.

"Why would she drive here alone to tell me that if it wasn't true?" She ducked her head back through the doorway to look at him. "How could she be okay with what happened if they were together?"

"Takes all kinds, Margo," he mumbled. "Just. What if they have a casual thing going? And you take him back, and he's up there, and they continue their casual thing?"

Feeling naïve, stupid—really—Margo swallowed hard and drew a deep breath in through her nose. She hadn't considered that. It was possible. Anything was possible. But Julie had seemed so sincere. Never mind the fact that Margo was jealous of the friendship between Julie and Jess, now Duncan had to go and plant more doubts.

"This is why I don't talk to you, Duncan," she said quietly. "You can't let me have anything when it comes to Jess."

"I don't wanna see you get hurt."

"Then leave me alone," she whispered. "Don't watch this. Because it hurts, Duncan. I know you and Stevi are all hearts and flowers, but you have to remember how it hurt you when you thought she wasn't in love with you."

"So you are in love with him?"

"I don't know." She shrugged. "I don't know what this feeling is, but I need to figure it out. And you're no help."

Duncan looked away, and Margo felt guilt stir inside again. She hated pushing him away. She hated the thought that a relationship with Jess would change her relationship with her stepbrother. But she wanted something with Jess. Something more than co-parenting.

She felt like a weasel for doing it, but she couldn't possibly stay here and close with them. For one thing, watching Stevi and Duncan flirt and talk and treat each other with respect only reminded her of what was absent in her life. And the possibility of Duncan spouting more wisdom or advice made her want to run. She crossed back to the bar, set her beer down, and hurried over the floor to the stairs.

"I'm going home. I'll be back in first thing to set up for the book club."

"Margo—"

"Duncan, leave her alone."

She didn't look back when she heard Stevi's voice. Instead, she rushed up the steps to the office to grab her purse. She had a flash of memory of that first day Jess had shown up here to see Berkley. The tense conversation between them up here in the office. Seemed like such a long time ago, already.

When she went back downstairs, she heard Stevi and Duncan talking, obviously in the kitchen. She heard her name, and though she knew both of them were concerned about her, she didn't appreciate that she was the topic of their conversation.

"Margo, wait!" Duncan called. "I'll walk you out."

She rolled her eyes as she slipped out the back door and headed to her car. She didn't need Duncan to walk her out to her car, for God's sake. It was twenty steps out the back door, and she'd been making that quick walk for over four years now.

"Margo!" Duncan had followed her out. She dropped into the driver's seat and looked up to find him on the sidewalk behind the bar, hands propped on his hips, his head tilted as he watched her. She had probably just pissed him off.

She didn't care.

Her hands shook as she started the car. She didn't need Duncan to walk her out. But she knew it made him feel better to walk each of them out when it was late, after close. She'd just taken that responsibility from him, so probably he was upset with her for that, too.

Wasn't that sort of what Jess had said? She didn't need him.

She didn't. She was capable of doing anything that needed done. She didn't need Jess around to change a tire on her car. She didn't need him to call and have a serviceman come out to the house to look at the furnace. She didn't need him to mow the yard.

She hadn't needed him to deliver their baby. After all, she had done all the work. She had carried Berkley for nine months, and it was her body that endured seven hours of labor. The grueling contractions. An hour of pushing. She'd delivered a beautiful healthy baby girl with Leah and Stevi's support. All she'd needed Jess for was making her baby girl.

Well. That and because she loved him.

She might not need him to do things for her. But she had needed him there with her. Because she loved him. Always had.

SHE HAD A TEXT WHEN SHE WOKE UP, AND HER HEART jumped when she saw it on her screen. It was from Stevi, though, and she stifled the disappointment as she shuffled out to the bathroom. She would forgo the coffee at home, since she was heading to the Queen to get coffee and pastries ready there for the book club meeting. She was muttering, though, as she stepped into the shower. What the heck kind of book club met bright and early on Saturday mornings? Seemed a bit crazy to her.

The bad feelings from the night before lingered. She felt bad for the exchange with Duncan, but on the other hand, she meant what she'd said. She had to figure this thing out with Jess, and having Duncan watching over her shoulder, leaning in now and then to share his opinions wasn't going to help anything. The text from Stevi said Duncan felt bad about last night, too, but Margo knew him well enough to know that he probably felt bad because he hadn't reached her. He hadn't made her see just how bad Jess was for her.

After her shower, she dressed in jeans—Leah and Stevi teased her often about her extensive denim wardrobe—and an oversized black tunic. Makeup was a necessity today, since she hadn't slept well again. Whether it was tossing or turning or dreaming of Jess—good and bad—she hadn't been sleeping much at all lately. She added low-heeled gray suede booties to the outfit and called it good enough.

She grabbed her phone and her purse and hurried out to the car. The weather had turned cold. With Halloween over, Margo felt like winter had begun. She didn't need a date on the calendar to say so. Once in the car, she hesitated. Maybe Stevi and Duncan were sleeping. Maybe they were busy doing things she didn't want to picture her cousin and her stepbrother doing. But she couldn't just ignore Stevi's text.

Me too, Stevi, but that doesn't change anything.

The Queen, as always, was welcoming. She flipped lights on as she walked through the kitchen. Rather than going upstairs, she simply slung her purse behind the coffee bar and then got to work. She started the coffee first, out of necessity. Her phone buzzed as she dug out the ingredients she would need to make chocolate chip muffins for the club. She had assumed they would want blueberry, but they had requested chocolate chip.

She considered turning on music while she worked, but the silence was comforting.

Would Julie have come down here to talk to her if she and Jess were involved? No. Women didn't work that way. They were territorial. Even if Julie and Jess were only casually involved and Julie didn't have a problem with Jess fucking around with Margo when he was here, she would have told Margo that. She would have staked her claim, made it clear that Margo knew Julie warmed his bed in Greenville, but when he was here, Margo could have him.

Still. That didn't mean it had never happened.

And even if it hadn't, Margo still didn't understand how Jess had gotten so close to the girl. Sounded like he'd given her more of his heart, his mind than he'd ever given Margo. Margo had his child, but Julie had his presence. After all, he'd quit drinking when he moved to Greenville. He hadn't done it for Margo or Berkley.

CHAPTER 25

IT WAS FOR THE BEST. FOR ALL OF THEM. HE AND JULIE still weren't speaking, and he and Margo were going to have to hammer all of this shit out between them before Julie would want to come back to Adam's Bay with him. If she ever wanted to. He'd stopped at the work site this morning. The guys were working a skeleton crew, finishing up the job. Jess had talked to Derrick for a few minutes to make sure he didn't need him; they'd talked about it yesterday. Derrick had insisted that Jess go to Adam's Bay to see Berkley.

Julie had pulled into the drive alongside Jess' truck as he was backing out. He'd waved, and he'd hated the feeling that he was doing something wrong as she stared at him sadly and then fluttered her fingers in a half-hearted wave. She had been the one to overstep, and he had the right to be angry with her.

And even if he did forgive her, that didn't mean he had to trust her again. Did it?

Margo hadn't answered his texts this morning. He hadn't heard from her since she had asked him last night if he was in Adam's Bay and he told her no. The worry over what he would find with her and Berkley had settled between his eyebrows, and a dull ache pounded through his head. He didn't think she would suddenly decide he couldn't see Berkley. She seemed sincere about her desire for Berkley to know him. And Margo was into family.

But after the visit from Julie, and the same old sex and the same old fight and the comment he'd left her with on Halloween, he wasn't sure Margo would want to see him. In fact, he wouldn't be surprised if she shut the door in his face. But he hadn't slept well, and so he'd climbed out of bed around six and hit the shower and the road, suddenly in a rush to see her.

Except now that he was on the outskirts of Adam's Bay, without Julie as a buffer and as his friend here to support him, he was a little bit afraid of what would go down. Maybe Margo would hand him Berkley and shut the door in his face. No, because she wouldn't trust him with their daughter. The last time she had decided she couldn't face him—the day after they'd had sex—she had vanished and had Stevi babysit him while he hung out with Berkley. Talk about feeling like a pussy. Stevi had to know the whole story, and the fact that Margo didn't trust him with Berkley, and Stevi watching him, thinking about the things Margo had said—

Her house was closed up tight, and there was no answer when he knocked. He rang the doorbell just to be sure, but the house felt quiet and empty. He checked his phone again as he hoisted himself back up into the truck. Nothing from Margo. He tossed the phone to the passenger seat, and it hit him that it was Saturday morning. Stevi had been trying to set Margo up on a date. What if that had happened last night? What if Margo had had such a good time on her date that she'd spent the night with someone else?

Wasn't like he could say anything. As long as she wasn't parading guys in and out in front of Berkley, and he didn't believe for a second that she would do that. Still. The thought of Margo with another guy pissed him off. He slammed the truck into gear, but then he reminded himself he had no idea where Margo was, and even if she'd spent last night with a guy or even two guys who had blown her mind, maybe they both deserved it.

Rage surged through him as he sped away from her house. He didn't want a speeding ticket, but he couldn't help the heavy foot. She wouldn't do that, would she? Margo was the most adventurous woman he'd ever been with, but that didn't mean she would sleep with someone on the first date, did it? That didn't mean she would get involved in threesomes or—

Her car was in the lot behind the Queen. Jess felt a shudder of relief rip through his body. Of course, Margo hadn't gone home with a stranger last night. Moms didn't do that kind of stuff, did they?

Then again, she could have gone home with someone and already been home and showered and come to the Queen. Hell, for that matter, she could have had her back pressed up against the wall back here with a stranger's hands fumbling between her legs. Hadn't Jess engaged in that very thing the night Berkley was born?

The back door was unlocked, and he yanked it so hard, it threw him off balance. Once inside—the bar was dark—he blinked to orient himself and then stood for a moment wondering where she was. Probably the office, he decided, but before he could head toward the stairs, he heard someone in the kitchen.

He wasn't sneaking, but he moved quietly to the kitchen door and then stood with his hands tucked in his hip pockets, to watch her at the sink.

"What're you doing?" he asked. Margo, her back to him, jumped and slopped water all over the counter and the front of her shirt.

"Jesus, Jess. You scared the hell out of me."

"I texted you," he said as if that excused him for scaring her here.

She shook her head and muttered something that he didn't catch about Stevi and Duncan.

"What're you doing?"

"Washing dishes."

He rolled his eyes when she glanced at him. Watched her step back up to the sink and plunge her hands back into the water.

"I see that. But why?"

"Book club meeting here in less than an hour," she mumbled.

"You're in a book club?"

"No." She shook her head. "But we started opening for stuff like this in the mornings. Business breakfasts. Retirement breakfasts. Book clubs. Whatever."

"And you have to deal with it?"

"I run the restaurant," she answered quietly.

"Do I smell coffee?" He lifted his head to sniff the air.

"Yeah."

"Can I have a cup?"

She nodded, but she didn't answer him, and that thought weighed heavily on him as he went in search of the mugs. He snagged one under the bar and looked around to see if Margo had a cup somewhere. When he didn't see one, he poured some for her, too, and carried them back to the kitchen.

"Why're you here so early?" She met him at the doorway, drying her hands as she spoke. Jess watched her duck her head and dab the dishtowel at the small spot on the front of her shirt. He considered sucking up. Telling her he had wanted to get an early start to the weekend, to spend as much time with Berkley as he could. It wasn't a lie. He hoped there would come a time—soon—when Margo would let him take Berkley without needing someone to watch him. But it wasn't the truth, either. Not the real reason for driving down here so early, and he didn't want to start today off with a lie.

"Couldn't sleep."

She tossed the dishtowel back to the counter and took the mug he offered her.

"Thank you."

"Can I stick around?"

"Berk spent the night with my parents, Jess."

He nodded, even managed a smile, when what he wanted to do was ask if Margo had spent the night alone.

"I could help you out here," he offered.

"Since when do you wait tables?"

"Can't be that hard."

Margo tipped her head and narrowed her eyes at him. "You might wanna watch it, Jess. We work our asses off here."

"I didn't mean to suggest otherwise. Just that you have a controlled group today, and I'm assuming a small menu."

He realized he didn't just smell coffee. Something was baking, and it smelled delicious. His stomach growled.

"Where's Julie today?" she asked after a few moments of quiet passed between them.

He sighed, took a drink, and then set his mug down on the nearest table. Margo watched him shrug out of his coat and toss it over the back of a chair.

"Don't you think we need to talk?"

"I don't think there's anything to say." Her voice was thick, but she cleared her throat. "The only thing we ever did right was sex, and you let me know the other night that you're not interested."

"You are so good at twisting things I say to suit yourself."

Rather than argue, Margo looked away and slipped past him. Jess watched her for a few seconds and then followed her to the bar.

"She didn't come today?"

"No."

"Why not?"

"Because I didn't want her to." He shrugged. "Because we had a blowout last night."

Margo stared at him with sad eyes. "You were with her? When I texted?"

"She had just left."

"Your place. She had just left your place, after you had a blowout."

"She said she told you there's nothing going on between us."

"Jess." Margo sighed.

"Twice, Margo. It happened two times when we were together. It was wrong. I was wrong. And I'm sorry. I am so sorry I hurt you."

He waited to see if she would argue, if she would interrupt him. But she avoided his gaze, her glassy eyes trained on the bar.

"The second time it happened was the day Berkley was born." His voice was gruff as he continued. "*After* Stevi called to tell me you had delivered her. Do you know what that did to me? Getting that call *after* she was born? And then for you to tell people you kicked me out because I was with another woman when you were—"

"You ever given birth, Jess? Have you been huge and unattractive? Legs spread wide open with a guy's hands inside you to guide a baby out?" She pressed her lips together. "I didn't want you to see that. I couldn't keep you interested in me before I gave birth. That was a moment for a woman and a man in love. Bringing their baby into the world. I needed a man there that thought it was beautiful. I didn't trust you to think that."

He nodded. Opened his mouth to speak, but he had to clear his throat before he could find his voice.

"I know." He nodded. "And I didn't give you a reason to trust me."

"I'm sorry. For taking that away from you. I know you want to be part of her life."

"Margo." He groaned. "I want—"

"Did you put her up to coming here?"

"What?"

"Julie."

"No." He dragged his hand over his eyes and down over his mouth and cheeks. "No. Julie had no right to do that."

"What are you afraid of?"

"What do you mean?"

"What do you think she told me? That makes you so angry?"

"Nothing!" he yelped. "It's just…"

"Just what?"

"Would you want Leah or Stevi to tell me everything you've ever told them in confidence?"

Rather than calm her as Jess had intended, his words seemed to upset her further. Margo flinched and rubbed at her eyes, careful not to smear her makeup.

"I thought…" She cleared her throat. "Never mind. I don't know why I—"

"You thought what?"

So desperate to know what Margo was thinking or what she thought at any given time, Jess reached for her. He brushed her hair back from her face and traced her cheekbone with his thumb.

"Tell me, Margo. Tell me. Because I can't read your mind."

"When you left—"

"Stop." He shook his head.

"What?"

"I didn't leave. Stop making it sound like I made the decision to leave you. You asked me to go, and I did."

"You made a decision to leave me every day, every night you didn't come home to me."

Jess sucked in a deep breath and then let it out in a long, frustrated sigh.

"When I asked you to leave," she started. She slipped off the stool, but she lingered there, so close he could feel her thigh touching his bent knee. "I thought you would...I hoped you would go somewhere. And stop drinking. And come back—"

"I did."

"I thought you would come back for both of us. Not just Berk." She sniffled and pursed her lips. A moment of silence stretched out between them. Jess wasn't sure he heard her right. "So imagine what it did to me when you showed up with Julie."

He sank back in his chair like she had sucker punched him.

"Margo—"

There was a tentative tap at the front window. Margo dragged her eyes from his and looked over her shoulder. She groaned and set her coffee on the bar and moved away from him.

"Margo, wait. You can't just say that and—"

"Time to go to work, Jess."

CHAPTER 26

HE STAYED.

At first, Margo was angry that he wouldn't leave after she'd opened her mouth and the truth—the god awful, embarrassing truth—had spilled out. She hadn't meant for that to happen. She didn't want him to know she'd spent the past year waiting for him to come back, because that sounded too much like saying she loved him. And she did. The more she thought about it, she realized she'd loved him from the beginning. She just hadn't known how to tell him, and she'd made the mistake of thinking he knew, that being together, that living together meant that she loved him. That she wanted him around.

She loved him now.

But that didn't mean she wanted *him* to know that. If Jess was armed with that truth, with her truth, he had all the power, and he'd already hurt her more times than she could count.

She'd greeted Peggy Lewis, the woman who had reserved the Queen for the book club meeting, assuming Jess would slip out the back door. Instead, Jess had introduced himself to Peggy—Margo's friend, he'd said, and that had both thrilled her and hurt her, because they needed to be friends, though it would never be enough—and donned an apron and helped her serve the nine fussy older women coffee and muffins. He'd moved with ease around the table, talking with each of the women, taking a few moments to make each of them feel special. Flirting, she supposed, though today, she knew it was harmless.

The women were charmed by him, though Peggy had expressed disappointment over the fact that Margo didn't have Berkley with her. Margo had held her breath, waiting for Jess to jump in and tell them that he was Berkley's father. But he hadn't. He had been on his best behavior, and he'd listened to Anita Smithers gripe because Margo didn't serve vegan butter and he'd listened to Barb Stroud's long-winded tale about her husband's latest hunting trip.

When they were gone, she had hidden in the kitchen, again washing dishes. Earlier she'd cleaned up her mess from baking the muffins. Now, she was washing the dishes the ladies had used, rather than putting them in the dishwasher. There weren't enough to bother with running it, and besides, if Jess insisted on sticking around the Queen, then she had to be busy.

"Do you want me to call Mom? Have her bring Berkley in?" she asked when she heard him wander into the room behind her.

"I would love to see Berkley," he said simply, "but I'd really like to finish that conversation we started earlier."

"I wouldn't." She looked up at him boldly, slightly amused when she saw him chowing down on a muffin.

"Did you make these?"

"Don't act like I can't cook."

"I'm not, but you baked these. For breakfast. You never made me breakfast."

"Maybe that's because you were never home for breakfast or you were hung over most mornings that you were home."

"Julie is hung up on a guy named Brent." He popped the muffin into his mouth and chewed it slowly, wiggling his eyebrows as he savored the treat. "He's a douche. Nice-looking guy, but he treats her like shit. Nice to her when he wants something. I didn't realize until last night that that included sex."

"Yeah?" Margo leaned her hip on the sink and tipped her head. "Were you curled up in bed with her when she told you that?"

"I have never laid a hand on her." He spoke calmly. Margo's heart jumped when he stepped toward her, but he only reached around her to grab the dishtowel. "I'm not attracted to her. At all. She's not attracted to me."

Margo swallowed hard and turned her attention back to the water.

"What?" He leaned into her when she didn't say anything.

"It doesn't make me feel any better."

"What do you mean? Julie and I are friends—"

"First of all, I don't know if I believe that. Second, what if you were attracted to her? Would you keep your hands to yourself? What if she decided to seduce you? Would you tell her no? And why can you be friends with her and not me?"

"Wait." Jess rested his hands on the counter, the dishtowel hanging from under his left palm. "Now I can't be friends with other women?"

Margo felt a furious blush climb her neck. It did sound stupid when he said it that way. They were too old for this argument, this behavior.

"I just...it hurts me," she started. She scrubbed at a plate that was already spotless. "It hurts me that you can give Julie so much of yourself. Your heart. When you wouldn't give it to me."

"Margo, you had me. You had all of me, and you didn't want it."

"I didn't have you. Every goddamned bar in town had you, Jess. I got what was left after a hard night of drinking. Or a fun night of drinking. Or an okay night of drinking."

She chanced a glance at him when she felt his body go rigid beside her. He hung his head, but he swung his gaze up to meet hers. His eyes blazed with anger.

"Julie's dad is my boss."

"I know." Margo nodded. "She told me."

"I don't know how she knew it. Maybe we look alike."

"What?"

"Users. Drunks. Selfish bastards."

"Am I supposed to stop you?"

"It's like she saw me and just knew. And—I don't know. Maybe she made it her job to save me. She just started talking to me. At first, I just wanted her to leave me the fuck alone. I was so angry, Margo. I was so mad at you. I was so mad that you took her from me."

"I didn't take her from you," she insisted.

"I know that now. Because of Julie."

"Yeah? What did St. Julie do to make you see the light?'

"Her dad's an alcoholic," Jess said simply. "And she told me some really horrible, ugly stories from her childhood. I mean, Derrick is good now. He and his wife are happy. He's healthy. They don't drink. But Julie shared really awful things, Margo. That made me think. If we'd stayed together, if I hadn't quit drinking, I could have done all of that to you. I did do a lot of it to you, and I wouldn't have changed."

"Then I guess it's a good thing we broke up, huh?" Tears burned her eyes, but she refused to swipe at them now. She wouldn't give Jess the satisfaction. She concentrated on the dishes again. "You got clean. You'll make someone a nice—"

"Why are you doing this?"

"You just said if we'd stayed together…and let's not forget that on Halloween night, you told me you weren't interested in sex."

"Hey." Leah knocked as she stepped into the room. "How'd the book club meeting go?"

Margo turned away from Leah, but that left her staring at Jess. She'd lost control of the tears. Jess handed her the dishtowel and then skimmed his fingers down her back and rested them on her hip.

Finally in control of herself, Margo nodded. "Good."

"Hey, Jess." Leah apparently realized she had interrupted something. "I'm sorry. I didn't mean…to barge in."

"It's fine," Margo sniffled. "Jess was just leaving."

"No, I'm not."

His hand was almost comforting on her hip, and they stood close enough that she could feel his breath on her forehead.

"I'm gonna go up to the office," Leah announced. "Trace dropped me off. He was going to run a few errands."

Margo nodded. "Are Stevi and Duncan here?"

"Not yet." Leah cleared her throat. "I could finish the dishes, and you guys could go up to the office, if you need to talk."

"No. We're good."

"Or you could go get lunch. We've got it covered here for a while."

"We're fine, Leah," Margo spoke louder this time, but her voice was gruff.

"Okay."

"How did Stevi and Duncan have time together? We've been interrupted twice in one morning."

"I'll call Mom." Margo shook her head. "And um…I don't know. I guess you could take Berk—"

Jess closed the fingers of his other hand around her wrist and tugged her closer. His lips were soft and warm on hers. He stroked them over hers twice and left them pressed to the corner of her mouth.

"I never said I wasn't interested in sex."

Eyes closed, Margo sobbed quietly. "You did, Jess. I wanted you to stay. Just to talk to me. To hang out. And you flat out refused me, and told me you weren't—"

He cut her off with another kiss. This one was wet; his mouth open over hers, and the inside of his lips were hot on hers. Margo gasped with longing. Jess moved his mouth over hers, soft and tender. Desire shot through her and left her weak in the knees. And the heart. She needed more from him. More than another crazy, wild night of sex.

She wanted the Jess that Julie knew.

Margo slid her hand up over his arm, her fingers digging into his skin.

"I told you I didn't want to be your stud boy, Margo. That doesn't mean I don't want to be with you."

"Dammit, Jess." She sobbed again and ducked her chin. She wiped her free hand on her shirt and then swiped at her eyes. "I can't do this. I can't do this with you."

"What do you mean?" He scooped a handful of her hair from her shoulders and then cupped the back of her head. "Margo, I worked my ass off this past year to get back to you. I want—"

"You broke my heart." She leaned into him, rested her forehead on his chest. "Every time you didn't come home. Every time you took a drink. Every time you were with someone else. You broke me, Jess."

"I'm sorry." He pressed a kiss to her forehead. "I'm sorry I hurt you, Margo. I was an idiot to treat you like that, and I'm sorry."

"I can't love you." She lifted her head and looked up at him. "The things you said to me the night we were together. I just…I can't do this again. I can't sit here and wait for you to hurt me."

"Sweetheart." He gathered her in his arms. Gathered her. He'd never done it like this. Never made her feel protected and safe. "Margo, I can't walk away. You and Berkley are all I want. And I need to know you want the same thing. I need to know you want to be a family."

"I can't, Jess." She shook her head as she stepped away from him. "I can't start over with you. I can't pretend those things didn't happen. I can't pretend—"

"We don't have to start over."

"I don't even believe Julie, and she came to me herself to tell me you guys—"

"We go from here. Start right where we are. Because we can't erase the past." Jess stepped closer to her. Margo heard footsteps, and she offered up a silent prayer that if it was Duncan he stay out of the kitchen. "We can't erase the past, Margo, because of Berkley. And because those mistakes made us who we are now."

"It won't work," she argued.

"I have to earn your trust." He cupped her chin in his hands and rubbed his thumb over her lip. "I know that. I will. I'll do anything I can to make you believe me."

"Anybody know…"

Margo dropped her head back and groaned when she heard Duncan's voice in the bar.

"Margs, you here?" Duncan bellowed. "We can't do this, Margo. We're never gonna—"

Margo looked over her shoulder when she heard Duncan's voice right behind her.

"Oh."

"Can you give us a minute, Duncan?"

"Is Leah here?"

"Leah's upstairs. Trace is running errands. The book club meeting was a hit. And we need a few minutes."

Duncan's gaze jumped from Margo to Jess and back.

"Sure."

She waited until she heard glasses clinking at the bar before she turned back to look at Jess.

"This isn't the place." She took a shaky breath. Maybe they did have a lot left to say to each other, but they couldn't continue this at the Queen. Not now.

"You're gonna let him call the shots?"

"That's three interruptions," she said softly. "It has nothing to do with Duncan."

"If I walk out of here now, you'll freeze me out later."

She stared at him silently.

"It's what you do, Margo. When you're hurt and angry."

Overcome with feeling—anger, grief, longing—Margo stepped away from him. She ducked her head and rubbed her forehead, trying to push the headache away.

"So, we're back to blaming me." She sighed and looked up at him. "Is that it?"

"It's not what I'm saying," he argued, "but it's true. If we don't finish this now, you'll push all of this aside and act like you didn't just tell me I broke your heart. You'll go back to—"

"So what do you wanna do?" She shrugged and tipped her head. "Stand here and have it out where my family's gonna be in and out and part of the conversation? Go to my house where we can cut loose and scream at each other?"

"I wanna hold you, Margo," he mumbled. "I want to feel you right here." He tapped his chest. "And I want to put my arms around you and hold you."

"What good is that gonna do?" she whispered. "We've got so many fights to have, what's that—"

Jess cut her off again. This time, he tossed the dishtowel down and reached for her. No kisses. Just his arms around her, her face pressed to his hard chest, and his chin resting on top of her head.

"I'm not naïve. I know we can't just wave a magic wand and fix everything. I know there're some hard things we both need to say to each other."

Margo closed her eyes. He was warm and solid, and standing in his arms brought back all the nights during the past year that she'd spent wishing for this moment. Afraid, suddenly, that it would end—that Jess would let her go or that Stevi would choose this moment to need her for something—she closed her arms around him and held on.

CHAPTER 27

As much as he wanted to dig in and get to the heart of their relationship, Jess knew that pushing her now would backfire. When she'd given in earlier, at the Queen, and put her arms around him, he'd had to squeeze his eyes closed and wait out the burning sensation. It wasn't enough; there was so much more work for both of them to do to heal themselves and each other. But it gave him hope.

He let her go when she stirred in his arms. Helped her finish up the dishes and the kitchen. Waited at the bar while she was upstairs talking to Leah. Even mumbled to Duncan when he asked if he wanted a drink. He chose to believe Duncan was going to offer him a soda or more coffee, and not that Duncan was fucking with him, hoping to tempt him into drinking. When Stevi came up from the cellar, Jess wondered again how things had developed between her and Duncan. She was a pretty woman, and he supposed he was man enough to say Duncan was reasonably attractive to a woman. But he didn't get how someone as sweet as Stevi could love a jackass like Duncan Marks.

He'd reminded himself it wasn't his business, and he had been happy to stand there and talk to Stevi while he waited for Margo. They'd talked about business, but then Stevi had shifted the conversation to Berkley, and Jess was over the moon to listen to stories about his daughter. Stevi pulled her phone out of her back pocket and swiped through a bunch of pictures until she found what she wanted to share with him.

The picture of Berkley with her bright blue eyes and her black curls and lavender boots that Trace apparently brought back for her from Nashville made his heart swell with love and pride and hope. He wanted that precious little girl with the beaming smile to call him Daddy, and he wanted Margo to love him, and he wanted to be a part of this family.

Duncan and all.

They left the Queen just after noon. Margo drove, and she was careful not to bump him or touch him in anyway. But Jess read her skittish behavior as nerves more than a sincere wish that he would disappear. She called her mom on the way over to the house, and they picked Berkley up and took her for a drive to the park. It was chilly, but Berkley was bundled up in a heavier coat and a yellow stocking cap, and Jess was thrilled just to be there, so the cold didn't bother him.

He pushed Berkley in the one baby swing at the park. Her squeals of delight rendered him speechless. Margo stood to the side, propped against the chunky plastic sliding board, and watched them. Shoulders hunched and hands tucked in her pockets, she looked cold. But her cheeks and the tip of her nose were red and adorable, and whenever he dared to look at her, she offered him a small, almost shy smile.

They took a short walk after Berkley got tired of the swing. But the wind picked up, and Margo was worried that it was too much for her, so they packed their daughter up and Margo steered the car to her house. Jess had noticed earlier—when they were talking in the kitchen at the Queen—that she'd asked if he wanted to go to her house. Not their house.

He wondered if he would ever be welcome the same way again at the house. If he would share her bed for more than an occasional night of sex. Inside, Margo announced that she would fix something for lunch, but she had to change Berkley first. Jess offered to take Berkley. The silent moment between them—Berkley rattling in a singsong voice and patting Margo's cheeks—lasted a bit too long for Jess' comfort, but finally, Margo passed his daughter to him and turned her back.

Jess stood for a moment and watched her peer into the fridge, but he decided to move before she changed her mind. He carried Berkley to her room and stood her in her crib. Her smile blew him away as he searched for and found a clean diaper and the tub of wipes.

"What do you think, kid?" he asked, amused by the way her eyes grew wide with wonder when he spoke. "Need some new pants?"

She shrieked with delight—typical female, he decided, excited to get new pants—and tried to jump up and down. She wobbled on her feet, and Jess scooped her up and smooched her cheek. Her giggles were so real, so full of life, he felt his eyes burn for the second time in one day.

She let him change her diaper. Played with a stuffed monkey as he worked with pretty steady hands. He looked over his shoulder once to see if Margo was in the doorway monitoring him. Surprised that she wasn't, he decided not to get cocky about one easy diaper change. He knew the next time could be a totally different story.

Margo had sandwiches grilling in a skillet when he carried Berkley back to the kitchen. She glanced at him and then eyed the baby, a soft smile playing at her lips. Jess belted Berkley into her highchair and then washed his hands.

"Do you know him?" Margo asked suddenly. Jess dried his hands and watched her flip the ham and cheese sandwiches.

"Do I know who?" He tossed the towel down and propped his hip on the counter. Margo made a show of checking the sandwiches, wielding the spatula like a weapon to hold him at bay.

She finally set the turner down and looked up at him, someone's name on her lips. Jess leaned in to kiss her. Just a soft kiss, only the slightest touch of his tongue against hers. Margo seemed flustered when he pulled back, which made him remember that Julie had said those kisses were the best. The ones that snuck up on you, maybe. The subtle *I love you, and I want to be here with you* kiss, rather than *I want you naked, so we can do dirty things together.* Definitely a time and place for those kind, too. Margo had never tried to hide that she liked those kisses.

But this stuff. The soft, romantic stuff. It had never occurred to him that Margo would be into that.

She blinked at him now, but Jess' gaze was drawn to the tip of her tongue, currently outlining her lips.

"The guy Julie's hung up on," she mumbled. Jess dragged his eyes back up over her face to meet her gaze. She wasn't done up for the night yet. Just a hint of eye shadow. Maybe some mascara. No heavy eyeliner, no lipstick.

Damn, she was beautiful.

Jess's turn to blink. She stared at him expectantly, reminding him that she'd asked him a question.

"No." He shook his head. "I know who he is. Never met him. Guy just seems like a dick."

"Where'd she meet him?" Margo turned back to the skillet. She flipped the sandwiches and gave him the side eye. Jess glanced at the sandwiches, noted a few burned spots around the crust. He grinned.

"I think they went to school together," he answered. "Why're we talking about Julie?"

She answered with a dramatic shrug. Turned the burner off and moved the skillet. Jess watched her set the spatula down and reach to open a cabinet. He grabbed two small plates and set them on the counter.

"She told me she's twenty-four," Margo continued. "She looks seventeen."

"You look beautiful." His voice was gruff. Margo ducked her head, but Jess wanted to kiss her again. He bumped her hip and captured her mouth in another kiss when she looked up at him.

"Don't," she whispered. "Not in front of Berkley."

"Berkley's too young to know what I'm doing," he answered.

"Still." She rested her hand on his chest to hold him back or push him away, but she kissed him back. "She's never seen anyone kiss me."

"Yeah?" Jess drew back from her with a small smile. "She's never seen anyone kiss you?"

"No." Margo sighed wistfully when Jess stroked a trail from her lips to her collarbone.

"Does anyone kiss you now? Other than me?"

"Nice try." She laughed softly and gave him a gentle shove. Jess grinned, but he took her hint and backed away to give her space. "I guess...I just need to know more about Julie, because I feel threatened by her. I don't like that feeling."

She busied herself with their sandwiches, plated them and then carried the plates to the table. Jess stared at her in disbelief. It made sense that she would doubt him, but not Julie. And for her to admit to him that she felt threatened was totally new.

"Especially when she looks so young."

"She's an only child." Jess watched from his place at the table as Margo dabbed a bit of baby food on a little red plate for Berkley. "Why don't you eat your sandwich while it's hot?"

"Um." She shrugged and shook her head, ready to argue. Maybe to say that Berkley wanted her lunch. But she stopped when she saw that Berkley appeared perfectly content in her highchair playing with her bib. Jess felt an arrow in his heart when his little girl looked up to find her mother staring at her. Berkley turned on a one hundred watt-grin and beamed up at Margo.

"My God." Margo rolled her eyes, but she chuckled. "What you do to the ladies, Jess. You just make us all so happy."

"Yeah, until I don't," he mumbled.

Margo left the jar of baby food and Berkley's plate set, but instead of sitting down, she went to the refrigerator for the pickles and ketchup.

"So her dad was a drunk?"

Jess eyes her silently for a second. Is that what she thought of him? Did she tell anyone who asked about Berkley's father that he was a no-good drunk? Jess had come a long way in the past year. He had stopped drinking. He had recognized that he had a problem, because of the memories Julie had shared with him. He wasn't mean when he drank. He didn't drink until he passed out. But he drank too much, every night. He let the partying and drinking keep him from what was important to him, and they were sitting at the table right now. No sense in arguing his case when Margo was right.

"Yeah." He nodded when she glanced at him. "Yeah. He was."

"Was he abusive?"

"No. I think he was just always falling down drunk. Either her mom had to go get him from his favorite tavern, or he stumbled in the morning after."

"Did he cheat? On her?"

Jess broke the eye contact and picked up his sandwich for a bite.

"Yeah."

Margo took a deep breath and nodded. He waited for her to say something, to compare Jess to Julie's dad, but she didn't.

"Julie saw him with other women when she was little. Watched her mom struggle to make ends meet. Watched her make excuses for his behavior. Look the other way and pretend to be oblivious to the women."

"And he's clean now?"

Jess answered with a curt nod, but when he realized Margo was staring at him expectantly, he mumbled yes.

"If you had ever laid a hand on me, I wouldn't..." Her voice trailed off. Jess sat back in his chair and studied her. She shrugged, apparently uncomfortable with his attention. "I would never allow you around my daughter."

"I know." He nodded. "You know I would never do that, Margo."

"Yeah. I know. I don't think I ever saw you mad, Jess. You never even got mad enough at me to fight with me. It was like you didn't care. My house was a place to live. My body was a body to—"

"Don't." He tipped his head and shot a look at Berkley. "I know I made mistakes, Margo. I made a lot of mistakes, and yes, in my opinion, the worst was that I never fought you."

"Because I wasn't worth it?"

"Because I was afraid to rock the boat."

She arched her eyebrows, but again, she was quiet. Her stillness made him fidgety. Margo was always in motion; it bothered him when she slowed down to think.

"What does that mean?"

"You called the shots." He took another bite of his sandwich and then set it down. Margo looked up quickly when he stood.

"Where're you going?"

"Nowhere."

He grabbed glasses and filled them with ice water, Margo's stare heavy on him as he moved.

"Does it bother you?"

"What?" He sat as he handed her a glass.

"Not drinking."

It was his turn to feel flustered. It didn't bother him. Not that much now. But it had. He wasn't sure he wanted to go into that struggle with her. Not yet.

"It did at first."

"Does Julie drink?"

"Not much. Not around me anyway."

Margo picked at her sandwich, eating small bites and then letting it sit for minutes on end. Jess finished his. Realized that even though Margo had put the jar of pickles on the table, she hadn't brought a fork over, and neither of them had even opened the jar.

"I should go in tonight," she said quietly. "I worry about Leah being on her feet so much."

Jess hated the thought of Margo working tonight. Of leaving her house. Saying goodbye to Berkley and heading home to his parents' house. Felt a little bit like high school days, and that coupled with the conversation made him feel like a pussy. He hated that he would be slinking out of here with his tail between his legs, but on the other hand, he had to walk the line and play his cards right or Margo might decide he wasn't worth the effort.

"Is Leah okay?" he asked after a few moments of quiet.

Margo glanced at him. "She had some complications early in her pregnancy. But I think she's doing well now." Rather than hold the eye contact, she squeezed her eyes closed and pushed her hair off her face. "I still worry about her, though. After what happened when she first found out she was pregnant, and then with Trace leaving…"

"Trace left her? When she found out she was pregnant?"

Now, that was a shock. That guy seemed rock solid.

"No. He left to help his brother out. Played part of Tanner's tour with him, and then he had to go back to Nashville to check on his mom. It was just a rough time for Leah. Especially with Kenzi's stroke so fresh in Leah's mind."

"Play Tanner's tour with him?"

Margo smirked and dropped her hands to her lap. "You have no idea who Trace is, do you?"

"Should I?"

"Ever heard of Tanner Dixon and the Lightnin' Congregation?"

"No."

"'Major country music star," Margo told him, though Jess didn't think she sounded too impressed. "Trace is a songwriter."

"Really?"

"Yep. He's got a lot of songs out there."

"Wow." Jess grinned. "And here I was overly impressed with Stevi dating Duncan."

"Duncan's in love with her."

"If you say so." Jess shrugged. He cleared his throat. "So. Do you want me to take off? So you can get back to the Queen?"

Margo opened her mouth to answer him, but she closed it without uttering a word. Jess watched her when she stood and carried their plates back to the sink. She rinsed them and set them in the dishwasher.

"Do you …" She started and stopped. Sighed. Jess watched her curiously as she slumped against the counter and folded her arms over her chest.

"Do I what?"

"Do you wanna…watch Berkley?"

"Are you asking me if I want to babysit my daughter?" Half thrilled that she had just extended him the opportunity to spend more time with Berkley, and half irritated to be used as a babysitter—rather than just a father spending time with his child—Jess scooted his chair back from the table. Berkley's constant chatter stopped at the harsh squeak.

"Jess." Margo stared at him with sad eyes. "I'm trying."

He nodded and groaned out loud. He stood at a safe distance from her for a second, but he was too far away.

He wanted to feel her breath on his face. At the very least, he wanted to smell her hair and her lotion.

She sucked in a sharp breath when he stood directly in front of her and propped his hands on the counter on either side of her.

"I asked you not to do this."

"I'm not kissing you," he argued, his voice low and tight. "Make no mistake that I want to kiss you right now. I want my mouth on yours, and I want your tongue on mine. And I want my hands all over you. But you asked me not to kiss you in front of Berkley, so I'm not."

A flame of desire flickered in her eyes. Jess stared at her boldly, daring her to look away.

"I can take her back to Mom's."

"I would love to be with her tonight. If you can function at work, worrying about me here with her."

"I know you wouldn't hurt her."

"Never."

"I hate this," she whispered. Jess swept his gaze over her face, watched her close her eyes, her brows drawn in a deep, unhappy frown.

"That I came back?"

"That you're so far away."

"We can fix that." He lifted his left hand and traced his fingers over her cheekbone.

"Don't kiss me." She opened her eyes as if she was afraid he would try to sneak a kiss.

"Pretend like I am," he suggested. "Pretend like my lips are barely touching yours."

She licked her lips and sighed that same wistful sigh again. Jess felt her breath on his face, felt it down his spine and into his toes.

"Where are your hands?"

"My arms are around you," he said softly. "Holding you."

SHE HAD TOLD HIM HE COULD TAKE BERKLEY TO SEE HIS parents. She'd even packed the diaper bag, just in case he decided to go. She left the car seat on the kitchen table. Kissed her baby girl goodbye, and then she'd looked longingly at Jess, wishing she could kiss him, too. She didn't want to do that. Not yet. It was too soon to show so much affection for him in front of Berkley. It didn't matter that Berkley was just a toddler; she would sense that there was something safe and special about Jess. She already had.

And besides.

It was too soon to be that free with her affection for her sake.

She loved him. But that didn't mean she was ready for anything else. She had to walk around her daily life and let that thought, that feeling sink in. She had to think about him. About what he might feel for her. Even if Jess said he loved her, it didn't mean he was ready to commit to her. After all, he'd had a key to the house and a place in her bed, and there'd been no commitment.

"What's wrong with you?" Stevi asked when Margo tapped a beer and ended up with a glass over half full of foam. "That's the fourth time you've done that. I saw you serve someone Riesling earlier instead of chardonnay."

Margo shot Stevi a grumpy look and then turned her attention back to the beer in her hand. She dumped most of it, eyes on the thick foam as she poured it out of the glass.

"Jess has Berkley." She shrugged. Afraid Stevi would think she was stupid for trusting him, she hesitated to look at her again. When she did, she found her cousin with a small smile on her face.

"That's awesome," Stevi said quietly.

Margo gushed a big sigh of relief and slumped her shoulders. "Do you think so?"

"Of course." Stevi rubbed her shoulder. She reached for the glass Margo was still holding. "Let me do this. The dude's gonna die of thirst."

Margo handed the glass over willingly.

"I just keep wondering if they're okay. If she's scared. If he remembered to take her blanket when they went to his mom's house—"

"Margo?"

"Hmm?" Margo finger-combed her hair away from her face.

"Breathe." Stevi grinned. "I think Jess will be fine. And that baby girl is nuts about him."

Margo laughed softly. "Yeah. She just lights up when he's in the room."

"So do you," Stevi said quietly as she slipped away with the glass in her hand.

Margo turned and watched her go. The Queen wasn't crowded yet, but there were enough people here early to suggest it might be a crazy night. She was relieved she had come in so that Leah and Trace could slip out when Leah was tired. But she worried that Jess would end up annoyed with her for being gone so long.

"Hey." Trace looped his arm around her neck and dropped a kiss on the top of her head.

"Hey." She grinned and sagged against him.

"Leah told me she sent you home earlier today and told you not to come back."

Margo tipped her head back to look at him. "She did."

"You came back for her." He said it as a statement, not a question, but Margo answered with a slow nod. "She's feeling good, but she does get tired."

"Oh," Margo chuckled and patted Trace's chest. "I remember that kind of tired, Nashville. She'll get some energy back for a while, and then right before she delivers, she's gonna be drained."

Trace's smile was warm and sincere.

"I'll take care of her," he promised.

"I know you will."

Her phone buzzed in her back pocket and made her jump.

"Excuse me." She flashed him a smile and ducked away from him as she tugged the phone from her pocket. She had texted Jess about an hour ago to say hi. He had seen right through her fake hi and told her they were fine. Sent a picture of Berkley on a pile of blankets in the middle of the living room, surrounded by what appeared to be every toy she owned.

This was a text from Joe, not Jess.

Jess texted me, Margo. Good job.

She ducked over to the restaurant. Only one table was still occupied; they would close in less than thirty minutes. Should she answer Joe? And say what? She didn't want kudos for giving Jess time with their daughter.

So what did she want?

Reassurance that she'd done the right thing. Well, Stevi had given her that, right? And she trusted Stevi more than most people in her life. Maybe a little reassurance that Jess wasn't going to hurt her, because she had no doubt that he would do anything for Berkley. But she wasn't sure what to think when it came to her and Jess.

I'm stupid, Joe. I can't break again.

She set her phone on the bar and waited for him to respond. Didn't take long. She wondered what he was doing right now. What did a married man whose wife was physically disabled and at least currently mentally incapacitated do on a Saturday night? He was probably with the kids. Addelyn and Liam were social kids; Margo had no doubt they kept Joe busy. But even if they were out, Joe would most likely be home with Edison.

Give him a chance.

Just like Joe to tell her that. If she shared her worries with him, he would probably send her inspirational thoughts about living life to the fullest. While she understood where Joe was coming from, she wasn't in the same spot and she had always approached life—at least her emotions—a bit more cautiously.

Her fingers shook as she touched her screen again to send another text.

She wanted to connect with Jess. Of course, part of it was nerves, the need to know—again—that Berkley was okay. But it was more than that. She hadn't admitted that to Stevi, but the butterflies in her belly were about more than her nerves over leaving Berkley with him.

Who knew I would like pretend kisses...

She hesitated, her finger over the send arrow. Her heart wanted her to do it. To send him the message. She wasn't ready to just throw caution to the wind and tell him she didn't want to live without him and invite him back into her home and her heart. But she wanted to flirt a little.

Not to string him along.

But to let him know she wanted to pursue...something with him.

"Why're you hiding out over here?"

She jumped when she heard Duncan's voice behind her. Her finger skimmed the screen of her phone, and she looked down, heart in her throat, to see that she had sent the text.

Because of Duncan.

She almost laughed, but she schooled her features into a blank expression when she looked at up at her stepbrother.

"Joe texted."

Duncan winced. "Everything okay?"

"Yeah." She nodded, but it hit her that she'd had her head so far up her own butt, she hadn't even asked after Kenzi lately.

"Berkley okay?" His voice was gruff and his shoulders were stiff, and he looked like he could chew a mouthful of nails.

"She's fine."

She bristled under Duncan's once over. Stevi must have told him Jess had her.

"You know what?"

He arched his eyebrows.

"It could be you. As many women as you've been with, it could be you slinking back to try and have a relationship with your child."

Anger flared in his eyes, but he kept his mouth shut tight, his jaw clenched.

"This is about more than Jess having a relationship with Berkley." He forced the words out through gritted teeth, his jaw still clenched with anger.

"It is," she agreed. "Stevi could have left. You know that? Right? She could be working a bar in Nashville right now."

"Jesus, Margo." He threw his arms up in frustrated defeat.

"But she believed in you," Margo reminded him. "She loved you."

"Are you really calling me a heartless bastard?" Duncan stepped closer to her. Margo's heart pounded up her throat both with regret over the words she and Duncan were throwing at each other and with the anticipation of what Jess would say to that flirty text. "Comparing me to him?"

"No." She shook her head, but she lowered her gaze. The eye contact was too painful. "I'm saying maybe you don't know him as well as you think you do."

"Margo. I just think you're making a mistake," he said quietly.

"He's my mistake to make, though, isn't he?" She slipped around him and hurried back to the bar. If she weren't going home to him, if Jess weren't watching Berkley tonight, she would have a drink. But no matter what happened tonight when she got home, and she doubted anything would happen, she didn't want alcohol on her breath.

She might at least get a goodnight kiss.

Jess texted her back about fifteen minutes later. Margo was mid pour with two glasses of Dykstra when her phone buzzed. She managed to play it cool long enough to finish the pour, hand the glasses over the counter to the two women waiting, and then step back out of the spotlight for a moment.

I like pretend kissing you almost as much as I like kissing you.

Okay, so she should take it easy. Flirting didn't really mean anything. Still. She and Jess knew how to talk dirty, but they had never really done the fun, sweet, and sexy flirting. It was hard not to get caught up in the fun, the anticipation.

He followed that text up with another picture of Berkley, this one in her car seat in his truck. She had her coat on, pointy hood sticking up in the air, a big grin on her face.

Certainly didn't seem like she needed to worry about Berkley missing her.

The rest of the night passed quickly. The Queen stayed busy enough that she didn't have to worry about conversation with Duncan. She and Leah talked for a while, the conversation interrupted several times as they moved through the room, waiting tables and talking to customers. They swapped pregnancy stories, Margo careful not to preach or over share. She had hated when pregnant women had done that to her, just as it annoyed her when the mother of a preschooler decided to impart wisdom now. If she asked, it was one thing. But Margo figured she was reasonably intelligent, she'd been raised by a more than capable, loving mom, and she made every decision in Berkley's life based on how much she loved her.

Leah and Trace left before eleven. Once Duncan locked the front door, Margo put her head down and busied herself with clean up. She didn't particularly want another run in with Duncan, and even more than that, she was anxious to get home. There had been no emergency phone calls, and Jess texted her through the remaining hours of business, so she knew Berkley was okay. But she was still anxious to get home and see her.

And him.

Stevi asked her how the night had gone, and while Margo wanted to talk to her about Jess and their time together earlier, she wasn't going to get into it now, with Duncan around. Instead, she simply said it looked like Jess and Berkley had had a good night. She found herself wondering what they'd done, though, as she worked. Surely, he had taken her to his mom's house, since he had sent the picture of Berk in the car seat. Had his sisters been there? Did they still hate her the way Duncan hated Jess? Would it ever change? And if it didn't, could she and Jess move forward at all with a relationship?

She left the Queen around 12:30. Stevi and Duncan were still finishing up the close, but Stevi scurried her out, knowing she was dying to get home. Margo reminded herself there wasn't much left to do. Maybe Duncan would run upstairs and run through the office to make sure everything was in its place. Stevi would walk through one more time to make sure the tables were cleared and the bar clean. They would take the deposit by the bank tonight or tomorrow. Duncan had always been the one to take care of it, because he didn't want the girls dealing with night deposits.

Jess' truck was parked in the drive, same place it had been when she left for work earlier. The house was quiet when she slipped in the back door. The lights were out, but the TV flickered in the living room. Margo set her purse and keys on the counter and tiptoed into the living room. Jess was sprawled on the couch, eyes on the TV, where he appeared to be watching a Jason Bourne movie.

Margo's heart and belly squeezed and flip-flopped when she noticed the baby monitor on the end table. He would hear Berkley if she fussed, even without the monitor. But the fact that he'd thought to bring it to the living room with him sent a rush of love and grief through her. How could she have taken away the first year of his daughter's life? Yes, they'd had problems, but he was a good guy at heart. His family was a good, hardworking, compassionate family, and she'd hurt them all when she'd sent him away.

He twisted his head around now to see her standing there watching him. It occurred to her that he had gone into her bedroom to get the monitor from her dresser. She wondered if he'd lingered. If he'd spent any time remembering the things they'd done in the bed.

As if he had to be in the bedroom to think about their sex life. They'd been all over each other in every room in the house, so there wasn't really anything special about the bedroom. Except that they'd slept together night after night. Something about sleeping side by side suggested vulnerability and trust.

Not particularly romance, but then, Margo decided she might be too old to care about romance. Maybe they were both at the age when vulnerability, humility, and trust were more important.

Jess blinked at her and hitched his lips up in a lazy grin. Her body tingled with the memory of those soft, sweet kisses earlier in the kitchen.

"Hey." On his back, he propped himself up on his elbow and regarded her curiously. The lazy grin still there, Margo had to remind herself not to go to him and climb into his lap.

Okay. Maybe she would like a little romance. With Jess Covey. They hadn't tried that route to begin with, because she'd been all badass and bossy, and she thought she was above needing it in her life.

Maybe she was wrong.

"Hi."

Jess sat up and swung his legs over the side of the couch. He rubbed his eyes and then pushed his hands up through his hair, making it stand on end in places. His jacket was slung over the end of the couch, and his boots were stacked on the floor, one of them tipped sideways. His gray t-shirt stretched taut over his shoulders. Margo almost thought she could see a twinkle in his eyes, but she decided that was a line out of a cheesy romance novel.

"She is so incredible." He spoke quietly, his voice a little gruff with emotion, and Margo wondered if she was wrong. If that was a twinkle in his eyes, because he was over the moon for Berkley Nevin Covey.

Maybe she'd been wrong about a lot of things, she decided as she moved closer to him. The problem was learning how to swallow her pride, because it was big and a little rough around the edges, and say she was sorry.

CHAPTER 29

M_ARGO_ MOVED CLOSER, BUT SHE STILL KEPT HER DISTANCE, and she watched him like she was weary of getting too close. For a second, Jess felt a jab of worry. What if while she was gone, when she was at work, she decided she didn't like the idea of Jess being responsible for Berkley? What if she'd been about to leave several times, to come home and take over, but Stevi had stopped her?

Or…what if she had been on the fence about the whole thing, and then Duncan had said something and pushed her, making her decide that Jess watching Berkley was a mistake? That seemed likely.

Then again, she had texted him about pretend kisses.

"What's wrong?" he asked when she didn't say anything.

"Nothing." She dropped her head back and took a long, deep breath. "Nothing. And you're right. She really is incredible."

"She's so smart." He leaned forward and propped his elbows on his knees and again ran his hands over the scruff on his face. "She just watches everything, and she learns so quickly."

"What'd you guys do?"

Margo glanced at the recliner, and Jess had to clench his jaw shut to keep from saying no, asking her to sit closer to him. She eyed him for a second, and then she crossed the room to sit near him on the couch.

"We played with her toys for a long time." Jess watched Margo unzip her boots and slide them off, one at a time. "She called you on her cell phone a few times."

Margo laughed softly.

"And we read a lot of books."

"She loves books."

"Well, she spent a lot of time looking at me when I was reading."

"Typical woman." Margo grinned. "Can't keep her eyes off you."

"Right." Jess rolled his eyes. "Maybe she was wondering where you were."

"Maybe she recognizes your voice." Margo met his eyes, but she quickly looked away. "From being around when I was pregnant."

The suggestion hit him hard and took his breath away. His chest expanded with the possibility, and he felt all puffed up with hope. And fear. What if Margo was messing with him?

"Is that possible?"

"Well, yeah. My doctor said it was when she was born. That she recognized my voice. I mean, it's been a while… but. You're her father. You were here."

"Not enough."

They sat for a moment, Margo apparently lost in thought, and Jess lost in regret.

"So." She cleared her throat and bravely met his eyes again. "Did you go see your parents?"

"We did." He grinned, and that same surge of happiness that had been hitting him all night ramped up his heartbeat again. "We spent quite a while over there."

When she didn't say anything, he held his breath. Should he ask if it was okay with her? Did he have to ask? He didn't have custody of Berkley. He didn't have visitation rights. He had nothing but Margo's gift of time she was giving him with his little girl. He didn't want to be a pushover, but he didn't want to push her too hard, either.

"Is that okay?" It pained him to ask, but for now, he didn't want to rock the boat.

"Yeah." She nodded quickly. "It's good. Were Lori and Melissa there?"

"They came over," he answered. They had cried. There had been a few times through the evening that Jess had felt his eyes burn a bit, but he'd held himself together.

Until he brought Berkley home and got her ready for bed. When he'd rocked her to sleep and carried her to her crib, he had let a tear or two go.

"Good." She nodded again as if that was the end of the conversation. Jess didn't want to leave. He was tired, and he figured Margo was beat. He wasn't sure how she'd done it the past year; the single mother gig alone had to wear her out, even if she thought it was the best job in the world. But balancing that with running a business with Leah and Stevi—a bar, no less, where she put in long, late hours—had to be exhausting.

But he didn't want the evening to end. They'd had an okay day; they'd made some strides—at least they'd talked a bit. Didn't mean they were in the free and clear, but surely, if they kept talking, they could work through the distance and the bitter feelings between them.

"How was your night?"

"My night?" She flopped backwards to rest on the couch and yawned. "It was good. I don't work a lot of late nights these days. They always want me to get home for Berk. And I do love being home with her. I think it's important that she wake up to me and that I'm putting her to bed most nights. But the late hours are too much for Leah. And it's not fair to put it all on Stevi and Duncan."

"You worked with him tonight."

When she didn't respond, he nudged her knee. She was sitting too far away to bump her leg with his. He wanted to remedy that, but he didn't want her to think he was putting the moves on her. As good as it would be—and his dick sure as hell perked up at the thought—it just wasn't enough.

She rolled her head on the couch and nodded.

"Did he know I had Berkley?"

"Stevi told him."

Again, he could keep going. Say something rude about Duncan. But he didn't want to. Wasn't likely that he and Duncan were ever going to stand at a grill in the backyard and shoot the shit while they flipped burgers for their families. But he was tired of that, too. Like it or not, Duncan and Margo were close. If Jess had any thoughts about a future with Margo, he would have to deal with Duncan, too.

"Do you want me to go?" He twisted around to get a good look at her face. In the nearly dark room, she looked tired, but content. She shrugged one shoulder. "What's wrong, Margo? What're you thinking?"

"What am I thinking?" She raised her eyebrows and breathed deeply. "I'm thinking how wrong I was for what I did to you. And your family."

He was shaking his head before she finished her sentence.

"We talked about this. If you hadn't given me the ultimatum, I wouldn't have seen what I was doing as wrong. I wouldn't have changed. And the last thing I want to do is be that guy, that dad who never keeps his promises because he was drunk when he made them or drunk when it came time to deliver."

From the corner of his eye, he saw that Margo was about to say something, but he shook his head quickly and held up his hand to stop her.

"I don't wanna hurt you anymore, either. I never wanted to hurt you." He sighed and covered his face with his hands. He was lying. That last line was a lie, and he could either take it back now or push forward while he carried that lie around. "You know what? That's a lie."

"What's a lie?" she whispered.

"I did want to hurt you." He huffed out a cathartic sigh. "Not all the time. Not every day. Not when I was having one more at the bar before I came home."

"Then when?" She sat forward, but rather than get up, she leaned into him and scooted sideways on the couch.

"I don't know. But there were certain times, certain things that just made me so mad. Things you did. And instead of confronting you, instead of fighting, I hurt you."

"When Berkley was born."

"Well. Yeah." He climbed to his feet and paced across the room. "That was the big one. But there were other times, too. All the times you insisted you didn't need my help. You didn't want me to do anything for you; you handled everything yourself. The upkeep on the house. Fixing the faucet in the kitchen. Replacing the furnace filter. Running to the post office to mail a bill."

"Jess."

"Sex." He linked his fingers behind his neck and then turned slowly to face her.

"Sex?"

All in, he reminded himself. He'd gone too far not to finish now.

"You always have to touch yourself first. You never gave me your first orgasm. You didn't trust me to know your body well enough to make you feel good, so you did it first. Just in case."

"Did I say that?" She sounded sad, rather than angry, as he feared she would be. "I mean…when we were together. Did I really say that?"

"Are you saying I'm wrong?"

He watched her struggle to answer him. Felt his heart break again when she finally relented and shook her head.

"Even after all the times we were together, you had to be in control for the first time. Because you didn't trust me. Maybe you were trying to remind me you didn't need me in the bedroom, either."

"Jess." She sobbed. He watched helplessly as she swiped at her eyes and then pushed her hair from her face. "I didn't mean to emasculate you."

"No, I don't think you did. And I'm not saying I don't love watching you pleasure yourself or that I wouldn't love to see you do it right now. I'm just saying after a while, it hit me that you didn't need me. For anything. Maybe you still don't."

She sniffled and licked her lips.

"You got the only thing you really needed from me." He nodded pointedly at the baby monitor. She winced, silent tears sliding over her cheeks.

"My mom was…completely dependent on my dad." She gathered her hair in her hands and held it at the back of her neck for just a moment. "I mean, she couldn't fill her car with gas without his help. She needed him to do all the upkeep on the house. He balanced the checkbook. He did their taxes. He did car maintenance."

Jess dropped his hands to his sides.

"I've never seen that in your mother."

"She learned," Margo whispered. "When Dad left."

Her mother had learned to trust or rely on no one. And so had Margo.

Jess smoothed his hand over his jaw again.

"I guess I did, too." She stood slowly. "Maybe I thought the less I leaned on you, the better. That you wouldn't feel smothered."

"Or maybe you felt like you couldn't trust me to do what needed to be done."

She was going to argue, but Jess saw the truth in her eyes.

"Maybe."

"I should've pushed this. All of it. Before I left."

Margo cleared her throat. "Would you still have left?"

"Yes." He nodded. "Because I had to grow up. You weren't the only one concerned about my drinking. About my careless attitude. I hated you for making me leave, but it was the best thing anyone has ever done for me. Yes, I regret missing the first year of her life. And I will be here now for the rest of my life. But if I hadn't walked away to grow up, I would have hurt you again and again. I'm sorry, Margo. For that truth."

She nodded and dashed at her eyes.

"But I don't want to move forward with any lies between us."

"Why are you telling me this now?"

"I had every intention from the time I left...after I got over being pissed...I had every intention, every hope of coming back to you and Berkley. Julie was key in making me see that you and I both made mistakes, and when she asked if she could come along to meet you and Berk, it never crossed my mind that you would think we were together."

"I had it in my head." Margo narrowed her eyes and sniffled. "I had it in my head every time we talked on the phone, every time you would text me about your progress, your job, I thought you would come back for both of us. And it killed me to look up and find her with you."

"Margo, I love you."

His throat was tight, and his chest burned with the need to breathe, to gasp a deep breath. He'd said those words to a few girls when he was younger, and he supposed he meant them then as much as a young kid with no clue for a future could. But he had never said them and meant them so much, so deeply in his life.

"How many women were you with, Jess? This past year?"

"The other night with you is the first time I've had sex since I left."

Margo stared at him with a touch of suspicion, but she slumped her shoulders and dropped her head forward to cover her face with her hands.

"I was with someone," she whispered. "Last year around Halloween. I was just…so angry with you. And so…needy." Jess didn't miss the sharp bitter note in her laughter. "I wanted you back, but I was still so angry."

"Did it happen more than once?"

She shook her head and slipped away from him. She paced the floor to stand at the front window.

"No. I mean…it was…" She didn't look at him when she shook her head and shrugged. "Lousy. He was a nice guy. We knew each other from the bar. That night with him killed any attraction I might have felt for him. Killed our friendship, too. He moved to St. Louis. And I was miserable because I wanted to justify what I did. I wanted to point out to anyone who asked that you and I weren't seeing each other anymore. And that you had cheated on me, so you deserved it anyway."

Jess agreed with her. To an extent. But he also wanted to

throat punch the bastard she'd brought home from the bar.

"Did someone ask you about it?" He tipped his head. "Like Leah and Stevi? Joe?"

"No one did," she said quietly. "So I had this ongoing argument in my head and my heart. Which made it worse."

"Margo." A year ago, he would have been embarrassed at the raw need in his voice, but tonight it didn't matter. In fact, he wanted Margo to hear it, to hear his desperation.

"I'm scared," she whispered.

"I don't want that to come between us now."

She nodded and then waved the concern away. "But I'm scared of us. I'm afraid I can't be who you want me to be. I'm afraid you'll find someone else."

"I love you," he repeated.

His heart pounded slow and loud in his throat and his ears, and Jess counted every beat as he waited for her to say something. Anything. Preferably a vow of love, but watching her watch him as she was terrified him.

Because he didn't have a plan B. He had worked his ass off this past year to come back to Adam's Bay and claim both Margo and Berkley as his. If Margo didn't want him back, he would still be Berkley's father, and he would be the best damned father a little girl could have. But he would be such a better man if he had Margo's love.

Finally, she gave him a quick, decisive nod. But she still didn't say anything. Jess propped his hands on his hips and dug his fingers into his waist. Margo hedged closer, eyes on his, sad but bold.

"I love you, too," she whispered.

"Sweet Jesus." He huffed out a hard sigh of relief and bent over at the waist, gasping now as if he had just run five miles to get to her.

"But, Jess."

He straightened slowly and met her eyes. The tremble in her voice unleashed a new wave of nerves.

"It's enough." He cupped her face in his hands and studied her eyes. "It's enough to know we love each other. We owe it to each other and ourselves to take the next step."

"The next step?" Her voice faltered, and her brows arched in surprise. "What does that mean?"

"Nothing big," he promised her. He offered her a cautious smile, afraid that she would think he was pushing her. "No big over the top gestures here, Margo. I thought I'd kiss you goodnight. And you could walk me to the door. And I'll be back tomorrow. Maybe Berkley and I can build a house again for you with her pink baby blocks."

Her laughter was soft, followed by a hiccup and a small sob.

"I could fix you breakfast," she offered. Jess' heart pounded up into his throat again when she covered his hands on her face with her own.

"I'd like that."

She was moving, leaning into him before he could kiss her. He wanted to lift her in his arms and march her down the short hall to her bedroom. To undress her and spend the next several days and nights worshipping her body, earning her trust and proving to her that he knew how to love her body.

But somehow, it felt wrong. Maybe this time he would take control and slow it down. Maybe he would earn her trust out here, in the real world—outside the bedroom—and prove to her that he knew how to love her heart and soul, before he loved her body.

Maybe he needed to earn the privilege of loving her body.

Maybe if he proved that he was here for the long haul, Margo would let her guard down and let him see she needed him, too.

CHAPTER 30

Berkley's face lit up with a smile when Margo's ringtone—"Rhinestone Cowboy"—filled the kitchen.

"What? Is that?"

Margo snorted when Jess whipped his head to look from Berkley to her.

"'Rhinestone Cowboy.'" She rolled her eyes. "Doesn't everyone know that?"

She leaned over to drop a kiss on top of Berkley's head—her black hair soft on Margo's lips—and stretched to grab her phone from the table. She glanced at the screen to see that it was Stevi calling, but she had bacon frying in one skillet, eggs in another, and biscuits in the oven. Stevi wouldn't mind if she let her go to voicemail; in fact, if she knew she was fixing breakfast for Berkley and Jess, she might encourage it.

"Well, yeah, I know the song." Jess laughed. "But. Why? Is it on your phone?"

"Trace." Margo put her phone down on the counter and checked the bacon. "He takes my phone all the time and messes with me. Either he's putting selfies on it or changing my ringtone to country stuff."

"Selfies, huh?"

Margo shot Jess a quick grin over her shoulder.

"I'm not complaining."

"That guy's right off a movie screen." Jess pulled his eyes from their daughter to look at Margo. He sounded a little bit awed by Trace, but his smile was all about Berkley.

"Stage," she corrected him. "And look in a mirror, Jess."

"Right." He nodded. "Okay, so, Trace messes with you. But Berkley likes that song?"

"She sure does," Margo agreed. The timer for the biscuits had less than two minutes to go, so she took plates from the cabinet, set them down, and then turned the skillets off.

"So she likes Glen Campbell and purple cowboy boots."

Margo turned again to watch him as he watched Berkley pick up a small bite of banana. The look of joy, the anticipation of laughter on his face as Berkley squished the banana too hard and pushed it in her mouth, made Margo's heart hurt.

"She does." Margo nodded. "And Willie Nelson."

"The work I have to do," he groaned softly, the look of joy turning to an ornery grin when he flicked his eyes to Margo. "Berkley, we're gonna find some AC/DC to listen to."

"She likes AC/DC," Margo admitted. "Really, she loves music. And Uncle Trace."

"Well, at least you have good taste in uncles, kid." Jess looked back at Berkley and winked. Margo continued to watch them as she carried two full plates to the table. The oven timer beeped, and Berkley's face molded into a mask of surprise. She squealed and clapped her hands together.

"Chew your banana." Margo clucked her under the chin as she made her way back to the oven. "And she's crazy about Uncle Duncan, too."

"Yeah, I figured," Jess mumbled. "Did you need to take that call?"

"It was Stevi," Margo answered. "I'll call her back when we're finished with breakfast."

"Maybe she'll be a musician." Jess scooped up a healthy bite of eggs and devoured them quickly.

"Stevi?"

He rolled his eyes, making Margo laugh.

He'd hung his coat up when he came in earlier this morning. Most likely, he hadn't meant any big deal with the act. Wasn't like he was marking his territory or planning to carry in a duffle bag or two to unpack and move in. But he'd hung up his coat, and Margo had felt a little flutter of something unexpected—though welcome —in her belly, watching him, and then again when he stepped away from the small closet in the living room and she'd caught a glimpse of his black leather mixed in with her coats.

He wore long-sleeves today, an emerald green thermal that somehow made his cheekbones appear razor sharp and his golden eyes pop. Or maybe that was just her. She'd slept last night after he left. After a kiss to seal the conversation and their walk to the door and the goodbye kiss. The goodbye kiss itself had been a mix of sexy and intimate and sweet and soft.

It filled her heart and left her wanting.

"Those eggs aren't going anywhere." She eyed his plate and then met his gaze. "There's no rush."

He laughed as he shoveled another bite in his mouth.

"I'm hungry." He put his fork down and sat back to study her as he chewed. Mouth closed, he was still grinning. "I was having so much fun with Berkley last night, I didn't eat much."

"But you ate. Right?"

"Yeah." He nodded and waved her concern away. "Yeah. Mom made chili. It was good. But." He shrugged and reached for his coffee.

"You need something hardy that'll stick to your bones."

He arched his brows at her over the mug.

"You always did." She shrugged, suddenly a little self-conscious under his stare.

"Tell you what I'd like to stick to my—"

She cut him off with a loud peal of laughter, and when Berkley imitated her—dropped her head back and cut loose with her own laugh—Margo and Jess only laughed harder.

"Maybe she'll be a singer in a rock 'n' roll band." Margo picked up a piece of bacon and held it for a moment before taking a bite.

"Over my dead body." Jess frowned and put his mug down. "You know what goes on when musicians are out on tour. Guys grop—"

"Oh, this is funny." Margo couldn't fight the smirk on her face or the hint of sarcasm in her voice. "How ironic that Jess Covey now has a baby girl to fawn over. You would have been the first in line to paw at a hot little chick in tight leather pants."

"Do you have leather pants?" He crunched his own bacon and then leaned forward to open the tub of butter on the table. Margo watched him dip his knife into the tub and then slather butter on the top of his biscuit. "We could do some role playing."

"You wish." She wiggled her eyebrows.

"When I said she might be a musician, I meant…like the harp or…grand piano or something."

Margo snorted and rolled her eyes.

"Never know."

"True," she agreed. Berkley finished her banana and smacked her pudgy hands on the highchair tray. "She might be a motorcycle ridin', foul-mouthed tomboy who can sink half court shots, too."

Jess' face lit up at the image, and he laughed, but he sat back again and sank his teeth into the biscuit.

"You'd be okay with that?"

"Which part?"

"Um." He nodded his head back and forth and stared at Berkley for a minute. Seeing she had his attention, Berkley shrieked and then rattled off a line of baby talk that ended in something that sounded suspiciously like Jess. Margo felt the word like a knife in her heart. "Well. Any of it. But the...foul-mouthed tomboy thing?"

"You don't want your little girl to be tough?"

"I want my little girl to grow up and be the kind of woman her mother is," he said simply. "Strong and independent."

Margo whooshed out a deep breath and nibbled on her lip. "Some guys find that a turn off."

"Some guys just need to open their eyes and appreciate what they have when they have it. Or maybe those kinds of girls and guys should just look for balance."

Uncomfortable again, Margo looked at Berkley. She had gooey banana smeared over her lips, so Margo leaned in to dab at them with her bib.

"No, no." Berkley shook her head emphatically, drawing a soft laugh from her father. Margo's hand trembled at the thought of Berkley picking up on who he was, calling him by name—weren't Leah and Stevi going to love that? Should she push it or was it time to tell Berkley Jess was her daddy?

Did it matter when she was so little?

Of course it did. Margo couldn't let her learn to call him Jess and then if he was still around three years from now, switch things up and have her call him Daddy. Talk about messing up your kid.

But. Would he? Still be around in three years? Next month? Five years? When Berkley was ten?

"What're you thinking?" He sounded concerned, like he sensed that her thoughts had turned dark and serious. Margo untied Berkley's bib and tossed it to the table.

"I would be thrilled if Berkley grew up to be a foul-mouthed tomboy who could shoot three pointers from half court, play the harp, and speed skate on ice." She took a sip of her coffee and lifted her eyes to meet his. "All I want for her is to be happy and to love herself just the way she is."

"Me, too." He held the eye contact. "Margo, I want you to be happy, too."

Stomach suddenly jittery and her breakfast not settling, she jumped up and started stacking dishes to carry to the sink. Okay, so she could admit to herself that she loved him. That she was in love with him. But she also had to face that fact that she didn't trust him. She wanted to. But she didn't.

Not yet.

"I didn't mean…" He sighed. Margo set the plates in the sink and then stood, shoulders hunched, ready for him to back step all the way out the door and deny that he meant what he said last night. To say he changed his mind. To announce that no strings attached sex was more his style.

"You didn't mean what?" Her voice was gruff, a mix of hurt and anger. She cleared her throat and waited, hands fisted on the counter, holding the weight of her body and her world, waiting for him to leave.

"Last night."

The chair squeaked quietly when he stood. She held her breath when she realized he was going to join her at the sink. Why? If he was about to break her heart yet again, why did he have to watch the hurt play out on her face?

"You didn't mean last night?" She turned to look at him, her voice sharp and aggressive, because she'd rather get her digs in and hurt him first than let him fire away at her.

"No, no, no." He pressed his body down the length of hers and leaned in to kiss her forehead, just along her hairline. "I love you. I meant that. I plan to be here forever. I meant that. I just…I said a lot of things to you that might have made you think I blamed you for everything that went wrong. I didn't mean that."

She swallowed hard, and her whole body sagged with relief.

"I don't want you to change because of what I said. I love you because you're you."

"Something's got to change, or we won't make it this time, either."

"Maybe we both do, just a little." He tipped his head and stared at her with wide eyes. "Maybe if I'm here, you can learn to lean just a little. And if you lean, maybe I'll do better. Do more. Be more for you. And then maybe we find out we make a good team."

Tears burned her eyes, and she nodded slowly. "Maybe."

"Takes two."

"I feel like you've ingested a library full of self-help books. You're coming at me with all of this wise, deep thinking, and here I am, still being that bossy, bitchy woman who would rather get herself off than let the man she loves do it."

"Um." The corner of his mouth tipped up in a lazy smirk. "Well, Julie spoon fed me real life examples that made me...more aware of who I was and who I wanted to be. And you've been busy. You've been the greatest single mom to a fantastic kid and a kickass business owner."

Margo dropped her gaze to the plates in the sink.

"As for getting yourself off—again, it's the hottest thing I've seen. But maybe now and then, you could let me do it. First."

Her face in flames and her chest too tight to breathe, she could only nod.

"Maybe we could go on a date one of these times when I'm home."

His hand was on her ass suddenly, but he wasn't grabbing or rubbing. It was just there, his thumb hooked in the back of her jeans and his hand there, almost protectively.

"Dinner. Dancing." He shrugged his eyebrows. "Or maybe dinner here and some building blocks and a story, and we could tuck Berkley in and then…go to bed together."

"She's a pretty sound sleeper," Margo mumbled, but she couldn't help the grin.

"If that's a challenge, I'm more than ready to take you up on it."

"You didn't want to last night," she reminded him.

Jess dragged his hand up over her back and then squeezed her shoulder. "I don't wanna do that empty, hard sex and then walk away. I want to make love to you, Margo."

"Dammit, Jess." Her laugh was shaky. "You're not playing fair."

"Sounds good, doesn't it?"

"Yes." She nodded, and then even knowing Berkley was still in her highchair, knowing Berkley had gone silent so she had to be watching them, Margo turned to him and pressed herself against him. She buried her face in his neck and pulled in a slow, deep breath, warmed by his familiar scent.

"I know you have doubts, Margo, but give me the chance

to show you how much I want you back in my life. Let me love you."

She wondered again about Berkley and when the right time would be for Margo to refer to Jess as her daddy. Not a decision to be made lightly. Not when it involved her daughter's heart.

"I want you to love me, Jess," she whispered, eyes closed. "I've always wanted you to love me. I didn't know how to ask."

"There's something I have to tell you."

"See? This is the stuff that scares the hell out of me, Jess. You say these incredibly romantic things, and you make me hope for the real thing, ya know? The joy I see Leah and Stevi live now with Trace and Duncan. I want that, too. And you tempt me with it and follow it up with a line like that?"

"Margo." He rubbed his chin over her head and then eased her away just enough that he could see her face. "It's not bad. I don't have something bad to say. But I do want to tell you this."

She scraped her teeth over lip and answered with a reluctant nod.

"I put my notice in with Derrick." He cupped her chin in his hand to hold her still. "I gave him my notice a while back. He told me to work until I couldn't. Until I had to get home to you."

"He knows about me? And Berkley?" she whispered, a little bit breathless with hope.

"Every guy on every roof with me knows about you and Berkley."

Margo sniffled and reached to swipe at her tears.

"What're you gonna do?"

"I'm coming back to Adam's Bay," he said simply. "I can't stand this seeing you and Berkley on the weekends."

Her lips formed a surprised O, but she didn't make a sound.

"I'll work with a construction crew," he continued. "I'm not worried about finding a job. I have a solid work reputation here, and Derrick will give me a good reference."

"Okay."

"But, I thought I might look for something more."

Margo felt a stab of guilt. She used to nag him to find something better. If he had a degree, she would tell him he should have an office job. Not necessarily for bigger money, but maybe less physical stress on his body.

She blinked as she stared at him and then she touched his face. Smoothed her hand over the scruff that even Berkley found fascinating and pressed her thumb to his lips.

"If that's what you want," she said quietly. "But don't do that for me. You like that kind of work. Don't let me take that from you."

Jess curled his fingers around her wrist and kissed her thumb.

"Thank you."

"Where will you live?"

He shook his head. "I'm not rushing back into your house."

His words sucked the hope from her heart again.

"Margo, babe, I don't want to push you. I don't want to rush anything. I am going to walk the line this time. I don't wanna do that to Berkley. Let's be in love and date and hang out."

"Is that all you want?"

"No." He lowered his head to kiss her. "But the next time I move in here, you'll be wearing a ring and your name will be Margo Covey."

She gasped out loud and then laughed a little self-consciously.

"You wanna marry me?"

"Yes."

"What makes you think I'll say yes?"

"I don't, yet." He rested his forehead against hers and took a deep breath. "That's why I want time to earn your trust. And make you crazy in love with me."

She slipped her arms around his waist and stepped closer.

"You're already half way there, Jess."

Berkley cut loose with an angry screech, apparently tired of being ignored. Margo laughed softly, but she kissed him back when he snuck a quick one before backing away from her.

"The boss speaks." Jess turned to Berkley and then glanced at Margo.

"You don't have to ask me, Jess," she whispered and nodded toward the highchair. She watched him slide the tray out and then unbuckle her. All smiles, Berkley lifted her arms for Jess to pick her up.

Margo's phone sounded again, and the same look of delight lit her little girl's face.

"Oh." Jess groaned and shook his head. "That's just so wrong."

"She likes to dance," Margo told him as she picked up her phone to see Stevi's number again. She glanced back at Jess with a frown. "Stevi again. Hang on."

"Hey, Stevi." She kept her eyes on Jess as he two-stepped—sort of—around the kitchen with Berkley in his arms. Margo wasn't sure whose smile was happier, his or Berkley's. "Everything okay? Is Leah okay?"

"Hey." Stevi sounded out of breath. "Yeah. Everything's good. I just loaded groceries in the car. I hate grocery shopping."

"Me, too. I just fixed breakfast."

"Bowl of cereal and a glass of orange juice?"

"No. Bacon—"

"No, no. Never mind breakfast. I wanted to tell you I set you up with someone. Take a shower and put adult clothes on. You have a dinner date tonight."

"Stevi." Margo groaned. "Who? That Shawn guy? I told you I don't wanna do this. I don't need a date. I took it back. Remember?"

Jess stopped moving and watched her with intense eyes.

"Margo, I can't just tell him you changed your mind. Just go out on one date. Nothing says you have to go out with him again."

Margo sighed and stared helplessly back at Jess.

"Jess is here."

Margo was mildly pleased that Stevi seemed speechless for a second.

"Like…Jess is there, and you guys had breakfast in bed?"

"No."

"Okay, so what's the problem? Just go out on this one date. It's dinner. Surely Jess can deal with that, right? He'll be heading back to Greenville tonight, anyway. He always leaves on Sundays."

Margo pressed her lips together and turned away from Jess.

"I can't believe you did this to me, Stevi."

"Well, you kind of put me in a bad spot, Margo."

"Fine." Margo ducked her head and rubbed the back of her neck.

"Good. I told him you would want to be home early for Berk. I'll babysit."

"Glad you thought of everything." Margo hoped Stevi heard the sarcasm in her voice. She ended the call and then stood for a moment, dreading the questions Jess was going to have.

"I heard her." He spoke quietly. It sounded like he was still standing in the center of the kitchen. "At the Queen one night. Talking about setting you up with someone."

Margo nodded and breathed deeply as she turned to look at him.

"I'm sorry."

Berkley lay with her head on his chest. The sight of her pudgy hand wrapped around his arm—Margo knew how hard and strong that bicep was under her baby girl's fingers—gripped her heart and squeezed it tight. This was everything she had ever wanted for Berkley, for Jess to come home and love her.

"Well." Jess sighed. Margo wondered if he realized he was rocking gently, his big hand splayed over Berkley's back. "I mean. It's one night."

Margo swallowed hard, but she could only nod.

"It's not even a real night. It's Sunday."

"You're really not upset about this?" She tipped her head and frowned. Tiny sparks of doubt warmed her belly. If the guy who was in love with her didn't mind that she was going out with someone else, didn't that seem to be a red flag?

"Margo." He nuzzled his cheek over Berkley's curls. "I want to stay. And answer the door. And rip the guy's nuts off and shove 'em down his throat."

Despite the rollercoaster of emotions, the thrill of the conversation, and the misgivings that still plagued her, she snorted softly and mouthed the word *wow*.

"I don't wanna go," she whispered. "And I don't want you to go."

"C'mere." He reached his hand out to her, and Margo's eyes filled when Berkley reached out to her, also. She dabbed at her eyes as she went to him, forgetting her rules that he couldn't kiss her in front of Berkley. It wasn't a sexy kiss, but it was intimate and possessive. Berkley wound her fingers in Margo's hair and then patted her head.

"I don't want another man to look at you." Jess kissed a trail from her lips to her cheekbone. "But you're a beautiful woman who runs a bar. And every guy in that bar every night has his eyes all over you, thinking about what it would be to put his hands on you."

"Jess—"

"It's okay," he continued. "You own a bar. I'm gonna have to deal with that. And this is Stevi. You guys were doing this before I was back, so I get it. Stevi went out on a limb for you. Go out for dinner. Tell him if he touches you, I'll cut his dick off and feed it to my dog."

"You don't have a dog," she reminded him. She was laughing softly, eyes on Berkley, who was thankfully too young to catch anything Jess was saying.

"I'll get one. Just for that. The meanest goddamned dog I can find. With big, sharp teeth."

Margo swiped at her tears again.

"It wasn't before you were back, though." She shook her head. "We had talked about it, but I didn't give her the okay until you walked into my bar with Julie."

"It's okay." He pressed his lips to her face again. "It's gonna be okay. I have to go back anyway. I'm gonna start packing. So I get back home."

"You're going back to Julie." She rolled her lips inward and stared at him with sad eyes.

"And I'll tell her that if she tries anything, you'll cut her boobs off and feed them to your dog."

Margo laughed and shook her head. "Jess."

"I love you. If we're gonna make this work, we have to start now. Please. Trust me."

"Well, I want to, and I don't wanna feed Julie's boobs to a dog, because I like her. She's a good kid. I don't want to dislike her because of you—"

"You don't have to." He shook his head. "I promise you."

CHAPTER 31

Jess left before five. Margo had no idea what time the mystery date was supposed to show up, and even though they'd had a good day together—she and Jess and Berkley—she was still irritated with Stevi and herself, too, since she'd started the whole mess, when she opened the front door at six to find Duncan on the porch. She looked over his shoulder for Stevi, but when she didn't see her, she turned her attention back to Duncan.

"What? Is she afraid to see me after this squirrely move?" she asked Duncan.

"Hey, Margs."

Margo turned her back to Duncan when she heard Stevi holler from the back door.

"What're you doing?" Margo called to Stevi. She looked back at Duncan with exasperation and then stepped around him to close the door when he came inside.

"Here to babysit." Stevi appeared in the doorway from the kitchen.

"Are you guys fighting?" Margo looked from Stevi to Duncan and back to Stevi.

"Nope." Stevi shrugged out of her fleece jacket and draped it over the arm of the recliner.

"Is that how you dress for dates?"

Margo whipped her head around, ready to rip on Duncan for the comment. He dragged his eyes down over her gray cowl neck sweater and her skinny jeans tucked into her long, low-heeled black boots.

"What does that mean?"

He answered with an exaggerated shrug. "You look like a mom."

"I am a mom," she reminded him.

"Steefi!" Berkley squealed. Despite the overwhelming feeling of anger and dread for what was to come, Margo had to laugh.

"Berkley!" Stevi was already on the floor with Berkley. Margo watched Stevi scoop Berkley up and kiss her cheek. "How's my favorite little girl?"

"Are you ready?" Duncan nudged Margo with his elbow. She looked back at him quickly.

"I'm not changing, if that's what you mean," she snapped. "He can take it or leave it, Duncan. Stevi, who am I supposed to be going out with tonight?"

Stevi, legs stretched out in front of her and Berkley plopped in her lap, stared at Margo innocently.

"I'll take it," Duncan told her. He nudged her again and nodded to the door. "Are you ready? Where's your coat?"

"What?"

"Duncan's your date, Margo," Stevi said quietly.

"Duncan's…" Margo mumbled. She turned her back to Stevi and stared at Duncan sadly. "What?"

"C'mon." This time, his nudge and his voice were gentle. Her eyes burned with emotion—whether it was more dread and anger or maybe a little guilt this time, she couldn't say. She took a deep breath and answered him with a small nod. She stepped around Stevi and Berkley, now both with their heads bent over Berkley's toy cell phone.

She wondered where Duncan planned to take her. Her stomach churned so much, she couldn't imagine eating anything. Maybe it was time to do this, to talk to her stepbrother. But the weekend with Jess—as good as it was —had drained her. She would have liked a day or two to get herself together before this happened.

The memory of Jess hanging his coat in the closet earlier in the morning when he'd first come over slammed into her when she pulled the door open. She missed it already. She missed him; she missed the feeling of contentment she'd felt today, having him here with her and Berkley. She reached for her own jacket, wondering if it was too soon. If she was setting herself up for heartache. The thing was, it was her decision to make. And with it being so new, again, she wasn't ready to defend herself or her choices to Duncan.

She pulled a lightweight leather jacket on and wished it were Jess' coat. She could use a little bit of him with her right now. Speaking of Jess, he was probably wondering what was going on here. Who she was going out with tonight. Duncan stood with his back against the front door, arms folded over his chest. He didn't appear sullen or angry, though. In fact, he was watching Stevi and Berkley, with the hint of a smile on his face. Margo wondered if he wanted kids. She snatched her phone from the end table and then reached for her purse.

"Leave it," he told her with a firm shake of his head. "I'll buy."

So, they were doing this. Going on a date. Where she was going to have to sit and talk to him. About Jess.

The pre-Stevi Duncan didn't want kids. Had nothing against them. In fact, he loved Berkley; he was the perfect uncle. But he'd never been the type to commit to any woman, let alone a lifestyle or a family. She supposed it was perspective, because now that he was with Stevi, Margo could picture him in the future with his own child.

"Hey," Stevi called as Margo neared the door and Duncan pulled it open. Margo glanced at her, Berkley still in her lap. Margo wanted to text Jess, but first she had to tell Berkley goodbye. She shoved her phone in her pocket and then squatted down and held her arms out.

"You be good." She laughed softly as Berkley flopped forward and crawled toward her. The three of them watched as Berkley pulled up on her knees, took Margo's hands, and climbed up to stand before her.

"Say, Mommy, I'm always good." Stevi met Margo's eyes.

Berkley rattled something, the look on her face earnest as if promising to be on her best behavior.

"I love you." She kissed Berkley's head and smoothed her hand over her daughter's curls. But she held Stevi's gaze, still a little stung at the setup.

"Bring me something to eat, Duncan Marks." Stevi lifted her eyes to look at him over Margo's head.

"You bet."

Margo turned Berkley in her arms and then held her hands as she toddled back to Stevi. When Stevi took her, she grabbed Margo's hand and squeezed it. Under Stevi's desperate look, Margo gave her a half-hearted squeeze back and then stood. She pulled her phone from her pocket as she stepped outside.

She silently dared Duncan to comment as she texted Jess to let him know she was with her stepbrother. He didn't, though. Didn't even roll his eyes or mutter something sarcastic as they walked to his car. Margo rolled her eyes at him when he slipped around her to open her car door, but she thought about Jess, about the things he'd said about her not letting him do things for her. Not exactly the same, but maybe it wouldn't hurt to try and relax a bit.

Her phone buzzed in her lap as she buckled her seatbelt.

Really not sure that makes me feel any better.

She laughed softly as she texted back that she would talk to him when she got home. Duncan started the car, but he was looking at her. Again, she expected him to deliver some biting remark about Jess, but he only asked what she was hungry for.

"I'm not, really, Duncan," she mumbled.

"Good. Then I get to choose." He flashed her a grin and drew another quiet laugh from her.

"Whose idea was this?" she asked after he'd navigated a few streets and stoplights.

"Mine."

She wasn't sure if she was surprised or not. Part of her had expected that, but she wouldn't have been surprised to find out Stevi had cooked it up. She had always been close to Leah and Stevi, and she still talked to them. But as close as she was to Duncan, she had learned early on with Jess not to say too much about him to Duncan.

"You couldn't have just come by?"

"You know how many times I've tried to talk to you lately? You either want to argue, or you blow me off."

"I don't like lectures." She stared out her window, not willing to look at him. "That's why I quit school."

"I don't like lectures, either," he answered. "But I like knowing what the hell's going on with people I care about. I like talking to my sister."

"Where are you going?" She leaned forward to look out the windshield.

"I'm dying for pizza. And that'll be easy to take back to Stevi."

She didn't care. In fact, if she were being honest, she would admit she was a bit hungry, and pizza did sound good. Still out of sorts, she didn't admit that to him. Instead, she rested her head on the seat and stared silently out the window.

Since it was a Sunday, Little Italy Pizza wasn't busy, and all too soon, Margo found herself at a table, with nowhere to look but at Duncan. They spent a few minutes looking at the menu, but they'd known each other too long to pretend they didn't know they both wanted pepperoni and sausage on thin crust. Duncan asked for a draft beer, and when he tipped his head and gave her a frown when she asked for a glass of water, she added a draft beer, too. Once the waitress was gone, menus gone with her, Margo figured they would get down to business. Which, she assumed, was bashing Jess.

Duncan propped his chin in his hand, though, and spent a few minutes staring out the window above their table.

"Can you believe it's November already?" He finally moved. Chin still in his hand, he twisted around to look at her. "Have you started Christmas shopping?"

"No."

"Imagine what it'll be like in another year or two with Berkley." He grinned.

"She'll be a monster with all the toys," Margo answered.

"I don't know what to get Stevi."

Margo studied his face, interested in the creases in his forehead. He seemed…concerned wasn't the right word. Pensive, maybe. Definitely had something on his mind.

"Get her some sexy shoes," she suggested, and she sat back when the waitress returned with their beers.

"She has more shoes than Nordstrom." Duncan cut her an are-you-freaking-kidding-me look?.

"Girls can never have too many shoes."

"There's no more closet space for shoes, Margo. Unless I start getting rid of my stuff."

Margo grinned and reached for her glass. "Just how much do you love her, Duncan? Maybe you should have a garage sale?"

"I think most people would prefer it if I continued to wear pants on a daily basis."

"Me being one of them," she said with a quick nod.

She lifted her glass for a drink.

"Stevi wants kids, doesn't she?"

"What?" Margo choked on the cold beer as it slid down her throat. She put her glass down with a thunk and then slapped her hand over her chest a couple of times. "What did you say?"

"Does she?"

Margo coughed and then ducked her face to her hands. What the hell? She had assumed Duncan was going to give her hell for being with Jess. She certainly hadn't expected this conversation to happen.

"And don't give me that line about how all women want kids—"

"I'm not gonna give you that line, Duncan." She shook her head. "Besides, not every woman wants kids."

"But Stevi?"

Margo puffed her cheeks up with air and then let it out slowly. "Yeah. Yeah, I think she does."

Duncan gritted his teeth, but he nodded.

"Um. It's really not that bad, just so you know." She reached over the table and touched his hand, but she was quick to pull hers away. "Berkley's the best thing that ever happened to me."

"You know I'm crazy about your kid." He rubbed his hands over his face and then back up over his bald head. "And I don't think it's a horrible thought. It's just…six months ago, Stevi and I were, like, best friends and hanging out and having fun. And then we were flirting."

"Yeah, saw that." She nodded, arched a brow and hoped he heard the sarcastic note in her voice.

"And now…I can't imagine not waking up with her every day. And—"

Margo snorted.

"What?" Duncan asked quickly. He dropped his hands to lay flat on the table.

"Nothing, Duncan. It's just…you and Stevi." She giggled and then covered her mouth to hide it. "I love it. I love you guys, but it's just so weird. To think of you guys waking up together. Even weirder to think of you going to bed together."

"No." He shook his head. "Don't. Don't think about that. I'm just saying that as crazy as this all seems, what's even harder to believe is that I lived so much of my life without her love."

Margo coughed again and reached for her beer.

"Too much?" He laughed.

"It's very sweet," she admitted. "It really is. Like I feel sick to my stomach it's so sweet."

He rolled his eyes and took his first drink.

"Don't panic because she wants kids. Duncan, she loves you. She's not gonna just…up and leave you if you don't want babies."

He huffed out a quick breath and nodded. Stared at something behind her.

"I mean." He shrugged his right shoulder with practiced nonchalance. "I never said never."

Margo chuckled. "This is entertaining."

"What?"

"I thought you brought me out to kick my ass about Jess, and instead, you're feeling me out about having a family with Stevi."

"I'm not feeling you up."

Margo shivered. "I didn't say that, and it's a good thing. Because Jess said he'd like to…um…let's see…knock your teeth down your throat."

"Wait. What?" Duncan suddenly sat up taller, as if someone had kicked him in the ass. "He's gonna knock my teeth down my throat?"

"Oh God! No!" Margo laughed and shook her head. "My date's. Before he knew it was you. He also said if my date touched me, he would cut his dick off and feed it to his dog."

"He doesn't have a dog."

"No, but he said he'd get the meanest dog he could find."

Duncan's lips twitched, and the move carried the same disdain an eye roll would.

"So he can fuck around on you, but God forbid, someone ask you out."

"And here we go."

"He hurt you."

"He did." Margo shrugged. "Yes, he hurt me. You hurt Stevi. Leah hurt Nashville."

"It's not the same."

"Kind of," she argued. "Look, this isn't your fight, Duncan. It's not your choice. You don't control me."

"I don't want to control you. I just want to protect you."

"Well, you can't. I'm a grown woman. I have to make my own choices and live with the consequences."

"Stevi said you're in love with him."

"When did she say that?"

Duncan waved his fingers impatiently. "Before she and I were together."

Margo sighed and nodded. "I am, Duncan. I didn't know it. Or maybe, I felt it and fought it. I don't know. Jess and I both made mistakes, but they aren't your business—"

"Because—?" He shrugged. "Why? Because I'm a guy?"

"What does that have to do with it?"

"You talk to Stevi and Leah."

"Well, they don't go all superhero on me and try to shield me from life."

"So you admit it. You tell them things you don't tell me."

Margo sighed and sat back in the booth.

"Why isn't it enough that I love him?"

"You tell me. Why wasn't that enough for him?"

"That's not what I meant."

"Here's the deal." Duncan started, but he stopped talking when the waitress returned with their pizza. She put it on the table between them and asked if they needed anything else. Neither of them looked at her when they shook their heads. "If you're in love with him. If he's gonna be part of Berkley's life. Make me understand it."

"Why? Why do I have to defend how I feel to you?"

"I'm not asking you to defend your feelings." Duncan groaned. Margo took a moment to serve them each a steaming piece of pizza, careful not to lose the melted cheese that wanted to slide off the server. "I don't want to lose you. To lose a friendship over this. If he's back in your life, make me get it. Tell me something redeemable about him."

"He's over the moon for his little girl."

Duncan nodded to grant her the point.

"Look. Jess cheated." Margo pushed her plate away. "And that still hurts. But…maybe things I did…"

"Do not tell me you're to blame."

"He cheated," she repeated. "But I wasn't perfect. I want to be with him, Duncan. What do you think I've waited this whole year for? I wanted him to come back. Not just for Berkley. But for me, too."

CHAPTER 32

WHEN JESS HAD MOVED OUT OF MARGO'S HOUSE, HE HAD boxed his belongings up and left most of them in the storage room of his parents' basement. Why bother dragging everything with him to a temporary apartment for what he had hoped would be a temporary phase? Maybe he had been pissed when he left, maybe he had spent as much time muttering and moaning about Margo being a cold-hearted, independent bitch. But he'd also known—even then, even before Julie had befriended him and shared her stories about her father—that Margo was a little bit right. And even more importantly, Margo was the mother of his child. He would do any damned thing in the world to be in Berkley's life.

He paced his small place now. Completed maybe the seven hundredth lap around the place since he'd come back to Greenville and left Margo to go on her date. He trusted her. He had never worried that Margo would play around, not even back when he saw her at work—talking and yes, flirting, with male customers. He'd known then that she could have any guy in the bar if she wanted. He'd known, too, that she didn't.

So, no, he hadn't truly worried that she would invite her date back to the house and get crazy with him. The whole drive back to Greenville he had replayed memories of the weekend. Helping Margo at the book club meeting had been fun. The intense talk while they had done the dishes together—before the whole damned crew had shown up and interrupted them—still made him feel a little hot and bothered. Telling her he loved her, when she'd come home from the Queen. Wanting to undress her and lay her down and slide into her familiar heat—that had been unbearable. Walking away that night, leaving her wanting had been harder than hell, but when he'd come back this morning and she had greeted him with a kiss and fixed breakfast—he'd known that he'd done the right thing.

Waiting could be hell. Waiting to get back to her. For the right time to really propose to her, because when he did it, he was going to do it right. Waiting to hear from her right now was killing him. No, he shouldn't be jealous of time she spent with Duncan.

But he was. First of all, he didn't want Margo with anyone else. Even for a drink. Or a basket of wings and a football game on TV. He wanted all of her attention, her conversation, her laughter. He wouldn't monopolize her time when he returned. Jess would never keep her from her family, even Duncan. But at the moment, everything between them was new again, and he wanted to breathe her in and share every moment with her.

And no, it wasn't like her stepbrother would put the moves on her. Jess had worried before he had known it was Duncan taking her out that Margo might kiss her date goodnight. No lingering, intimate kisses. But if Stevi had set her up with someone she knew, she might feel obligated to participate in a goodnight kiss. Or if he was a friend, she might want to kiss him, the soft, gentle kiss of affection, nothing more.

Jess yanked open the refrigerator door, determined not to picture Margo's pale pink lips puckered and touching some other guy's cheek. He didn't want a beer. He didn't need it. Didn't need to drown his sorrows. Nothing like that. He just needed a distraction.

No. Not even that. He just needed to know that Margo loved him enough to stand up to her stepbrother. And then he needed to pack up his meager belongings that he'd brought with him to Greenville, tell Derrick and the crew thank you, and point his truck and his heart back home to Adam's Bay.

He swung the door closed when he heard the knock on his door.

Okay, he forgot about Julie. No question it was time to move on. To go home to his girls—God, but he loved the sound of that. But he didn't want to leave things the way they were with Julie.

He realized she wasn't going to walk in now. Not after the things they'd said the last time she was here. Feeling like a jerk for being so angry at her, he crossed the open living space and opened the door. Back to him, she whirled around and stared at him with big eyes. Her phone was pressed to her ear, and she was listening intently, but she almost smiled at him.

Jess leaned on the doorframe, feeling like a heel when she apparently remembered they were made at each other. Her trademark look—wholesome and happy—faded, and the smile didn't happen. Instead she held up her finger, as if asking him for a minute. Jess shrugged and turned away from her with a sigh. He left the door open so she would come in when she was ready.

Not for the first time, not even the tenth time, he eyed his phone on the kitchen counter and told himself to leave it alone. And then gave in and reached for it. No new texts. He wondered how desperate he would look if he texted her now. He wondered if he cared. Why would it be a bad thing to let her know he was anxious to hear from her?

"Are you busy?"

He pushed his phone away and turned to the door again when Julie spoke. She stepped inside, closed the door, and lingered there, as if she was afraid to look at him, to get close to him.

"No."

"I just had a date," she said quietly. He couldn't help the once over. Guy thing. Protective guy friend thing. Whatever. Julie was dressed in workout clothes ninety percent of the time. Tonight she wore skinny jeans, gray Cons, and a black turtleneck with a stripe of Buffalo Plaid through the center. Not Margo's style, but cute.

"You went out with him?"

"What? Who?" She tossed her purse on the end of the couch and moseyed her way to the kitchen. "Brent? No."

"Good." He felt bad, even as he said it, but he couldn't help it. He hated the thought of leaving Julie to a dick like Brent to use. She deserved someone better.

"Wow." She cleared her throat. Jess watched her wiggle her way onto one of the wooden stools at the breakfast bar.

"You can do better."

She breathed deeply, like she was telling herself it wasn't worth arguing with him. Jess watched her smooth her fingertips over her forehead.

"You know what, Jess? Sometimes the heartache doesn't matter. When the guy you've crushed on for years looks, you're ready to do what you can to keep him interested."

"You shouldn't have to use that to keep his interest."

"He's good in bed," she said simply. "I mean. Why is it okay for you? I haven't had sex for—"

Jess held up his hand to stop her. "We've covered this. I'm thrilled that Brent rang your bell, Julie, because yes, sometimes we all just need that. I don't want to know details. I don't like him. I do like you. I do think you deserve a guy who'll bring you a berry mango smoothie just to surprise you. You deserve a guy who wants to play catch with you in the park. You deserve a guy who touches all the right spots and makes you come unglued and then stays in your bed overnight. And brings you breakfast in bed."

"Know of any guys like that?"

"No, but let me remind you, you're young."

Julie opened her mouth to argue, but Jess shook his head to silence her.

"You are young. I'm not being a dick. I'm not trying to sound wise. I'm young, really. Yeah, I've fucked a lot up in my time, and that makes me feel old, but the point is, we've both got a lot of time to figure it out. You could bump into your guy tomorrow at your smoothie place. It could be five years from now. That's okay. There's no expiration date on meeting someone."

She pressed her lips together.

"And," he continued, hands propped on the counter, "if you have a fling or five between now and then, that's cool, too. I'm not being a dick and saying you shouldn't enjoy yourself. Even though, no, I have not done that since Margo and I split up, except with Margo. So please don't casually throw it out there. Don't justify fucking Brent for kicks because you think I'm a man whore. I cheated on her, and I have absolutely no excuse for the first time. It was stupid. And not worth it. And even though the second time was about revenge and wanting to hurt her because I was angry, it was stupid and so not worth it."

She blinked at him, but she waited to see if he was finished.

"He's not good enough for you." Jess shrugged. "I don't care if the guy gives you four orgasms a night. He's stupid for not seeing how wonderful you are."

"Um." She raised her eyebrows. "Never four, and is that possible?" She tipped her head. "Are you telling me you can do that? Because I'm a little bit jealous now—"

Jess laughed and shook his head.

"Thank you," she whispered. "I appreciate you saying that."

"I'm not just saying it," he mumbled.

"Are you still mad at me?"

"Kind of."

She nodded. "So, it's still not okay that I wanted to make sure she knew I wasn't sleeping with you?"

"I appreciate that you wanted to make that clear. But. She should trust me. I need her to trust me."

"You're right," she whispered. "I'm sorry."

"I mean." Jess sighed. He paced the kitchen again and then turned to look at her. "Did you—? The nights we sat outside all night and talked? When I told you about the time she had the flu and she was throwing up everywhere and determined that she would get everything done? She did the laundry. She cleaned the house, and she called for Leah to watch Berkley…"

"What're you asking? If I told her that stuff?"

"Did you?"

"No, Jess. I told her that we were friends. That when you decided you were coming to see Berkley, I asked if I could come. To see Berkley. To meet Margo. And that the minute she laid eyes on me, I knew what she was thinking."

"The day her car wouldn't start. And she couldn't get in touch with Duncan. He was on his way back into town. From a liquor expo. Couldn't get a hold of her dad. And she called that mechanic guy to come down to the Queen. They towed her fucking car. She never called me. I could have taken care of it."

"I know." Julie nodded.

"I helped her in the kitchen. At the Queen. I used to help with her prep work. I helped her meal plan sometimes. I helped her with anything she needed, but she wouldn't ask me. Like she was a fucking superhero determined to do every damned thing herself. But if Duncan offered to do something, hey, thanks, that's great."

"I didn't tell her any of that, Jess. I didn't share anything you told me. That's private. Between friends. I get that."

Jess glanced at his phone again.

"We talked this weekend. I didn't…go into this stuff. But I mean…I told her how much I hated that she would never lean on me. That she'd never trust me to help."

"Good."

"She's out on a date right now."

"What?"

"She thought Stevi set her up, but it was just Duncan. So instead of wondering if she's kissing someone goodnight, I have to wonder if he's reminding her what kind of ratjack asshole I am."

"Did you sleep with her? This weekend?"

"No." He dragged his fingers back through his hair. "Are you hungry? I'm hungry. I need to do something with my hands, because I want to punch the fridge."

"That might hurt, and no, I just had a date." She flashed him a grin when he looked at her. He rolled his eyes and opened the fridge again.

"I had Berkley while she was at work Saturday night. Took her to see my parents."

He grabbed the eggs and a bag of shredded cheese and turned to set them on the counter. When he realized Julie hadn't reacted, he looked at her over his shoulder.

"Really?" She offered him a big smile.

"Yeah." He nodded, aware and uncaring that the grin on his face probably made him look like a ten-year-old.

"That's awesome, Jess."

"My sisters came over to meet her."

"Did she get scared at all?"

"Um." He dug around in the meat drawer of the fridge until he found a packet of sausage links. "Maybe a little. She was a little clingy with me."

"Not that you minded."

"Not that I minded," he agreed. He set the sausage on the counter and then hesitated before moving to grab a skillet from the cabinet. "There's no word for the feeling…when she grabbed a handful of my shirt and buried her face in my neck."

Julie grinned. "She trusts you. That's instinct."

"I would fight dragons for that little girl."

"I know you would."

"Feels good when Margo hangs on like that," he mumbled, careful not to meet Julie's eyes. "But this is a different feeling."

"Of course it is. You're her daddy," Julie reminded him. "My daddy is still my favorite guy in the world."

Jess laughed and nodded, still avoiding her eyes.

"Which is why I made it my mission to…make you see Margo. And Berkley. And get your ass back home to them." Julie spoke quietly. "And if I overstepped the other day or any other time, I'm sorry, Jess. I guess I just wanted Berkley to have her daddy in her life."

Jess squatted in front of the cabinet, but he hesitated again. Nodded his head back and forth and finally sighed.

"I know, Julie. And I appreciate that you care." He cleared his throat and glanced at her. Their eyes met for a second, but both of them were quick to look away. "I mean, maybe if you hadn't taken the time to tell me about your dad… maybe I wouldn't have gotten my shit together."

"You would've," she said, "but not so quickly."

"So. How was the date?" He leaned into the cabinet and grabbed the only skillet he had. He looked at her as he stood and set it on the burner. Julie watched him as he gathered a bowl and a whisk to scramble eggs.

"It was okay."

"Just okay?" He shot her a quick look as he cracked an egg into the bowl.

"Eh." She turned her nose up. "Yeah."

"What'd you do?"

"We had pizza."

Jess laughed softly and shrugged apologetically.

"If you had the perfect date, who and what?"

"Chris Hemsworth. I think we'd stay in."

Jess snorted. "Okay. Moving on."

"No, how about you? Perfect date? Who and what?"

"Margo and Berkley. And we would stay in. Berkley and I are pretty good builders. And Margo and I—"

"Your phone is buzzing."

He let go of the whisk so quickly that it flipped out of the bowl and flung scrambled eggs over the counter.

"Margo." His heartbeat spiked.

"I see that." Julie grinned. "I'm gonna go. Talk to you tomorrow."

She patted his hand as he put his phone to his ear.

"Hey." He watched Julie grab her purse from the couch and slip out the door without a backwards glance. "I was afraid you wouldn't call."

"Hi." She sounded tired, but not frustrated. Which could be a good thing for him or a bad thing. Maybe she wasn't frustrated with him, but then again, maybe she'd had a good night with Duncan and so, now, maybe she wanted to blow Jess off. Go back to the way things were last week. Two days ago.

"How was it?"

"Well, thankfully, you don't have to resort to violence. I don't wanna pack my baby up to visit you in a jail cell."

His laugh sounded dry and forced. She wasn't giving him much to work with. His stomach now a twisted mess, he didn't want the eggs. He picked up the skillet to put it away.

"That's good. I'm not really into violence."

"I know that." Her voice went soft and sweet here, and Jess felt his heartbeat kick up again. "I wish you were here."

"You do?"

"I do. I don't like this now. You being so far away at night."

"What did Duncan say, Margo?"

"When can you come back?"

He slumped against the counter at his back and let his shoulders sag with relief and guilt and sadness and need.

"I'll talk to Derrick tomorrow."

"This weekend was..." Her voice trailed off, and he wondered what she was doing. Was she at home now? With Berkley? Had Duncan left? "Perfect, Jess. You here with me and Berkley."

"For me too."

"Is it bad that I want you here now? I want you in my bed. Tonight. I want to be with you, Jess. I hope it's okay that as much as I love you as her daddy, I need you, too."

"What're you doing?" He looked around the counter and almost laughed when he realized he was looking for his phone, the one pressed to his ear. The clock on the stove said ten after nine.

"I'm lying on the couch, wishing you were here."

"Are you touching yourself?"

"No. But I want to."

"Jesus, Margo. You're gonna give me a heart attack."

"We've never had? phone sex."

"Are we gonna do that now?"

"I want to."

"Tell me about Duncan."

"I told Duncan that I love you, and that the mistakes you and I made together...mistakes we might still make...are between us."

"And does he want to kill me? Did he forbid you to see me?"

"Forbid—?" Her voice was sharp. "Are you kidding?"

"I've been dying to hear how this night went. I was about to climb the walls when Julie came over."

"Julie's there?"

"She's not now. She came by to tell me about her date."

"And how was it?"

"To quote her, eh." He gave up on the mess in the kitchen and slipped around the counter to sit on the couch.

"That sucks."

"I don't want to come between you and Duncan. But I'm not gonna back down, Margo. I want you in my life."

He gritted his teeth when he heard her moan softly.

"Don't start yet."

She laughed softly. "I'm not. I just turned to my side. Duncan is concerned. But. He wasn't like...total badass about it, either."

"You're saying he gave you the thumbs up?"

"Nope."

He heard her yawn, and then laughed at himself over the sudden yearning to be back at home with her and Berkley.

"I don't know if you guys will ever be besties, but he seemed…easier now. Like. In tune with—"

"Emotions?" Jess offered.

"Stop it." She laughed again. "Maybe he's changed."

"Seems so unlikely."

"He's in love, Jess. I've never seen him like this."

"I hope he doesn't hurt her."

"Jess. I just spent the last few hours telling him that as much as I love him, he has no right to be involved in anything between us. It's not our business what goes on between him and Stevi."

Jess sighed and closed his eyes.

"I think we should get Berkley a guitar."

"You think what?"

He grinned. "Surely, there are toy guitars. Santa could bring her one. She could go on stage with Trace."

"Oh my God," Margo gushed.

"Can't you see it? He could sing "Rhinestone—"

"You've been thinking about this? You think about me and Berk when you're there?"

"Margo, I don't think about anything else when I'm away from you."

CHAPTER 33

"How's Jess?" Leah sauntered up behind Margo at the bar.

"Good." Margo nodded, head bent over her iPad. She and Tony had started looking for new soup recipes after the other night, the date with Duncan. When he had reminded her it was November and asked if she had started Christmas shopping. Because she hadn't. Done anything. She had been so wrapped up in Jess suddenly appearing at the Queen, in her life, and she'd been so desperate to hold onto her anger with him—she'd given that a lot of thought, too, and it hurt her to admit to herself in those dark, lonely hours when the rest of the world, including her baby girl, was asleep that she needed to be angry because she was afraid. Afraid to let him back in, afraid that he would say all the right things and she wouldn't, simply because she didn't know how. And he would go looking for company somewhere else again.

And then she'd had to wonder and worry about Julie. And feel guilty over that one night of incredible sex—the night she and Jess had fought again—

She'd been running. Margo realized that the night she and Duncan had shared a pizza and small talk over draft beer. She had dreaded the hell out of that night, but in fact, it had slowed her down. Woke her up.

Seize the day. Yada, yada, yada.

Time was passing her by, and she decided she was through with wallowing.

"Good?" Leah rested her chin on Margo's shoulder and her hand on her hip. "Are you gettin' some? Because you have this smile—"

"What?" Margo snorted and pushed back at Leah, trying to shove her off.

"I told Nashville the other day that we didn't need to turn lights on here. Your smile lit the place up. I figured you and Jess had a fun weekend."

"We did, but not like that," Margo answered. She chuckled when Leah gave her hip a gentle squeeze and rubbed her tiny baby bump against her back. "You have a baby bump."

"I know." Leah gushed and stepped back. "Trace says he sees it now."

"Does he talk to the baby?"

"Yeah." Leah nodded. "All the time. Did Jess?"

Margo glanced at Leah, a little surprised by the question. "Of course."

Leah smiled wistfully. "He says my boobs are bigger now, too," she mumbled. "I'm okay with that, but they kind of get in the way."

"Of what? They're there for your pleasure right now. How can that possibly get in the way?"

"Yeah, they're extra sensitive right now." Leah tipped her head.

"I'm going to assume you're talking about body parts I don't want to know about." Duncan appeared at the end of the bar, arms straining with two big boxes, one of them a case of wine. "Unless we switch lanes and talk about Stevi."

"Pour me a drink, Duncan, and stop talking." Margo eyed him expectantly.

"I can't button my blouses anymore."

"You don't have a big baby bump yet." Duncan shook his head. He bent his knees and lowered his armful to the floor behind the bar.

"What're you doing?" Margo asked him.

"Trace and I have a surprise for you ladies," he announced.

"I was talking about my boobs," Leah told him. Margo snorted when Duncan, still squatting at the boxes, ducked his head and then shook it slowly.

"I thought we said we weren't going to talk about those body parts."

"You interrupted my conversation with my cousin. I'm having boob issues."

"Oh, dear God." Margo groaned. She pushed her iPad away and stepped around Duncan to open the glass door of the wine case. She selected a bottle of Sylo Louis Malbec—something new that their wine rep had just brought in for them to sample—and studied the label as she stepped over Duncan again.

"What're you drinking?"

Margo glanced at Leah. "Sylo Louis," she answered. "I'm a bit frightened but intrigued."

"Hope it doesn't taste like moonshine."

"Homemade wine isn't awesome, either," Leah agreed with Duncan. "And anyway, we weren't talking about my boobs. Not at first. I was asking Margo if she got some last weekend, because she's been really cool and laid back this week."

"There's so much wrong with what you just said, I can't. Just." Duncan stood. He looked at Leah and then Margo. "Here." He reached for the bottle, but she didn't hand it over.

"What?"

"I was going to open it and pour you some."

She eyed him silently for a moment, half tempted to argue

that she was perfectly capable of opening the bottle herself.

"I don't know. If this conversation is going to continue, I'm thinking I might go straight to tequila."

"Do you remember the movie *Tequila Sunrise?*" Leah asked with a quiet giggle. Margo rolled her eyes and leaned on the bar to study her cousin.

"Stop it."

Leah's grin only spread wider over her face. "God, how many times did we watch that scene?"

"What scene?" Duncan asked them. Margo realized she was still holding the wine. She was capable of opening it herself, but she had asked him to pour her a drink, hadn't she?

"Where's Stevi?" Margo asked him.

"That movie's like, twenty years old. You were kids when it came out."

"So, we watched it when were in high school."

"And?" He took the bottle when she handed it off. Set it on the bar and reached for the opener.

"We had a Mel Gibson thing for a while," Margo mumbled. "Let it go."

"So there was a hot scene in the movie?"

"Mm." Margo shrugged. "Leah sure thought so."

"Did Stevi?"

"Did Stevi what?" Stevi asked as she came down the steps across the room. "I just got off the phone with Todd Barber at KABR. We're all still onboard with the radio advertising for the holidays, right?"

"Yep."

Margo was amused by the way Duncan watched Stevi approach the bar.

"Do you like to watch hot scenes in movies?" he asked her.

Stevi's face flushed, and Margo and Leah laughed.

"You have to ask?"

"Not those kinds of movies." He wiggled his eyebrows. "Like. Regular movies. Dramas. Thrillers. The hot scenes."

"Of course I do." She rolled her eyes as she climbed up to sit on a barstool.

"Okay, so. Back to Margo." Leah took a step backwards and slid onto the stool at the end of the bar.

"You okay?"

"I'm fine." Leah nodded. "But if we're gonna sit here and have a good old-fashioned talk, I'm gonna sit."

"We never talked about your boobs before," Duncan reminded them as he worked the cork out of the bottle.

"Why are you talking about your boobs?" Stevi looked at Margo with a frown.

"We're not," Margo said simply. "We're talking about

Leah's. They're so big, they're getting in the way of things."

"Pretty sure you're not gonna hear Trace complain." Duncan turned his back to them and reached for a glass.

"Is that a veiled complaint from you?"

"Do you think I have any complaints about your body, Stevi Hague?" Duncan shot her a look over his shoulder.

"Yep. I need tequila." Margo groaned.

"So." Leah yawned. "Duncan, can I have a soda?"

"No caffeine."

"I know."

"Okay. Stevi, you want some wine?"

"Please."

"Margo. When was the last time you guys had sex?" Leah asked with a grin.

"And now I need tequila." Duncan splashed the deep red liquid into two glasses and then recorked the bottle.

"You did ask me why I don't talk to you."

"I'm changing my mind." He shrugged and handed her and Stevi both a glass.

"It was a few weeks ago," Margo told Leah. "When I asked Stevi to come over and hang out at the house the next day."

"You guys didn't make love last weekend?"

Duncan hung his head and folded his hands behind his neck.

"You okay?" Margo nudged him with her elbow. She winked at Leah and Stevi.

"Yep. Hanging. I'm hanging in. I am doing this. I can be your best girlfriend. Tell us. Why didn't you and lover boy get it on last weekend?"

Margo snorted. She sipped her wine and then studied the glass, letting the wine sit on her tongue for a few moments. Leah watched her expectantly. Duncan finally moved to get Leah something to drink.

"We. Talked. A lot." She swallowed the wine, still not sure what she thought of it. "Some arguing. Some talking."

"That's all ya got?" Duncan frowned and shook his head. "Dude, just be ready. You guys ask me about me and Stevi, I'm gonna tell all. We get dirty."

Stevi covered her face with her hands and shook her head. Duncan laughed as he filled Leah's glass with ice and white soda.

"C'mon. Hit me." He dared Margo. "If this is it, hit me. I can take it."

"Remember your forehead kiss?" she directed her question at Leah, and Leah gave her a slow, sweet smile.

"I do."

Margo shrugged and arched her eyebrows.

"Wait." Duncan handed Leah the glass and then reached for the wine bottle again. "Wait. What was that?"

"What?"

"What's a forehead kiss?"

"Duncan." Stevi rolled her eyes. "C'mere, babe." She climbed up to sit on her knees and leaned over the bar to kiss his head when he stepped close enough.

"And that's a big deal?"

"I think that's when I fell in love with Nashville," Leah said quietly.

"Where is he?" Stevi looked around.

"At home. He's got some issues with a song he's writing. Something isn't just right. I told him to stay home and come in later."

"Do we not have a forehead kiss, Stevi?" Duncan turned to her. Margo bit her lip, ready to say anything to diffuse this argument about to happen.

"Duncan, I realized I was in love with you the night we were over there on the steps, and you pulled me into your lap."

"And grinded on you." Duncan nodded. "Wow. I am an utter dick, aren't I? I couldn't be a nice guy and give you a forehead kiss."

Margo swallowed more wine, not even giving herself time to taste it.

"You did, actually," Stevi said softly. "The night you sent me home when we were dancing. I didn't see it at the time, but..."

"What do you mean?"

Margo met Leah's eyes and saw the same look of desperation she figured she wore.

"We had phone sex Sunday night," Margo blurted out. "After my date with Duncan."

Speechless, Duncan turned his head slowly to look at Margo.

"I totally...did not...hear you say that."

"You asked."

"Leah did."

Margo shrugged. "Have some wine."

"Is it good?" Leah asked her.

"I'm not sure," Margo admitted. "I'm sort of just slamming it now."

Stevi chuckled.

"You weren't...like...thinking about that. When we were talking. Were you?"

"No, Duncan. I wasn't." Margo smirked and rolled her eyes. "I got home. And I put Berkley down. And I called Jess to let him know you didn't put some spell over me and make me hate him. And." She shrugged. "I missed him."

"You started it?" Duncan yelped.

"What was that?" Leah giggled. "Oh my god. You are a girlfriend, right now, Duncan. Oh my God." She bent over and snorted, shoulders shaking with laughter.

"I didn't...girls do that? I mean." He looked desperately to Stevi for help.

"You like it when—"

"Uncle!" He threw his hands up and shook his head. "Uncle. Done. Let's have some wine and read the Bible, ladies."

"When he's coming home?" Leah asked Margo.

"He talked to his boss on Monday. He already gave his notice, but the crew is a man short right now. So Jess is sticking with one last project. He started packing, but he said he didn't move much. He left a lot at his parents' house."

"Will he be here for Thanksgiving?" Duncan asked with a frown.

"Yes." Margo nodded. "He will. Please don't be a dick to him. Just avoid him if you have to, but—"

"Look, sister, I am trying to deal with this!" He laughed and shivered. "Remember that? Two minutes ago, you dropped that phone sex bomb, and I gotta think of who was on the other end of that call. I'm working on it."

"I am so in love with him," Margo said sincerely. "I know I never said that before, but I am. And I just want him back home with me. And Berk."

"Berk sure loves him," Stevi mumbled.

"You're not gonna let him make her hate Uncle Duncan, are you?" Duncan tipped his head.

"No. But he was pretty floored with the whole 'Rhinestone Cowboy' thing. Said he's going to play her some ACDC."

"See?" Duncan smacked his hand down on the bar. "Me and the old boy agreeing on something right there. Already."

"Hate to tell you, but Trace likes hard rock, too." Leah shrugged.

"Well, then, maybe we'll all be a happy little family here at the Queen."

Margo heard the sarcastic tone in Duncan's voice. She met his eyes and frowned.

"I hope so, Duncan," she whispered. "More than you can ever know."

CHAPTER 34

THE SNOW STARTED LATE IN THE AFTERNOON. JESS HAD left Derrick's office around two. Funny, he couldn't wait to get back to Adam's Bay and start this new life. Dating Margo. Loving Margo. Being around Berkley every day. But there was a small part of him that would miss the little life he'd made here in Greenville, too. He'd lingered in the office with Derrick long after the older man had shooed him out and told him to get home to Margo. They'd talked a little about everything, same as always. Jess supposed one day he'd find a lesson in Derrick's story about buying the used pick up when he'd first started the business seventeen years ago. Derrick had finally kicked him out, told him he was going to run by the Myer residence and take a look in the attic to check for leaks before they made any further plans on the roofing project.

He'd given his notice a long time ago, but he'd done it again earlier today at the office. He would still need to make a trip or two to finish the final move, but he was done working for Carmichael Roofing. Jess was already at his place, loading the last of his few boxes into the back of his truck. He would come back for the furniture over the weekend; he was ready to get home to his girls. Head tipped back, he watched the big flat flakes falling, so pretty against the black sky. He stood for a moment, hands resting on the back of the truck, and wondered if it was snowing in Adam's Bay. If it was, he wondered what Berkley thought of it. Margo wouldn't have her out now, not in the dark, when it was so much colder. But earlier today, before the hours grew late and the sky had darkened, he would bet that Margo bundled her up and took her out to see the snow.

Enough wondering, he told himself. The sooner he finished with the boxes and smaller items—he was pretty sure he could strap the end table into the bed of the truck —the sooner he would be on the road to home. To the girls.

He wasn't worried about the snow. There wasn't much accumulation in the forecast, and Jess had been driving for sixteen winters. He wasn't afraid of the drive; he just hoped there wasn't enough moisture to get into the boxes in the truck. Again, it wasn't like he had anything precious packed away in the boxes; everything in them could be replaced. Some CDs and movies. Towels and linens. A few kitchen items. No pictures in albums or frames. No keepsakes from his school days. No framed diplomas or personal files. Still. Wet cardboard was a pain in the ass to deal with.

With a shiver, he ducked back inside. He liked Thanksgiving. And he especially liked a cold, snowy Thanksgiving. The holidays at home with his sisters when they were younger—including Thanksgiving—were days for being outside in the snow, building forts and throwing snowballs. His sister Lori had been into snow angels, but not him or Melissa.

The year he and Margo first started dating, they had had a killer snowball fight. She had a hell of an arm, and she clocked him three times from half-court. And then later, when they'd gone inside her house, she'd gone down on him and he'd forgotten all about the snow that had melted down his back and made his collar and t-shirt wet. Her hands had unbuckled his jeans so fast, all he could do was grip the counter behind him and watch her work his dick.

That had been a first. He adjusted himself now as he looked around the living room. Didn't look that different since he had lived pretty basic up here. Margo had never wanted him to return that attention. She never let him linger too long, his face between her thighs, her skin warm and soft on his cheeks. But she'd always been hungry to do him.

He hoped what he had said, the things they'd talked about wouldn't change her. He loved her fiery wickedness in the bedroom. He just hoped she would give him the chance to love her the way he wanted to, also. They'd made progress. They had talked through their differences. Jess was so relieved to have shared his feelings with her and even more that it hadn't turned into a fight. In fact, she heard him. He knew she'd heard him and taken his words to heart. Just as he finally realized why she'd held him at a distance and loved him that way.

If they'd worked through those things, if Margo wanted him to be there with her, maybe she would let him make love to her the way he wanted to.

For now, he needed to get moving. They'd made plans to go Christmas shopping. They'd probably pick things up for Stevi and Leah, too, but mostly, they had made plans to shop for Berkley. Jess was thrilled at the thought of picking things out for his little girl. He prayed he would be around on Christmas morning to watch her open her toys. He wanted to be Santa Claus, and he wanted that more than he'd ever in his life wanted Santa to come to see him.

He'd driven down a few times through the last couple of weeks. Hadn't even told his family he was there. He would go straight to Margo's, and she would greet him with a hug. Maybe a kiss. Even in front of Berkley. They would eat dinner together. Twice, she had dinner ready for him, and once, they grilled outside together, even though it had been damned cold outside. Berkley had been adorable bundled up so tight in her parka that she could hardly even wiggle.

As much as he wanted to stay, to crawl into bed with Margo, he didn't. He needed it to mean something when it happened again, and he was pretty sure it was going to mean every damned thing, and Margo might wake the neighborhood, not just Berkley. But he had to get back to Greenville each time, finishing up the last of the crew's little odds and ends projects to help Derrick out.

Derrick kept giving him shit each day he showed up. Kept telling him to get out of town and get home to his women. Jess' whole body thrilled at the words. His toes curled, and his blood pressure spiked, and hope expanded so wide in his chest, it hurt to breathe.

Julie had taken the news of his notice and his plans to move with a grin and a nod of approval. They were at her place, eating tacos and watching American Ninja, alternately ripping on the contestants and cheering them on. When she told him that she knew he was leaving, that her dad had mentioned it in passing, Jess felt a stab of guilt. He should have told her himself, but he'd been worried she would be pissed.

Stupid worry. She'd eventually thrown her arms around his neck and held on tight for a few moments. Kissed his cheek and wished him well and drew away from him all so fast that all he had time to do was blink and nod. She'd changed the tense in what she was saying about their friendship, though, as if he planned to never look back. He would. He hadn't made a big deal of it. *Tender moments, blah blah blah.* Besides, he was still a guy, and talking about friendships and stuff was still awkward. But when he left her place that night to go home, he'd told her not to delete his number because he would sure as hell be checking on her to make sure he didn't need to kick Brent's ass.

Julie's laugh had been sweet, sounded like a bell trilling, and she'd tipped her head and told him she hoped he would send a picture now and then of Berkley. He'd promised. He thought Margo would be okay with that, too, since she'd seemed to like Julie even when she felt threatened by her.

His phone buzzed in his pocket, so he drew it out to look at it, assuming it was Margo. It was already after six; he should've left by now. He and Margo were planning a movie night. She was at the Queen right now, but she would head home soon, stopping to pick Berkley up at her mom's house. From there, home, where she would stick a couple of frozen pizzas in the oven and they would curl up with Berkley and watch movies. Jess didn't care if they were watching Little Einsteins or Smurfs or static on the TV. He couldn't wait to walk into the house and get kisses from his girls.

Berkley's kisses were sometimes wetter than Margo's. Definitely stickier. Never sweeter, but sweet all in their own way. The text on his phone was from Julie, not Margo.

I need you.

Seemed a bit dramatic. He wondered if she had decided she did want him to kick Brent's ass. Not that he would. He was done with all things bar brawl and alcohol. He would give his right arm to be part of the crew at the Queen, but he had no desire to pick up a bottle or to draw his arm back to throw a punch.

He flipped his light off, head ducked over his phone to dial. He would just call her. Tell her he was on his way out. Maybe she just needed to talk about Brent. Or a bad date. Hadn't she had another date last night? This guy was a yoga instructor, if memory served. Jess flinched, hoping like hell he wasn't going to hear details about how limber the guy was.

"This is Julie. Leave a message."

With a sigh, he started to tap out a quick text. He'd tell her he was on the road, and she could call him when she had a chance. He had time to listen while he drove. And anyway, he could talk to her once he was in Adam's Bay.

He texted Margo, too. Told her he was just leaving and apologized for running late. Sent her the stupid heart-eyed emoji because that's how she made him feel. She answered immediately with the emoji blowing him a kiss. Warm from the inside out, he tucked his phone in his pocket and thought about what to get her for Christmas.

Oh, how he wanted to buy her a ring. He would. He would buy her a ring right now, if he didn't think she would balk. But he knew Margo too well to think she was just quite ready. Besides, he wanted to do the ring and the proposal outside of another big day. No Christmas Eve stuff. No Valentine's Day. Just a day. When he and Margo and maybe Berkley were together, having fun.

For now, he could get her earrings. Or a necklace. He wondered if Berkley would bother a necklace? Margo had never been big on jewelry; he hadn't noticed that she'd taken up wearing much since he'd been gone.

Wasn't even so much that he wanted to claim her, mark her, so all the guys that had their eyes all over her ass at the bar knew she belonged to him. Well, maybe that was part of it. But mostly, he wanted to give her something special, something pretty. Something that wasn't necessary. Their first Christmas they spent together, he asked her what she wanted for Christmas and she told him she needed a new vacuum. He had been frustrated with her; even then she had pushed back at his attempts to be romantic. Now, he decided he was mad at himself for that. He could have given her the damned vacuum and something personal. Why had he let her push him away and hold him at a distance? Why hadn't he seen the fear behind her control?

Yep. A necklace. Maybe Berkley's birthstone on a pendant of some sort. Or maybe one of those necklaces with the infinity symbol. Didn't they have those? He was pretty sure his sisters had oohed and awed over—

A loud knock and then banging on his door made him jump so hard, he nearly dropped his phone.

"Damn." He laughed at himself and reached for the door just as it banged open. A flurry of snowflakes whipped in on a gust of wind; a woman's hand pushed at the door. Julie appeared, eyes swollen and bloodshot. Tears streaked her chapped cheeks. Jess felt his heart throw a beat so hard, he thought it would pound out of his chest. He lunged for the light switch and reached with his other hand to grab her arm and yank her inside. "What happened? What's wrong?"

"I know you're leaving," she sobbed and swiped at her face, but she fought him and refused to come inside. "But I need you, Jess."

"Okay. What happened? What's wrong?"

"It's my dad. Mom's not home. She went to Chicago with my aunt. I called her. She's coming back, but I—"

"Jules, what happened?"

"He was on a ladder," she sobbed. "At the Kearny house."

"What? What the hell—"

"In the attic. He was in their attic—"

"On a ladder?" Jess asked quickly. "That doesn't make any sense."

"He was checking something for leaks." She pushed her hair off her face and reached for his hand. "He fell. They don't know if he had a heart attack and that made him fall. Or if the fall caused him to have a heart attack."

"Oh, Jesus." Jess pushed her gently toward the door. "Let's go."

"Myer Kearny called for an ambulance. He called me. I was at the gym, getting ready to go home. They're going—"

"Let's go." Jess repeated. He stepped outside behind her and closed the door. Julie headed to her car, but after making sure his door was locked, he directed her toward his truck. "I'll drive."

She nodded and climbed in without arguing. The roads weren't bad, and traffic wasn't terrible, but Julie nearly rode the dash on the short drive to the emergency room. Jess wanted to comfort her, tried to talk to her and keep her calm, but he knew she was terrified. He would be, too. He hoped her mom got back soon, though the drive back from Chicago was long and it would be close to midnight if they drove straight through.

He needed to call Margo, but he would wait until they got to the emergency room. No need to make Julie worry over him or feel guilty for keeping him from Margo and Berkley. He would stay with her until her mom was back in town. He had no qualms with that; she was just a kid, and no one wanted to sit in the ER waiting room alone.

But he had to let Margo know what was going on.

Julie sobbed quietly in the passenger seat across the cab of the truck. The radio was on, turned down low. Journey's "Separate Ways" played quietly. Jess watched the snowflakes fall on the windshield, but from the corner of his eye, he saw Julie sit up straight and swipe at her eyes as the squat but sprawling gray hospital building came into view down the main drag.

When he parked, Julie scrambled out of the truck before he could yank the keys from the ignition. He hurried around to her side to help her, but she was already skipping up the curb to the sidewalk. Jess locked the truck and then tucked his arm around her as they raced inside.

Greenville wasn't a big city, but their ER and hospital in general did its share of business. The waiting room was already half full. Three older ladies gathered near the triage desk, talking to the nurse there. Two security guards stood watch, and Jess noticed a group of young guys decked out in bright red bandanas and leather jackets. They didn't impress him; in fact, they looked like spoiled kids trying to look mean. But when he saw them notice Julie in her yoga pants and sports bra with just a lightweight sweatshirt hastily thrown over it, he decided he was glad security was watching them and glad he was with Julie.

She stepped up when the older ladies moved to the corner to sit. The boys in the bandanas watched them for a moment. Jess fisted his hands, but he stayed by Julie. When two of the five swung their attention back to Julie, he shrugged out of his coat and set it over her shoulders. She glanced at him as the nurse at the desk checked the computer for information about her dad.

"Put it on," he told her, his voice firm. "And zip it up."

She frowned, but she did as he told her and then looked back at the nurse when she spoke to her.

"They're working on him now, hon." The nurse sounded apologetic.

"What do you mean?"

"Stabilizing him to get him up to the cath lab."

Jess eyed Julie carefully. She was a health guru, had a degree in nutrition or something, so she obviously knew what a cath lab was.

"Can I see him?"

"Not right this minute," the nurse said quietly. "Let them do their thing."

Julie nodded, but when she turned to him, he saw the way her eyes roved the walls frantically, as if she was determined to find a way out of the waiting room and back to see her dad.

"I'm so scared, Jess." She bit her lip, but she still cried. Jess slipped his arm around her and pulled her away from the spotlight. He led her to the wall opposite the triage desk and put his arms around her. "What if he—"

Jess shook his head and gave her a squeeze. "Say a prayer, Julie. Stay positive."

CHAPTER 35

"W͟HAT'RE YOU STILL DOING HERE?" L͟EAH ASKED AS M͟ARGO poured a bottled beer into a tilted pint glass. "Thought you had plans with Jess."

"I do." Margo eyed the amber liquid carefully as she righted the glass, so there wouldn't be excess foam at the top. She tossed the empty bottle and handed the beer over the bar to a guy who'd been hitting on her all night. She avoided his eyes as she took his ten and glanced at Leah. "He said he's running late."

"Oh." Leah pursed her lips. "When was that?"

"Um. I don't know. Maybe thirty or forty minutes ago."

"So he should still be home soon."

Margo grinned. Home soon. She liked the sound of that, and she'd stopped trying to hide how she felt from any of them. She hadn't lied to Duncan about the recent nights when Jess had driven down just to hang out with her and

Berkley, but she didn't share how happy, how perfect it all felt, either. There weren't any dirty details to share, but she didn't tell him that she and Jess had spent long minutes that felt like hours curled up together on the couch, kissing like horny teenagers, either.

She had liked kissing like that when she was a horny teenager. Somewhere along the way, she'd lost the desire for and enjoyment of those kinds of kisses. She'd been all about the sex. The grind and the explicit touching. Getting off. She'd never been one to give that kind of control over to anyone. Since her first time in the basement of a high school boyfriend's house when that boyfriend had bumbled around like an idiot and skipped any sort of touching to make sure she was ready, and then ridden her to his climax and left her wanting, she'd taken matters into her own hands.

Now, after Jess called her attention to her control issues, she wanted a chance to be different. She'd let him lead, let him slip his hands in her shirt and her bra and play. What she'd realized had shocked her. Jess might love touching her that way, but she'd forgotten how good those soft, gentle touches could feel. And she'd forgotten how good those long, slow kisses tasted.

All things she told Leah and Stevi, but not Duncan. And she didn't feel bad about keeping secrets, either. It was enough that Duncan understood that she was in love with Jess and wanted to be with him.

"I know. I'll go soon."

"Doing dinner?"

Margo chuckled. "Frozen pizza."

"Oh, yum."

"Right? It was his idea. Throw a frozen pizza in and kick back with Berkley and watch TV."

"He loves her."

"I need to tell her he's her daddy. I mean…at this point, it won't be…earth shattering to her. But if he's here, and I let this go for a while and then tell her…" Margo shrugged.

"You're sure." Leah smiled. "I love that, Margo. I'm so happy for you."

"Thank you."

"Why don't you go ahead? Go home and do something sexy for him while you're waiting."

"I don't think phone sex is legal while driving."

Leah laughed out loud, but she slapped her hand over her mouth when Duncan looked her way from the other end of the bar.

"Not what I meant." She rolled her eyes. "Shower. Put some perfume in some mysterious places. Do some chocolate covered strawberries."

Margo wagged her eyebrows at Leah. "I don't know what you guys do in your spare time, but I don't just have chocolate and strawberries sitting around waiting for a romantic night."

Leah pursed her lips. "Have any canned whipped cream?"

"Oh my God." Margo snorted. "That's so high school."

"Actually, it's not," Leah said with a shrug. "It's pretty much just the other day."

"Nashville does whipped cream?"

"Oh, he does whipped cream so good." Leah sighed, eyes closed on a private moment.

"God, I need to go home and have a date with my battery-operated boyfriend before Jess even gets home." Margo groaned. "Stop it. You're standing at the bar in the Queen looking like you're five seconds from an orgasm."

"Five seconds from an orgasm?" Trace slipped up behind Leah and dropped his hands on her shoulders. "Can I play, too?"

Leah grinned. "Go home, Margs." She waved her fingers at her as if to shoo her away.

She decided she would go on home. They were busy, but with Leah and Trace still here, and Tanya waiting tables with Stevi, the crowd was manageable. Still, even after telling Duncan and Stevi she was leaving, it took her another twenty minutes just to get upstairs to get her purse from the office. She checked her phone again as she pulled her keys from the bottom of her bag. Nothing new. She would run by her mom and dad's to get Berkley and then head home. And wait for Jess.

Margo stood at the top of the stairs for a moment, content to watch the crowded bar from afar. They'd done well for themselves. They might still struggle to make ends meet sometimes, but Margo understood that was the nature of the beast. They had to stay relevant. Revamping their special nights, pulling in new musical talent—funny how that wasn't a problem with Nashville around—and keeping the menu exciting and the food good. But mostly, the one thing that Margo thought made a business like theirs thrive or die was the people involved.

They had good people. Twice, they'd had to let employees go. Well, one of those times, said employee—kitchen help—had decided to make his own hours and finally called one night just to announce he was too busy to work for them. None of them had blinked twice over that loss. They'd fired a waitress for her poor attitude with their customers. After all, their customers were their lifeblood. If people chose to spend their time and hard-earned money here at the Queen, then they deserved to walk inside and feel at home.

Margo saw Stevi look up at her. She smiled and lifted her hand in a small wave. Their granddad would be proud. She'd worried at first. Well, they'd all worried about the expenses, throwing their trust money into a building that needed an overhaul and opening another bar in a drinking town. But Margo had dropped out of college. Not because she wasn't smart enough to do it. But because she didn't want to waste her time. She had been restless as a student, and once she'd quit school, she'd been restless with worry over what Granddad would think of her.

Now she knew. They'd done something worthwhile with his money, and the Queen lived in his name. She moved when she realized Duncan was watching her. One foot in front of the other, down the steps. The drummer hit the last beat as she reached the bottom step and swung wide around the staircase to slip through the crowd. She waved at Stevi and Duncan again as she passed them at the bar. Leah blew her a kiss from the end barstool, and Nashville, who stood behind Leah, turned and walked her to the door.

"You don't have to walk me out," she told him with a smile.

"Kidding me?" He turned a deep frown on her. "Duncan would have my ass if I didn't walk you out."

She chuckled and nodded her agreement.

"You ever gonna marry my cousin? Make this whole thing official?" She tipped her head to look up at him as they walked.

"I want to marry Leah yesterday," he told her as he dropped his arm around her shoulders.

"What about Stevi and Duncan?"

Trace turned his nose up a bit and shook his head. "I'm more of a one guy one girl kinda guy."

"Nashville." She slapped his chest playfully. "Do you think they'll get married?"

"I do." He nodded. "I think the idea is sort of rattling around in Duncan's head, and he's kind of trying to ignore it. But he'll end up asking her."

"You think? Does he talk to you?"

"Oh, I'm not touching that." Trace held his hands out in front of him as if to hold her off.

"Guy code?" she teased.

Trace shrugged, but his lips were tipped up in a smirk.

"If you're pleading the fifth, or guy code or whatever you wanna call it, I'm going to assume you guys have talked about it."

"Why all the marriage talk?"

Margo opened her mouth, but he had caught her off guard. Heat burned her cheeks so she ducked her head and shrugged.

"Did he ask you?"

"No."

"But?"

"I mean…" She sighed and glanced at him again. "He's said the word a time or two."

"And?"

Margo leaned on her car and folded her arms over her chest. Rather than look at Trace, she tipped her head back to study the stars. The air was crisp and cold, but the night around them was completely still.

"I don't know."

"You don't want to settle down with him? Be a family?"

Margo drew in a deep breath and blew it out slowly.

"I do. I really do. We've talked a lot, Trace. Since he's been back. And I'm ready to put it behind us. To move on. I love him so much."

"So what's wrong?"

"Berkley," she whispered. "If I screw this up, if I trust him again, and things go wrong, he's not just gonna hurt me. He's gonna hurt Berkley."

Trace, who had come outside in shirtsleeves, shivered.

"Is he, though?" He shrugged, watched her with intense green eyes that she knew must make Leah's heart race. "First of all, I know I wasn't supposed to, but I like him."

Margo smiled sheepishly.

"The guy had balls, just showing up like he did."

"I thought southern gentleman didn't say things like that."

"Southern guys got balls just like everyone else, darlin'." He winked. "He came here a while back, uninvited. Unwelcome. He stood up to every one of us. To see you."

"To see Berkley."

"And you." Trace raised his eyebrows. "Maybe he hurt you before. I don't hold with infidelity, Margo. You know how I feel about that. I wanted to mop the floor with your stepbrother's ass when he was dickin' Stevi around."

Margo snickered and started to tease him again.

"I'm a guy." He grinned apologetically. "And he was dickin' her around, and it pissed me off. I think the most basic place for a guy and a girl to start is respect. So yeah, I get it. He hurt you. We all do that. We all hurt the people we love the most in one way or another."

"I know."

"I see how he watches you. The way he looks at you when he thinks no one is watching. He's in love with you, and he's busting his ass to earn your forgiveness and your trust. And even if things don't work out between you, Jess Covey's not gonna hurt his little girl. Because he's just as wildly in love with her as you are."

Margo sighed.

"I know what you mean." Her voice came out in little more than a whisper. "But I'm her mother, Trace. It's my job, it's the most important thing I will ever do. Protect her."

"I'm just trying to tell you that you don't have to protect her from her daddy. He's one of the good guys."

Margo's eyes filled, but she smiled at him.

"Don't let Duncan hear you say that."

He laughed and reached to hug her.

"I'm not scared of Duncan, Margo, and neither is your guy."

"Thanks, Trace."

"Be careful." He dropped a kiss on the top of her head and then backed away from her.

On the drive to her mom's to get Berkley, she turned the radio off. The silence in the car was peaceful. She hadn't needed Nashville's approval, but she felt so much lighter, so much more at peace after talking to him. Leah and Stevi would have said all the same things to her. Both of them had come around, and while that had surprised her in the beginning—after Jess had come into the Queen with Julie—it didn't now. Maybe Leah's hormones had been to blame when she'd first started hinting that maybe Margo should give Jess another chance. But both of them had seen what Margo had seen when he'd first turned her head. Not just the thick black hair and the golden warmth of his eyes. Jess was a family guy, and she'd unknowingly walked all over his need to love her.

No, she hadn't needed Nashville's approval. She didn't need anyone's approval. She'd been making her own decisions for a damned long time. But Jess had reminded her that it was okay to lean, to ask for help or advice, to talk. Maybe there was strength in knowing you were capable of doing anything that needed to be done and still being able to accept the support and love of family.

She visited with her mom for a few minutes, but she was fidgety and anxious to get home. Jess might even be there by now. She'd given him a key the last time he had come down. Not for a big moving in day, but so he could let himself in on nights like this one if he beat her to the house.

Berkley seemed to sense how anxious she was to get home, because she resisted every attempt Margo made at leaving. First, she had a fit when Margo packed her diaper bag with her toys. Then, she demanded a cookie and screamed when Margo said no. Of course, Margo's mother gave her a little banana cookie. Margo bit her tongue, slumped against the counter to wait while Berkley nibbled the cookie with the grace of a queen and the pace of a snail. In between bites, Berkley made a show of straining to see into the living room, where Margo's dad was watching an old cowboy movie.

When she finished the cookie, Margo bundled her into her coat, Berkley going board stiff and fighting as if her life depended on not wearing the coat.

"Berk." Margo sighed. Her mother stood at the kitchen sink, back to her, but of course she was hearing everything: the cajoling Margo did and the sassy fit-throwing Berkley did. "We have to go home. Do you wanna see Jess?"

Her little girl's eyes lit up at the mention of his name. Margo's heart hurt with the knowledge that Berkley was crazy about him and that she didn't know him by the name Daddy.

"Do you?" Margo tilted her head.

Berkley nodded and rattled something, again ending with a word that sounded like Jess.

"We need to go, sweetie. We're gonna go see your daddy."

Her mom dropped something in the sink. Margo glanced at her, met her eyes when her mom looked at her over her shoulder. She held her breath, hoping her parents would be on board with her decision. A tiny smiled played at the corner of her mom's lips. Margo turned back to Berkley who was picking at the zipper of her coat.

"Do you wanna go see Daddy, Berkley? Jess is your daddy. He's coming home to see you again tonight."

Berkley whispered *Jess* again, chin still tucked to her chest as she worked at her zipper, and then she lifted her head and beamed a beautiful smile at Margo.

"Daddy." She said it clearly, and she nodded firmly as if to say she approved. Overcome with emotion—joy and sadness and guilt—Margo's eyes filled again, but this time she let the tears slide.

CHAPTER 36

BERKLEY SANG SOFTLY, HER SWEET VOICE FILLING THE kitchen and living room as Margo loaded her few breakfast dishes in the dishwasher. She kept an eye on her, since she hadn't put her in her playpen, but Berkley seemed content on the blanket spread out over the floor, surrounded by toy blocks, stuffed animals, and a couple of board books.

Margo put the pizza in the oven after eight, assuming Jess had gotten a later start than the late start he'd texted about. When the pizza was done, she let it sit on the stovetop as she wandered the house, dreading the truth she felt in her bones.

He wasn't coming. And he hadn't called.

She would give him the benefit of the doubt, but the more minutes ticked by on the clock and she didn't hear from him, the harder it was to believe in him. By nine, the pizza was cold, and she wasn't hungry, so she threw it away.

Seemed like she'd done this same routine many times when they had lived together.

Her throat was hot and tight as she got Berkley ready for bed. Before, when she and Jess lived together, she'd done the wasted dinner scene so many times, she'd learned not to cry. Something Jess had zinged her for recently, as if it didn't matter what he did, because she didn't feel anything anyway. Tonight, she cried when she rocked Berkley to sleep. Twice, Berkley struggled to sit up in her arms. Margo let her, heart breaking each time, when Berkley looked around the room and then turned sad eyes back to Margo.

She was looking for Jess, too.

Her friends and family had all been so sure that even if she and Jess didn't work out, he wouldn't hurt Berkley. But this was the beginning of heartache for her baby girl. A daddy who said one thing and did another. Margo swiped at her eyes, at the tears on her face, and tried to sing Berkley to sleep.

But Berkley rubbed her eyes and squirmed, restless. Margo didn't mind holding her longer, snuggling with her. She moved her to her shoulder and closed her own eyes when Berkley popped her thumb in her mouth. She prayed that Jess was okay, and she prayed that he would eventually call with a reasonable explanation, and finally, after she put Berkley down and it was midnight, she called him.

Maybe he was testing her. Maybe she should have called him again hours ago, but she got caught up at the bar and then talking to Trace. Talking to her mom and Berkley. At first, she'd been caught up in hope. Dreams. Lala land, apparently. And then, the sinking feeling, the realization that it was happening again pulled at her, weighing her down, and she was caught up in dread.

She had long since changed from her jeans to comfy pjs, and because she feared what would happen when she called, she brushed her teeth and removed her makeup. Checked on Berkley again, careful not to wake her. She stood for a long time at the crib, thinking through the past several weeks. The way she'd grown used to Jess' presence in her home again.

The way Berkley had fallen in love with him.

She sank to her bed, one knee bent under her as she stared at her phone. Her heart pounded so hard it hurt. Setting her phone on her knee, she wiped both palms on her fleece pants, and took a deep breath.

Was he drunk? Or just sloppy? Hanging on a girl at the bar? Or was he entertaining a room full? She'd found it didn't matter to him; he loved the attention. Didn't matter to her, either. His need for attention had been more important to him than their relationship.

"Dammit, Jess," she whispered. She picked the phone up and tapped the screen to see her missed calls. After the text, he had called two different times, forty minutes apart. No messages. And then nothing.

Her fingers shook as she tapped his name on the missed calls list. She hesitated, took a deep breath for courage, and pressed the phone to her ear. Her stomach twisted in knots as she counted the rings, and then her heart lurched when it stopped in the middle of the fourth.

"Hello?"

The voice was gruff with sleep, but Margo recognized it.

"Julie?"

"Hey."

"It's Margo. Why are you answering Jess' phone?"

She ducked her head and pressed the heel of her hand between her eyes. Well, stupid question, wasn't it? She knew damned well why Julie had answered Jess' phone. But she was going to be a masochist and sit here and listen to one of them or both of them stumble through excuses.

"Just a sec."

Margo could hear Julie murmuring softly. Then she heard the sound a cushion—a pillow or mattress, maybe—made when someone was shifting around on it.

"What?"

She bit her lip when she heard Jess' voice, also thick with sleep.

"Margo's on the phone."

"Oh, shit."

She pulled her phone from her ear and tossed it on the bed. She could hear him clearly now; obviously, Julie had given him his phone.

"Margo? God, babe, I'm sorry."

And just like that, she was starting over again. Same guy. Same heartache. Only that much worse because he'd made her believe in him. He'd reached inside her and made her admit that she loved him.

Why wasn't that enough?

"Margo? Margo? Please listen? Please."

Margo flopped backwards to rest her head on her pillow. Tears slid from her eyes to her hair. Jess was still calling out to her. She reached for her phone and tapped it to end the call. Tossed it to the floor and then curled into a ball and cried.

NO ANSWER, SAME AS THE LAST FOURTEEN TIMES HE'D called her since midnight. In fact, this time, there wasn't even a ring. This last call went straight to voicemail.

"Dammit, Margo." Jess threw his phone across the cab of the truck, glancing at it when it crashed to the floor against the passenger door. He took a peek in the rearview and dropped his foot on the gas pedal. He would drive ninety to get to Adam's Bay—didn't give a damn about a speeding ticket, except for the time it would take, and it was already after eight.

He'd stayed at the hospital with Julie. Waited when they took her dad up to the cath lab. Held her hand when the cardiologist spoke to her in a reverent tone and explained that Derrick had two major arteries almost completely blocked and would need bypass surgery. Her mom hadn't made it back by then, but each time anyone gave her an update, Julie called her.

Derrick had been admitted, naturally. And Julie's mom and aunt had finally come crashing into the waiting room close to midnight. He'd been sacked out on one of stupid vinyl-covered loveseat torture devices. Julie had been in her dad's room. He stirred enough to watch them huddle and talk, thought about calling Margo—he had hated that he missed their night. He'd tried to call her, but of course she was busy on a Friday at the Queen—but he was too damned tired to move.

Julie had watched her mom slip out of the room and then crashed on the loveseat next to him. The furniture was probably worse than the floor for comfort, marginally better for cleanliness, he supposed. Trying to get Julie comfortable, he'd urged her to lie down and rest her head in his lap.

And then apparently he had dozed off again. And Julie had been the one to hear his phone buzzing, since he'd tucked it under his thigh when he'd settled Julie down to rest.

The seventy-three minute drive from Greenville to Adam's Bay took him less than an hour. He needed a shower. He wanted coffee. Real sleep.

But the only thing that mattered to him right now was Margo. He kept his speed under control in the neighborhood, though his heartbeat was erratic and choppy as he pulled into her driveway. He had a bad feeling that she wasn't home when he noticed the drapes on the windows were closed.

Either that or she was still in bed.

Doubtful. She liked to linger in bed some days, but he figured Berkley had her up and going most mornings.

He rapped his knuckles on the door and then shoved his hands in his pockets. It was cold here, but it hadn't snowed. Not even a dusting. They had about an inch of snow back in Greenville. His boxes had gotten wet since his truck was parked outside in the hospital lot. He didn't care. Just hoped he still had a reason to unpack them.

When she didn't answer, he knocked again. Debated on using the key she'd given him, but after last night and her phone call, he thought it might be a bad idea. It was obvious what she thought.

"Margo," he called quietly, banging the door hard enough to make his knuckles ache. She wasn't home. Who knew? Maybe when he hadn't shown up last night, she'd packed Berkley back up and gone to Leah or Stevi. The thought of Margo being at Stevi and Duncan's right now, of having to get through Duncan to talk to her, made his head pound. His blood raced through his body as if he was pumped to deliver the first pitch on opening day.

Whatever. He'd break down a brick wall to get to her. Duncan didn't scare him. Turning away from the door, he shoved his fists into his coat pockets and hurried back down the drive to his truck.

He started the truck and dropped it into gear. It was possible she was with Stevi and Duncan, but it was entirely possible that she was at the Queen. They might all be at the Queen, rallying around her, ready to defend her against the lying, cheating bastard who had shown his true colors again last night.

He would try the Queen first. He'd walk through all of them to get to Margo; he'd walk through hell to get to her. Just had to find her first. His phone buzzed on the floorboard of his truck, and adrenaline surged through him. Maybe she had been at home, and she'd watched him knock and then drive away. And now she'd changed her mind and wanted to talk to him. True, she would be ready to fight, but they had to start somewhere. And as far as Jess was concerned, they were worth fighting for, and he was ready.

He swung the truck into the empty lot at Brassfield Elementary, jammed it into park, and reached for the still buzzing phone. He couldn't reach it; in fact, at the moment, he couldn't see it. Muttering with disgust, he sat up straight, popped his seatbelt, and flung it off. He had to twist so that he was nearly lying on his stomach across the cab of the truck.

"Fuck." He groaned out loud when the buzzing quit. She'd given up. The thought lit a fire of anger in his gut. She'd given up so easily. Maybe she loved him, but she didn't trust him. True, he'd hurt her before; but he'd walked the line this time, and still, she was ready to believe the worst and walk away.

Still stretched out across the cab, Jess groped blindly for the damned phone. His fingers finally bumped it and knocked it over from leaning on the door to laying on the floorboard. With a sigh, he snagged it, sat up, and looked at the screen.

Not Margo, after all.

Julie.

Fingers of his right hand curled around his phone, Jess draped that arm over the steering wheel and ducked his chin to his chest. He dragged the fingers of his other hand back through his messy, unwashed hair, and muttered in exhaustion and defeat.

Julie had been a wreck this morning. Not about her dad. But Margo. Julie had insisted on walking with Jess down the hospital corridors and out to the parking lot. Jess appreciated the support, but his heart was pushing out his chest with rage (at the situation) and fear (that Margo wouldn't listen) and worry (for Julie and Derrick) and sadness (for himself). His only thought had been to get the hell out of the hospital and point the grill of his damned truck in the direction of Adam's Bay.

Get there.

He loved Julie and owed his current happiness (well, happiness as of twenty-four hours before) to her wisdom and generous heart. But at that moment, all he wanted was to get the hell back to Adam's Bay, to the mother of his child.

The love of his life.

He almost tossed the phone away again, as he pressed the brake and put the truck in drive. But he noticed Julie left a voicemail. What if something had changed in Derrick's condition?

Rather than listen to her message, he tapped her name and waited for her to pick up on the other end.

"Did you talk to her?" Julie answered on the second ring.

"What?"

"Margo." Julie sounded hushed and nasally. Jess wondered if she was in Derrick's room.

"I can't find her," he answered. "How's your dad?"

"What?"

Now he heard movement. The rustling of clothes. Footsteps. Someone murmuring in the background.

Margo had heard Julie pass him the phone when they'd both been asleep on the loveseat in the waiting room. Julie sounded groggy, and they'd whispered as she passed him the phone, and then Jess probably sounded groggy—given what he'd done to her in the past, what was she supposed to think?

She was supposed to believe in him. To think something unavoidable had come up and that he would get home to her as soon as he could.

"What do you mean you can't find her?"

Now she spoke a bit louder, so Jess assumed she'd slipped

away by herself so she wouldn't disturb her mom and aunt or her dad.

"She wasn't at home. How's—"

"So, where is she? What're you—"

"Dammit, Julie, I'm going to the Queen. Let it go. How's your dad?"

"Stable," she mumbled, and then she rushed on, "let it go, Jess? Really? You guys were on the way back together. You're moving home to be closer to her. To your baby. And now she really thinks you and I slept together? I can't let that go. I don't want to come between you—"

Jess closed his eyes as Julie gushed, her voice thick with tears and regret.

"It'll be okay."

"If I were her, and another woman answered your phone—"

"Julie," he interrupted her. "It's okay. If I had the same choice to make all over again, I would go with you to the hospital. This will work out."

"What if it doesn't?" she whispered. "What if I ruined your chance of reconciling with her? You love her, Jess. You've—"

"Then I guess I'll be a loser, living in his parents' basement again, and maybe at least getting supervised visits with my little girl." He was overdoing it, trying to ease Julie's worry, but the words were pathetic, and the fact that they were true left a bitter taste in his mouth.

"Jess—"

"I have to go, Julie. I gotta think while I drive. I gotta get my shit together—"

"I'll talk to her—"

"No." He was careful not to snap at her, but he was firm. No way did he want Julie involved in this conversation. Fight. War. Whatever happened, it was between him and Margo. There was no more room for Julie than there was for Duncan or the rest of the gang.

"Okay." Julie sniffled. "Thank—"

"Don't thank me," he said gently. "I needed to be there with you, with him, as much as you needed me."

CHAPTER 37

Rather than stay at home and have a pity party of two or one and a half—Berkley sensed her sadness, but Margo didn't want her to feel it, too—she'd packed the diaper bag up and headed out of the house bright and early. She debated on texting Leah and Stevi, but she drove straight to the Queen without alerting anyone about what had happened.

Or what hadn't happened.

She lugged Berkley and the diaper bag and her own purse in and up the steps to the office. Set the playpen up in the office but changed her mind and carted Berkley into the break room with her. She plopped her in the highchair and arranged a few Cheerios on the tray. Berkley squealed with excitement, banged the tray once, and then hit Margo square in the heart with a sweet little smile.

"Do you want some bananas?" Margo leaned over to drop a kiss on top of Berkley's head, touched by her soft, silky curls on her lips. Such a precious little bit of life right here that was bigger than her entire word. How did Berkley not mean as much to him? How could he say all of those things, the words about forever and marriage and loving Berkley and being a family and then turn around and choose someone else? Again?

"Nanas." Berkley nodded.

Margo laughed softly as she stepped away from the highchair. She made coffee first and then while it brewed, she dug out? a jar of bananas, a little pink rubber tipped spoon, and a bright yellow bib from the diaper bag.

"Does Berkley like bananas?" Margo asked in a singsong voice as she leaned over her baby to put her bib on her. Berkley was slumped forward chasing a Cheerio on her tray. She finally managed to pick it up when Margo dropped into the folding chair in front of the highchair. She stuck her hand out, the cereal piece pinched between her thumb and index finger.

"You want Mommy to eat it?" Margo tipped her head. Berkley grinned and nodded.

"After all the work you put into getting it, you're giving it to Mommy?"

"Mommy."

A burst of warmth and love surged through her. She leaned over so Berkley could feed her the cereal, Berkley's fingers warm on her lips.

"Mmm." She drew back and smiled at Berkley, heart

breaking at the beautiful smile on her little girl's face. "Thank you, Berkley. That was yummy."

"Ummy."

"Yes, it was yummy. How about some bananas?" Margo twisted the lid off the jar and picked up the spoon.

"Jess."

Margo dropped the spoon. It banged on the edge of the tray and fell to the floor. She kept her eyes on Berkley as she leaned sideways to retrieve it.

"What?" She started to stand, but when Berkley said it again—Margo was both thrilled and sickened that she was saying Jess' name—she spun around to look at the doorway behind her to see if Jess had snuck in downstairs. No one there.

Of course not. Jess was probably just waking up. Julie in his arms. Her hands on his skin. Her mouth—

She bit her lip and gave herself a mental shake. She'd believed that little brat when she'd said there wasn't anything going on between them. She'd believed in Jess, in all of those promises, the dreams he'd spun for her about the way things would be between them from now on.

"He's not here, baby girl," she said quietly. She rinsed the spoon off and then took a second to pour herself a cup of coffee when the machine beeped. She hated him at the moment. She'd lain awake all night, thinking about him with Julie. Wondering why he had gone through the whole damned song and dance with her, giving her more this time, and making her believe in him. Why wasn't she enough for him? Why weren't she and Berkley enough for him?

Maybe he just couldn't commit. Maybe he was scared.

She snorted at the direction her thoughts had taken as she turned back to Berkley. Nope. She wasn't going to break. No benefit of the doubt. Not after what he'd done the first time. She hated him. From the top of his head of thick, dark hair, down to his boot-clad toes, she hated Jess Covey. And she wouldn't forgive him.

He might be Berkley's father, and she wouldn't take that from him.

But no way in hell would she let him back into her heart.

When Berkley finished the bananas, insisting that Margo try a bite, too, Margo took her back to the office and set her in the playpen right in front of the desk. Berkley watched Margo with intense blue eyes, following her every move as she pulled toys and books from her diaper bag and put them in the playpen with her. Margo laughed softly when she pulled the last toy from the bag—the stuffed hot pink cell phone—and Berkley reached for it, her face lit up with a big smile.

Margo set the bag on the couch and then slipped around to sit at the desk. Berkley cut loose with a screech and baby babbles and then lifted the phone to her ear to rattle away. Margo watched her for a few moments, wondering again how Jess could be so willing to give it up. Then again, maybe Jess was crazy about Berkley and not her. Maybe Jess had visions of those fun family times they'd been sharing, only instead of making those memories with her, he wanted Julie in the picture.

Her eyes welled with tears, but she was already frustrated with herself and the tears and the way it hurt so badly to draw a deep breath. She swiped at her eyes, turned her attention to the computer on the desk, and decided she would search for fun holiday ideas for appetizers and entrees. They would throw a holiday party again this year; last year's had been a big hit, and their profits had far exceeded their expectations. Margo figured the sky was the limit with festive nights at the Queen now that Trace Dixon had become a permanent fixture here. Either he could do a set—oh, but the ladies still poured in night after night to get a look at him, though they often left disappointed that they didn't turn his head—or he knew someone who was willing to drop in to their trendy little bar in Adam's Bay. Trace Dixon had put them on the map, no doubt about it.

Eventually, Margo emerged from her plans—three pages of detailed notes as detailed as wine pairings suggested for particular menu items and ideas for decorations once Thanksgiving was over—to hear voices downstairs. Though she'd been deep in thought, she'd glanced at Berkley from time to time, and when she'd noticed her little girl had snuggled in the fetal position and closed her eyes, she'd tiptoed out from behind the desk to cover her with a small fleece blanket.

The voices were Stevi and Duncan. Margo couldn't hear them well enough to overhear their conversation, which she figured she should be grateful for. But on the other hand, she hoped they'd noticed her car in the lot out back, because she didn't want to overhear any dirty talk, or even worse, sex. She happened to know that the two of them had gone for the gold a few times at the Queen. It had been strange at first to hear those sorts of stories from Stevi, about Duncan, but Margo decided early on, it wouldn't be fair to Stevi to cheer her on with Duncan but at the same time not want to share in her cousin's happiness. Still, Margo was relieved that Stevi kept the details to a minimum. For instance, Margo knew they'd had sex in the cellar, but she didn't know exactly where or when and she was okay with that.

That thought led her back to Jess. The nights they'd hidden up here in the office, making out like stupid kids on the sofa across from the desk. They hadn't ever totally lost control here, but Margo thought it could be fun. Sexy. A little bit daring.

Not with Jess.

Not now.

But before, maybe.

She tossed her pencil down and winced when the tip broke. Dashed at her eyes when she heard footsteps on the stairs outside the door. Whether it was Stevi or Duncan coming up to find her or get a jump on paperwork, Margo didn't know what she was going to say. As angry as she was—no, that wasn't right—as hurt as she was, there was a part of her that didn't want Duncan to know what had happened.

And it wasn't because she didn't want to hear *I told you so*.

She didn't want Duncan to hate Jess any more than he already did.

Why the hell did she want to protect Jess now? Sure as hell wasn't because she loved him. Nope. That wasn't the reason.

Maybe because no matter that she'd had enough of the lies, enough of Jess' bullshit, she still wanted Berkley to have a relationship with her daddy. No matter what had happened or ended between herself and Jess, he was still always going to be a part of her life because of Berkley. She wouldn't take that from him; even now, after another long night without him—knowing he was with someone else—Margo still felt guilty for taking Berkley's first year of life from him. No matter that he said he wouldn't change it if he could. She still felt wrong for keeping Berkley from him and his family.

"Hey." Stevi appeared in the doorway and wandered into the room. Margo saw the way her eyes slipped to the right so she could take a quick peek at Berkley before zeroing in on Margo. "I thought I smelled coffee."

Margo flashed her a weak smile, getting away with it because Stevi was preoccupied with Berkley.

"She loves that thumb."

Margo turned her attention to Berkley, thumb in her mouth, completely zonked.

"Do you think I should worry about it?"

"Didn't Leah suck her thumb when she was little?" Stevi, still not looking at Margo, asked. "Until she was like five?

Pretty sure Mom and Dad have talked about that. Who's got a more beautiful smile than Leah?"

"You." Margo shrugged.

Stevi finally turned to her with a sheepish grin. She rolled her eyes.

"What the heck are you doing here so early? I figured you would be enjoying breakfast in bed this morning."

Margo smacked her lips together and answered Stevi with a slow blink. At a loss for what to say, she lowered her gaze and examined the notes she'd written so far. Perfectly small, neat handwriting filled the page. All bullshit notes that really weren't necessary. Just something to keep her mind off of Jess.

Or maybe Jess would say the notes were something she could control, since he had decided she was a control freak. Made her wonder again about Julie. What kind of woman she was when she wasn't looking another woman straight in the eye and lying about the nature of her relationship with a man.

"Oh, shoot." Stevi sounded disappointed. "Did you guys get into it?"

Margo couldn't bring herself to look at Stevi. Bad enough that it had happened the first time. How stupid, how gullible could she be to have fallen for his lies the second time? She had to say something, though, to get Stevi moving. She swallowed hard—her throat tight and hot with tears—and then she heard Trace's voice downstairs, and she did hear him say *darlin'* so obviously Leah was here, too.

She didn't want to be on display. She thought she'd wanted to talk to Leah and Stevi. But not here. She couldn't do this here. Knowing that Jess and Julie were probably lying together musing over what they'd done to her—who was she kidding? Jess was probably balls deep inside Julie's tight little snatch right now, Margo Nevin the furthest thing from his mind—was humiliating enough. Announcing that fact to the people she loved most in the world—besides Berkley and Jess—made her feel like an absolute failure as a woman.

"Margs?"

Margo dropped her face to her hands as the dam broke. Not just tears. Big, ugly sobs shook her body, and then Stevi was there beside her, hand on her back and her shoulders. Fingers in her hair. Gentle and strong, at the same time, because Stevi—like most women—could do both, and apparently, Margo couldn't.

"He didn't come," she whispered into her hands. "He didn't show up."

She heard Stevi groan with disgust.

"Hey!" Leah's cheerful voice boomed through the room. "Oh. Sleeping baby. Shoot. We need a red light you can— what's wrong?"

"Close the door," Stevi said softly.

"What? Why? What's wrong?"

"Leah!" Stevi's voice was sharper this time. Margo licked her lips and dropped her hands. Leah glanced at her and then moved back toward the door.

"What's going on?" Duncan slapped his hand on the door before Leah could get it closed. Margo watched him push the door back. He looked from Leah to Stevi and finally, he turned his full attention to her. Her stomach flip-flopped, and her chest was tight, and she loved Duncan to the moon and back, but...

She loved Jess, too. And yes, there were times when she needed Duncan to flex and show his stepbrother muscles and protect her. The thought shot her straight back to the day Jess had walked into the Queen six weeks ago and she'd wished for her army to protect her.

But there were times when she needed girlfriends to know exactly what she was feeling. Love and hate. Right now, she was a volatile mix of love and hate and grief and yearning, and she needed a soft touch while she cowered here to lick her wounds more than she needed a parade of macho masculinity, the promise of protection.

"Dammit, Margo." He groaned.

"Did you fight?" Leah whispered. "What happened? What did he say? Everything was so good, Margo. What happened?"

"He didn't show last night," Stevi told Leah. Margo, eyes still locked with Duncan's, noticed his brows shoot up in disbelief.

"He didn't—? But maybe there's—"

"I called him after midnight." Admitting it made Margo feel like a desperate kid, begging her boyfriend to come back.

Rather than walk out, Duncan crossed the room to stand with Stevi. Margo waited for the lecture to start, but he simply slid his hand around Stevi's back and curled his fingers around the curve of her hip.

"Remember the way I fucked everything up?" He leaned into Stevi and kissed her head, but his eyes were still on Margo. Of course, she remembered. Rather than ask Stevi to explain an old note he'd found, Duncan had treated her badly in front of a bar full of patrons and the Queen's crew. That night had ended with Stevi throwing a spiked red heel at him and then she and Leah curled up with Stevi, hoping to ease the heartache.

As much as Margo wanted their comfort, she realized now how stupid, how useless that had been. Leah and Stevi could wrap themselves around her to hold her together, but no one was going to fill that lonely, empty space inside her that Jess had made again in just the past few weeks.

She nodded, shocked by Duncan's calm.

"Julie answered his phone." She sniffled. "After midnight. When she passed it to him, I could hear..." Margo dropped her gaze again; humiliation flamed in her cheeks. "I woke them up."

"Dammit, Jess." Leah's whisper was harsh and sad at the same time.

"He doesn't deserve you," Duncan mumbled.

Margo struggled for a moment to control her emotions, the ones bursting to break free of her throat. The need to fall apart and rail over this happening again was so real, her body practically vibrated. She hadn't done that. When Berkley was born and she asked Jess to leave, when Jess had stared at her with those goddamned soulful golden eyes and packed his bags and left without a fight, without a word, she'd folded her feelings up and swallowed them and then lied to everyone, including herself, that she was okay without him.

"I feel so stupid." Her stomach hurt. Missing him, needing him. Knowing he had made a choice, knowing that she'd lost out to another woman—again—was a physical ache in her belly. She lowered her gaze again, stared at her notes until they blurred. "I lied before. When he left. I lied to myself. I love him. I've loved him from day one. When he gave me that grin over the bar. He lit me on fire with just that smile."

"Margo."

She didn't look up when Leah spoke, nor when she moved. She listened to the sound of Leah's clothing rustle —made her think of the sounds of sheets rustling and cushions moving—and her boots on the hardwood floor.

"I tried not to need him. I didn't want to tie him down, make him feel responsible for me. But, oh my God, we had so much fun," Margo continued. "Turns out I did everything wrong. He said so. So this time, I let go. And I loved him."

She sent a quick glance at the three of them, both appalled and comforted at the shared misery on their faces.

"I really thought we were gonna work this time." She shook her head. "I wanted him here. With me and Berkley. I wanted…to be a family. I wanted what you guys have. I'm sorry. God, I'm sorry. I love that you guys are happy, but I don't get—"

"Margo!"

She shivered when she heard Jess' voice all the way from the first floor of the bar.

"I can't do this." She shook her head and covered her face with her hands. "I can't."

"You have to do this," Stevi spoke gently. She leaned over and dropped a kiss, half on Margo's cheek and half on her hand that covered her face.

"Let him explain?" Leah whispered.

"Margo?" Jess bellowed again, but his voice was closer now. He was coming up the stairs.

"How do you explain chronic infidelity, Leah?" Margo dropped her hands and tipped her head to look at her cousin. "Don't I deserve more than that?"

"Of course you do, Margo." Leah flinched. "God, yes, I wanna strangle him. But." She shrugged. "He loves you. Even I saw it this time."

"It's not enough," Margo argued.

"Guys?" Trace called. Margo figured he was right behind Jess on his way to the office. No doubt he was curious why Jess was stomping through the bar like an elephant on a steroid rage, but he had no idea what had happened, so Margo didn't fault him for not barring Jess from the stairs, the office.

"Margo."

She looked up as Jess stepped into the office. Black leather jacket pulled on over a wrinkled t-shirt. One she knew well. Faded, worn jeans that sculpted his powerful thighs and made her a little jealous, because she would never touch him again. His hair was mussed, and his eyes were bloodshot with fatigue. She assumed he'd thrown some clothes on and rolled out of bed after a morning romp with Julie. Maybe he'd come to do another acting job with her. Or maybe he'd come to make sure fucking Julie wouldn't fuck his chances of being Berkley's daddy.

At least Julie was warm and sweet and friendly. Margo would rather Berkley have a stepmom like that than some of the other women she'd seen hang on Jess.

Then again, Julie had no trouble looking Margo in the eye and flat out lying her ass off about sleeping with Jess and then climbing into bed with him after those empty promises. Margo wasn't sure she wanted her daughter to learn behavior like that. Then again, maybe learning to lie, to be the aggressor and the cheater—the other woman— would protect her baby girl's heart. She didn't want that, though. She didn't want Berkley to ever feel this pain, but she didn't want her to be the kind of woman to hurt others for her own gain.

Pain and sadness surged through her. She dragged her eyes away from Jess and looked at Berkley, still sleeping—though she had flopped over on her back. Just like her daddy, one arm tossed up carelessly over her head.

"Oh, boy."

Trace sounded a little guilty, a little defeated, and a little uncomfortable.

"Margo. We need to talk."

Margo, eyes still on Berkley, breathed deeply. She dabbed at her tears again and shook her head.

"I have…nothing to say to you…Jess Covey." She finally found her voice, but her words were choppy and breathy and barely more than a whisper.

"Then you can listen."

CHAPTER 38

Margo held her breath, eyes on Berkley. She wanted to believe that it meant something. That Jess dragging himself out of a warm bed with a warm, willing woman, to drive an hour down to see her meant something. But mostly, she didn't believe it meant anything beyond her being stupid and desperate.

He'd come charging down this morning to make sure she wasn't going to threaten him with losing the right to see Berkley. His name was on her birth certificate. He could take her to court. She wouldn't take Berkley from him; she didn't want to hurt Berkley.

Berkley, who had learned to say Jess.

Her stomach jolted when she remembered she had told Berkley last night—in front of her mother—that Jess was her daddy. Not that Berkley got it right now, but given a few more weeks, maybe days, Berkley would learn to say it consistently.

Daddy.

Leah lingered at the front of the desk; Duncan stood behind Margo, silent and brooding. Margo appreciated the support, but this had to be done, and it had to be done in private. She looked up when Stevi leaned over the playpen and carefully picked Berkley up. Margo's heart hurt when Berkley mumbled in her sleep and then ducked her face into Stevi's neck.

She watched Stevi slip out of the office, noted the way Jess watched her go. The yearning in his eyes when he looked at Berkley. Trace stood just inside the door, a pained expression on his face. Margo couldn't bear more pity, so she didn't make eye contact with him. When Leah moved, Trace followed her out without a word.

Margo closed her eyes, expecting Duncan to go off on Jess. She didn't want it. She didn't want the raised voices or fists. She didn't want her stepbrother and her lover—ex-lover, again—to stand here and fight over her. About her. Around her.

Because she needed this to be over. Again. The longer Duncan lingered, the longer this was going to take.

Duncan moved suddenly, squeezed her shoulders hard, and then stalked from behind the desk to stand in front of Jess.

"You fuck with her right now, and I'll—"

Jess lifted his chin to stare at Duncan, eyes burning with anger. "Fuck off. I'm here to talk to Margo."

Margo held her breath, eyes on Duncan, ready for him to throw a punch or at the very least, shove Jess up against the open door. Her shoulders sagged with relief when he only stared for another second or two and then walked out of the office without another word.

Jess stood in place for what felt like an eternity. Margo's heart, her head pounded, waiting for the final goodbye to begin.

Finally, he moved. With calm, deliberate motions, he stepped back and closed the door and finally turned to her.

"Get. Out." She breathed deeply, hunched up over the desk. Afraid, humiliated, she didn't want to look at him and remember the lies he'd fed her—the ones she'd swallowed like candy. Instead, she ducked her chin to her chest and rested her forehead on the heels of her hands.

"I'm not leav—"

"I don't ever wanna look at you again."

"Margo—"

"Get out!" All of the pent-up emotion tore through her and exploded on a shout. "Get out of my office. Get out of my life."

My heart. Get out of my heart.

"We need to—"

"I don't want to talk, Jess. Not this again. I don't wanna know anything. I don't care if it just happened. If you decided you needed to fuck her before you moved. If you've been sleeping with her for months. I don't care what you do or who you fuck, but it won't be me again."

"I didn't fuck her!" His face was twisted in a grotesque mask of emotion. "Nothing happened. Nothing's ever happened with her."

"I waited. Last night. I sat and waited for you, and you didn't show up. You didn't call me—"

"I texted you. I told you I was running late. I called you—"

"That doesn't count. You can't make those obligatory phone calls and get off fucking scot-free, just because I was busy here. You could have left me a message. You could have called me again." She stood and shoved the chair back hard enough that it bounced off the wall behind her.

"Margo—"

"Do you know what that did to me?" She moved around the desk and stepped up close to him. "Hearing Julie's voice when I called your phone at that hour? Do you know how much that hurt, Jess?"

"Let me explain—"

"Fuck you." She threw her hands out and slapped them on his chest. "Fuck you. I'm done with this. I'm done with you. You don't love me. And if you think you do." She shook her head and shrugged. "I don't want that kind of love. I can't raise my daughter with half a heart, Jess."

"Margo—"

"I hate you right now." Hands still on his chest, she fisted them, gathering his shirt and his skin in her fingers. "I hate you. Why did you do this? Why did you come home and say those things to me? If this is how it's gonna be?"

"It's not gonna be like this, because it didn't happen." He grabbed her wrists and held on tight when she struggled to get away from him.

She shook her head. "You asked me to love you. To need you. And I do. Goddamn you, Jess Covey, I do. But I'm not gonna live like this."

Tears streaked her face, but Jess still held her wrists, so she had to let them go.

"I was walking out of my apartment." He spoke through gritted teeth. Closed his hands around her wrists even tighter. She would have bruises tomorrow.

Some that would never heal.

"Look." She sniffled. "I told her last night."

Jess looked up and around the office. "Who? Leah? Stevi? Is that why the cavalry was here? You believed in me enough to call the guard dogs in the first time something comes up?"

Margo yanked her right wrist free of his hold and swiped at her eyes.

"The first time?" she repeated. "It's not, though, Jess. Is it? It's not the first time you decided to forget me and fuck someone else."

"Margo." He let go of her other hand and rubbed his own eyes. "Goddammit, let me talk." He shoved his hands back through his hair and then linked his fingers behind his neck.

"I picked Berkley up from Mom's. So we could go home and get ready for a night with you." Margo licked her lips. "She was being…" She blew out a harsh breath. "Stubborn. So I told her we had to go home. To see you."

Jess' eyes filled.

"She says your name now. But I told her last night that you're her daddy."

"Margo." He sighed. She turned to storm away from him, but his hand flew out and caught her again. This time he dug his fingers into her waist and tugged her back to stand closer to him.

"I won't…" Margo closed her eyes, because there was magic or voodoo or something so desperately lovable in his golden eyes that it broke her heart to look at him. "I won't keep you from your daughter. But you will never… I'll never give you myself again. There's no more us, Jess."

"I was leaving my apartment—"

"I need you to leave." She blinked her eyes open and stared at him coldly.

"And I need to say this!" he roared with anger. Margo flinched and sobbed out loud when he tugged her closer, still, and cupped her face in his hands. "I need to say this. And you need to hear it."

"I don't wanna know how I compare. I don't wanna know what you love more about her—"

"Stop it." He shook her gently and leaned in to press his forehead to hers. "Goddammit, Margo, shut up and listen."

"Why did you do it?" Eyes locked, faces so close she could feel his breath on her face, her words were no more than a whisper. "Why am I never enough for you?"

"I love you to the fucking moon and back." His thick lashes were wet with tears. "I love you."

His words were a knife in her heart. In her throat. She sniffled and squeezed her eyes closed. She hated him. But she hated herself more, because when she felt his lips hovering over hers, she parted her own and waited. And kissed him back when he finally kissed her. The soft, gentle press of his lips to hers quickly became desperate and hungry and hard. When she sighed—she hated the longing she felt, the longing she heard in her sigh—he deepened the kiss, his tongue hesitantly stroking hers and then when she kissed him back again, boldly claiming her mouth.

"Stop." She tore away from him and shook her head. His hands still cupped her face, and her traitorous hands were suddenly on his neck. His skin was warm. She felt his Adam's apple bob as he worked to control himself. "Please just stop. I don't wanna do this anymore."

"I texted you to tell you I was running late." The words, spoken in a ragged voice, came out fast, his hands still desperately holding onto her. "She showed up just as I was ready to go. She had just texted, but I thought it was you."

Margo closed her eyes and wished him away. Wished the last day and night away.

"It was snowing. I was thinking the boxes in my truck might get wet, but it didn't matter as long as I had a reason to get back here and unpack them. To stay."

Margo shook her head. "You don't. Not for me."

"Baby, don't say that." Jess' insistent voice made her open her eyes.

"Don't call me baby."

"Her dad had a heart attack," he ignored her demand and continued. "She's an only child. Her mom and her aunt had just gone to Chicago for the weekend. Derrick was in an attic, inspecting for leaks. I didn't get the whole story, because I didn't get to talk to Derrick. He was in the ER and the cath lab. I think I fell asleep before he was admitted."

Margo jerked her chin from his hands and stepped back.

"He was on a ladder or something. In the attic. He fell. They don't know if the heart attack caused the fall or if the fall caused the heart attack. She was scared to death that he…that he would die."

"And so what?" Margo shrugged. She wiped her palms on her jeans and turned her back to him. Jess was quiet as she walked across the office, around the playpen, to stare out the window Stevi liked to sit in. "You had to fuck her to keep her calm? Or did you just get turned on because she needed you?"

"This goes both ways, you know."

Margo looked at him over her shoulder as a sarcastic laugh rumbled up from deep in her belly.

"What the hell does that mean? Do you think I've been screwing around on you when you're gone? Or did I drive you to sleep with Julie? Is that it?"

"If you love me." He arched his eyebrows and shrugged. "If you love me, Margo, you have to trust me. I told you I fucked up before. I handled things wrong. I cheated on you, and I am sorry. I thought we were passed that. I thought you'd forgiven me, and we'd moved on."

She felt a stab of guilt. He was right.

"Yeah, well, when I call your phone after midnight, and get Julie's voice...thick with sleep, and then hear you both rustling around, what am I supposed to think?"

"We were in the waiting room at the hospital. Yes, she was sleeping on me, but we were on a loveseat built in the seventies. Not made for comfort. Sure as fuck not made for sex."

"Why didn't you call me?" she whispered.

Part of her longed to gobble up his explanation as gospel. Part of her still wanted to tear him limb from limb. She turned her back to the window and stared at him, desperate to feel his arms around her again.

"I did call you."

"You didn't leave a message."

"I wanted to talk to you. Not leave a message." He shrugged and laughed bitterly. "I guess I knew you wouldn't believe me. You would think it was a bullshit excuse because I was either shooting longnecks at some bar or cheating."

"So you're gonna turn it around and blame this on me?"

Jess stared at her sadly, silently for several long seconds.

"No." He huffed out a sigh and shook his head. "I don't wanna drag this out and keep fighting. I'm here because I love you. And all I want is to be here with you and Berkley."

"Jess." She swallowed back the tears and the words she wanted to say. *I love you. Come home.*

"Maybe if you're still so sure I would do this…" He shrugged. "Maybe you don't love me."

"I do love you, and that's why this hurts. I can't live like this, Jess. I can't wonder if you're out doing—"

He shook his head as he pushed off from the front of the desk. Margo watched him as he walked closer to her.

"And it hurts me that I love you and you don't believe me. She needed me—"

"Yeah, I know now that you're a sucker for needy women."

Jess ignored the biting comment, which only made Margo feel worse.

"She's a kid. And she was scared. What kind of dick would I have been to blow her off? She's scared to death for her dad, and now she's worried that she fucked things up between us."

"You could have called me. Later."

"I should have," he agreed with a nod. "I'm sorry I didn't. I fell asleep."

Margo looked up when he stood directly in front of her.

"You can call her. I'll give you Ginger's cell number, and you can call her and ask if her husband is in the hospital. You can call the hospital and ask for Derrick's room." He shrugged. His lips were set in a grim line, his jaw clenched. But his eyes were sad. "But I can't live like that, Margo. I can't do this if you don't trust me."

Margo sniffled. She considered throwing back the same old argument. The drinking and the other women. But she bit her lip until the urge passed.

"I'm not asking you to forgive me." Jess cupped her chin in his hand and rubbed his thumb over her lip. "Because I didn't do anything wrong, Margo. I stayed with a friend who needed me. The same as you would do."

Margo closed her eyes when he pressed his thumb to the center of her lower lip.

"I'm asking you to believe in me."

"Is he gonna be okay?"

"They admitted him. Two major arteries blocked. He'll have open heart surgery this week."

Margo winced. She opened her eyes when Jess drew his hand away. He fiddled with something in his pocket and finally pulled his phone out.

"What?" she asked when he handed it to her.

"Do you wanna call Greenville Memorial or Ginger?"

Margo stared at him boldly. She didn't think about the first time, when she'd stubbornly held her head high after asking him to leave. Instead, she focused on the last several weeks when Jess had been around. When Jess had been Berkley's daddy. And the three of them had been a family.

He'd said he wanted to marry her. Stubborn independence and all.

She took the phone from him and held it in a tight grip.

"Which one do you want to call?"

"Please don't do this again, Jess," she whispered. "Please."

"Margo."

He moved cautiously to settle his hands on her hips.

"Berkley needs you."

"Margo, please—"

"She's so in love with you." She reached up to stroke the scruff on his face.

"I want you, too, Margo. I want both of you in my life. Always."

"So am I," Margo whispered. She lifted her head to look him in the eye. "I'm so in love with you."

"Always?" Jess stepped closer. She sighed wistfully when he combed his fingers up through the back of her hair to cup her head. Margo parted her lips, but he didn't kiss her there. She closed her eyes when he pressed his lips to her cheek and then her forehead, sliding his free hand around her waist.

Weak in her knees, her stomach filled with butterflies, and her heart throbbing at the base of her throat, she wrapped her arms around him and pressed her face to his. Skin to skin. He was warm, his jaw rough with scruff against her cheek. She ducked her head to bury her face in his neck.

"Always."

The End

Thank you for reading Always, Jess. Please consider leaving a review on your favorite bookish site.

Loved You More, Lorelei Bluffs, Book 8

A Lorelei Ending, Lorelei Bluffs, Book 9

I Do, Lorelei Bluffs, Book 10

Truth Is, The Williams Legacy, Book 1

Other People's Ugly, The Williams Legacy, Book 2

Omissions, The Williams Legacy, Book 3

Contemporary Romance Novels:

Destiny's Calling: Your Future Is Waiting

Wedding Day Shenanigans

Holiday Fling

The Kiss Off

Something Like Love

Plus One

Hold Onto the Stars, Book #5 in Blue Collar Romance series

The Jane Thing, Book #2 in Meet Cute Book Club series

Shameless Santa, Book #7 in Welcome to Kissing Springs series

Sunshine & Soulmates, Welcome to Kissing Springs, Sunshine Season

Bourbon & Bedposts, Book #7 in Welcome to Kissing Springs, Bourbon Season

Doctor Divine, Doctors of Eastport General, Season 2

Beach Daze, Flamingo Island

Moonlight in Montreal, The Vagabond Series

Christmas and Other Inconveniences, Betting on Christmas Collection

Eggnog in Amesbury, Christmas in Amesbury Series (Sweet Romance)

A December Wish, Wishing for Love Series (Sweet Romance)

A Naughty Lesson

The Santorini Sack, The Vagabond Series

Love, Nashville, The Mississippi Queen Trilogy, Book 1

Forever, Duncan, The Mississippi Queen Trilogy, Book 2

Always, Jess, The Mississippi Queen Trilogy, Book 3

Gettin' Hitched, The H Books, Book 1

Hookin' Up, The H Books, Book 2

Holdin' On, The H Books, Book 2.5

Intoxicate Me, 515 Whiskey, Book .5

Taste Me, 515 Whiskey, Book 1

Scrooge Me, 515 Whiskey, Bonus Short Story in Let's Get Naughty V 3

Contemporary Romance Novellas:

Indian Summer

Dear Jaclyn Perris

French Stuff

Holdin' On (The H Books)

End in Flames

Mistletoe Mishaps

Toasted: A New Year's Eve Novella

Endless Summer (Timberton Hounds)

Homeless Holiday (Timberton Hounds)

Restless Hearts (Timberton Hounds)

Timberton Hounds Novellas Boxset

Boone's Girl

Intoxicate Me (515 Whiskey)

Seducing You (Welcome to Kissing Springs and Lockland Distilling: Keys to Love)

Kissing You (Welcome to Kissing Springs and Lockland Distilling: Keys to Love)

Swipe for Fangs

Swipe for Ghouls

Feels on Wheels (Love in Motion Duet, Book 1) (Sweet Romance)

Rings on Wings (Love in Motion Duet, Book 2) (Sweet Romance)

Love in Motion Boxset

Other Novellas:

The Devy Man, A Horror Novella

Today, Again (Sweet Love Story)

Women's Fiction Short Stories:

India Falls

Luther's Cross: 87,600

The Candy Cane Tree of Willow Lane

Delays

Same Time Next Year

Contemporary Romance Short Stories:
Perfect Pictures, The Wine Tasting Series, Traminette (Sweet)
Coming Home, The Wine Tasting Series, Edelweiss (Sweet)
Save Me Every Dance, The Wine Tasting Series, Rosé (Sweet)
Marry Me, The Wine Tasting Series, Shiraz (Sweet)
Birthday Wishes, The Wine Tasting Series, Muscat (Sweet)
Dad Jeans, The Wine Tasting Series, Vignoles (Sweet)
The Wine Tasting Series Boxset (Sweet)

Peppermint Lane
Priceless Memory (Timberton Hounds)
Truly Dante, A Mississippi Queen Trilogy Short Story
Strawberry Wine
Love Letter
Leaving You, A Lockland Distilling: Keys to Love Short Story
Sambuca Santa
Deadman's Hollow

ABOUT THE AUTHOR

Tracy Broemmer is the author of several contemporary romance novels including the 515 Whiskey Series, the Welcome to Kissing Springs: Bourbon Fever Collection, and the Mississippi Queen Trilogy. Tracy also writes women's fiction and is the author of the Williams Legacy series as well as several stand-alone titles.

Tracy's books have been called gripping, emotional, and timely, and readers describe her characters as real and relatable.

Tracy lives in Midwestern Illinois with her husband of 31 years. Visit her on the web and sign up for her newsletter at www.broemmerbooks.com